The Last Scion of Ra

By

K.Aten

Dedication

This one is for all my fan fiction lovers out there, especially folks who love and support Archive of Our Own. The platform is superb, the stories full of limitless possibilities, and the support I've found there is unmatched anywhere else.

I hope you fall in love with my characters just like I did.

"Well, Scion may have saved me, but Kaelen-Ra Evon, you are my hero."

If you know, you know.

Credits

AO3 for their well-maintained platform and author protections. The Supergirl TV show for character inspiration. Actresses Katie McGrath and Melissa Benoist for their on-screen chemistry, because there would be no Supercorp without them. And finally, my fans. Thank you for following, pushing, prodding, suggesting, and aiding me, as well as dropping all those beautiful comments straight into my writing soul. I appreciate you because you inspire me.

Prologue

Kaelen's heart pounded with terror while their high-level home shook all around her. She stumbled and nearly fell aws she moved away from the windows toward the interior. Tremors were a regular occurrence in Kypl City but today was different. The magnitude and frequency of the quakes had steadily increased throughout the afternoon until debris rained down from above as the structures began to fail. Kaelen had experienced nothing like it in her thirteen *vosans* of life. She frantically called, "*Liu?*"

Her mother was supposed to be working, but when Kaelen looked out the balcony entrance after the first unexpected tremor hit, she saw many shuttles landing on home platforms. Kaelen yelled for her father, thinking they may have taken the tunnels home instead. "*Kre?*" Still no answer. She stumbled again and fell to the floor, crying. "Wex!"

"Do you have a request, Kaelen Ra-Evon?"

"What is happening? Where are my parents?"

Wex hovered closer. The smooth, white exterior of the robotic construct was a familiar sight in their home and soothing with its presence. *"Please remain calm. Your parents will arrive shortly. They asked that you change into your ship suit, the one you received before your last trip with Evon Ra to Tahn."*

The most recent round of tremors stopped and Kaelen used that opportunity to stand. Trained from a young age to obey Wex's orders, she ran to her room. She was disconcerted to note the large cracks throughout the floors and walls of their home on the way there.

Kaelen assumed her family would seek refuge off world while the abnormal quakes continued. So, she filled a small satchel with items that she'd need, much like she'd do for any of her scientific trips with her father. Just the bare essentials.

The only exception she made to the necessities was to add a few personal items she couldn't bear to see destroyed in case the worst should happen. The bonding torques she received the day after her guild induction ceremony, even though a mate hadn't yet been chosen for her. Kaelen also picked up a holo-cube that held information about her family, images, and videos. Lastly, she selected the shimmering black and silver cape gifted by her *zodha* and *ghun*, Brev Ra and Disu. Brev Ra was her father's father, and head of their house.

Once her pack was complete, she slung it across her thin shoulders then made her way through their home to the balcony and the approaching family shuttle. The small ship touched down as tremors struck again. Mags on the landing rails engaged, slamming the shuttle against the metal decking. The door opened and her father yelled, "Hurry!"

Kaelen sprinted the short distance and less than a dozen breaths later, she was secured as they lifted into the air. "What is happening? I thought the engineers announced that they found a way to stabilize Argon's core but these tremors indicate that is not the case." Her parents shared a glance before her father spoke.

"The solution failed catastrophically yesterday, triggering the rapid degradation of the planetary core cooling rods and an imminent system-wide collapse."

"Are we heading to the tech center to work on a solution?"

"No. Our priority right now is to keep you safe. It is our duty to the eldest heir of the house."

Kaelen gestured out the window of the shuttle, taking note of the delicate spires crumbling and falling to the streets below. "Look around us! Nothing here is safe."

Clovi Ze-Est said, "Everything is going to be fine."

Her mother's declaration was ludicrous, and the lack of public warning left Kaelen unsettled. "There have been no announcements of this failure made across citizen bands. You didn't think to tell me yesterday that our planet was in imminent danger? The Thinker Guild should have warned everyone so they could evacuate if needed. Why hide something this catastrophic?"

"There aren't enough ships on Argon that could get everyone—"

Her father interrupted from his place in the other seat. "We were trying to protect you, *eina*—"

"Protect me? What about everyone else, all the other houses, guilds, and people below us in both station and rank? Who will safeguard them?" She received a thin-lipped stare while the shuttle flew toward a part of Kypl City she'd never visited before. "Where are we going?" Evon Ra met Kaelen's furious and heartbroken gaze. "We thought we'd have more time…to fix it or to plan in case we couldn't. There is one procedure we can attempt to slow the meltdown, but probability of success is low. In the meantime, we have to do what we can to be sure *Dolem*-Ra survives."

Clovi picked up where her *mhinez* left off. "We're meeting Brev Ra and Disu at a private lab. Your *zodha* decided that you're to be sent off planet, where you'll be safe, until we can handle this crisis."

"No! I can help—"

"I'm sorry, Kaelen, but the head of our house has made up his mind and we agree with him. While you may have full rights intellectually under Argon's laws with your induction into the Thinker Guild, you're still biologically a minor in society and our responsibility. But rest assured, we've prepared for this exact eventuality."

Throughout their flight, Kaelen could tell whenever the tremors would begin and end based on the amount of damage to the infrastructure below. Luckily it was calm again when they landed. All three exited the shuttle as Brev Ra and Disu rushed over. They moved fast, despite their advanced age. Kaelen's *zodha* and *ghun* looked as worried as her own parents. Brev Ra said, "We must hurry. I fear this lab won't remain sound for long and if it collapses before the ship can lift off—" Another tremor hit and they all staggered.

"It's unfortunate that you had no son to carry on the house name but alas, nothing can be done now."

Kaelen's shoulders hunched at her *ghun*'s critical words. She looked around and saw a small, personal ship prepped with it's clear cover open. Her father's earlier comment about preparation, and the convenience of the shuttle struck her as odd. "When did you start planning for this?"

"Kaelen—"

"How long have you known this was a possibility?" Clovi looked down, and Evon Ra's eyes darted away. Their guilt was easy enough to read and the betrayal was like a kick to her middle. Her *zodha* remained silent though the call to send her away was ultimately his.

Evon Ra sighed and his shoulders slumped. "Nearly a *vosan*." He rushed on with an excuse before she could respond. "It was never regarded as a serious concern. You know as well as we do that every scientific indicator and projection model gave the stabilization program a high success predictability score."

Brev Ra nodded. "It's true, little one. Failure was a faint possibility at best."

Her father waved toward the ship. "This was a worst-case scenario that we never fully planned out. That's why we only have the one personal pod."

Kaelen's mother grabbed her hand and pulled her closer to the ship. Once they stood next to the gleaming vessel, her mother begged, "Please, *eina*. This is hard enough without worrying about you." Kaelen looked around the group of four then nodded. After all, her elders were telling her to go and there wasn't much one small girl could do in the face of such a massive planetary failure. She unslung her satchel and placed it in a compartment near the head of the ship. Then she climbed inside and lay back, trusting the cushioned surface to form snugly around her body.

Evon Ra gently grasped her hand. "We are sending you to a planet called Terra. It is a long journey for this type of craft."

"How long?"

"A little over ten *vosans*—"

"What?"

Her mother grabbed her other hand. "Please, Kaelen. If we manage to stabilize Argon's core, we'll send the code to bring your ship back. If we don't, we'll help others evacuate then follow your coordinates and pick you up with a larger interstellar vessel. With any luck, our separation will be short either way."

Kaelen pleaded. "But why Terra? Why not one that is closer?"

"Reports from the Tau Ceti in our sector mentioned the technologically primitive planet and its yellow sun. They've been protecting it for generations but will allow refugees under certain circumstances. We only discovered Terra because of rumors that the Hogath ruling family may have fled there when the Argon Military Guild took over for a few years during the war."

Kaelen was confused by his statement. "I thought they died?"

"Yes, it was later proven that King Logar and Queen Aheer perished before they could land. We didn't make this decision lightly. After running experiments, Brev Ra and I suspect why they wanted to go there. The Tau Ceti data and our own testing indicates that the unique radiation signature of their yellow sun may provide some sort of enhancement to Argonian cells. We had theories that our race would be stronger and more powerful than any of the humans, aliens, or their mutant hybrids, the Chromodecs, but we ran out of time for further testing."

Kaelen shook her head as tears welled up and ran down her cheeks. "I don't want to be more powerful. I want to stay with my house."

"*Eina*, you will always be with Ra because our house will live on in you." Her father touched the glowing emblem on her ship suit. "The war with Hogath did more than damage our planet. It severely weakened us in this sector and Argon has enemies that would love to pillage the Thinker library and tech center. It's vital that we send you someplace safe where you won't be found in case the worst should happen here. The new planet can still be dangerous, so you need to be strong." She didn't know if he meant stronger there, or stronger in general for what she was sure would be the destruction of their home.

Clovi spoke with her own eyes full of tears. "Please trust us, *kimea*. Take care of yourself on the new world and we'll join if we're able."

"Okay." Kaelen read the sadness in her parents' eyes and had a bad feeling about their plans and machinations. She'd studied the ideas and designs for technology that could stabilize their planet's core and didn't see how they'd be able to reverse what had clearly reached a critical point. But she relied on her parents to stay true to their word to help others evacuate and follow if things were beyond repair.

With one last wave, her ship closed and the flight system came online. Kaelen was happy to hear Wex's voice filling the small space inside, indicating the house-bot's program was installed as both teacher and guide for the journey. Another shudder collapsed part of the opening as debris rained down.

Kaelen felt the slight tremor as the engine cycled and her ship smoothly lifted. She mourned the deaths that had occurred since the tremors began, and feared for the rest of her people should they continue. Her ship had just cleared the exosphere when it rocked violently. Kaelen brought the rearview screen online and gasped as glowing cracks appeared all over the surface of the planet. The tiny ship was exceptionally fast though and was clear of danger when Argon exploded and the shockwave hit.

"No!" Kaelen covered her mouth with both hands and sobbed as she watched the end of everything she'd ever known.

She wasn't allowed to grieve long before Wex spoke. *"Apologies, Kaelen Ra-Evon, but I have orders from your father to begin your education immediately if they failed to prevent the destruction of Argon. Prepare yourself for hypnopedia in one* dendir. *"* Before she could fully process what Wex was saying, Kaelen was put into a deep sleep and her Terran education began.

One year after the destruction of Argon

Leah rose to consciousness slowly, pulled from dreams that had become either a respite from the waking world, or a terrifying reminder of the last time she saw her family. Two weeks and as many surgeries had passed since the accident and Leah already hated the persistent beeping that was jarring and loud in the private ICU room. The last clear thing she could remember from that night was joking around with her brother before a crack of lightning shook the car. Horrendous *screeching* preceded her entire world turning end over end after their car was struck and they tumbled down an embankment.

Leah lay there until the sky grew light, unable to turn away from the unseeing eyes of her parents. She was pressed up against Mads, but he wasn't moving and didn't answer her cries. After a few hours his body grew cold below hers and she knew that he too was dead.

No one told her the cause of the wreck, but she heard nurses whispering outside the door that police suspected it was a Chromodec. The mystery of why remained because the other person found at the scene also died. Either way, Leah didn't want to think about the accident. Unfortunately, every morning she woke in the hospital alone served as a reminder of her losses.

Leah looked out the window and saw that it was already late afternoon and she'd slept nearly the entire day away. It wasn't like there was anything else for her to do other than wish she had died with her family. Who was she to survive when everyone she loved was gone?

After a short while, someone knocked on her door before pushing through. Leah recognized her father's personal lawyer, Dan Desmond. The other two looked vaguely familiar but she couldn't say why. Even though Leah Lockheed was only thirteen, she was in fact a genius. She'd already graduated high school and had been taking college courses for more than a year. Leah was frightened of her future, but she wasn't unaware to the reality of her situation.

"Hi, Leah. You already know who I am."

"Hello, Mr. Desmond."

He gestured toward the man and woman that stepped into the room after him. "I'd like to introduce you to Charlie Tuck, and his wife, Doctor Ellie Tuck." Ellie moved closer to her hospital bed. "Hi, Leah. You probably don't recognize us. We haven't seen you since you were about four years old. With me heading up the Lockheed International labs in Los Angeles, I'm afraid we don't make it to New York very often."

She gave them a curious look. "If you're a doctor, are you going to help me with my legs?"

"Your legs, dear?"

Leah poked one of her skinny thighs. "I can't feel anything. The doctors said my spinal cord was severely compressed in the accident, causing irreparable damage."

"Oh!" Ellie put a hand over her mouth, stifling the reaction.

Dan cleared his throat. "Actually, Charlie and Ellie are your godparents. Marlin left instructions that if anything were to happen to him and your mother, they would take you and your brother in and raise you."

"What about Lockheed International?"

"You don't need to worry about that—"

Leah would not be dissuaded by Dan's placating tone. "I said, what about my family's company?"

He sighed and the Tucks remained silent. "Contingency plan L-47 was initiated upon your parents' deaths. Lockheed's headquarters will move to Los Angeles, closer to the Tucks. Ellie was assigned as your proxy until you come of age, at which time you'll receive your full inheritance and take over as CEO, provided you've achieved the stipulated education and training. Until then, you'll be moving to the Tuck's house in Sello Bay. It's a small town slightly northwest of Los Angeles. You'll live with them and their daughter, Madison."

Her mouth dropped open. "But what about school? I was supposed to start MIT this fall!"

Dan shook his head and lifted his hands in a gesture of helplessness. "I'm afraid I don't know—"

He was interrupted by Charlie. "MIT has a satellite campus in Los Angeles. I know it's not the same as living the dream in Cambridge but it's certainly better than nothing for the time being…at least until you're more settled."

"I see."

"Honey," Leah swung her gaze to Ellie, and something about the woman's tender smile and overall bearing calmed her. "I know we're not your real family, but we'll do everything we can to make you feel welcome with us."

Leah looked from one to the other, then turned her head to meet Dan's dark brown eyes. "Okay." It wasn't like she had a choice. Her father used to say that life didn't slow down for anyone. You either kept up or fell behind. Leah had never fallen behind on anything and she wasn't about to start.

Leah spent a total of six months between the hospital and rehabilitation center before she was released to relocate across the country to live with the Tucks. As a result of the distance, she'd only met Ellie and Charlie a few times before the move and had yet to meet their daughter. It was a difficult journey in more than distance. With all that happened, Leah fell into depression and a therapist came to the house twice a week, paid for with her family's money. She had outpatient therapy at a place in town, to help with the physical side of things.

Lockheed funds also paid to renovate the house in Sello Bay to accommodate Leah's wheelchair. It was an older, three-bedroom home located on twenty acres about fifteen minutes from town. It was a modest house, despite the fact that Ellie and Charlie could certainly afford something larger and newer with their successful, high-profile careers. They kept it because the house had been in Ellie's family for generations, and they never wanted to move.

Ramps were built to each entrance, a lift for the stairs was added, and Maddie's upstairs bedroom and bathroom were expanded to make it more accessible. Ellie previously mentioned that she hoped having the girls share a room would help them develop a bond with each other, as well as give Leah a companion in the unfamiliar house.

All the changes would have been tolerable to the resilient girl, but Madison hated Leah immediately and wasn't shy about it.

Ellie introduced the two with a hopeful smile. "Maddy, this is Leah Lockheed. She's part of the family now and I'd like you to treat her as such. Would you like to show her around?"

Maddy rolled her eyes. "Not likely."

"Excuse me?"

The teenager crossed her arms. "You expect me to be sunshine and roses but it's not like I got a say in any of this. Then you blow out the spare room to make my bedroom and bathroom bigger, and I'm stuck sharing with some rich brat!"

"Madison Shiloh Tuck, you apologize this instant!"

Ellie's body was stiff with fury and Leah wanted to sink into her chair and cry. But she was tired of crying. She didn't blame Maddy, really. Maddy was two years older and an only child. Even Leah could see it had to be difficult for the girl to wake up one morning with an "instant" sister. Leah attempted to placate Maddy. "I'm sorry, I'll try to stay on my side and not bother you."

"Oh, goody!" Sarcasm fairly dripped from Maddy's words before she stomped into the kitchen. A door slammed somewhere, and Leah assumed it was a back door to the house.

"She doesn't mean it, honey. Maddy is just…she's been going through something for a while now and we haven't been able to get through to her. She'll come around."

Leah muttered, "Before or after she pushes me down the stairs?"

"What was that?"

"Nothing, Mrs. Tuck."

Ellie squatted down so she could look Leah in the eye. "Please, none of that. I meant what I said about being part of this family. You can call me Ellie. Now, how about I show you around the house. After that, I'll make us some homemade chocolate chip cookies. With my expanding duties at Lockheed, I'm going to be busy and I don't know when I'll have the opportunity for baking again outside the holidays. At least Charlie will be around to help now that he's officially retired from the CORP science division."

Leah sighed, staring off in the direction that Maddy had gone. "Okay, Mrs—Ellie." She quickly amended after seeing Ellie's finger waggle.

She and Maddy continued to butt heads for the next few months until one day Maddy took it too far. "I can't believe I have to share my room *and* my family with you. Things were great until you came along!"

That's when the quiet and affable Leah snapped. "It's not like I had any more choice in this than you. And at least you still have your family! You didn't wake up one morning with everyone you loved gone, on top of everything I have to deal within this stupid body!"

Maddy blanched. "I—"

"Did you know I have nightmares nearly every night?"

Maddy shook her head.

"I press my face into the pillow so you can't hear and tease me. I loved my brother and you're nothing like him. You might have a similar name, but you're just, just…cold! The only time he was ever cold was when I was pressed against him for hours in the car and I realized that he'd died. He was my big brother and now he's gone." She started to sob, not caring any more if Maddy hated her. Maddy was blocking the doorway to the room so Leah couldn't even leave to hide her breakdown, providing more fuel for mocking.

Instead of doing any of those things, Maddy went silent. Leah looked up to see her staring wide-eyed. Realization twisted Maddy's features, followed quickly by a look of guilt. "Oh my God, Leah! I'm so sorry." Maddy rushed to her side and knelt down next to Leah's wheelchair and held out her arms like she was going to hug Leah.

Leah flinched away, unsure of what to expect. "What—"

"I didn't mean any of it, honest. I'm just… I'm clearly the biggest asshole to ever ass."

Leah's tears abated, part from shock that Maddy was apologizing, and partly from hearing her call herself an ass. She sniffled. "Can you say that last bit again?"

Maddy gave her arm a light pinch then pulled her into an awkward hug. "I'm being serious here. I just," she sighed, "I suppose I'm a bit jealous that you came into my family and you're getting all this attention. Dad quit the stupid CORP for you and it's great having him around now, but he never did that for me. Not that I blame them. You're brilliant and I see the way my mom is amazed by you. You even humor Dad by working out in the garage with him on all his crazy experiments."

"You're not stupid, Maddy. Ellie tells me all the time how smart you are. You're only two years older than me and you're a senior in high school because you skipped grades when you were younger. I think that also qualifies as brilliant."

Maddy rolled her eyes and pointed at herself. "High school," then pointed at Leah. "MIT. I think that proves my point."

Leah grabbed Maddy's finger and gave it a shake, still in awe of the sudden transformation of their relationship. "We're both still kids. Mads used to say that no matter how smart we were, both of us were still kids and allowed to be stupid once in a while. Of course, he usually said that before trying an experiment that he knew we'd get in trouble for." She sighed wistfully. "He always took the blame though."

"You miss him a lot, don't you?"

"I feel like part of me is empty without him. I mean…part of what I have left." She frowned and gestured toward her lower body.

Maddy grabbed her hand and held it between both of hers. Her eyes were down when she cleared her throat, but the words sounded heartfelt. "Um, I know I've been a real bitch to you. I've been trying to figure some stuff out, something, uh, that I'm not sure how to deal with and you came along right in the middle." She looked up to meet Leah's hopeful gaze. "But I'm making a promise to you right now that I'm going to fix this. Can we have a do-over?"

Leah gave her a tentative smile. "I'd like that."

"I know that you've lost your brother and he can never be replaced, but I'm going to try to be the best big sister that I can starting now. What do you say?"

"Promise?" Leah's bottom lip quivered.

Maddy let go of Leah's hand and held up a single pinky. "I pinky swear."

"Maddox used to say the same thing and he always kept his word." Leah hooked her pinky around Maddy's, feeling lighter than she had since the death of her family.

Chapter One

Meanwhile, two thousand miles away, a small, sleek ship landed in a clearing near Zeeland, Michigan. The intended interstellar journey had been shortened to little more than a year because of a wormhole created by the cosmic forces of Argon's explosion reacting with a pocket of dark matter.

The field was part of a ten-acre parcel belonging to Paul and Shelly Miller. Paul had a bird's eye view of the landing from his hunting blind. He forgot all about the buck that had been in his sights less than a minute before. Sure, the venison would have been nice but ignoring things like alien ships wasn't an option. Shelly was there with him and the sound of a motor winding down brought them out of the blind into the chilly November air.

"What the blazes?"

"Paul…"

Rather than answer, he double checked that his barrel was empty and the safety was on before taking the rifle back into the blind. He returned to see Shelly pointing toward the ship that had landed no more than thirty yards from their location. "I think something is happening."

"I'm gonna go check that out." He glanced around, knowing they were in the middle of their property with their nearest neighbor miles away in the opposite direction of the house. "You should probably stay here."

"Oh no you don't, Paul Miller! You are not leaving me by myself while you traipse off into a field to look at some crazy ship. I'm coming with you."

With ten years married, and sweethearts since they were fourteen, he knew better than to argue. "Alrighty then."

It didn't take long to reach the gleaming silver vessel. The cover looked like a type of glass but it was opaque enough they couldn't see inside. "Well, I'll be damned."

"Do you think it's aliens or Chromodecs?"

He shrugged. "Could be refugees, or even CORP. The government's always got secret stuff floating around up there."

Further conversation on the nature of the craft was interrupted as they both heard a loud *psshh* sound of depressurization, and the cover along the top slowly lifted on a vertical hinge. "It's opening!"

Paul muttered drolly, "Ya think?"

Shelly slapped his arm. "Hush, you!"

"Now Shelly, whether this is an alien, Chromodec, or the government, let's agree now not to go near whatever is in that thing until we know it's safe."

"But Brandon says most aliens are refugees and harmless."

"That's easy enough for your nephew to say. He's a fully-trained CORP agent with an entire team to back him up. We've neither youth nor some fancy Chromodec power to our names. Let's be smart about this."

"But what if they're hurt—" The sound of a crying child interrupted whatever Shelly was going to say. She broke into a run toward the craft. Paul was hot on her heals. "Oh! It's a baby…a toddler." She tried to get closer only to be pulled back by her husband.

"Shelly, wait! We don't know anything about that babe, or where it comes from. No matter how much it looks like us, it could be dangerous to humans."

Suddenly the toddler's crying stopped as he noticed the two people watching him. The child hiccupped a few times then pulled himself to stand within the cushion of the ship. He reached out a chubby little hand toward them in an age-old sign of "want," one that neither Miller was able to ignore. The blanket slipped from the nude baby and Paul scratched at his stubbly cheek as he amended his statement. "Correction, where he comes from."

Shelly looked up at Paul while she moved to lift the child into her arms. "You better call Brandon. The CORP needs to know about this and he's probably the quickest way to get through to someone official."

Paul sighed and pulled the phone from his insulated orange camo coat. In the end, the couple made the decision to take the baby up to the house at the edge of the property. It was a tight fit to get both adults and the child on the four-wheeler, along with all their gear, but they managed. They were told to expect agents out of the Chicago office since that was closer to their house than Detroit.

Four hours after the call, a black SUV pulled up their driveway. Brandon exited the passenger side of the vehicle and slammed the door shut.

"Uncle Paul and Aunt Shelly!" He gave both of them a hug and stepped back to introduce the others. Brandon gestured toward the driver, who was a tall and lanky woman dressed in a black suit. "This is Pathos, and the ugly guy over there is Stinger."

The older couple followed Brandon's gesturing hand as he introduced his fellow agents. Shelly's eyebrows lifted when she met the obscenely handsome man with the codename of Stinger. With his high cheekbones, bright green eyes, and deep red hair, he could have graced the cover of any fashion magazine. "My boy, you better have your eyes checked."

Stinger held out his hand when he reached the porch. "Ignore Pulse. He's just jealous I get more dates from both genders than he does. My real name is Shaun Kinney and I've heard a lot about Brandon's family. You seem so nice. I can't believe he shares blood with you."

Brandon made a face. "Rude."

The female agent didn't join in their antics. She was all business. "Where is the child?"

Paul gestured toward their front door. "Please, come in. We just got him to sleep after more than an hour of fussing. Shelly thought he may be teething."

"An alien child?"

Shelly shrugged as the CORP trio followed her inside. "Seems human enough in both appearance and actions. I put him down in our spare room. Sorry the house is such a mess. We were out hunting all day."

"You mean I was hunting. You were reading your romance novels."

Shelly waved him off. "Oh, whatever!"

Brandon looked around the space. "Where's Tate?"

"He's spending the weekend at his buddy's house. Got some new game or something that they've been dying to play."

Paul snorted. "Probably ask for it himself for Christmas. I swear, back when I was a ten-year old kid, we kept it simple with things like Legos and Mario Kart on the Wii, not this fancy VR crap."

"Yeah, yeah, and you probably rode your scooter uphill both ways to school, right?"

Paul shook a finger at him. "Keep it up, kid, and I'll tell Shelly not to bring that apple crumble you like so much to Thanksgiving dinner."

Brandon held up his hands, understanding when he was beat. "You win! At least for the next week."

Stinger laughed outright and Pathos merely shook her head before turning to Shelly. "The child?"

"Follow me." It was obvious Pathos was the agent with the most seniority. She motioned for the other two to stay in the living room with Paul. The house wasn't large, just a small three-bedroom ranch but it did feature a full basement. It was big enough for the small family of three with a little extra space for Shelly's craft projects. She stopped in front of a closed door. "Paul found Tate's old crib in the basement and brought it up to my craft room. We figured it would be quietest in there with all the material and whatnot absorbing sound."

"Good thinking. And the ship?"

"We left that in the field. Didn't have a way to bring it up to the house. It's pretty secluded out there, not much will bother it but some wildlife."

They quietly crept into the room and stood near the crib peering down at the sleeping child. His skin was deeply tanned and he had a thick mop of fine black hair. Pathos took off a black glove and held her middle finger to her temple while staring intently at the baby. Shelly assumed she was using her Chromodec power but didn't know what it was. Probably something mental.

Pathos lowered her hand and kept her voice to a whisper. "Has he displayed any abilities?"

"Nothing. Just looks and acts like any other baby that I've seen."

The agent rubbed her chin. "Hmm…the CORP doesn't exactly have the resources to take in an alien refugee this young."

"You mean this has never happened before?"

"Not like this, no. There have been other refugee babies in the past, but they were sent down to live with guardians. This is a different set of circumstances we're dealing with here." Pathos gestured toward the door. "I need to make a call."

They returned to the living room and Pathos went outside, leaving Shelly to join the conversation in progress.

"What did Tate say about the ship and baby?"

Paul shrugged. "We didn't tell him. No sense interrupting his time with his friend over something that will be in and out of our lives faster than most of his gaming missions."

Shelly glanced toward the front window where she could see Pathos gesticulating wildly while speaking into the phone. "I'm not so sure about that."

"What do you mean, honey?"

She met his gaze. "I don't think the CORP is equipped for something like this. Doesn't sound like they have anyone to take care of an alien child, a potential child of power."

"She's got a point, Uncle. It's not like we can take him back to the downtown CORP headquarters. That's no place for a kid let alone a baby that young."

"So, what's going to happen to him?"

Stinger looked around the house and Shelly watched the way he paid closer attention to the family photos that littered the walls. Tate's school pictures, sports teams, his artwork, and plenty more of their family and extended family. He nudged Brandon's arm. "I've got a twenty that says they ask your aunt and uncle to take him in."

Brandon snorted. "Here in Zeeland? No way. They'll bring him back to Chicago and put the kid in a home where they can keep an eye on him. I'll take that bet."

Paul and Shelly made eye contact, appearing to speak without speaking. She tilted her head and he shrugged. She blinked back and he nodded.

Stinger looked back and forth between them. "Did I miss something?"

"Ignore them. My aunt and uncle have this weird thing they do and they're always on the same page. Mom says they're like two peas in a pod. Poor Tate can't get away with anything."

Paul shook his fist at him. "I'll pea your pod."

Their laughter quieted as soon as Pathos came back into the house carrying a tablet. Mr. and Mrs. Miller, the CORP has a proposition for you."

"Well, shit!" Stinger laughed at Brandon.

Shelly gestured toward the doorway leading into the kitchen and dining area. "How about we have a seat in there? I have a feeling this discussion will go better with some coffee."

It didn't take long for Pathos to lay out the CORP offer. They'd be given a stipend in exchange for raising the child. "The only caveat is that you send monthly reports on his progress, and immediately report any powers that develop."

"What about the boy's family?"

"Obviously, we'll want to know if anyone comes to claim him or if you get any other alien visitors." The Millers quietly mulled over the offer after reading through the fairly straight forward fostering contract. The CORP would cover any medical costs or damages incurred should the child become dangerous or destructive. They'd lose the stipend if they adopted the boy, they falsified documents, or broke any laws while serving as foster parents.

Pathos looked concerned that they hadn't answered yet. "The CORP can also provide parenting guidelines and other reference material if you need—"

Shelly cut in, "I've raised one boy successfully to the age of ten, I think I can make it at least that far on my own with another. You can save your pamphlets and whatnot." She turned to her husband. "Paul?"

He narrowed his eyes and pointed to one section of the digital contract. "Make it quarterly for those reports, and I don't want to spend ages filling out your stupid forms. Simple is better. And what about the ship?"

"The CORP would take—"

"It technically belongs to the boy. It may be all he has to connect him with his people."

Pathos blew out a breath and nodded. "You've made good points. Give me a few minutes, please."

Brandon stood next to Paul with his arms crossed. "Tate is gonna freak out and you're going to lose your craft room, Aunt Shelly."

Shelly smiled. "The craft room can be moved back to the basement, not that I'll have much time for it with a baby in the house. And Tate asked a few weeks ago why we never had any more kids. He said he wished he had a little brother."

Piercing cries broke the quiet of the house and Brandon laughed. "I bet he regrets those words."

Paul shook his head. "Tate's a good boy. He'll be fine."

"I'll go get him." Shelly caressed Paul's shoulder as she stood and left the room.

Another minute went by before Shelly walked through the doorway with the boy on her hip. He was once again wrapped in his blanket and looked around the bright kitchen with fascination. Pathos refreshed her tablet screen and displayed an updated contract. She also brought up a single short form. "This is what you'll be requested to fill out once every three months. After you sign and provide us with your bank information, the CORP will initiate the first monthly deposit for the child's care. If you consent, the CORP will build a secure storage solution on your property and you'll be given the access code."

"That will work as long as I get a say in the where of it. But I have a suggestion: there's a hidden sublevel beneath the barn that I think would easily hold the ship."

"Of course. If you take us to the ship when we're finished, we have the equipment with us to get it moved."

"What about his name?" Shelly asked. "He'll need that for some sort of citizenship proof, right?"

"The CORP hadn't planned on—"

"Absolutely not! If the CORP is going to contract with us to raise a child in the United States, they need to give us documentation of citizenship. What if his family never comes to get him? He'll need to make a life here on Earth."

Pathos rubbed her forehead. "Give me another minute please." She typed away at her tablet and waited for a response from whomever was on the other end. It came back less than a minute later. The stern agent's fingers hovered over the keypad. "Rocket agreed. What do you want to call him?"

"Us?"

Pathos waved around the room. "Someone needs to name him and it's not going to be these two clowns."

"Hey!"

Paul spoke quietly. "If you want to name him that, I'll support you."

"Name him what?"

Shelly looked up at her nephew. "We didn't tell many folks but Tate was born as a fraternal twin. There were multiple complications during their birth. His brother had a nuchal cord and didn't survive. I also suffered severe uterine bleeding and the doctor was forced to perform a full hysterectomy to save my life."

"Oh. Does Mom know?" Brandon asked.

"She was one of the only people we told because I struggled to deal with it all. But I think it's time to make a good memory with that second name we chose." She looked toward her husband. "We've got one beautiful boy named after my dad. I think it would be nice to have another named for your pop."

Paul pointed toward the tablet. "Write down Michael Allen Miller. That's what we're going to call him."

An hour later, the small spaceship had been stowed beneath the barn and the SUV was gone. Brandon left Paul and Shelly with a promise that he'd seem them the following week for Thanksgiving at his mom's house. Shelly stood in the middle of the living room, cradling the boy that appeared to be close to a year old. "Looks like we have some shopping to do."

Paul scratched his stubble and glanced down the hall where the door to Shelly's craft room stood open. "And some rearranging."

A gurgle came from the babe and Shelly ran a finger along the soft cheek below a bright hazel eye. "Welcome to the family, Michael."

* * * *

"I have to tell you something. Can you promise to keep a secret?"

Maddy and Leah were in their room getting ready for bed after celebrating Maddy's seventeenth birthday earlier in the day. "You spend half your nights helping me through my nightmares. I'd say we can trust each other pretty well by now."

"I'm serious."

Leah gave her a worried look. "Is this about the adoption? You know I didn't ask them to do it."

"It's not that. I actually like the idea that you're gonna be my sister for real and asked them to announce it tonight after we cut the cake."

Leah threw a pillow at her. "Sure, you say that now. I thought you were going to push me down the stairs when we first met."

Maddy grinned and shrugged.

"So, what did you want to tell me?"

"Will you promise not to tell Mom and Dad? I've gotta be ready and I'm not yet."

Leah rolled closer to Maddy's side of the room and held out her hand. "I pinky swear."

Maddy hooked their little fingers together and gave a tug. Then she shoved her hands beneath her thighs where she sat on the bed, but not before Leah saw them shaking. Rather than call Maddy on her nerves, Leah waited.

"I'm gay."

It took less than a second for Leah to respond. "Uh huh."

Maddy's head jerked up and she met Leah's gaze. "What?"

"I said yes, as in I'm agreeing with you."

Maddy's mouth dropped open in surprise. "You knew!"

"I went to an all-girls school for years and everyone was older than me. You don't think I know what it looks like when a girl likes another girl? Like you and Dani last year?" She delighted in the blush that colored Maddy's cheeks. "If it makes you feel any better, I'm bi."

"Yeah, I knew that. You've got as many pictures of boys as you do girls on your wall." Maddy paused then shook her head and laughed as she turned to look at her own wall over her shoulder. "We're idiots, aren't we?"

Leah sniffed and gestured toward the academic accolades sitting on her dresser. "Speak for yourself." The pillow came flying back toward her head and she easily caught it. "We can tell them together when you're ready."

Maddy stood from the bed and came over to Leah's side of the room to give her a hug. "Thanks…sis." When she pulled away, her brows furrowed. "Do you think they'll be cool with it?"

"I think Charlie will be over the top supportive."

"Yeah?"

Leah grinned. "I bet you ten dollars."

Laughter rang through the room. "I know for a fact you're good for more, but I'll take that bet."

Maddy appeared pretty happy to lose the bet a week later when both girls came out, Maddy as a lesbian and Leah as bi. Ellie simply baked two cakes and Charlie frosted them to look like the flags he found online.

Unfortunately, death came knocking a year later over the winter break. Everyone was home for two weeks, even Ellie. Lockheed always shut down its North American facilities to give its employees paid leave to spend time with their families. Maddy had begun premed studies in her third year at UCLA, maintaining her level of prodigy. She pulled up the drive of their Sello Bay home to see her dad outside splitting logs at the side of the house nearest their woodshed. After parking, Maddy grabbed her suitcase and ran over to give him a bear hug. "Why are you doing all this by hand? Don't we have a log splitter?"

He chuckled. "We do. I didn't feel like hauling it out today."

Maddy looked at his sweaty red face. "You should probably take a break before you give yourself a heart attack, yeah? I'll come out and split a pile later after I put my stuff away and steal some cookies."

"How do you know there are cookies?"

"Mom always makes cookies on my first day home." He swatted at her and she danced away. "Smarty! Remind me later to show you what I built in the garage." She rolled her eyes but was genuinely curious.

"What is it this time, a portal to another dimension?"

Charlie aimed another swat at his daughter's shoulder. "It was one time that I tried to do that and yet you never let me forget it!"

"Dad, you blew all the fuses in the breaker box and we were watching the final episode of Seventh Sister!"

He held up his hands in defeat. "Fine, I'm sorry for ruining the last episode of your witch show. But I promise, this isn't something so pie in the sky. I created a new chair for Leah, one that will float off the ground rather than roll. It's custom molded and it will give her more freedom of motion."

"Like the one the comic book guy has, Professor X?" He nodded. Maddy glanced toward the front door of the house, then looked back at him. "Did she ask you to do that?"

He lowered his voice. "No, she didn't. But Maddy, you know how it is. Her dream isn't only to take over her family's company in a few years. She wants to work in the labs and bring all those ideas she has to life. You and I both know that labs aren't really tailored to a person who doesn't have full freedom of motion." He sighed. "It's more than that though. Even now, years after the accident, I still hear her talking to Ellie about her nerve damage. She's constantly keeping tabs on the biomedical community to see if there have been any advancements in nerve and spinal cord regeneration. I wish I could fix that for her but it's not my field of expertise. I'm just an engineer." He swallowed and looked away.

"You're more than that and you know it. I think it's thoughtful of you, Dad."

When he looked back, his eyes shimmered with unshed tears. "I figured if I could make things a little easier for her, I could give back some of the mobility that was lost in that accident. As I said, the new floating chair is incredibly high tech, sleek, and small. It can raise and lower to bring her to whatever level she needs."

Given her own pre-med studies and learning about patients with varying degrees of spinal injury, Maddy was interested in her dad's latest invention. "What about rough terrain or stairs?"

He smiled. "It can easily traverse both. I actually used Lockheed's new batteries and agreed to share the design if I could borrow one of the company's experimental hover-fields. Leah may be getting the prototype of this new chair, but with any luck thousands of others around the world will benefit as well."

Maddy shook her head and gave her dad another hug. "You continue to amaze me."

"Yeah?"

"Absolutely! Now, I'm gonna have some cookies with my sister, then I'll come out and set up the log splitter. So, you can put that down now." She pointed at the ax in her dad's hand where it was leaning over his shoulder. He merely winked at her and stood watching as she grabbed her duffle bag and jogged up the front steps and into the house proper. Maddy heard the sound of him splitting wood again when she was out of sight and she shook her head.

An hour later Maddy slid her chair away from the kitchen table. "Hey, I promised Dad I'd split some wood. Can you clean up and tell Mom I'll shower before dinner"

"Sure."

Less than a minute after Maddy walked out the front door, her scream pierced the cool morning air and brought Ellie and Leah out of the house. "Dad!"

Ellie called out, "Maddy?"

Maddy had already stumbled through the scattered wood pile and was on her knees performing CPR. "He's in cardiac arrest, call 9-1-1!"

Ellie ran inside to grab her phone while Leah sat frozen in her chair, breath fogging as she took in the sight of Maddy compressing Charlie's chest. Ellie was on the phone with the emergency operator as she ran down the stairs toward her daughter and husband.

"Mom, I need you to give breaths while I do the compressions." Leah broke out of her fog long enough to roll down the long chair ramp and sat helplessly at the bottom.

"Leah," Leah turned to look at her adoptive mother. "Take the phone and talk to the operator, let them know where to have the ambulance turn off from the main road so they can find our place. I'm going to go help Maddy, okay?"

"Okay." She took the phone from Ellie and nearly dropped it on the ground as fear made her hands shake. "Hello?"

"Hi, can you tell me who I'm speaking with?"

"This is Leah. My mom is helping my sister give my dad CPR. Maddy said he's not breathing and in cardiac arrest."

"Thank you, ma'am. The ambulance should be there in about fifteen minutes."

She begged, "Please, they have to come sooner. She's already been working on him for a few minutes and the human brain can only survive for so long. She's going to tire soon."

"Do you know CPR? Can you spell her for a bit?"

"I…" Leah looked at the ground where Charlie had fallen. One of the wood piles had been knocked over creating a debris field of split wood that her chair would never navigate. She wished more than anything that she had one of the rugged chairs built for trails, but she'd never been particularly outdoorsy. "I'm in a wheelchair and they're in an area I can't reach. I'm sorry."

The kind person on the other end of the call prompted, "How old are you, Leah?"

Her voice wavered, the memory of another time and another accident bringing tears to her eyes. "I'm sixteen."

"Hold on the line for me, okay? Paramedics will be there soon."

Hours later, Leah was at a loss, sitting next to Ellie and Maddy as they clung to one another and cried. Even with her sister's knowledge of CPR, there was nothing they could have done to prevent the massive heart attack.

The three Tuck women leaned on each other during their grieving period. They all cried when Maddy unveiled the new chair her father had told her about. Leah was grateful that she had Charlie in her life for as long as she did. But while Leah had plenty of therapy dealing with the loss of her first family, it was a new and traumatic experience for her sister. Maddy spiraled into depression and began drinking enough that her grades dipped.

The real turning point in Maddy's healing came about six months after Charlie died, when she was home on summer break from UCLA.

Maddie came downstairs and fixed her plate after Ellie and Leah were both seated at the table. When they were nearly finished eating, Ellie rested her fork on the side of the plate. Leah tried to stay quiet because more often than not, Maddy snapped at everything like a hurt animal. Too many times over the past few months, dinners with the three of them ended with an argument between Ellie and Maddy.

"I got a letter from the university today."

Maddy glanced up and went back to eating. "Oh joy."

Ellie sighed. "How are you failing molecular biology? That's one of your favorite subjects."

Leah sucked in a breath in shock. "You're failing bio?"

Maddy stood abruptly, her chair scraping loudly across the wood floor. "So what? We can't all be perfect little geniuses!"

"But I'm not—that's not what I meant."

"Save it. I'll be in the garage if you need to lecture me some more."

"Madison Shiloh Tuck, you get back here and apologize to your sister!"

Rather than obey her mother, Maddy shoved through the screen door that led out the back of the house. The spring creaked, then snapped the wood frame back to slam into the door jamb, startling Leah. She looked down at her own half empty plate and pushed it away. "I'm not hungry anymore. May I be excused?"

Ellie scrubbed her face with her hands, then her soft brown eyes met Leah's gaze. "Sure, honey. I'll clean up here." She paused for a moment before asking, "Are you going to check on her?"

Leah glanced out the door toward the garage where her sister had gone. "Yeah."

"Maybe give her a little time to cool down first."

"Okay. I'm going to study for the exam I've got coming up."

"You know you don't have to take classes all summer, right? You should live a little, appreciate the time off."

Leah shrugged. "I like to learn. It's something I'm good at and it makes me feel…normal. Worthy instead of worthless."

She watched as Ellie tensed and narrowed her eyes. "You are not worthless. You would never be worthless! I don't want to hear that kind of talk from you, okay?"

"But—"

"But nothing, Leah Avery Lockheed-Tuck! You are kind, brilliant, beautiful, and destined for greatness and nothing can convince me otherwise."

"I don't want to overshadow Maddy."

"Maddy carries greatness within her as well, but in a different way. You're both the most important people in the world to me and I want you to be happy. Give your sister some time then see if you can talk to her."

"I will."

An hour later, Leah made her way out to the large garage where Maddy often retreated while she was home from university after Charlie's death. She knocked on the door but there was no answer, so she turned the handle and moved her hoverchair inside. Maddie was wrapped in an old flannel shirt of her father's, drunk and crying in his favorite chair.

"Go 'way."

Leah ignored her. Instead, she maneuvered closer and pulled Maddy into her lap and took her back into the house. It was nice that she no longer had to mess with the chair lift, the hover capability making her ascent smooth as could be. Once in their room, Leah was able to shove Maddy off her lap into her sister's childhood bed. She got a glass of water from the bathroom for her, then sat and held Maddy's hand while she sobbed.

"Why did he leave me?"

Leah wiped her own tears with a free hand. "I don't know why they leave."

"I miss my dad."

"I know. I do too."

Once Maddy was all cried out and appeared to sober up a bit, Leah returned those words from years before. "I know that you've lost your dad and he can never be replaced, but I'm going to try to be the best little sister that I can starting now. What do you say?"

Maddy squeezed Leah's hand and gave her a watery smile. "You already are. Thanks, Leah. Love you." Then she closed her eyes and passed out.

"Ugh, it sucks being an intern. I'm glad I was able to make it for dinner." It was Leah's eighteenth birthday and Maddy had a rare night off from the hospital.

Ellie smiled at Maddy. "Susan says Los Angeles General Hospital has the highest treatment rate in the emergency department, but they're also busy."

Maddy nodded. "One of the reasons I was hoping I'd land that one. And yeah, busy is an understatement."

"You look tired, honey. Are you getting enough sleep?" Ellie reached across the table to feel Maddy's forehead and Maddy gently slapped her hand away.

"Mom!"

Leah snickered at the fussing and Maddy pointed a finger at her. "Hey, not all of us can intern at a cushy job like Lockheed International."

She shot back, "You seem to forget that I've managed to earn two doctorates and a master's while doing my internship. You can't even manage sleep." She stuck out her tongue. Maddy started to flip her off but put her hand back down when Ellie scowled.

"Girls, can you play nice this evening? It's a momentous occasion."

Maddy smirked across the table and Leah fidgeted at the familiar look.

"So, how does it feel?"

Leah's apprehension was replaced by confusion. "How does what feel?"

"Being a rich bitch again."

"Madison Shiloh Tuck!"

Leah laughed and shook her head. "Ha-ha, you got middle-named! And you're still an asshole."

"But I'm the best sister, admit it."

"Never!" Leah slapped Maddy's arm, and Maddy slapped hers in return.

Ellie shook her head at their antics. "Children, do you think we can make it through dinner now? We have an early start tomorrow, first to the lawyer to sign the paperwork for Leah's inheritance and CEO assumption, then off to L-I where she'll be officially introduced to the board. They're all in Los Angeles for this transition."

Leah made a face. "Fantastic."

Ellie put her hand on top of Leah's where it rested on the table. "Honey, you can wait to make the transition, no one will force you. I'm happy to have you take over if you want it, but if you're not ready, say the word."

"No, I'm ready. I'll be fine. I'm inviting clouds into a clear sky." All three of them smiled at what had been one of Charlie's favorite sayings. "As long as I have you as my VP of Operations, I should be fine."

"When is Miss Pérez set to start?"

Leah smiled at the mention of the woman she met while attending classes at the MIT satellite campus in Los Angeles. They were fast friends, even though Ana was five years older and in her last year of school at the time. To be fair, everyone was older than Leah. Ana was part of a special program for lower income students and was pursuing a double major in Business Technology and Accounting. She was over the moon to be offered a job at Lockheed International when she graduated a few years back.

Leah smiled at Ellie. "I told her to take a few days and relax before she starts in the corporate finance department next Monday. I would like to put her in as David Stein's second. A little bird told me he's thinking of retiring in a few years."

"Who's David Stein?" Maddy took a sip of her water and made a face. Leah knew Maddy had been drinking for years at college but didn't dare in front of their mother or in a public place because she was still a year below legal drinking age. Leah never told their mother about finding Maddy drunk in Charlie's garage that night. "He's the chief financial officer."

Maddy raised a dark eyebrow at that. "Your friend is pretty young to fill the size of those shoes."

"Ana is brilliant with finance and insight in regards to the direction of technology in the world, so I'm not worried about her being able to do the job once she knows what's expected. I've met some of the board members already. Too many of them stare at me as though I'm fresh meat in the piranha tank. I'd prefer to have people I can trust implicitly in the important positions."

Ellie nodded. "She's right. The board is a mixed bag this quarter. Phasing out all weapons manufacturing from the company and switching over to information technology, biomedical, and green energy projects within the first five years after the accident put some of the old guard's panties in a bunch."

"I know it wasn't easy for you, Ellie. But after reading about all those lawsuits over the years, I couldn't in good conscience keep doing things the way my father did. The mass shooting with David Roger Coleman was what, maybe six years ago? It was all over the television right before the accident."

Maddy and Ellie both frowned. "I've never been involved in that part of the company as the Los Angeles labs have always focused on the biomedical side of the business. But I remember that Coleman's lawyer tried to say he snapped because of L-I's marketing campaign at the time that glorified gun ownership and equated weapons with nationalism."

"That was no excuse for him to take a fucking duffel bag of semiautomatic pistols and assault style rifles to a peaceful Earth Day protest in New York. The loss of life that day, hundreds of people dead and injured, including kids. It makes me sick as both a human and a doctor!" Ellie didn't correct Maddy's language. It was a sore subject for everyone.

Leah sighed. "I mean, obviously Coleman was at fault because, ultimately, he pulled the trigger. But where does the blame end? He wasn't wrong about Lockheed at the time. I may have been young but I wasn't stupid. I looked it up a few years ago and didn't like what I found."

Ellie patted her hand. "I'm sorry, honey. I didn't think you were paying attention to all that back then, what with the accident and recovery to deal with."

"You were stuck in the middle of it, and you never said a word to me at the time."

The older woman gave her a sad smile. "I didn't want to bother you. It was my job to deal with the fallout and that's why I agreed with your request to phase weapons from Lockheed's business portfolio. The board initially agreed because splintering that part of the business and selling to companies like Guardian Technologies brought in dividends to all the stockholders, despite the shakeup and market loss caused by your father's death. As for Lockheed International, obviously we had the best lawyers and none of the lawsuits from the families came to fruition. It was, as you said, ultimately the responsibility of one man."

"No matter what the judge or jury said, I don't believe that. I can't. We have a responsibility to the world, to fight against those who would make money off the backs of the poor, the disillusioned, and the victims." Leah thumped her fist into her other palm. "I want Lockheed International to be a force for good, starting now."

Maddy gave her shoulder a little shove. "With you and Mom heading the company, it will be."

"I'm well aware that some folks on the board aren't fans of Lockheed's current direction or the fact that Leah is going to take over at such a young age. That's the main reason I agreed to serve in a dual capacity as senior VP of Operations and director of the Special Projects Lab."

Ellie shook her head and her lips twisted with a scowl. "Some were bad before, always pressing about profits and trying to make deals behind my back. But a few of them started to show their colors four years ago when the Alien and Chromodec Equal Opportunity Employment Act passed. Many on the board aren't fans of ACEOE and doubled down on their ignorant comments when L-I put out an announcement that we were willing to hire all applicants, regardless of origin and power profile. A few were voted out by shareholders but others remain."

Maddy used a fork to stuff a shrimp in her mouth. She commented through half-masticated seafood. "Good, vote them all out! Anyone on that board who still wants to discriminate after the uprising and reparations thirteen years ago are assholes."

Ellie shrugged. "I understand though, Maddy. The world went crazy when Colonel Marek Maza started the Chromodec uprising. The CORP has done a lot to regain the country's faith in their ability to control both aliens and Chromodecs who go rogue. But people remember the damage and death that occurred because of one deranged man with a demented view of reality."

"Still." Maddie grumbled.

"You know they tried to pin that one on us too?" Both Maddy and Leah shook their heads. "The CORP found a lot of Lockheed gear as well as crates of high-tech rifles that were barely out of prototype. Officially they were reported stolen but…"

Leah sucked in a breath. "You don't think my father had anything to do with it, do you?"

"I knew Marlin for a long time and can't imagine that he'd cut a deal with the likes of Maza. No, it was more than likely someone lower down the food chain trying to make some fast cash. Either way, with the reports of theft filed before the uprising, the company came away unscathed. Let's just say I'm glad that we're done with all that business because it would have weighed heavily on my conscience otherwise."

"Me too. Thanks for supporting me, Ellie. I'd forgotten about the uprising."

Maddy snickered. "That's because you were a baby at the time."

Leah raised her eyebrow. "I was five at the time and already spoke three languages, thank you very much. Like you're one to talk. You were only seven."

Maddy shrugged and gave her a lopsided grin. "It's true. And honestly, I don't remember it that well either, other than what I learned in school."

"I wish I didn't remember it. We're lucky that we had the hero members of the CORP, especially Nova and T'ala available to quell it. But the things they had to face with Congress after…despicable." Ellie shook her head. "I was scared for your father when all that happened. He wasn't even an active agent at the time. Charlie mainly worked down in the labs. They actually put him in the field right after, can you believe it? Tensions were high and public opinion was low against the CORP."

"You know Dad could handle himself, he was a fully trained agent."

"Trust me, girls. I know better than either of you. Maddy, with you being so young, the two of us stayed in Sello Bay the entire time until things calmed down. I was frightened that the world was going to burn. Things were bad, really bad. Not many of us in my generation forget so easily, despite all the reconstruction and education that came after."

Leah scowled. "That still doesn't excuse Jones's and Strathmore's behavior on the board. I saw the recording of that last meeting. Real healing on all sides can't happen unless we give people a chance."

Maddy nodded and pointed at Leah. "Old soul right there and folks better listen. And on a lighter note, I'm glad that you're taking your rightful place as the head of Lockheed International." She swallowed and met Leah's gaze. "You are the embodiment of hope and progress and deserve this, sis."

In a rare moment of insecurity, Leah asked, "You think so?"

Maddy leaned over to give her a quick, one-armed hug, before straightening again and stabbing another shrimp with her fork. "I know so."

Ellie lifted her glass of wine and the other two followed with their sparkling waters. "To the future that stretches before us like an unending blanket of stars."

Both daughters echoed portions of her sentiment. Maddy called, "To the future," At the same time Leah smiled and recited, "To the stars." It was a good night for the Tuck family.

Chapter Two

*Five years later and a little more than ten years
after the destruction of Argon*

Kaelen woke to Wex's voice. *"We are entering the Terran solar system and will begin the landing sequence as soon as we reach low planetary orbit in approximately twenty-six minutes. I have activated the distress beacon that will allow us to land on Earth unhindered by any of its Tau Ceti protectors."*

Kaelen recognized the foreign language called English right away. She assumed that Wex had switched over to the regional language to help her acclimate to the local customs and culture. "Earth? I thought I was going to Terra."

"Earth is the native name for the planet. Terra is Tau Ceti terminology."

"How long was I asleep?"

"Kaelen Ra-Evon, your journey has lasted for ten Earth years and four Earth months. Your ship is currently on a trajectory to land in the far northern part of the continent called North America. Our records indicate that the United States of America is the most powerful nation and grants its citizens the greatest amount of freedom. They also have the highest population of aliens and powered individuals they call Chromodecs."

She felt strange and realized that both her mind and body had grown while she slept in ship stasis. Kaelen didn't have memory of the experience necessarily, but the way the learning worked was immersive, with lessons growing systematically more difficult and emotionally demanding to fully prepare her for adulthood on a foreign planet.

Kaelen left Argon a thirteen-year-old girl. She arrived on Earth as a twenty-four-year-old woman. She was clean and healthy as a result of the onboard nutrient tanks and the nanotechnology programmed to maintain a body during long space travel. The grief of her lost world was still there in the back of her mind, but it wasn't as sharp or painful as she remembered at the time of the explosion. Kaelen assumed part of the education included therapeutic emotional adjustment as well.

She mentally catalogued the languages she'd been instructed in that were part of Earth's cultural make up. English, French, Spanish, Russian, Arabic, Chinese, German, and Japanese. "The languages… there are so many!"

"Those are but ten of hundreds."

"Hundreds? How do these people even communicate with each other?"

"Is that a question for me, Kaelen Ra-Evon?"

"No, Wex. Is there anything else I should know?"

"Ship sensors detected an Argonian beacon pulse shortly after entering the star system."

Kaelen felt hopeful. "That means someone has landed and is seeking contact. Could it be my parents?"

"I have no way to make a definitive determination but probability is low since the craft is already on Earth and anyone that escaped Argon would have left at the same time, or just after you."

She hated that her AI was so logical sometimes. "I suppose that's true. Can we track the signal once we land?"

"Unfortunately, private pods are not equipped with the technology needed to track a microsecond-long coded communication burst that only broadcasts once every six Earth weeks. Perhaps you can use Earth science to aid your efforts."

"Isn't Earth supposed to be primitive?"

"Your new planet is, but you are not. Your training on Argon put your mind far above anyone else on Earth and thus you should be able to make use of the natural resources and primitive technology to fashion a beacon receiver and decoder."

She scowled. "Why is everything so complicated?"

"It is to prevent Argonian enemies from preying on weak or distressed ships."

Kaelen sighed and considered the standard protocol she'd learned from her father, regarding exploration of a new world. "Do I have any objectives when I reach Earth?"

"Objective one, hide your Argonian ship. Objective two, apply for asylum in the nearest major country. Objective three, hide your yellow sun-given powers. Objective four, exchange the minerals located in the front compartment of the ship for local currency to fund your new life on Earth. Objective five, contribute to society in a meaningful way that doesn't advance Earth's science too far or too fast."

"Why do I need to hide my abilities in a place populated by other powered individuals and aliens? And what are these Chromodecs that my father mentioned? The Terran history on the subject was vague."

"Earth Chromodecs are a human/alien hybrid, though records indicate the alien portion of their genetic makeup was originally human stock, tampered with centuries ago by the Tau Ceti. They can be quite dangerous."

"Dangerous?"

"Earth suffered from a Chromodec uprising eighteen years ago, primarily located in the United States of America. Evon Ra and Brev Ra received the most recent data about Earth from the Tau Ceti shortly before Argon's demise. It indicated that Earth became more welcoming in the eight years that followed, but powerful individuals could still seek to do you harm. You must keep your abilities hidden from all."

Kaelen sighed. There was a lot to do before she could begin to create a home for herself. The light shining through the clear cover of her ship was brighter than the rose hue she was familiar with. It made her skin tingle and she felt strange. Different. "Wex, what will my yellow sun powers be on Earth?"

"There is no data to supply an answer for you, Kaelen Ra-Evon. You will have to discover them and learn to control them after you land."

A short while later, the ship began to shake as it hit Earth's upper atmosphere. Unlike the last time she was near a planet, Kaelen felt no fear. After all, she couldn't lose everyone she loved a second time. The ship made a controlled descent, though Kaelen was annoyed the angle of approach prevented her from seeing the surface of the planet through the clear cover.

Kaelen touched a button to bring up an image of the land below and gasped. "Trees!" She recognized what they were from her Terran education programmed into the ship, most likely garnered from Tau Ceti scout ships. They were similar to the ones in Argon's history books. She'd seen trees before on other planets, but nothing like the expanse below. The area which she descended in looked to be covered with them, like great spindly green fingers reaching toward the sky. And the sky, it was light blue like the oceans of Tamarae. "Great Vos, this land looks as beautiful and unspoiled as any I've seen with my father."

"While Earth has parts that are untainted, such as the region we will be landing in, other urban areas suffer from overcrowding and pollution. It is the bane of many fossil-fuel driven industrialized nations."

"Where are we landing in the United States of America?"

"Calculating..." There was a brief pause before Wex answered her question. *"Unfortunately, systems indicate that a robust airspace defense led by an organization called the Chromodec Office of Restraint and Protection, exists over the most powerful nation so I am altering our course for the other major English-speaking country in North America. The new destination is called Canada, specifically their Northwest Territories. It is a remote location, and you should be able to hide the ship sufficiently to prevent discovery."*

Kaelen was already considering the list of objectives. Because of the instruction she was given and her Argonian perfect recall, she could readily picture her new world, and the country of Canada. "That's hundreds of Earth miles from the border of the United States of America. How will I travel there with no means of locomotion? I still need currency to procure items such as clothing to better fit in with Earth society."

The ship abruptly slowed, and Kaelen felt a little bump as it touched down. *"Prepare for atmospheric depressurization."*

The cover seal broke with a *psshh* sound and Kaelen breathed her first lungful of Earth air. She sucked in a few breaths while she continued to lay back in her ship. "It's different, a little heavier."

Wex responded. *"While their atmospheric makeup is very similar to Argon, you'll find slightly higher levels of oxygen and carbon dioxide from what you're used to. Their gravity is ninety-eight percent that of Argon. Size is relatively the same. Earth suffers from occasional geothermal shocks, though they typically follow the major fault lines along the continental plates."*

Having delayed long enough, Kaelen slowly sat up. Wex had warned her that she may have trouble controlling her physical reactions with the new powers. There were no issues yet but she made a conscious effort to be gentle with everything, as if she were holding a data puck. She carefully climbed out of the ship and turned in a circle to look around. A cacophony met her ears. "What is that sound and why is it so loud?"

"I'm not reading abnormally loud phonics in this region. Perhaps this is one of your new yellow sun powers."

Kaelen winced at a particularly loud shriek and clapped her hands over her ears. "If it is, I'm not enjoying it."

"I may have a temporary solution, Kaelen Ra-Evon. There are communicators that fit inside one's ear canals within the left front panel of the ship. Perhaps they can help block some of the sound. I will note this sensitivity in the log. You will most likely be susceptible to high decibel sounds so you must beware."

Kaelen carefully leaned back into the ship to retrieve the items Wex spoke of. Once she had them in her ears the sound quieted. A smile broke over her face. "It's beautiful! Are the trees singing?"

"Those are birds, the avian species living all over the planet. They have been extinct on Argon for thousands of Earth years."

"Birds…" Kaelen whispered.

"Kaelen Ra-Evon, perhaps you should perform a series of tests to discover what other abilities, and weaknesses, you may have."

She sighed at the familiar notion of experimentation. "Okay. How would you recommend I do that?"

Wex's voice came through the communicators in her ears instead of the ship system. *"I would recommend stepping away from the ship first."*

Kaelen walked carefully to the center of the clearing. Tall trees surrounded the space. They were of the coniferous variety according to her new Earth education. "Okay. What now?"

"Start by performing a short vertical jump."

Kaelen bent her legs slightly and did as Wex suggested. Rather than lift a few inches from the ground the way she'd expected based on every childhood game she'd played on Argon, Kaelen shot straight into the air. She rose so fast that a booming sound echoed around her as she broke the sound barrier. "Wex!" She eventually stopped but continued to float in place in a disconcerting manner.

"Kaelen Ra-Evon, it appears as though you have the power of gravity independence on this new world."

She muttered, "Gravity independence, it says…" Kaelen gave an experimental kick of her feet and moved slightly forward. "Does this mean I can fly like the birds that sing in the forest?"

"My calculations indicate that your power of flight will be nothing like the avians of Earth, or even the mechanical constructs created by the humans. Speaking of which—"

Kaelen suddenly heard the whine of an engine approaching through the dampening effect of the communicators. She craned her head around and panicked to see a flying craft heading in her direction. "Wex, there is an Earth jet coming toward me. How do I return to the ground?"

"I have no such knowledge in my database."

She certainly didn't want to sit there to be hit, Kaelen began kicking as though she were in one of the off-planet oceans she'd visited with her father. She barely made it clear of the plane's flight path, the wind of its passing sending her tumbling through the air. As soon as Kaelen thought about how much she wanted to stop the chaotic motion, she came to an abrupt halt. "Oh." She stuck a fist out and mentally pushed forward. It worked.

"Kaelen Ra-Evon, it appears as though you've mastered the motions of gravity independence."

She moved in a circle, then looped, spun, and dove downward. When Kaelen neared the ground again, she reversed her body so she could touch down with her feet. Unfortunately, she didn't properly calculate her speed of approach and sunk nearly two feet into the soil. She made a face and carefully lifted herself out of the hole.

Even though the landing was less than ideal, Kaelen knew she'd improve with practice. And the thought that she could fly was too exciting for her to feel anything but joy. "You can say flight, Wex. I was flying and it was amazing!"

"Well done, Kaelen Ra-Evon. Would you like to try another experiment?"

Kaelen took a deep breath and readied herself. "Yes. What do you recommend next?"

"Please place your hand over the scanner on the inside of the ship." She complied and waited for the contact analysis to complete. Wex spoke a few seconds later. *"It appears as though you have a near field of invulnerability around you, though I am unable to tell the extent of such a field."*

"Invulnerable? I can't be hurt?"

"Based on the molecular structure and density listed in your scan, yes."

She had many concerns about the results. "How far outward does it extend? Is it on all the time? Can I turn it off?"

"Apologies, Kaelen Ra-Evon. I have no answers for those questions. There is a large stone located approximately one hundred Earth yards south from your position. Please proceed to its location."

Kaelen was about to ask which way was south but closed her eyes instead. She was elated to discover that she could sense the electromagnetic field of her new planet. Once she had the direction in mind, she strode the required distance through the trees until she came to a large boulder. "I'm here. Now what?"

"Scans indicate that the boulder has a small enough base for you to sufficiently grab onto it. Please attempt to lift the stone."

She was skeptical at Wex's statement and made a face. "This boulder is larger than I am. I can't lift such a thing!"

"Please comply with the experiment."

Kaelen squatted down to attempt the impossible. She wedged her fingers beneath the soil and gave a quick pull, mentally preparing herself to struggle…only to watch as the large granite formation shot into the air, much like she had done with her first jump. Unsure if there would be other flying craft in the vicinity, Kaelen flew upward to follow the boulder and bring it back down. She misjudged her trajectory and plowed face first into the stone instead, exploding it into pieces. She shook her head to remove loose stone and gravel from her hair and ship suit, then floated in place for a few seconds.

"Enhanced strength is another one of your yellow sun powers, Kaelen Ra-Evon. A tremendous discovery."

Kaelen snorted at the sheer amount of understatement in Wex's declaration. She flew back down to the clearing, landing cleanly near the ship, and smiled proudly.

"Your next task is to run, though all signs lead to the hypothesis that you will be enhanced in this manner as well."

Kaelen had already assumed as much so used care when choosing the direction that she sprinted. She took a breath and suddenly found herself many Earth miles away. Luckily, Wex said the ship's standard short-range capability was equal to that of her line of sight between the ship and her communicators. The higher the ship, the farther the range it had because the system could compensate for the curvature of the Earth. Otherwise, Wex could access one of the orbiting Earth satellites and use it to reach the communicators, but there would be a slight lag if utilizing that method.

"Maximal speed, strength, hearing, and invulnerability. That is your list of abilities I have recorded at this time. Would you like to continue with the experiments, or begin the steps needed to achieve citizenship in the country of Canada?"

She looked around the clearing. "What more can we possibly do in such a primitive setting?" Kaelen caught motion out of the corner of her eye and saw a large, furred form lumbering toward her. Sudden fright had her scrambling backward. She tripped and went down on her backside. It didn't hurt but made it a lot more difficult to maneuver. Kaelen forgot about her invulnerability, as well as all the other powers she possessed under the yellow sun. Instead, she froze with fear as the age-old fight or flight reflex kicked in, one clearly not limited to humans. Her eyes grew warm, and vision took on a yellowish-red hue, much like she remembered from living on Argon.

"Kaelen Ra-Evon, sensors indicate a high level of light radiation building up in the vicinity of your pupils. The Earth bear cannot harm you. I recommend closing your eyes to prevent possible damage to the

local flora and fauna."

Kaelen complied. She grew aware of the warmth emanating from her eyes and worked to slow her breathing. As she calmed, so too did the heat. Kaelen spoke from her place on the ground, eyes still closed. "What if it damages my ship suit?" She heard the creature *whuff* from someplace nearby and didn't move. Soon enough, the sound of its passing faded in the opposite direction from which it had originally approached.

"Your ship suit is comprised of high-density nanofibers with a service layer of nanobots and will repair itself as soon as any damage occurs. The technology will also allow you to reprogram the suit appearance and shape."

"I will do that once I've seen current Earth garments. That will save me from having to purchase clothing or carry excessive baggage wherever I travel."

"That is a logical plan. The ship suit will help protect you from impacts, energy emissions, and keep your body clean during times of prolonged use, even without a connection to an Argonian ship system. The nanobots derive power from a variety of sources such as kinetics, solar radiation, impact vibration, and body heat. After all, it was designed to withstand long-term space travel and planetary exploration."

Kaelen opened one eye, then the other and confirmed that she was once again alone. "Do all creatures of Earth roam around freely in such a manner? It's a bit disturbing."

"Usually in rural areas, though you will see some movement in urban areas as well. If you recall in your training, the larger cities have zoological centers where they seek to preserve rare and dying species."

After taking a few more calming breaths, Kaelen stood. "I think we've got a sufficient understanding of my powers now, Wex." She glanced up to see the sun had moved beyond its zenith and knew the day was waning. "I think it makes the most sense for me to begin the acclimation process. Do you know if this place is secure enough to leave the ship? If not, can you recommend somewhere else?"

"Please stand by while I utilize satellites to scan the region."

Something fluttered nearby, startling Kaelen while she waited. It looked like a flower but came steadily closer. Unsure what it was, she tried to blow the creature away. It froze in midair and dropped to the ground. "Oh! Wex, what did I do?"

"The external camera and sensors on the ship indicate you've discovered yet another power gifted by the yellow sun, Kaelen Ra-Evon. You have the ability to freeze things with your breath. This will come in handy when you hide your ship somewhere on the east face of Mount Nirvana. You should take it soon before daylight is gone."

Kaelen was too concerned about the frozen thing to pay much attention to the AI's suggestion. "Did I kill it?" She knelt down to the ground and gently picked up the small creature with iced wings. It didn't move.

"Earth records indicate that some species of butterfly will reanimate once they are no longer frozen. Perhaps you can practice breathing normally to warm it."

Kaelen tried a forceful breath against her hand and noticed the cold of it right away. She tried a softer puff and felt the difference. Armed with her new knowledge, she gently exhaled against the frozen insect and watched as its wings began to move. It took another minute for it to warm up then the butterfly flittered away. "I did it!"

"Well done, Kaelen Ra-Evon. Are you ready to transport the ship?"

She stood and gazed worriedly at the last connection she had to her home. "You're sure I'll be able to communicate with you once it is hidden?"

"Yes, Kaelen Ra-Evon. My communications system can work through the rock of the mountain range. However, it will not work through the deeper layers of the Earth's crust. As I said before, for a circumferential connection I can utilize the primitive satellites above. Their security is inferior to that of Argon technology."

She nodded. "What is the best method to relocate it?"

"Your strength and flight capability ensures that you'll be able to carry the ship to the mountain face. I would recommend using your newly discovered laser vision to melt an artificial cave in the rock and place the ship within. Then solidify the opening with your freeze breath, to prevent detection from humans that brave the elements and wander too near."

Kaelen wondered if humans often ventured to the top of mountains, but she didn't say anything to Wex. Plan in place, Kaelen retrieved the satchel of her personal belongings from the head of the ship, then she moved to the largest compartment at the foot of the ship to retrieve the items her parents had left her. She paused before opening the small insulated door and took a shaky breath, contemplating the thought that they were the last things from her world, from her parents, before everything was lost.

Kaelen felt a brief pang of sorrow at the thought that she'd never see them again, but it was tempered by her dedication to duty. It was something all Argonians learned from a young age. To learn, forge ahead, persevere, and contribute in a meaningful way to society. Truthfully though, there was a much darker part of her heart that seethed at the lies and betrayal her own family had taken part in. She wondered if things would have turned out differently if they'd spent their time fixing the problem instead of pretending it didn't exist. Or if they'd thought to send a warning to all the citizens so that more could escape the planet.

Shaking free from her depressive thoughts, Kaelen opened the hatch. There were two containers inside, one medical kit and a capsule that must have been placed there by her parents. She picked up the larger one and opened it to see a variety of gems and minerals inside. While holding it in one hand, she reached into the compartment for the medical kit with her other and felt a wave of dizziness, then pain. She staggered back and dropped her parent's capsule. "What is happening?"

"Please stand by for scan."

Kaelen cried out and crawled farther from the ship. "Every joint in my body hurts like someone is stabbing me. Make it stop!"

"Kaelen Ra-Evon, scans indicate a radiation signature emanating from the compartment that is unique to anything else in my database. I will dispatch a drone to remove the dangerous substance."

She squinted through her pain and watched as nanobot clusters swarmed out of a tiny opening on the main console of the ship. They disappeared from sight as they moved down toward the compartment, and she heard the medical kit click open. A few seconds later, a small drone bot came into view carrying a vial of glowing orange liquid. "Is that healing serum? I've never seen it glow like that."

"I can confirm that it was Argonian regenerative serum, though it appears to have been altered somehow. I will run simulations on

causality of its radioactive signature while I have the drone take it away for disposal."

"Thank you." As promised, she felt better as the vial moved farther away. A few minutes later, Wex spoke with their explanation.

"After analysis, I have determined that the regenerative serum must have been affected by Galactic Cosmic Radiation, possibly due to poor pod shielding in the forward compartment. This is not something that would normally make a long journey in such a small craft."

Kaelen had nothing in her education that matched Wex's description. "What is Galactic Cosmic Radiation, and is this a result of something on Earth?"

"GCR, as it is referred to by the Earth science community, is a dominant source of radiation that comes from outside this solar system but primarily from within this galaxy. GCR is composed of a nuclei of atoms that had their surrounding electrons stripped and travel at slightly less than the speed of light. Your ship would have been exposed to it on the journey here."

Kaelen stared into the trees where the drone left the flasks and shivered at the remembered pain. "How could GCR affect the serum and not me or the minerals and elements my parents sent?"

"Argonians have been genetically modified for centuries to withstand most radiation without ill effect. I have insufficient data to explain why the serum would absorb the strong radiation to that extent but not the rest of the elements within the ship. It is my hypothesis that the Thinker Guild is unaware of the toxic results of irradiated regenerative serum to Argonian physiology. It would also explain why the ship suits are incapable of protecting you."

"Are there other such things on Earth?" The notion that something so painful could be scattered across her new planet concerned Kaelen.

"Nothing on Earth is likely to have been subjected to GCR. And it's improbable that the humans have created a similar serum. If you remember, they are quite primitive compared to Argon. Five minutes until you can lift the ship. The rest provided by your house will not cause harm."

Kaelen stood and approached the ship carefully but felt nothing like the pain she had experienced from the altered serum. The gems and minerals her parents included in the capsule were scattered on the ground from where she'd dropped them, but they looked ordinary. She couldn't understand why any would be so valuable on Earth. Kaelen shrugged, collected the dropped items and dumped them back into the container. She slid the capsule into her satchel. Five minutes later, the travel pack was secured across her shoulders, having also stuffed the nanobot drone inside on Wex's suggestion, and she skimmed the treetops toward the mountain her AI had indicated.

It took some time as she was instructed not to fly too high or too fast, to avoid detection by authorities of the North American airspace. Eventually she found Mount Nirvana. The sun was low on the horizon when Kaelen used her laser vision for the first time. She was amazed to see the rock turn molten and pour away and surmised that the heat she produced must be immense. Water from the melting snow and ice ran in rivulets and dripped across the opening. Once the space was large enough to fit her small, personal ship, she let it cool for a few minutes then gently placed it inside. After, she backed away and used her freeze breath on the running water to hide it again. The ice turned opaque, and she could already see snowflakes falling and sticking to its surface.

"Wex, can you still hear me?"

"Our communication remains uninterrupted, Kaelen Ra-Evon."

"Good. Where is the nearest large city to apply for citizenship, and to exchange gems and minerals for local currency?" Kaelen continued to float in the air in front of the mountain, uncaring of the temperature or buffeting winds. She was beginning to enjoy her abilities on this strange new world.

"According to the planetary communication web, the closest city that would fit your needs is Vancouver. It lies southwest, eight hundred and eighty-seven Earth miles from your current location. I have updated my technical data using Earth's global internet. Commercial aviation crafts stay below sixty thousand feet. If you fly above that you can make the trip a test of your maximum gravity independent speed."

Kaelen was skeptical. "Can I fly above that? Don't I need to breathe?"

"I have a theory that, along with your other yellow sun gifts, you also have a greater capacity to survive on less oxygen or go completely without oxygen for longer. I have already established that

Earth atmosphere is denser and more oxygen rich than that of Argon. I would recommend rising until you begin to feel discomfort to test the hypothesis."

Kaelen willed herself upward through the layer of clouds that hung above the mountains. She kept going until the world lay peacefully below her. Kaelen was so high that she could see the curvature of the Earth in every direction. While she was a little winded, she felt well enough. "What is my current altitude?"

"The sensors in your communicators indicate that your heart rate is marginally elevated, and you are floating at sixty-two thousand three hundred and forty-three feet, Kaelen Ra-Evon."

"Incredible. Why can't I see the Earth rotate below me?" Kaelen probably knew the answer, but the amazing view and strange circumstances kept her off balance. It was easier to depend on Wex for a quick answer.

"You are hovering in an envelope of air that is rotating at approximately the same speed as the Earth. There is no relative motion between you and the Earth's surface because you're both rotating at the same speed."

"Of course." Kaelen looked over the entirety of the planet below, then moved her gaze toward the stars. Somewhere out there would be an empty bit of space where she knew her planet once resided. But light travels significantly faster than even the fastest Argonian ship and the image of it would have disappeared from the sky years before her arrival to Earth. Her thoughts were interrupted by Wex's voice in her ear.

"I suggest now is the time to test your speed."

"What if I hit something?"

"Your reflexes should be increased along with everything else, sufficient enough to dodge any foreign objects in your path."

Without another thought, Kaelen shot forward, picking up speed in exponential increments. She flew around the world in two and a half seconds. The second lap took less than a fraction of that time. It was unreal but before she could ruminate on that fact, Wex directed her down toward a large seaboard city on the edge of the nation of Canada.

"While you cannot gain citizenship overnight, data obtained in my most recent update indicate that Canada participates in the special alien

amnesty project which provides a fast path to citizenship if a refugee were to meet the required criteria. Your first stop will be a business called the Vancouver Bullion and Currency Exchange. You can exchange a portion of the gold in your pouch for Canadian dollars.

"These dollars, they are currency I can use in the United States of America?"

"No. You will need to exchange them again when you travel to that country."

Kaelen grumbled. "That seems highly inefficient."

"Such is the way of this world, Kaelen Ra-Evon. Once you have attained funds tonight, you can purchase an evening stay at a hotel where you can find refreshment, a bed, and cleaning facilities for your body if you desire such. Tomorrow, I'll direct you to the nearest international bank where you can deposit your currency, as well as store the valuable gems you have on your person. They will give you plastic cards you can use to purchase goods and services in exchange for your currency."

"Will I be able to—"

"You will be able to use the plastic cards anywhere in the United States of America."

Kaelen blew out a sigh of relief as she hovered over a sign advertising one of the 4200 Earth religions. "Wex, this world is complicated."

"Kaelen Ra-Evon, your intellect is beyond that of anyone on Earth and thusly you are sufficiently capable of adapting and contributing to this society, complicated though it may seem at first. Once you are financially stable, you can register as an alien refugee. Based on previously recorded data, most paths to Canadian citizenship involving qualified aliens take less than a standard Earth month."

"What must I do to achieve the honor of becoming a Canadian?"

"You need to show that you are either employed or have sufficient wealth to support yourself for six Earth months. You will be required to pass a citizenship test. They will record your background planet of origin and will create a holo-still for the identification card."

"That sounds simple enough."

"It is. I will instruct you on what you need to know to pass their test this evening once you've purchased temporary lodging."

Kaelen took a deep breath and wrinkled her nose at the different smells that emanated from the brightly lit city below. "I thought it would be louder."

Wex answered at the same time her filters cut out on the communicators. *"It is."*

She clapped her hands over her ears and yelled. *"Ahh,* make it stop!"

"That is another thing you will need to learn, Kaelen Ra-Evon. You will have to acclimate to the sounds all around you, to temper your yellow sun hearing, else it will become a weakness should your communicators fail."

The sounds quieted again, and Kaelen began her descent to an empty section of streets below. "Tomorrow. We can work on that tomorrow." Wind blew her hair into her face for the thousandth time since she exited her ship. "I also need to find a way to cut my hair."

"You are of the Thinker Guild, not Explorer. There is no need for cutting your hair."

"Even so, I feel as though I'm of both guilds now that I'm here on this strange planet. I will comport myself as I see fit while I rebuild my life here."

"As you wish, Kaelen Ra-Evon. Though you are invulnerable, you may be able to use Earth mirrors and your laser vision to sever the strands. It will require study on your part to make the style sufficiently pleasing. Now, walk six of these building blocks forward, then go left another three. You should see the business you need on the right side of the street according to the authority called Google."

It was early evening but there weren't a lot of people on the streets since most businesses were closed for the day and it was more of an industrial area of the city. Kaelen got a few strange looks for her black suit with its glowing white symbol on her chest, but most continued on their way. She contemplated the mental list given to her by her father and mother. With any luck, she would have the first four objectives completed quickly and could begin her contribution to society, and try to find the location of the mysterious Argonian beacon. It was time for her new life to begin.

Chapter Three

Ellie frowned at the job application sitting on top of the pile. She pressed the speakerphone button and punched in a four-digit extension. It rang a few times before a man answered. "Yes, Boss?"

"Joe, what's with the first application? Your job is to weed out all the garbage and only send me viable applicants. The first page is almost blank, containing not one single bit of education or job experience. Is this a practical joke?"

Deep laughter rumbled from the other end of the line. "I'm well aware of the job you stuck me with, Ellie. However, I thought you would appreciate the oddness of that one. Did you see what the person did? Look at pages two and three."

The wrinkles between Ellie's brows deepened as she flipped to the second page. A long paragraph was written in precise handwriting that continued onto the third page. It was so small and neat that, at first, she thought it had been made by a printer. What gave away the fact that it was indeed handwriting was the single fingerprint smudge at the bottom of the last page indicating it had been written in blue ink. "What in the world…" She finished reading with wide eyes.

Joe's voice came back over the line. "See what I mean? This Kaelen Ra-Evon, citizen of Canada, refugee from Argon, and resident of Twenty-four East Lane Street, Los Angeles, California, in the United States of America, solved a previously unsolved theory on the last two pages of her job application."

"The Collatz Conjecture."

"Exactly."

Ellie sighed and rubbed her temples. Normally they wouldn't entertain the idea of bringing someone into the Special Projects Lab without proper references, a correct level of educational training, and most definitely a previous job history. From the looks of the application, this Kaelen Ra-Evon simply walked out of the ether. "My guess is that they are a recent refugee to Earth."

"I thought the same. And I know what the rules are, but can you imagine the level of intellect that put down that solution? Where are they from, how much more do they know? It's my job to make sure you have the most talented staff down there in SPL, and my gut is telling me this Kaelen could be Patel's replacement now that he's heading up the main lab in New York."

Ellie dropped the application back onto her desk. "I'll need to run this one by Leah. Tell you what, check both our calendars for an opening and schedule the interview. We may as well see for ourselves what makes Kaelen Ra-Evon tick."

"Will do, Boss." The line went dead. Joe never bothered with any other farewell.

Ellie punched the top number on her speed dial. She smiled at the voice on the other end.

"To what do I owe the pleasure? Are you getting bored down there in SPL?" They'd begun shortening the name of the Special Projects Lab years before and it stuck.

"It's never boring, you know that."

"Have you filled that opening yet? I'm hoping to see results on the nano project by the end of second quarter next year."

"Actually, that position is exactly what I want to speak with you about. Got a minute for an in-person chat?"

"For you, always. I'll tell Jenna you're on your way up so she can buzz you in. My next meeting doesn't start until three."

"Give me five." Ellie hung up and snatched the application from her desk before making her way out of the office and to the elevator.

Ten minutes later, Leah sat in her hoverchair. It was the fifth design generation, and significantly more comfortable than the original Charlie conceived of years before. The seat had been upgraded, and legs enclosed, both surrounded by a smart gel that improved blood circulation and oxygenation of tissue. Those improvements decreased how often she had to do pressure relief exercises. Ellie sat nearby on the guest couch. Dark red lips parted in surprise as the younger woman read the neatly printed pages and solution to the Collatz Conjecture.

"This is incredible!"

"There is no educational experience."

Leah pointed at the blue ink. "Did you see this handwriting?"

"Kaelen Ra-Evon also has no past job experience."

Leah snapped out of her gobsmacked daze and met her adoptive mother's eyes. "They solved the Collatz Conjecture within the space of two eight and a half by eleven pages. I want that brain in my company."

Ellie nodded, assuming as much. "I thought so. I already asked Joe to find an opening that would work for both our schedules to set up an interview. I guess we'll see what this Kaelen Ra-Evon is all about then. I mean, we got lucky with Clevna Trog—"

"You know he prefers Einstein."

"Sorry, but at least he had job experience and references, even if they were mostly off world."

"I agree, he was a boon for Lockheed. Perhaps you should arrange to have him sit in on the interview as well. It may be good to hear another alien's perspective."

Ellie smiled. "Excellent idea." She pulled out her cell and sent a text to the head of talent acquisitions and got a thumbs up emoji in return. "Joe's on it." She looked at the time on her phone and turned back to Leah. "I don't suppose you'd like to join an old lady for lunch?"

Leah rolled her eyes. "Old she says! Let's head down to the cafeteria, I'm in the mood for today's special."

"Sounds good, honey."

Three days later, Leah, Ellie, and Einstein were in Leah's office, waiting for one Kaelen Ra-Evon. Ellie and Einstein used the time to inform Leah of the latest findings on the nanotech project. Jenna's voice over the intercom interrupted their conversation. "Ms. Lockheed, Joe said that Kaelen Ra-Evon is ready for you in conference room six."

They made their way down the long hallway of the executive level. Conference room six was the smallest room but still had enough space for the four of them. Leah was first to go through the door but stopped as soon as she met Kaelen Ra-Evon's pale, blue-eyed gaze. It was like being struck by lightning, without all the pain. The moment felt heavy, important somehow, and she struggled to make her brain work.

Objectively, it appeared as though Kaelen suffered in the same way as her mouth dropped open. Suddenly she cocked her head as if she were listening to someone. She abruptly stood and approached Leah with her hand outstretched. "Hello. I am Kaelen Ra-Evon, citizen of Canada, refugee from Argon, and resident of Twenty-four East Lane Street, Los Angeles of California, United States of America. Thank you for allowing me the opportunity to interview for this work assignment."

Leah shook her hand gamely and snapped out of her daze when she heard a throat clear behind her. She gestured for Kaelen to return to her seat, then quickly moved to the opposite side of the table where one of the office chairs had been moved away. Ellie entered next, followed by Einstein. Kaelen stood again and leaned across the table so she could carefully shake both their hands.

Ellie smiled. "Please, you don't have to be so formal with us. We like to have a normal conversation in these types of interviews because you'll be working closely with the people in this room if you're chosen for the job. Be yourself."

Kaelen nodded, but her brows furrowed indicating confusion about Ellie's reassuring words.

Einstein gave Kaelen a calculating look. "You are Argonian?"

"Yes. May I appear in my natural clothing?"

"Go ahead."

Kaelen smiled with excitement and caressed her collar. Leah was surprised to see what looked like normal Earth clothing shift into that of a sleek black jumpsuit with a glowing symbol on the front that looked like a backwards Z. Kaelen asked Einstein, "You're familiar with Argon?"

He nodded. "I visited a planet near yours long ago. I was an intellectual youth at the time."

"Are you an alien refugee too?"

Einstein pressed a button on his belt and a metallic man with a gleaming chrome head sat in the chair, instead of one that looked like a typical Earthling. "I am an organic android from Donboth but wear a hologram inducer to make people more comfortable around me."

"Oh. The Thinker Guild had a lot of respect for Donbothian's, though I don't believe they were allowed near our planet."

He frowned. "For good reason. My people are known collectors of organics. You are a long way from home, Kaelen Ra-Evon."

She looked down to where her hands gripped each other on the top of the table. "Argon is no more so Earth is my home now."

"Gone?"

"Destroyed, yes."

It was rare for Einstein to display any emotion unless he was with his girlfriend. His face could move similar to a human because of his organic metal skin but he preferred a more stoic resting face the majority of the time. Despite that, Einstein frowned and hummed at the level of tragedy involved with losing an entire planet. "Are there any others?" Leah assumed he meant others that escaped.

"My ship—uh, I mean to say that it was rather sudden and I have reason to believe I may be the only survivor from the core meltdown. Regardless, I've mentally prepared myself for the challenge of living on Earth alone. *Kymeth sal ne Ra.*"

Leah leaned forward. "I don't understand." Those piercing blue eyes met her own and Leah felt short of breath.

"The creed of my House. With intellect we overcome."

It was apparent that Einstein had a lot of knowledge of Kaelen's people, so Leah let him continue to probe for her background with questions that they wouldn't know to ask or understand. He pointed at the glowing symbol on her chest. "That is the meaning behind your family crest, correct?"

Kaelen's eyes widened with something that looked like excitement. "You are familiar with *Dolem*-Ra?"

Leah interrupted. "What is that, doh-lem rah?"

"That is my family." Kaelen paused and tilted her head, as if she were searching for the right words.

Einstein answered for her. "Ra is her house name. The phrase '*dolem Ra*' roughly translates to 'house of Ra' but there is no exact match in human culture for all that entails." He looked back at Kaelen. "I have some knowledge of your house. They are mostly Thinkers, which I'm assuming you are as well."

Kaelen smiled. "I was the youngest to ever be inducted into the Thinker Guild. Unfortunately, I was forced to leave my home not long after. I learned about Terra—Earth during the ten-year long sleep that spanned the course of my journey."

Leah interrupted by raising her hand. "Hold on, there is a lot to unpack here."

Kaelen's brows furrowed. "On the contrary, there was nothing to unpack as I arrived with a minimal of material goods."

"No, I mean—"

Einstein explained. "What Leah is trying to say is that you've given us a lot of information, data that two beings of Earth would have some trouble coming to terms with since they are unfamiliar with extended distance space travel or hypnopedia learning." He addressed Leah and Ellie. "That is a mostly Argonian practice involving images and education sent directly to the cerebrum using a nano-aided bio-organic connection within their ships."

Leah's curiosity clawed its way up her spine, and she gave Einstein a hungry smile. "I trust that you'll explain to me in depth later." She turned back to Kaelen. "Sorry for interrupting. My thirst for knowledge exceeds my good manners most days."

"The person that lacks a thirst for knowledge is cursed to wither from intellectual drought."

Ellie smiled kindly at Kaelen. "That's a wise saying. May I ask how old you are, Kaelen? And can I call you that?"

"You may refer to me by my first name. That is common here, yes?"

"It is. If I may say, as a fairly new refugee to our planet, you speak very good English. Though it is a bit formal."

"Formal? There is more than one way to speak this English?" She paused again, her gaze going unfocused for a moment before nodding at Ellie. "I see. You are referring to slang, as well as formal and informal sentence structure. I will—" She sighed and drew in a deep breath, letting it out slowly. "I'll try to be less formal."

"You're doing fine, just speak in the way that's most comfortable. Let me make introductions. My name is Doctor Ellie Tuck but you can call me Ellie." She paused then added, "Doctor is my title, an advanced educational degree. My Donbothian friend here is Clevna Trog, though we call him Einstein down in the lab."

He explained. "Albert Einstein was among the most brilliant and influential human scientists of all time."

Ellie pointed toward Leah. "And that is Doctor Leah Lockheed-Tuck, the current CEO of Lockheed International."

"Uh, thank you, Ellie." Kaelen looked at Leah. "Doctor Lockheed-Tuck, does being CEO make you the head of your house?" She paused and assumed that look of listening again. Apologies, I realize you don't have houses here. At least not the way we did on Argon."

"You can call me Leah." She hesitated for a moment before voicing her observation. "Is someone speaking to you, Kaelen?"

"Besides you?"

Leah smirked. "Yes, besides any of us in this room. Your body language indicates you're hearing something that we are not."

Einstein nodded. "It does appear that way."

Kaelen's eyes widened with surprise. "I'm impressed that you noticed. No one has previously guessed such a thing. I have an artificially intelligent computer assistant that traveled with me from Argon. Wex is housed in my ship, but I have contact with it through my ear communicators."

She turned her head one way, then the other, showing them the small pieces of tech in each ear. "Wex was my instructor at home, and on my journey, and has been helping me acclimate to Earth society."

Leah's said, "Fascinating!"

Kaelen suddenly twitched. "Oh, apologies to Ellie. You asked me how old I am. I left Argon when I was thirteen and I'm approximately twenty-four Earth years now. At least to my best calculations."

"Are Earth years comparable to Argon's years?" Kaelen nodded and Ellie gasped, clearly appalled. "But…but that's your entire childhood!"

"I can assure you that my education was complete before the

destruction of Argon. The ship itself provided even more training and simulated experience within a multitude of scientific disciplines.”

Ellie frowned. “Weren’t you lonely?”

Kaelen appeared to consider the question before she shrugged. “I have no answer for you. I was asleep for the journey so lacked true conscious awareness of the time.”

Interested though she was in Kaelen’s attractive mind and fascinating gadgets, Leah did her best to steer the meeting back on track. “Why do you want to work for Lockheed International, Kaelen?”

“All my research indicates that this company is currently the best when it comes to cutting edge technology. They have an open policy for alien employment, a robust philanthropic presence with half your research dedicated to green energy, and it would be the best fit for my intellect and philosophical interests. I was raised to contribute to society in a meaningful way. I want to help enrich Earth with better ways to live and advance, to prevent the same overreach of resources and subsequent disaster that befell my own planet.”

Einstein raised a single pale eyebrow. “That is a—”

“Very good answer.” Leah glanced at Ellie. She could tell her adoptive mother was impressed, the same could be said about Einstein. Despite the fact that he tried to hide behind a stoic facade, Leah had learned to read the man over the past few years. She met Kaelen’s intense gaze. “You told us why you want to work for Lockheed. Now tell us why we should hire you?”

Kaelen lifted her chin. “Because I’m the smartest being on this planet.”

Einstein countered. “I am a twelfth caliber intellect, though admittedly I’m near the limit of my base programming.”

“My father, Ra-Evon, was an eighth when I was tested. I too rated at a twelfth caliber with an expectation of growth. But more than that, I am an Argonian specifically engineered to problem solve, and descended from a long line of Thinkers.” She smiled at Einstein. “I believe we could do good work together, Clevna Trog.”

He smiled back. “I concur.”

Kaelen turned to look at Leah, eyes moving down to take in the hoverchair, and stared for perhaps a bit longer than anyone was comfortable with. Before Leah could say anything, Kaelen asked, "Why do you use that chair for locomotion, Leah Lockheed-Tuck?"

Leah frowned at the invasive question but answered anyway, understanding that Kaelen was clearly still learning Earth culture and social norms. "I was in an accident when I was thirteen. My family died and I suffered a paralyzing injury. Ellie is my adoptive mother."

Kaelen leaned forward. "You also lost your family?" She touched her head then her chest in what looked to be a show of respect. "We are kindred in a way. Wex says I've probably made you uncomfortable, that it would be considered rude to ask such questions. I apologize."

"Why did you ask?"

"The question?"

"Yes."

Kaelen tilted her head. "If it is a nerve injury as you say, why wouldn't you use simple nanotechnology to repair it and restore limb function? It is a wonderful piece of equipment, but still quite primitive in some respects. I would love to see the design of it—" She paused and swallowed. "Um, I mean, should you hire me for this position."

Everyone in the room froze with the exception of Kaelen. Repairing nerve damage was one of the main goals of the SPL on Leah's direction, and they'd only just begun working with nanotech. Ellie and Einstein knew exactly what the research meant to her.

Kaelen spoke into the silence. "Did I say something wrong?"

Her comment broke the heavy pause and Leah dared to breathe again. "On the contrary, you said something very right. You're hired and your first project at L-I will be to work with Einstein on his current nanotech project, developing treatment that can repair nerve damage on a cellular level." She began to move away from the table but stopped at the sight of Kaelen's outstretched hand.

"Please, there is another reason I wanted to work for this company specifically. I know that a large corporation such as Lockheed International has resources that the average citizen would not, and would contain some of the most brilliant minds on Earth."

"Continue." Leah inclined her head, curious about what Kaelen was going to say.

"Wex cautioned me not to mention earlier that my ship detected an Argonian beacon when we first entered the solar system, and again after arriving in Los Angeles. I don't know if it's a fellow survivor of our planet's destruction, or an explorer on long assignment. My greatest hope is that it's a member of my house. Unfortunately, the computer system of my personal craft is insufficient to track a microsecond-long coded communication burst that only activates once every month and a half. I would like to ask for aid in my search for this other ship."

Leah thought about the problem. While aliens were living openly on Earth and had at last gained rights to citizenship across the majority of the planet, plenty of discrimination could still be found around the world. If there was another Argonian living on Earth, they could be well-hidden. "Once you've gone through your orientation, we'll all sit down together and discuss strategy to build the equipment you need to find the source of your mystery signal."

"Kaelen Ra-Evon, is it possible that the signal is one of distress?"

She frowned. "Wex insists it's a standard emission from another small pod craft like my own, which aren't meant to be long range explorers. They're usually part of a larger ship fleet."

Leah was fascinated. "Like a sci-fi escape pod?"

Einstein shook his head. "No, those are highly impractical. What use is escaping an emergency situation only to be floating in space with no resources available? No, Argonian pod craft are fully capable of long-range travel, they're just not ideal for the mental health of an individual unless they have a hypnopedia equipped AI onboard."

"Which most have unless they're assigned to the orbiting tech station—oh." Kaelen grew pale and covered her mouth with a hand.

Ellie leaned closer. "What is it?"

Kaelen's eyes filled with very human-like tears. "I just remembered all the families assigned to the Thinker Guild that lived there. It's all gone now, everything."

"I'm very sorry for your loss, dear." Ellie shook her head. "Mere words are insignificant in the scope of everything that has happened to you but they're all I have."

Leah's heart ached for her but before she could express her own sympathy, Kaelen drew in a deep breath and straightened in her seat. "Are you okay?"

"There is no point in mourning the things I cannot change, only honor those that came before me. I—I think I will be."

Einstein hummed. "Is it possible someone could have made the journey ahead of you by way of a spatial anomaly? The explosion of Argon could have affected dark matter pockets for lightyears around. If a ship went through one of those pockets while space was folded, it would have sped the journey immeasurably, taking months rather than years."

"I...I don't know. The planet itself was caught off guard by the speed of the core meltdown. Only a select few knew of the real danger. Any ships leaving from our orbiting research center would have been programmed to find the nearest habitable planet."

"What about your neighboring planet?"

"Hogath? That was no longer sustainable for life. Wex insists that the signal is most likely from an Explorer ship that somehow got lost and stranded here on Earth. My people knew about this planet from the Tau Ceti. It makes logical sense that an Explorer vessel would have set off to investigate the nature of it."

Leah moved around the table and closer to Kaelen. She reached out to take the woman's hand, then changed her mind at the last second. After all, she had no knowledge of Kaelen's species and thought it best not to assume anything about personal space or physical contact. She learned that from Einstein. "It will require some time with you and your AI to figure out exactly what and how the pod is broadcasting so we can build a detector—"

"And decoder. The message is also scrambled so people that would do Argonians harm can't find the pod."

"Decode and descramble then. Either way, we'll do our best to find any of your people that remain."

Kaelen appeared overwhelmed at Leah's words. She reached toward Leah's hand but pulled back at the last second. Leah closed the distance for her, and Kaelen delicately grasped her palm. "Thank you. In return I promise to do good work for you."

Leah smiled, a look that completely enamored the Canadian from Argon if the expression on her face was anything to go by. "Of that I have no doubt. Welcome to Lockheed International, Kaelen."

* * * *

While the brunt of the technical work for the nano project fell upon Einstein and Kaelen's shoulders, Leah and Ellie provided invaluable information and assistance regarding human biology. Kaelen was awed at the knowledge that the humans possessed, especially Leah. She brought it up one day while they were all in the lab.

"You're exceedingly intelligent and highly trained. It is a marvel considering the inefficiency of the Earth education systems. I myself find the human body fascinating and can't wait to explore more."

Ellie snickered and Kaelen observed Leah's cheeks grow warm with a blush. "Um, thank you. Despite how intelligent we all are, I'm glad you're working with us, Kaelen. You've pushed this project to the next level."

Einstein nodded over his analysis of a slide. "I agree. Your presence on this project has been most beneficial." When he was finished, Einstein walked over to the bench where Kaelen was working. "You mentioned that you had a nano drone taken from your ship. May I examine it?"

"Kaelen Ra-Evon, it is most unwise to—"

"If our project can benefit from the knowledge contained within my drone, then I see no reason not to let them look at it. I trust them, Wex." They couldn't hear the assistant's voice because Wex still spoke through the communicators. But no one said anything to her when she occasionally responded to it.

"It is against Argonian code to advance primitive world science beyond their natural capability."

"We will be careful." That was the end of the argument as far as she was concerned.

Kaelen retrieved the drone from her satchel. The other three scientists gasped when she instructed Wex to disassemble and reassemble it while they watched.

"May I study this?" Einstein held up a hand. "I promise not to damage it in any way or copy technology without discussing with you first." Kaelen smiled and handed it over. He made to walk away but paused and glanced back at her. "I put my initial design for the beacon receiver in the project file on the SPL network. I'd like you and Wex to analyze it. We still need to convert Argonian data waves to something comparable in Earth technology to program a fast receiver."

"I will. Thank you."

He nodded and walked away, already focused on the makeup of the nano drone.

A little over a month and a half later, or two signal pulses after hiring her into L-I, Leah sat Kaelen down and admitted that her algorithms still hadn't been able to triangulate the location of the mystery ship with their receiver, despite the chemical makeup of the Argonian personal craft's hull that Wex provided. The signal was hard to detect and their world was a large place.

"I have a backup option that will work based on the same frequency provided by your AI, but it's not practical. I pre-emptively approved a time allotment from one of Lockheed's geosynchronous satellites every month and a half to scan down to the surface."

"You know for certain this satellite will trace the signal?" Leah nodded. Kaelen's heart raced but she tried to temper her hope. "Why isn't it practical?"

"Unfortunately, the satellite can only scan a small area at a time, no more than twenty miles in diameter." She reached into a storage pocket of her hover chair and withdrew a small tactical flashlight and called out, "Room lights, ten percent." Overhead lights lowered until they were in near darkness. Leah pointed the flashlight toward one wall, then moved the cone of light across the surface. "The cone of light represents the satellite scan. I can make it broader and cover a larger area—" She moved the end of the flashlight so the beam spread out and became more diffuse.

"But the scan isn't as precise."

"Exactly. I'm sorry Kaelen, but I don't know how to speed up this process. It's like finding a needle in a haystack. Room lights, one hundred percent."

Kaelen tilted her head. "Why would you attempt such a thing?"

"It's a saying meaning that something is difficult or near-impossible. I know our technology will work, but we have to be "listening" to the right area to receive the beacon which seems like a daunting task. Checking a couple dozen miles every six weeks means it could take hundreds of years unless we get lucky and hit just the right spot." She shook her head. "I don't know about your race, but mine is not so long lived."

"What do we do? Wex, is there any other information you can provide that will make our task easier? How did you determine our landing coordinates on the surface of the planet?"

Wex's voice came through her communicators. *"Standard Explorer Guild practice dictates the appropriate landing region of a foreign planet."*

"What did it say?"

Leah gave her a curious look so Kaelen said, "Use the external communicator speakers please, Wex."

"Yes, Kaelen Ra-Evon. Appropriate landing region is one no closer than a dendol *of minimal atmospheric shuttle speed outside one of the top five population centers of a continent, but no farther away than one and a half* dendol.*"*

Kaelen explained, "My closest approximation of a dendol is an Earth hour."

"So, between one and one and a half hours outside a major population center. What is atmospheric shuttle speed?"

"Translated to miles per hour would be ninety-nine point two."

Leah had pulled a tablet from a compartment on her chair and began taking notes. "This is great, we can work with this. We're looking at a region between one hundred and one hundred and fifty miles away from one of the top five cities in North America. Let's see, Mexico City, New York, Toronto, Los Angeles, and…gah, is it Chicago or Houston?"

"It is Chicago, Leah Lockheed-Tuck."

Leah made a strange face at Kaelen when she answered Wex. "Uh, thank you." Then she brought up a map of North America and began drawing large circles around the cities she mentioned.

"How does this help us? That's still a massive area to search. Wex, are there any other details to the Explorer Guild guidelines?"

"The destination was broken into regions, either by the computer using geographic markers or established political boundaries. Destination should be closest to the midpoint of the most populous nation."

"That rules out both Canada and Mexico. Wait, how did you end up in Canada, Kaelen?"

Kaelen laughed. "Apparently, guild rules can be changed when the air space above the target destination is heavily guarded. Wex, where were we originally headed before landing in the Northwest Territories?"

"The target city was Chicago. It features a significant amount of air defense."

"I'll say! That's the current home to the CORP headquarters. I hope the ship we're looking for wasn't found by them."

Kaelen grew alarmed. "Are they bad people?"

"No, the CORP isn't comprised of bad folks any more. But it is still a government organization and would probably jump at the chance to take any crashed ship apart."

Kaelen shivered as she remembered the reports of what the humans did to the original stranded alien that led to the creation of their Chromodecs. "We should change our target and begin searching around this new city."

With a few keystrokes, Leah brought up a map of the United States and zoomed in on the Midwest. "Our job will be a little easier because we can probably eliminate the significant portion that is Lake Michigan."

"At one hundred to one hundred and fifty of your miles, it is still a large area to search."

Leah tapped her bottom lip then began typing furiously. She downloaded a map of the region then wrote a quick computer program to lay out circles the equivalent of twenty miles in diameter until the land was covered with no gaps. There were almost a hundred and fifty circles. She sighed and dropped the tablet onto her lap.

Kaelen frowned. "By my calculation, the new search could take as long as eighteen years to complete."

"Realistically, it probably wouldn't be the first or last place we scanned. There is a high probability we find it somewhere in the middle of that time period."

Kaelen gave her a helpless look. "Do you have any other options?"

"Nothing, I'm afraid. I'll write the code for a new search routine this evening. For lack of any other options, I'll direct the satellite to begin at the farthest point of land in our perimeter, east of center. I'll program it to scan in a clockwise direction." Leah pointed toward the map. "Someplace called Pentwater."

Kaelen nodded. There was a small part of her that secretly hoped the mystery ship was one of her immediate house, perhaps her mother or father. It was small because she knew the odds were extremely low that any of the four elders that she left behind were able to get to a ship before the explosion. Her heart hurt to think on it so she shifted her focus back to Leah. She looked into Leah's eyes and froze much the way she'd done the day she was interviewed. There was something about Leah that drew her attention like nothing else.

Kaelen was discomfited at being thrown into an entirely new world filled with complex and unique social cues, but there was one bright spot to her existence in Los Angeles. Once she got control of her maximal hearing, Wex stopped filtering the sounds of the city for her. At first, it was disconcerting the way she always knew the location of Leah. Kaelen would never admit it to anyone, but sometimes at night when she worried for her future and found her thoughts fixating on the mystery ship, she would listen intently until she could identify the sound of Leah's calm breathing and heartbeat among hundreds of thousands around her. It was soothing and made her feel safe.

Her heart sped to match Leah's as they continued to stare at one another. Kaelen's reverie was broken by Leah's question. "Is something wrong?"

She ducked her head slightly and looked up at Leah, feeling shy. "No. Everything is well. Thank you."

A few nights later found Kaelen humming an old Argonian song while she worked on a nano generator after standard lab hours. She paused when she heard the sound of Leah's heartbeat grow closer, and her own heart raced with excitement. The elevator gave a ding down the hall, and she knew the owner of Lockheed International was coming to visit, as she often did after her corporate day was finished. Kaelen enjoyed working late since she didn't have anything to do at her apartment other than remember all the people she'd loved and lost. She'd already spent too much time staring into her holocube.

Kaelen didn't mind the interruption because she spent most of her evenings drowning in loneliness. Only four people had clearance to work in her lab and she often missed friendly conversation after Einstein left each day. She looked up with a smile to see Leah on the other side of the reinforced plas walls, scanning into the room via the biometric panel. "Hi, Leah. I heard you coming down."

Leah paused the hoverchair inside the door and gave her a curious look. "You heard me?" Kaelen nodded.

"Coming down the hall?"

"No, coming down in the elevator from your office."

Leah maneuvered over to the bench where Kaelen was standing. "Kaelen, my office is on the other side of the building…on the twenty-fourth floor."

Kaelen nodded in agreement. "Yes, I visited once so I'm aware of its location."

"People can't hear that far."

"I can." Leah sat in silence for a few seconds and Kaelen wondered if she had done something wrong.

The other woman tilted her head. "Humans can't hear that far. Does your enhanced hearing have anything to do with the fact that you're an Argonian?"

Wex gave a warning in her ear. *"Kaelen Ra-Evon, please be aware of your third objective. You were cautioned by your parents to hide your yellow sun powers on Earth, for fear that the humans would react negatively."*

"It's only hearing, and this is Leah. What harm could there be?"

Leah's brows drew together. "Are you speaking to me?"

Kaelen blushed. "Um, no. I'm talking to Wex. I'm sorry, it is reminding me of my objectives while on Earth."

Unsurprisingly, her words failed to clear up Leah's confusion. "What objectives?"

"I was given a set of guidelines created by my mother and father. Some I've already completed, such as hiding my ship, applying for asylum, and exchanging minerals for wealth. Others are ongoing."

"And why would Wex warn you about your objectives when I questioned your acute hearing?"

Kaelen knew how brilliant Leah was, that she was considered a genius on Earth, though the term was hard to quantify in regards to any other beings in the universe. She now understood the necessity of Wex's warning but still trusted Leah. "I seem to have gained certain abilities since coming to Earth. It has something to do with the yellow sun and the way my cellular structure reacts to the radiation it produces."

Leah's eyes widened and her respiration rate increased at Kaelen's admission. "And enhanced hearing is one of those abilities?" Kaelen nodded. "You have more?"

"Yes, but I can't disclose them. I'm sorry, Leah. Wex is most adamant. My guide says it is for my protection. I hope you understand."

Red lips opened with surprise and Kaelen stared hard at the colored skin, wondering if they were as soft to touch as they appeared. Wondering how the paint that gave them their dark color tasted. She was broken from her observations when Leah covered her hand with a warm palm.

"I would never ask you to divulge personal information if you're not comfortable with it. I'd like to think we're becoming friends and I will support you in whatever way I'm able." Leah paused before continuing. "And I won't tell anyone else about your hearing, or possible other powers."

Kaelen contemplated Leah's statement. "Are humans capable of verbal compliance without signing many wasteful pages of agreement?"

"Are you asking if humans are capable of telling the truth, or are we capable of making promises?"

"The second one. I understand too well that everyone has the ability to lie."

Leah nodded sadly. "How about this," she held up her smallest finger. "When my sister and I make promises to each other, ones that we never intend to break, we always pinky swear."

"Is this a special power, or legal agreement?"

Kaelen got a soft smile and gentle head shake for her question. "No, it's simply a promise from one person to another, words born from trust, affection, and respect."

"Okay." Kaelen held up her own hand with the pinky in the air, mimicking Leah's gesture. Leah reached over and hooked their pinkies together.

"I swear not to divulge anything about your yellow sun power, or existence thereof, without your express approval." Then she shook their hands slightly while the pinkies were locked.

The gesture may have been small, possibly insignificant in the grand scheme of her new world, but it meant something to Kaelen. Not only for the promise, but for the physical contact. One thing she had become painfully aware of was exactly how touch-starved she was since arriving on Earth. But with her new powers, Kaelen wasn't confident enough to initiate contact with anyone, fearing the amount of damage she could cause on accident. She whispered, "Thank you, Leah Lockheed-Tuck. You are my favorite person on Earth."

Leah's smile was wide. "More than Einstein?"

"Yes."

The conversation ended there and Leah released her finger. She moved to the computer station on the bench next to Kaelen, cursing as she had to lift the keyboard into her lap to log in. She quietly began her own work and Kaelen wondered why Leah didn't use the computer station across the room that was set up with easy access for a chair rather than the tall bench with cabinets beneath. Not wanting to say something insensitive, she stayed silent as she adjusted the replication settings for their second batch of nanobots.

A few minutes later, Kaelen walked over to one of the large cabinets on the far wall. She opened her personal drawer and frowned, then pulled out two empty boxes. "Quark."

Leah snickered and Kaelen wondered if she shouldn't have used the expletive that she'd heard Einstein utter many times. She glanced over at her. "Sorry, Leah. Apparently, my food stock has run out. I'll need to purchase more when I leave here but I'm unsure if the provision business is open this late in the evening."

"Don't you have any food at home?"

Kaelen shook her head. "I brought my last two boxes here since I work most of the hours of the day. I didn't realize my supply was nearly empty."

Leah held up a hand. "Wait. When you say food stock, what are you referring to?"

Kaelen held up the boxes for a popular brand of protein bar. "I like the chocolate one best, but they are all excellent. Wex analyzed my options in the business near my apartment and, given my inability to work with raw Earth foods, it recommended this product to meet my needs. I discovered them in Vancouver Canada and was happy to see Los Angeles also had them within the commodity stores."

"Kaelen! Are you telling me that you've been on Earth for more than four months and you've only eaten CLIF bars?"

"Yes. Is that…wrong?"

Leah slapped her hand against her face, something Einstein said was called a face-palm, and Kaelen briefly wondered if it hurt the other woman. She hoped not since she found the symmetry and texture of Leah's face pleasing.

"When you say you're unable to work with raw Earth foods, what exactly does that mean? You can't eat any of the native food stuffs?"

Kaelen shook her head, not sensing anything more than curiosity from her friend. "Things here are unfamiliar. Back on Argon everything was prepared for us. I don't know how to put the Earth foods together or how long to cook the ingredients to make them edible. I experimented twice and regretted both meals. Very much." She shrugged helplessly. "Everything about Earth is incredibly primitive. I never realized how much that would affect my life beyond basic science."

Leah's eyes widened with shock and Kaelen feared she'd made her angry until she spoke in a steady, kind tone. "Why haven't you gone to a restaurant after you leave work, or on your lunch break?"

"But I'm not tired when I—oh. Wex says those are eateries that provide prepared food."

"Oh, Kaelen. It's time we continued your Earth education."

"How will—"

"Log off your workstation and gather your things. I'm taking you out to eat."

Kaelen was confused. "This eating out, it is a good thing? Is there a difference between eating out and eating in?"

Leah blushed for an unknown reason, but she answered Kaelen with the same patience she always answered her questions. "Wex is correct. A restaurant is a place that prepares food for you. You can purchase the prepared food to eat on the premises, or to take home. Are you allergic to any Earth foods?"

Kaelen found the question confusing but Leah elaborated without asking.

"Can any harm you?"

"I don't think any food on this planet can harm me."

"Good. Now, gather whatever items you would normally take home with you, and I'll treat you to dinner."

"Do these restaurants have machines to combine and heat the foods? If so, can't I purchase one for myself?"

Leah snorted. "Come along, Kaelen Ra-Evon. I'm going to treat you to something a lot better than protein bars." She logged off her own workstation and waited by the door. Kaelen hurried with her shutdown routine then threw her empty boxes in the recycling bin before joining her. Leah glanced at her as they made their way toward the elevator that would take them up from the sublevel where SPL was located. "Do you trust me?"

"Implicitly." Kaelen's answer was immediate, and Leah gave her a wide-eyed look as her hoverchair moved into the elevator.

"Really?"

"Have we not pinky sworn?" Leah pushed the P button for the parking garage. Kaelen usually walked to work from her one-room apartment so had never been in the garage before.

"In most cases, informally, you usually pinky swear about a certain specific topic only."

"I gathered that. But I also know that if I can trust you about something that would be scientifically and medically enticing, such as enhanced hearing, I can probably trust you with the minor things of my existence."

The elevator dinged and they exited. "That makes…a lot of sense actually."

"Of course, it does. I'm logical and intelligent. I would hope to speak sensibly."

"You sound too much like Einstein."

Kaelen caught Leah rolling her eyes and assumed she said something else odd. While Earth languages on their own were easy to learn, local slang, idioms, and other odd turns of phrase often confused her. They stopped in front of a sleek looking van and Kaelen grew confused. "Will you operate this vehicle yourself?" She'd studied Earth vehicles after arriving on the planet, and all the ones she'd seen required hands and feet to operate.

"Do you see a driver inside?"

Taking the comment as a serious question, Kaelen focused intently on the van, trying to discern the existence of another person within. Her vision abruptly shifted, and she could see everything at once. She reeled and pressed her palms against her eyes. "No, no, no! Wex, what is happening?"

Chapter Four

"Kaelen, are you okay?"

Unheard by Leah, Wex responded. *"Kaelen Ra Evon, I cannot answer your question without more data."*

Afraid to open her eyes, Kaelen remained bent slightly with her hands covering her face. "Everything looks odd. I was trying to focus on the inside of the van and suddenly my sight spectrum changed and I saw through it, other vehicles, and even walls, with no regard to physical structure. How do I make it stop, Wex?"

"Through the walls, Kaelen?"

Leah's racing heart was loud to Kaelen's enhanced hearing and she knew that her friend was either frightened or excited by something. Perhaps both. "Sorry, Leah. I'm okay but I'm experiencing strangely shifted vision." She heard Leah move closer and felt a gentle touch upon her wrist.

"Are you suffering from visual difficulty or pain?"

"No, it doesn't hurt. Wex, do you have a suggestion?"

"Kaelen Ra-Evon, perhaps if you relax your focus, much like you've done with the laser vision power. I suspect this is another form of radiation emission from your eyes, one that your brain can interpret to provide an additional type of enhanced sight."

Leah's other hand rubbed Kaelen's upper arm as the hoverchair bumped up against her thighs. Kaelen shivered at the feel of Leah's touch, reveling at the sensation. "Relax, Kaelen. Your breathing has increased which probably isn't helping your panicked state."

Kaelen laughed. "You're giving me the same advice as Wex."

"Clearly we're both concerned about you then."

Heeding the advice of her AI and Leah, Kaelen took a few slow breaths, conscious enough of her powers not to activate another on accident. She cautiously opened her eyes. The first thing she saw was Leah's face near her own. Leah's clear, greenish-blue irises were mottled in their coloring, and her lips were parted as if she were either going to ask a question or had been staring in wonder. Once again, those soft lips caught and held her attention. With effort, Kaelen tore her gaze away. She was relieved to have her sight back to normal. "I'm okay now. Thank you for your care and advice."

"Always, Kaelen. I'm here for you if you need it. Not merely as your boss, but as a friend if you like."

Kaelen smiled, feeling an emotion expand inside her that she thought she'd never feel again after watching the destruction of her planet. "I would like that. I'd been considering you my friend but didn't know if you felt the same." She pulled away and stood straight again.

"I can assure you that I do. Can you tell me what happened? Is this related to the yellow sun power you discovered?"

"Kaelen Ra-Evon, it is unwise to divulge—"

Ignoring Wex, Kaelen answered honestly. "Yes. Apparently, this new ability allows me to emit radiation from my eyes and interpret the images returned, letting me see through objects in my immediate vicinity. As you can guess, it was previously undiscovered."

"You have x-ray vision?"

Kaelen contemplated her knowledge and vocabulary, then her understanding of what an x-ray was. "Perhaps something very similar."

"Fascinating!"

A loud sound emanated from Kaelen's stomach and her cheeks grew warm. "Sorry, again. I'm afraid that my caloric intake has been low for too long."

Leah hit a button on the keypad near her right hand and double chirps came from the van. Seconds later the top and bottom of the driver's side split open. She glanced at Kaelen. "Get in and buckle up."

Kaelen had ridden in Earth vehicles numerous times, though she didn't like them because of the rate they consumed precious fossil fuels. On closer inspection, she didn't see any exhaust ports. "Is this an electric vehicle?"

Leah grinned. "It is. All my private vehicles are, with the exception of the two executive jets. But even with those, I hired the best designers to come up with the lightest, most fuel-efficient hybrid aircrafts possible." She floated into the vehicle and Kaelen hurried around the van to enter the other side. Once seated, she gripped her knees tightly.

"Relax, I promise not to crash us. I got that out of my system ten years ago." She leaned over and patted the back of Kaelen's hand and smiled to show she was joking.

Mouth open, Kaelen looked back at her in shock. "You would jest about something as serious as the accident that permanently damaged you?"

Leah made a face. "Sorry. I forget that others aren't used to my brand of dark humor. It must come across as strange to you, given how relatively new you are to Earth and the way you tend to take things quite literally. I came to terms with my injury years ago, Kaelen. I've had a lot of therapy." She sighed. "At first, I was afraid to even ride in a car again. I'm still nervous about it, but I find that the experience is much more acceptable as long as I'm in the front and in control."

"Why is that?"

"Because I was a child at the time of the accident, sitting in the back of the car with my brother when we went off the road. It was one of the only times my father decided to drive us himself rather than use the family driver. My therapist suggested that having control might help me feel safe in vehicles again. She was right."

"Oh." Kaelen looked down, then reached across the expanse between them, the same way Leah had done minutes earlier, and carefully patted her friend's hand. "I'm sorry you had to go through that at such a young age. It is not an easy thing to experience."

Leah gazed at her intently. "No, it's not." Kaelen's stomach rumbled again and Leah smiled. "Are you ready to try my favorite food?"

"Is it coffee? You drink that all the time and I don't enjoy it."

Leah laughed and put the van into gear. "Nobody likes black coffee."

Kaelen gasped. "Why would you torture yourself like that?"

"Because coffee gives us humans a burst of energy, something that is vital when running a *Fortune 500* company." Leah stopped at the exit of the parking garage and glanced at Kaelen. "You've got a wrinkle between your eyes that usually indicates discomfort or confusion. What are you thinking about?"

Kaelen rubbed the spot between her eyes and could indeed feel the wrinkle in the skin there. "I didn't realize your company was only worth five hundred American dollars. It seems as though it would be more successful given the level of technology you produce."

Leah laughed loudly and seemed unable to explain what was so funny to Kaelen. "I'd tell you to Google it, but I know you don't own a phone. *Fortune 500* is the name of a magazine. Ask Wex to look up what is required for a company to make it onto their list."

"Okay." Twenty minutes later they turned into a parking lot. Kaelen looked up at the sign on the nearest building and said aloud, "Oh that makes a lot more sense."

"Lotus Garden?"

Kaelen glanced from Leah to the building and back. "Um, no. Wex explained the American financial system and how it relates to the corporate world."

Leah's eyes widened with surprise. "In twenty minutes?"

"Wex increased audio speed to twenty times the normal rate." Leah opened her mouth and closed it without uttering a word. She opened it again, then shook her head.

"I'm not going to ask. I'll assume this is another thing related to our pinky swear."

In that moment, Kaelen realized the dilemma of divulging information that seemed fairly innocuous, when in all actuality it wasn't normal by Earth standards. Leah was far too intelligent to miss such details.

"Leah Lockheed-Tuck has a surprising intellect for an Earthling, Kaelen Ra-Evon. She has dangerous potential."

Kaelen was suddenly glad of the pinky swear they'd made though Wex clearly wasn't as impressed. "Thank you."

"Let's go eat."

A few minutes later they were seated at a private table near the back. They were given menus and Kaelen picked it up to study one side. "This is a list of prepared foods, correct? How do I know what to order?"

Leah glanced up from her own menu. "Oh, you're looking at the wrong side. The English menu is on the back. Turn it around."

Kaelen frowned with confusion. "Why would I need to turn it over? Is the list different?"

"No, but the side you're looking at is in Chinese."

"Leah, I'm fully capable of reading Chinese. My Earth education provided by Wex in my ship was quite thorough and I'm able to read and speak the ten most common languages of this planet."

"Fuck me."

"I'm unfamiliar with that term—" She paused as Wex spoke into her ear.

"Kaelen Ra-Evon, that phrase is a demand for coitus."

"Wex says it is a demand for sex. Is that appropriate between friends or coworkers? The Lockheed International human resources handbook clearly states—"

Leah quickly moved around the table and placed a hand over Kaelen's mouth to stop her from speaking. She glanced around the restaurant, then made eye contact. When Kaelen had been silent for half a minute, she leaned away again and moved back to her side of the table. Leah facepalmed as Kaelen sat confused across from her. "It's just an expression. Strangely enough, even though fuck is considered one of the worst English profanities, it is very versatile and used by many. Basically, what I meant in this context was that I'm incredibly impressed by you."

"Oh. Okay. Can we eat now? When will the food come?"

"Kaelen, we haven't even ordered yet. Do you know what you want?"

Kaelen glanced down at the list in her hand. "I don't know what any of it is."

A woman that looked to be a few years older than Leah came over to their table. "Good evening, Leah. Will Eliza and Maddy be joining you as well?" She looked around as if searching for the other two women in the Tuck trio.

"Not tonight, Xiuying. Instead, I brought my friend Kaelen Ra-Evon."

"Excellent. Would you like to start with something to drink?"

"Sparkling water, please."

Someone from the counter called out in Chinese and their server answered before turning back to Kaelen. "It's nice to meet you, Miss Ra-Evon. And for you?" Excited to actually hear one of the languages she'd learned on the long voyage, Kaelen said something to her in rapid-fire Chinese. Xiuying answered her then turned to Leah. "Your friend speaks perfect Mandarin!"

Leah smirked. "Yes, Kaelen is full of surprises. What would you like to drink, Kaelen?"

Kaelen looked back and forth between the women. "I would, uh, like the same as you?"

"Do you trust me to order for you?"

"Yes. I'm interested in food experimentation." It was an odd statement coming from someone seated in a Chinese restaurant who had demonstrated that they were fluent in the language seconds before.

Leah looked up at Xiuying. "I'd like three, no, four orders of my usual, please. Kaelen has never had the food here and I think she is going to like it." She turned to Kaelen and smiled. "You can take home any of the leftovers."

A few minutes later, Leah demonstrated how to use the chopsticks. Kaelen immediately snapped hers in half.

Leah handed her own set across the table. "Try again."

Unfortunately, the position of the small sticks of wood was odd enough that she couldn't keep control of her maximal strength and she broke those as well. She frowned and placed the remaining pieces on the table. "I'm sorry, Leah. I haven't used any of your Earth utensils yet. I fear my new, uh, the changes I've undergone prevent me from the fine motor control needed to use chopsticks."

"Nonsense." Kaelen jumped slightly at Leah's exclamation. "I've seen you working on the smallest circuit boards and using the keyboard in the lab at speeds much greater than anyone else." Leah hesitated at Kaelen's look. "Yes, I did notice but I was waiting for you to bring it up as it wasn't my knowledge to hold. What I'm trying to say is that you have the potential to master this."

"You have a lot of confidence in me."

Leah leaned closer to the table, and Kaelen. "What is the most delicate thing you've seen since coming to Earth?"

"Something called a butterfly right after landing. I thought I'd harmed it with ice—uh, I thought I'd destroyed it accidentally, but it eventually reanimated and flew away."

"Tell me the pressure you'd use if you were to stroke a butterfly's wing?"

Kaelen held up a single finger as she contemplated the question, mentally going through her gathered Earth information to date. "My knowledge of entomology indicates that would be bad for a butterfly."

"What pressure would you use to prevent damage to the wings?"

"I calculate no more than eleven point three grams of pressure."

Leah nodded and gave her a smile. She grabbed another set of chopsticks from the jar on the table and removed the paper, then broke them apart. She handed the set to Kaelen. "Good. Now use that knowledge to apply the correct pressure, holding them in the manner I showed you. Once you can use them without breaking, gradually apply more pressure until you're able to lift things from the table." She opened another set of chopsticks for herself and positioned them for Kaelen to see. Five minutes later, Kaelen had already gotten the hang of the eating utensils. The food arrived shortly after that.

Kaelen looked at the table that was covered in delicious smelling items. "I don't know where to start."

Leah pointed toward one large dish with the hand not holding her chopsticks. "Start with the pot stickers and be sure to dip them in the sauce. Watch." She used her chopsticks to pick up and dip the dumpling, then took a bite of it while holding it over her plate. Kaelen copied the motion. As soon as the flavor hit her tongue, she quickly stuffed the rest of the dumpling into her mouth, cheeks bulging out. "That is delicious!" She looked at Leah excitedly. "This is my new favorite Earth thing."

"Aww, I thought I was your favorite Earth thing?" Leah sighed dramatically and threw her arm across her eyes. "I've been replaced by pot stickers!" From the look on her face, Leah clearly never expected a serious response when she put her arm down.

"Leah Lockheed-Tuck, you are my favorite of everything, here or anyplace else in the universe. I've never met anyone like you before and I'm glad that you've allowed me to be your friend.

Leah gave her a soft smile. "I feel the same way. Now, eat up. There are other foods here for you to try."

They spent the next hour at the restaurant with Kaelen marveling at how she'd been missing out on such wonderful combinations of flavor since landing on Earth. Leah programmed Kaelen's address into the van's nav system and drove her home after their late meal. Once parked in front of the apartment building, Leah gave her a smile. "Did you have fun?"

Kaelen couldn't put into words how much better she felt after eating something other than the Earth ration bars. For the first time since landing, she felt as though she could truly make a home on the primitive planet. "I did. I think I'll be returning there many times."

Leah laughed. "There are other restaurants too, Kaelen."

"I…" Kaelen grew distressed at the thought of venturing to a restaurant by herself, not knowing anything about Earth foods or eating practices. "I'm afraid that I don't know enough to go alone. Perhaps you could join me again? After business hours of course, in case it's frowned upon for someone of your station to fraternize with a lower status lab employee."

"On Argon, your house is higher than all the rest and thusly Leah Lockheed-Tuck should be honored to dine with you—"

"We're not on Argon, Wex! The status of my house doesn't matter here on Earth."

"Kaelen Ra-Evon, you could be a ruler on Earth with your power and intellect."

"I will do no such thing!" She refocused on Leah and shrugged, annoyed at Wex's input. The compassion shining in Leah's eyes was a lot to bear. Kaelen wished she could ask for what she really wanted, which was an embrace like the ones she used to receive from her mother, father, and even her grandparents before they all disappeared in the flaming wreckage of a dying planet. She pressed her lips together rather than speak aloud of her unattainable needs.

"Technically, you don't work for me, you work for Ellie. And I'm not sure if you've noticed, but as the boss I make my own rules. I don't value social status or appearances. You're a brilliant and irreplaceable member of the team, but you're also my friend. Now that we've put that behind us, I'll gladly share some meals with you, and I know Ellie and Einstein would as well. I've got the noon hour free tomorrow. We can all take a break and go out to lunch. How does that sound?"

Kaelen whispered, "It sounds amazing."

"Good. Now that we've established our friendship by making promises and breaking bread—"

"But we ate no bread."

"It's a saying that translates to eating together, Kaelen. What I'm trying to tell you is that I like to hug my friends and family goodbye, but I don't want to push you outside your comfort zone."

Kaelen's lip quivered for a second as she admitted, "I like hugs a lot. But I can't hug you."

Leah had already started to lean toward her when Kaelen's words registered. Taken aback, she said, "Why not?"

Shame drew Kaelen's gaze away. "I don't want to hurt you. I…you saw the chopsticks, Leah. Humans are very fragile."

Something in her words must have given her away because Kaelen looked back at her new friend in time to see her eyes widen and lips open with a tiny gasp. "Oh." Then she smiled. "Let's try an experiment. Get out of the van."

Kaelen exited the vehicle and moved onto the sidewalk, waiting for Leah to join her. "What is your experiment?"

Leah came as close as possible, then raised the chair so high off the ground she was nearly as "tall" as Kaelen. She held out her arms. "Now, step closer and let me hug you. I've learned a thing or two about hugging from the Tuck family and let me tell you, it's the best. No one should go without."

"Okay." Kaelen moved so the sleek side of Leah's chair pressed against her upper thighs. They were so close that Leah had no trouble leaning over and wrapping her arms around Kaelen, squeezing her as tight as humanly possible. Kaelen closed her eyes and reveled in the sensation. When Leah pulled away again, Kaelen gazed back at her with adoration. She felt the cool glide of tears running down her cheeks and reached up to wipe one with the tip of her index finger. It shimmered in the light of the streetlamps. "Thank you, Leah. You have no idea how much that means to me and I'll never forget it."

Leah gave her a tender smile. "Kaelen, I'm positive we're going to hug again at some point. And eventually, if you start coming to game nights, everyone will hug you."

"It may be a common enough thing on this planet, and amidst your friends, Leah Lockheed-Tuck, but that's my first hug on Earth, and the first of such from you specifically. I will treasure it."

"Me too. Good night, Kaelen." Kaelen nodded. "Good night."

Less than two minutes later, Kaelen was left standing alone on the sidewalk in front of her apartment building. Wex interrupted her peaceful moment. *"Leah Lockheed-Tuck is much smarter than anticipated considering she is merely human. It is unwise to divulge any more information to her than what you already have."*

Kaelen rubbed her arms where Leah had held her tight and muttered the first Earth saying she could think of that would express her displeasure at Wex's statements of the evening. "Shut up, Wex." After that night, Kaelen started removing her communicators during social situations, only leaving them in for work or when she was home alone in her apartment.

As promised, Kaelen continued to share meals with Leah, as well as Einstein, occasionally Ellie, and a few other scientists at Lockheed who she'd gotten to know through Einstein. Ellie treated her much like her own *liu* had, curiously the same way the older woman treated Leah. Kaelen asked Einstein about it one day and his answer was simple, straightforward.

"My girlfriend, Nalla, calls it found family. When people don't have a family of their own, whether from death or disowning, they will often come together with others and create a type of family unit that goes beyond the bounds of blood, code, house, or legal relationship."

Kaelen thought about his words while they worked in the lab. "It's a good feeling."

Einstein nodded. "Leah and her family have made me feel more at home than I ever expected. My past wasn't positive or beneficial to anyone except for my master."

"You were enslaved?"

"Yes, by a being who called themself The Collector. They were fascinated by all manner of technology and thought it grand to acquire a lone Donbothian on assignment in the Outer Worlds. Perhaps it was what humans call karma because of the way my own race has been known for doing similar to organic species."

Kaelen frowned. "I've heard that Donbothians have stolen entire cities. It's one of many reasons they weren't allowed on Argon."

"Exactly so. Because of my mistreatment, I'd given up ever making a positive connection to others, especially here on Earth."

"How did you escape The Collector?"

He tilted his head, as though he needed time to contemplate her question. Kaelen knew that his positronic android brain could compute much harder questions in picoseconds. "The Tau Ceti rescued me and in return for my freedom, I agreed to become a Watcher. It is a noble task but not where I've achieved my greatest existential joys. It is in the people I've found here in Los Angeles— Nalla, Leah, Ellie, Maddy, and others you've not met yet—they are all my people now. My family."

"Do they know that you've claimed them? Is this an official declaration?"

Einstein let out a rare laugh. She was fascinated by the organic sound of it, rather than the expected digital replication. Einstein was an enigma the way he mimicked humans as much as possible while maintaining his unique android mannerisms. "No, Kaelen Ra-Evon. It is an informal claiming, the same as they have done with me. We are all friends and we take care of one another. We look out for each other's mental, physical, and emotional well-being. Is that not what family does?"

Kaelen looked down at her bench. "I thought so. But I learned the hard way that family can also lie to those they love, and sacrifice innocents for their own wellbeing and status."

"Well then," Einstein slapped the table. "It's good that you have a new family now who would not treat you with such disrespect."

That garnered a smile from her at last. "It is. Thank you, Clevna Trog. You are a good Donbothian, and a better person." They resumed their work, but it gave Kaelen much to think about.

* * * *

"Can you believe she'd been living off water and CLIF bars since she landed on Earth?"

Ellie smiled at Leah. "Is that why you've started dragging her and Einstein out to lunch a couple days a week, and ordering in all the rest?"

Leah's cheeks warmed. "Perhaps." She sighed. "She seems so lonely, you know? She said something to me after that first dinner and I realized that Kaelen hadn't made any other connections with people since coming to our planet. Kaelen said she liked hugs but that she was afraid to touch anyone while on Earth. I thought she was going to cry when I hugged her goodbye."

"I'm glad she's making friends with you all. You do realize that with you devoting more time down in the SPL, I've been upstairs covering all those mandatory meetings."

Leah gave her a worried look. "You don't mind, do you? I can start picking up the slack again. You shouldn't have to get stuck with all the work I like to avoid."

"Honey, it's fine. I don't mind helping out and the way I see it, Kaelen needs a friend as much as you want this project finished. You and Einstein are good for her. You're right…she is lonely but more than that, I think she's taken a special shine to you."

"She doesn't have any friends here in Los Angeles other than us. She admitted the other day that she spends all her time in the lab or at home and I don't have the heart to force her to work less because I know she's still struggling to come to terms with loss and culture shock. I think she's happy to have someone to talk to."

Ellie gave her a knowing smile. "If you say so, dear."

Leah cursed in a rare display of frustration. "Damn it! Kaelen lost her entire world in an instant and instead of having anyone with her who could hold her and help her heal, she spent ten long years sleeping through Earth education and her people's equivalent of therapy. That Argonian AI may be one of the best in the universe, but you can't replace an actual person when you're dealing with love and affection." She shook her head and met Ellie's gaze. "My heart truly goes out to her.

She is so strong."

"She's also brilliant, more so than we first realized during that interview."

Leah knew that Ellie was impressed from day one. She nodded. "Hands down. It's not only that she has a brilliant mind, but she's full of compassion that I rarely see anymore, let alone someone who has suffered such a loss."

"And she's extremely attractive."

"God is she!" Leah froze and looked at Ellie with wide eyes. "Uh, I didn't say that."

Ellie burst into laughter. "It sounds as though you did." After a few seconds pause she added, "It's okay to like her, honey."

"Yeah?"

"Yes."

"I'll admit to you and nobody else that my infatuation with Kaelen is bordering on ridiculous. There was just…something about her from the moment we met. You know? And learning the depth of her intelligence hasn't curbed my interest in the slightest. If anything, it's only exacerbated my feelings."

Ellie nodded. "I felt the same way about Charlie."

"But it also feels wrong because I know she hasn't been on Earth long and she never really had a childhood, or an adulthood for that matter. Is she mature enough to understand human relationships? That's not even taking into account for societal practices, biological compatibility, and—"

"Sweetheart," Ellie's touch stilled the nervous rambling and Leah grew quiet. "Trust me, strange though Kaelen's circumstances may be, she is extremely mature and very much an adult. There is also more to Leah Lockheed-Tuck than CEO and scientist. You're human too, but you won't know what's possible unless you try."

"Some days I feel as though I only have half of me to offer. My relationships never work out so I've kind of given up. No matter how good the technology is, I wish I could still walk. You know what I miss most?"

Ellie frowned. "No, what?"

"We had this thick and luscious green lawn at the Lockheed Manor when I was a little girl. I remember removing my shoes after my tutor would leave for the day, then I'd run downstairs and outside and race through the grass, doing circles until I fell. Mads would make fun of me but he'd always smile. He told me that feeling the grass against my toes was as important as feeling the air between my fingers. I'd like to feel the grass again."

Ellie patted her arm. "You will, I'm certain of it." She gave her a wink. "I have a feeling Kaelen will be there when you do."

"Hey, looks like I caught you both and saved myself a trip downstairs."

"Maddy!" Leah spun her chair in place and zipped over to her big sister.

"Hey, Leah." Maddy had a bag from their favorite Thai place, clearly full of food for all three of them. She leaned down and gave Leah a hug, then set the food on the coffee table and gave her mom a hug as well.

Ellie patted the couch next to her. "How's the hospital?"

Maddy began unpacking the bag and handing out chopsticks. She shrugged. "Not too bad now that the full moon has passed. What is it about that time of the month that brings out all the crazies in Los Angeles?"

Leah opened her clamshell container and gave the potstickers an appreciative sniff. "Maybe it has something to do with primitive urges acting in concurrence with the greater tidal pull next to a coastal city?" Everyone snorted at the obviously BS answer. "Are you off today? Where's Tasha?" Tasha was Maddy's current girlfriend of more than a year. She was a social worker that Maddy had met during a hard case involving a minor at LAGH.

"She's good. I'm off today but she isn't. That's why I decided to pay my two favorite relatives a visit and run some errands."

"We're your only two relatives."

Maddy grinned and shrugged before slurping noodles into her mouth. "Even so." She moaned. "I love this place."

"More than Beast Burger?"

"Uh…"

Ellie laughed. "She got you there, Maddy. And honey, you and Tasha need to come over for dinner soon. I haven't spent nearly enough time with that delightful woman."

"We're pretty busy, Mom. We don't have many free days where we're both off at the same time—"

Leah interrupted Maddy's excuse. "Maybe if you'd stop banging like bunnies on those free days, you'd have more time to visit your mother."

"Leah Avery Lockheed-Tuck!"

Maddy snickered. "Now that is a nice change of pace. I'm glad it's you in trouble this time and not me."

Ellie turned to Maddy next and gestured with her free hand. "And you…are you really not visiting because you're too busy having sex with your girlfriend? Shouldn't you be past the honeymoon phase by now? I expect you to stop eating out and come over to my place for a home cooked meal sometime soon."

"Uh, I…" Maddy's face and neck flushed red.

Laughter filled the room and Leah was forced to set down her container so she didn't spill it. Even Ellie chuckled at the look on her eldest daughter's face. She winked at Maddy. "Gotcha. I may be old, but I'm not dead. I certainly know what young love looks like and how sex works."

Maddy scrubbed a hand over her face. "Okay, changing the subject now. How is Ana doing since she took over as chief financial officer?"

"Good, actually. She was a little worried that she wasn't ready at first but she's blossomed in the role. I'm glad I snatched her up years ago when she was fresh out of university," Leah said.

Maddy guffawed. "Listen to you! You were right out of university too!"

"Oh yeah? Well now I'm the youngest CEO to ever top the *Fortune 500* list two years in a row. So, you can take those eggs and suck 'em!"

Chapter Five

It was six months later…six long months of team lunches, dinners with Leah, Einstein, and Ellie, or sometimes dinners just between Kaelen and Leah, before the small group working in the SPL hit their first true milestone. They'd reached the testing phase for two separate cures, one nanobot solution and one serum designed by the scientists in Lab 12. The serum team discovered a way to artificially create stem cells and used those to make the treatment. Regulatory T-cells had long ago been proven to promote repair and regeneration of various organ systems.

Kaelen had been on the project for nine months at that point and cursed the lack of modern tools at their disposal. Einstein pointed out that what was modern for her, was nothing more than science fiction for the people of Earth.

The SPL trio, as Ellie had taken to calling Leah, Kaelen, and Einstein, were down in the lab going over the results from their live test of the specialized nerve regeneration nanobots. They ran the baseline tests the week prior and were simply running the next set to see if there had been any change in the rats' condition. Truthfully, because they were running two trials simultaneously, they had to examine both the SPL nanobot test subjects, and the Lab 12 serum ones.

The first trial started with eight lab rats with precisely cut spinal cords that they'd received from a local school. The rats were slated to be destroyed but Ellie found out and had them relocated to L-I from the university lab. Why waste perfectly good rats when their group could make use of them? Four were injected with a stem cell serum created by her other lab, and the other four were injected with the nanobots and a nano power generator. Leah wanted to see which treatment had the fastest results and the greatest improvement.

"I'm positive the nanobots will be more effective and faster than the serum. My calculations are dope, as was Einstein's programming." Leah snickered and Kaelen grew concerned that she'd used the incorrect slang. "Was that the wrong word in this context?"

"Not at all, it was just funny to hear you say. I think you're getting the hang of it."

Einstein nodded. "I concur with your assessment of the nanobot efficacy. In fact, I am so certain of our results that I made a bet with Jonah in lab twelve. It is too bad they're all at the convention in New York. I'm sure they would love to see the one-week results in person."

Leah pointed at the camera in the corner of the lab. "They'll see it, don't worry. Now, let's remove subject R1 and run the tests."

Kaelen opened the cage and gently cradled the whitest of the four rats in her hands. "I called him *Krigh*. Because he is whiter than the others."

"It is unwise to develop an attachment to test subjects, Kaelen Ra-Evon. As a scientist you should know this."

Einstein's words of caution met their mark and Kaelen nodded. "I know. It's just…we didn't have many personal pets left on Argon. They were considered a waste of precious resources, which had been severely depleted during the war." She stroked the fur along the back of the rat then carefully placed him in a special clear container inside the computed tomography scanner.

Once they had a full image set of the region where the spinal cord had been cut, she removed the rat and put it on the table for Einstein to hook up two sets of electrodes. He sent a series of electric pulses, not enough to hurt the rat, but enough for them to monitor a reaction. The equipment would pick up any test subject nerve activity. Once all the stats were recorded, Kaelen returned the rat and retrieved the next one from its cage.

Displaying her usual abundance of curiosity, Leah asked, "Do you have a name for that one?"

Kaelen smiled shyly and placed him in the CT box. "I call him Sleepy."

"That's adorable."

They repeated the process for all four of the nanobot test subjects, as well as the others in the serum trial, recording the data from each. Then Leah brought them up side by side on the screen. She frowned. "I thought we'd see more of a change. The circulatory function for both projects was marginally improved at best."

"It's only been a week, Leah. Not nearly long enough for the bots or the serum to work. I predict we will begin to see more significant results in a month when both have had a chance to replicate within the test subjects' systems," Einstein said.

Kaelen nodded. "I would say that time frame seems most plausible."

Leah smiled and leaned back in her chair. "Good. It's Friday and the last one of the month. Will I see you and Nalla later, Einstein?"

"Indubitably. Nalla says she will for sure kick your ass in Settlers of Catan." Leah lifted a dark eyebrow at his statement. He inclined his head. "Of course, those were her words, boss, not mine."

Leah smirked. "Of course." She turned to Kaelen who watched the interaction curiously. "What about you? I know I've asked many times before, but would you like to come over for game night?"

Kaelen hesitated. "I—"

"It's an informal gathering of my closest family and friends."

Leah had invited her many times, but Kaelen never felt comfortable socializing outside her small work group. "I don't think I'll do well with a lot of strangers. I also don't understand what a game night is."

"Kaelen Ra-Evon, Earth games can take a variety of forms that may include cards, boards, intricately carved pieces, or sometimes a combination of all three. Argon had similar forms of entertainment."

Wex's explanation made sense but it still didn't tell her about the ones they had on Earth. "Do you all play one particular game, this Settlers of Catan? I'm afraid I don't know how to play any, at least none here on Earth." She paused. "I also don't want to intrude on your family time."

"Kaelen," Leah waited for her to make eye contact to continue. "You're included in that group of family and friends. I would love to have you over."

"If you're sure…"

Leah smiled. "I'm sure. Don't worry about food, we'll have plenty of pizza and snacks." Leah must have seen something in Kaelen's expression, perhaps that confounded wrinkle she's always talking about. "What is it?"

"Will I like this pizza? I haven't tried that yet."

"Kaelen Ra-Evon, you have not had pizza? Nalla would say your Earth education is sorely lacking."

"Kaelen," Kaelen looked from Einstein to Leah again. "You'll love it. Trust me."

"Okay."

Leah grabbed a nearby notebook from the lab bench, tore a page out and wrote on it. She handed it to Kaelen. "This is where I live. You can recite it to any taxi driver and they'll deliver you safely." Einstein snorted and Leah amended, "Safe enough. Otherwise, I would guess that Wex could instruct you on the proper buses to take. I'd normally recommend something like Uber or Lyft but without a phone…" Leah shrugged.

Kaelen frowned. "I can simply walk there. I don't wish to hire a vehicle that contributes to Los Angeles's pollution levels."

Einstein proposed an alternative. "Have you considered purchasing a bicycle, or an electric scooter to increase your mobility? Los Angeles climate is moderate, and you would be able to ride it year-round, as long as it wasn't raining. I would estimate if you are walking to work, you don't live so far away that a bicycle would fail to be practical."

"Kaelen Ra-Evon, the Donbothian has an intelligent solution. Both are two-wheeled modes of transportation and require balance and dexterity to operate. Your superior stamina and reflexes would guarantee that self-powered mobility would be no hardship. But while both a bicycle and electric scooter would be excellent tools of conveyance, the wiring in your sub-standard domicile would not be sufficient to handle charging for any large appliance without risking fire. I'm afraid the scooter would be implausible."

Wex informed her daily that the quality of the apartment she rented wasn't fit for even a human and beneath her status as the last scion to *Dolem*-Ra. She smiled at Einstein. "That is an excellent idea. Where would I purchase a bicycle, and will they teach me to ride it? Wex says that I have no safe place to charge a scooter."

Leah looked at her smart watch then offered, "How about this? It's close enough to five to log out for the day." Einstein lifted a finger to refute her statement and Leah narrowed her eyes at him. "Don't argue with me, Trog. I'm the boss, remember?"

Her statement rang slightly false based on something she'd previously said to Kaelen. "But didn't you say that technically, Ellie was our boss?"

Leah raised an eyebrow and gave Kaelen an imperious look. "Who holds stock majority at Lockheed International."

"I researched that the same night Wex explained the financial system. You do."

"And who is the current CEO of Lockheed?"

Kaelen swallowed, fascinated by the look on Leah's face. It was intelligent, powerful, and a little arrogant. Leah looked like a proper Argonian and Kaelen's stomach clenched with something that wasn't fear. She whispered, "You."

Leah smiled. "Do you need anything from your apartment?"

Kaelen looked back and forth between Einstein and Leah. "Do I need to bring something for your game night?"

Einstein said, "You do not," at the same time Leah shook her head.

"Okay. I don't need to go back to my apartment."

"Good. You can ride with me to my place, and one of us can take you home after. Maybe Maddy and Tasha since they live on your side of town." When Kaelen hesitated, Leah added, "It's more efficient and less wasteful of resources." That garnered a nod from Kaelen. "Good! Now let's shut this place down and start the weekend. The work will still be here on Monday."

Einstein packed his laptop away in the messenger bag he carried daily and waved as he made his way out of the lab. "Nalla and I shall see you in a few hours, Leah. And you as well, Kaelen."

Kaelen hadn't gone many places on Earth since landing the year before. A rented room in Vancouver, her apartment in Los Angeles, Lockheed, a local grocery store, and a handful of restaurants. None of the locations had the look or feel of her home on Argon. While Leah's residence still didn't have the same aesthetic, the place had a majesty all on its own. Kaelen was impressed that her friend appeared to own the entire top of her building, a conclusion she came to after the elevator deposited them right into an entryway off Leah's main living space.

She turned in a circle, looking up at the high ceiling. It was bright white with light gray accents. It could have been considered sterile, but the decorations within were colorful and soft. "This entire domicile is your home?"

"It is."

Despite the large size, the room with couches appeared comfortable and warm. Kaelen's eyes moved throughout the open floor plan of the main section. Besides the sitting area, there was a spacious kitchen, not that Kaelen had mastered the art of preparing Earth food, a dining area, stairs that led to an upper level, a short hallway with a door off one side and a set of double doors at the end, and large glass panels on tracks which Kaelen quickly realized were doors that led outside.

She frowned. Leah's home was disastrously high for an external exit to be practical. She pointed toward the egress. "Isn't that dangerous for humans? It doesn't seem safe to leave your home from this altitude."

Leah laughed and gestured toward the doors. "I have a balcony. Come see." She led Kaelen over to the door and pushed a button on her hoverchair. One side slid open and Leah smoothly floated through into a large, walled-in space.

Outside Kaelen could see more furniture, a heat source, and lamps. What caught her attention most was the view from so high above the streets. Kaelen looked out over Los Angeles, remembering another prospering metropolis that spread out much the same way. Leah's balcony reminded her of the landing pad at her family home. Not only that, but the way the late afternoon sun shone through the odd cloud cover cast a reddish glow across everything. She missed the rose light of Argon. Kaelen whispered softly into the breeze. "Glorious Vos, thank you for gracing this day with knowledge and prosperity."

When she turned away from the railing, Leah looked at her with concern. "Are you okay?"

"I'm fine. Your view reminded me of the one I had from my family home."

"You miss it a lot, don't you?"

Kaelen took a steadying breath. "Longing is a wasteful emotion. Should I help you set up for this game night?" She made to take a step away but paused when Leah spoke.

"Kaelen, stop. Look at me, please?"

With a slow turn, Kaelen stood facing her. "Do you need something?"

Leah raised her chair and moved it over next to Kaelen. Then she held out her arms. "You look like you could use a hug."

Something in Kaelen broke and reformed at Leah's kind tone and selfless gesture. As promised, Leah had been hugging Kaelen more since that night outside her apartment. And over the past week and a half, they'd even worked up to Kaelen hugging her back. Tears welled and ran down her cheeks, and part of her felt ashamed to be so emotionally dependent. It wasn't rational or productive.

Leah broke Kaelen from her thoughts by reaching out and tugging at her sleeve. "You're overthinking again. Give me a hug."

Kaelen sank into the embrace, returning the smallest amount of pressure. "I'm sorry if I am being a burden."

Leah pulled back enough so she could meet Kaelen's gaze. "Hey, hey, look at me. You are *not* a burden. You will never be a burden. I want you to feel comfortable and safe here, okay?" Then she pulled Kaelen close again.

Kaelen sighed and shut her eyes to the sights of the city. "Okay."

They stayed like that for a few minutes until Kaelen felt grounded again. She stepped back and smiled. "Thank you. You continue to amaze me, reminding me of how much I like having you in my life."

"Ditto." An odd word that confused Kaelen. Leah pointed between her eyes with a smirk. "Wrinkle. What are you thinking about?"

Kaelen rubbed the offending spot. "I don't know what ditto means in this context and I put my communicators in my satchel when we left the lab." At Leah's curious look she added, "Some things I need to understand on my own."

"I get it. And ditto means 'copy that' or 'same.' Though I suppose I can make things even easier for you and say that I appreciate having you in my life as well." Leah grabbed Kaelen's hand with her free one and led her inside. "Now, we have some time before the others arrive. I'll call in the pizza order then I can show you how to play a few of the group's more popular games."

Warmth started in Kaelen's stomach and radiated throughout her body. She wasn't sure if it was because she was about to learn something new, or if it was from the feel of Leah's soft fingers clasped with her own. "I would like that very much. Can you tell me who else will be here?"

"I'll describe everyone you haven't met yet when I teach you to play Uno."

Hours later, Kaelen stood at a whiteboard easel with a black marker in hand. There was an even amount of people at the game night and Leah volunteered to be Kaelen's partner for all the team games since Kaelen had never heard of most of them. Despite her inexperience, everyone groaned as Leah easily guessed Kaelen's drawings during Pictionary.

"I'm sorry. I'm obligated to let you know that I possess perfect recall and superior spatial reasoning, both of which allow me to replicate whatever image I picture in my head."

Everyone groaned and one person threw a piece of popcorn at her head. "Boo! New game!" That prompted the group to move on to other games where Kaelen wasn't so skilled.

She'd been introduced to everyone as they arrived, and she recited each name in her head multiple times to make sure she had the new people memorized. It was odd that she had perfect recall for facts and figures, but names and faces sometimes eluded her. Maddy, Leah, and Einstein, were all familiar because she'd met them many times at work. While she'd heard about Ana, Nalla, Tasha, and Tasha's brother Devon, it was her first time meeting them.

"What is the purpose of this Monopoly? Does it teach humans how to effectively do business?"

Nalla laughed at her, then quickly clapped a hand over her mouth. "Sorry, Kaelen. To answer your question, this isn't at all like real business. It's a long, boring game where we all end up watching Maddy and Leah fight over first place.

Ana chimed in, "At least until one of them flips the board."

Kaelen looked back and forth between the sisters in question with wide eyes.

"Look who's talking, Pérez!" Maddy countered. "You've done your share of flipping too!"

Tasha snickered. "Babe, she's right though. It usually is you."

Maddy shot her a betrayed look, but Kaelen saw her features soften right before she kissed Tasha. Kaelen watched the kiss longer than she probably should have. Something about it made her think of Leah and wonder what it would feel like to kiss someone she loved. Kaelen glanced at the woman at the forefront of her mind. "Is your found family always so chaotic?"

Leah gave her a fond smile and took another sip of wine. "Don't forget, it's your found family too. I think it's pretty safe to say we've all claimed you by now, Kaelen." Kaelen felt her cheeks warm at the idea of Leah "claiming" her but listened intently as she kept talking. "And a great scientist once said that chaos, when left alone, tends to multiply."

"Kaelen, you would have appreciated Stephen Hawking, the man behind the quote."

She tilted her head at Einstein. "Was he on par with Leah?"

"Mr. Hawking was a theoretical physicist whose theory of exploding black holes drew upon both relativity theory and quantum mechanics. He also worked with space-time singularities." Einstein paused in thought before continuing. "Though I understand him to be a genius by Earth standards, he wasn't the same as you or I, or even Leah."

"Hello, I'm sitting right here."

"Yes, you are." Kaelen gave her a confused look. "We are in your home, where else would you be? Maybe I should amend my determination on your intelligence after you made such a basic statement."

Nalla crowed, "Oh my gawd, she did not!" She pointed at Leah. "She called you basic." The rest of the group started laughing, including Leah. Maddy shook her head and took a swig of her beer, while Tasha looked at Leah with concern.

Glancing around the group, Kaelen feared that she'd missed some social queue. "Sorry if I spoke out of line, Leah. Did I say something wrong?"

Leah shook her head and reached out to take Kaelen's hand. "Not at all, darling. I am often self-deprecating and accept light teasing from my friends and family. Nothing you said was incorrect. Not only that, but you don't even realize why what you said was funny."

Maddy interrupted before she could explain further, clearly curious about one of Kaelen's previous statements. "What did you mean when you and Einstein were referring to Earth standard genius? Are there more types?"

Kaelen looked at Einstein, hoping the Donbothian would explain. He merely nodded for her to answer. "Since you're all friends with Einstein, you probably know he was engineered to be a twelfth caliber intellect."

Maddy muttered, "A fact he never lets us forget."

"What most of you don't know is that I'm also a twelfth caliber intellect." A few people gave her a startled look.

"It is true. Kaelen Ra-Evon comes from a long line of thinkers, and we are well met in both thought and deed while working within the SPL."

Kaelen continued. "The numbers I use are actually based on the Donbothian intelligence scale. I think Einstein could explain them better in terms of how they relate to human intelligence."

"That I can do. Let's see, Donbothian's have recorded individuals all the way up to thirteenth caliber. The Collector themself insisted of a twenty rating but I never saw evidence of such a thing." He gave a sniff of disdain before continuing. "The lowest is the non-sentient intelligence. After that is first caliber, which is below human average, second caliber average, third caliber above average, fourth is gifted by human standards, fifth is exceptionally bright, sixth is genius— " He paused. "For context, the CEO of Varden Industries, Brian Strong, and fabled Detective Sherlock Holmes are both sixth level. To continue, seventh caliber would be considered super-intelligent, like Albert Einstein or Stephen Hawking—"

"Whoa, whoa, whoa…" Maddy broke in. "You mean more classifications exist after super-intelligent? Holy shit!"

Einstein and Kaelen nodded before he continued. "Eighth caliber intellect is what the average Donbothian rated."

"And my father, Evon Ra."

He smiled at her. "Yes, as I said before, I'd heard of your house. An above average Donbothian would rate as a ninth caliber intellect, a gifted Donbothian would be tenth, and an exceptionally bright Donbothian would rate as an eleventh caliber intellect."

Tasha held up a hand. "Didn't you say you were a twelfth caliber, Einstein?"

"Well, yes. And apparently so is Kaelen Ra-Evon, last of *Dolem*-Ra."

His words triggered the realization that, with the passing of all before her, effectually, Kaelen herself had become *the* Ra. It was a title held by the most senior of her Argonian house, which was previously her father's father. Many of her new friends appeared confused at the unfamiliar words so Kaelen translated for them. "*Dolem*-Ra means 'house of Ra.' I am the last of my house, and possibly of the Argonian people as a whole."

Nalla finished her drink and placed the glass down on the side table. "So, Kaelen, does that make you a princess or something?"

"No, Argon didn't have royalty."

Nalla tilted her head. "Well then, what does that make you if you're the last of *Dolem*-Ra?"

Kaelen swallowed and looked down, the words evoking a dark feeling in the pit of her stomach. "Lonely."

Leah reached over to squeeze Kaelen's hand and her next comment had everyone laughing again. "Are we all going to ignore how the average Donbothian is still calibers higher than the smartest Earth genius? How is that even fair?"

That got Kaelen to look up again. "There are exceptions to every rule, Leah. I was one such exception in the way that I surpassed all those before me on Argon. You are another exception."

Leah sucked in a breath and her lips parted. "Me?"

Einstein was already nodding. "Yes, I've long surmised that myself." He gazed at Kaelen. "I suspect eighth or ninth caliber. What say you?"

Kaelen looked at Leah, taking in her flushed cheeks and comfortable looking sweater. She answered Einstein with only half a mind on the question. "Yes, at least an eight but we would need testing equipment that I don't think exists here on Earth to be certain."

"It does not."

Maddy snorted. "Well, I feel like chopped liver now. How about the rest of you?"

Laughter echoed around the game room and Nalla scooped up the dice. "Time to get the world's longest game back on track." She groaned when she saw the number that came up. "Nooo!" Then she moved her piece to Leah's most lucrative property.

Leah grinned in a predatory manner and held out her hand. "Boardwalk with a hotel…that will be two thousand dollars, please."

Nalla sighed and gathered up the rest of her cash then thrust it across the board toward Leah. "You are a shark! It's not even fair playing this game with any of you. I'm always the first one out."

"Not true," Kaelen pointed out. "I lost all my money first."

Nalla rolled her eyes. "You've never played before and appear to enjoy watching the others. Not me. I'm going to refill my drink and grab another slice of pizza."

Kaelen's head jerked up. "There's more pizza? It's delicious and I can't believe I've never tried it until tonight."

Maddy laughed. "I've heard the stories, from these two," she pointed back and forth between Einstein and Leah, "and from Mom. Is there anything you haven't enjoyed since you arrived on Earth?"

"Kale!" Leah and Einstein called it out at the same time and Kaelen made a face.

"It's true. Kale is bitter and unpleasant. Why is it so angry? It's like…if coffee were a vegetable!"

Leah snickered. "She also doesn't like coffee unless it has enough sugar and cream in it to fall into a dessert classification."

Kaelen shrugged. "While I don't receive any benefits from the caffeine content, the caramel macchiato from The Bean Bag is delicious."

Nalla nodded. "She's totally right on that, best drink there."

Maddy rolled her eyes. "You're both children who clearly never hit a wall twenty hours into a busy thirty-hour shift."

Nalla pointed at her and winked. "And that's why I'm a reporter and not a doctor." She gestured to Kaelen. "Come on, Evon. Let's go raid the pizza boxes."

Chapter Six

The name startled her, and she brought it up to Nalla on their way out of the game lounge to the main living space of the home. "That was my father's name."

Nalla grabbed a piece of plain pepperoni pizza from one open box and sat on a stool at the kitchen counter.

"Evon?"

"Evon Ra."

"Ra…your house name is like the Egyptian sun god. I took Earth mythology in college and learned that Ra was the king of the deities and the father of all creation. Patron of the sun, kingship, power, heaven, and light…blah, blah, blah." Nalla waved her hand with the last few words to highlight how inconsequential she thought Ra was.

Kaelen wondered briefly if this mythological sun god, Ra, and her own ancestors were so different. Arrogant benefactors and leaders of their worlds. She deflected. "I'm no god, merely a refugee sent to Earth by her father." Her stomach twisted at the slight falsehood because Kaelen knew that her powers put her far above the rest of the planet, seeming as much like a god to humans as they would seem to a lesser species. Perhaps she held a bit of her house arrogance after all. "As for my name, descent and inheritance were patroclinous in Argonian society. Women carried their father's name for the rest of their lives, even after bonding."

"That's kind of bullshit."

Kaelen grabbed her own slice and sat down next to Nalla. "Why do you say that? You mentioned that you are Varian, what is your naming convention?"

"Because the connection to the psychic plane only manifests in female Varians, our naming follows the mother's family line. When my mother, Korana Bel, fled to Earth at eighteen, she met and married my father, who took her name."

"That makes logical sense. Do you have siblings?"

"Nope, an only child. I won't call you by your last name again if it makes you feel uncomfortable. But patriarchal societies rub me the wrong way. Ugh! What happened to free and equal? Women shouldn't be passed from man to man like cattle."

Kaelen thought for a few seconds. "I like your passion. And when you put it that way, it makes the women of my planet seem more like possessions."

"It's not like Earth is any better. Things are similar here but times are changing. Same sex marriage is legal, people can live how they choose, with whom they choose." Nalla paused and Kaelen grew curious.

The young woman was bright. Maybe not on the same caliber as an Earth genius, but she had a depth of emotional intelligence that few others could ever attain. Kaelen assumed it had something to do with Nalla's psychic powers. "What is it? You look like you want to say something."

"Have you considered changing your name, now that you're here on Earth? You said the rest of your planet and people are gone. You could do anything here, be anyone you want."

Kaelen frowned. "I...I couldn't do that. How would I carry on *Dolem*-Ra if I were to change my name? I am the last scion of Ra. I am *the* Ra"

"What does that mean?"

"I'm not sure. It has never happened before that one of the ruling houses on the Council would only contain a single member. I'll consult with my AI on the topic later."

Nalla nodded. "So back to the original subject, how do you plan to carry on *Dolem*-Ra? You said yourself that if you were to marry, you would retain the name of your father. If you were to change your name, then you could potentially pass on Ra much the way your father did."

Nalla got up to make herself another cocktail while Kaelen tried a different kind of pizza. She ate it fast while Nalla's back was turned and was busy wiping her mouth by the time Nalla came back to her stool. "To my knowledge, it's never been done before. Not that the subject will ever come up, as it is unlikely that I'll find a mate here on Earth. Argonian bonding, uh, marriages were arranged by a specialized computer program to guarantee compatibility. My people mate for life and some couples matched as early as birth. When the time came for them to have a child, their DNA was collected and put into the genetic birthing chamber."

Nalla opened her mouth to speak but no words came out and Kaelen grew confused. "Did I say something wrong?"

"Hold up," Nalla raised her hand, palm facing toward Kaelen. "You mean to tell me that Argonians don't actually, uh, have sex?"

Kaelen shrugged. "It wasn't necessary for procreation. Some did, sure. I'd read plenty about it in the science journals, but that wasn't the focus of joining houses. In fact, I've read many scientific texts that indicate the greater populace of Argonians felt no sexual desire. I believe this planet calls such people asexual. I learned about it on the way to Earth during the human biology instruction."

"Huh."

A thoughtful look crossed Nalla's face and Kaelen said the same words she'd heard often enough from Leah. "What are you thinking about?"

Nalla grinned and her expression was unfamiliar. "What about you?"

"I don't understand."

"Are you asexual, or ace as we call it?"

Kaelen thought about it, contemplating all she'd seen and learned since landing in northern Canada. Did she feel sexual attraction? "I—"

"How much pizza are you going to eat?"

The second Leah came into view, every bit of Kaelen's attention focused on her. Leah was smiling and her cheeks held an attractive flush. Kaelen's response came out as an awed whisper. "Leah."

Leah looked from one woman to the other. "Are you going to come back and play the next game? What are you even doing in here anyway?"

Nalla answered, wearing that same infuriating grin that Kaelen had yet to decipher. "Oh, not much. Just talking about smashing the patriarchy, and cultures with ace representation. Did you know that many Argonians were asexual?"

"Oh!" Leah looked at Kaelen when Nalla dropped that particular bit of information. "I'm sorry if I've ever said anything out of line. Are you, uh, are you ace, Kaelen?"

Nalla snickered and grabbed her drink before making her way around Leah and down the hallway. She called out over her shoulder, "She's definitely not."

"Is that true, Kaelen?"

Kaelen would swear she could feel the heat of Leah's intense gaze and she squirmed a bit, her third slice of pizza forgotten on her napkin. "I never considered it until…"

"Until what? You came to Earth?" Kaelen shook her head. "Until you came to Los Angeles?"

"No. That's not when."

Leah moved closer and rested her fingers on the white knuckles where Kaelen's hands were tightly locked together. "You can tell me; I won't judge you, promise."

Kaelen whispered, "Do you pinky swear?" She unlocked her fingers and held up a single pinky, which Leah immediately hooked her own around.

"Of course, darling."

"I'd never considered sexuality or attraction until I met you."

Leah sat there in silence for nearly a minute while they stared at one another. Kaelen could hear Leah's heart racing, and she feared that she had caused her friend distress. "Was I not supposed to say that? I value your friendship more than any other, before or after Argon. I wouldn't want to jeopardize that with useless self-realizations."

"Oh, no! You haven't jeopardized anything at all. I promised, didn't I? It caught me off guard because we've never actually discussed the more personal topics during meals together." She cleared her throat and looked away before coming back to the conversation head on. Kaelen appreciated Leah's forthrightness. "What did you mean when you said that meeting me made you consider your sexuality?"

"It means that with no fellow Argonians, and no program to determine a proper match, I assumed that *Dolem*-Ra would die with me.

It didn't occur to me that I could perhaps find someone on my own who would be worthy of my house. I certainly didn't expect that I would be drawn to someone the way my parents were drawn to one another."

"And you are…um, you're drawn to someone here on Earth?" Kaelen nodded but didn't say anything else. Rather than ask the obvious question, Leah's reasoning seemed to take a side tangent. "What did you mean when you said it was a useless self-realization?"

Kaelen frowned. "Even if I were to find a match worthy of my house, I'm afraid I can't act on my attraction. A physical relationship would be impossible."

Leah seemed surprised. "And why is that? Are you afraid that someone wouldn't want you, or be interested in return?" Kaelen shook her head. "Are humans and Argonians physically compatible?"

"Based on everything I learned during my journey, we have similar enough sexual anatomy and sexual response to make relations of that nature beneficial for both people involved."

A muscle tightened in Leah's jaw as her expression grew dark. "Do you think that whomever you're drawn to would be incapable of returning physical affection?"

"No, it's not that at all. It's…I can't say."

Leah's eyes widened. "Does this have to do with our first pinky swear?"

"Yes. I, uh—" Kaelen sighed. She wanted so badly to discuss all the changes wrought on her body by the yellow sun of Earth but she was still hesitant to go against one of the objectives set forth by her parents. Her shoulders dropped. "Leah, while my head and heart are still the same as they were on Argon, I'm afraid my body is too different to be safe with someone here. It's too…powerful." Her bottom lip quivered and she cursed Vos for her weak emotional fortitude. "I don't want to hurt anyone."

Leah moved closer and hugged Kaelen as tight as possible. She'd gotten good at understanding when Kaelen was feeling sad and overwhelmed, something Kaelen appreciated immensely. "I don't think you would hurt anyone. I have faith in you. But in the end, you have to do what is right for you and don't let anyone tell you different. Okay?"

Kaelen nodded and carefully returned Leah's embrace. "Okay."

When Leah pulled back again, Kaelen felt immeasurably lighter of heart. She didn't like talking about things she couldn't change.

"Better?"

"Yes."

Leah lowered herself and turned toward the game room. "Are you ready to rejoin the others and learn how to play Settlers of Catan?"

"Yes, that sounds like a lot of fun."

Kaelen was right beside Leah as they made their way down the hall. They could hear laughter and good-natured bickering coming through the double doors, though it was significantly louder for Kaelen. Right before Kaelen made to push through ahead of Leah, she stopped and looked back over her shoulder. "Leah Lockheed-Tuck," Leah met her gaze and waited. "If I could choose anyone to join *Dolem*-Ra, the best one, I'd choose you." Then she was through the door in a flash, the image of Leah's face frozen with shock permanently burned into her memory.

Game night continued for a few more hours, though Leah was a bit quieter than normal after Kaelen's declaration in the hall. Kaelen feared that she'd upset her friend and endeavored to keep certain things to herself going forward. Part of Kaelen wanted to retrieve her communicators from her satchel and ask Wex about human sexuality and social norms. Then she feared Wex would caution her away from friendship with Leah.

Eventually Nalla and Einstein left, then Devon and Ana. As promised, Maddy agreed to give Kaelen a ride home after they helped Leah clean up the game room and kitchen.

"Are you ready, Kaelen?" Maddy and Tasha had already given out hugs and goodbyes and waited by the elevator off Leah's living room. Kaelen stood in front of Leah, nervously shifting her weight back and forth on each foot. She was fearful that her own hug would be rejected because of her unsettling words to her friend from earlier.

Leah held out her arms. "Come here."

That was all Kaelen needed to fall into another one of Leah's exceptional embraces. A minute later they pulled apart. Kaelen whispered, "Thank you."

"You don't have to thank me, darling. Now, I'll see you on Monday, okay?" Kaelen nodded. "I have meetings all morning but I'm planning to come downstairs in the afternoon."

Kaelen felt a wave of emotion at her words. "I can't wait to see you then. Good evening, Leah." She stepped back and gave a little wave then made her way over to Maddy and Tasha. "I'm ready now, thanks for waiting."

Tasha looked from Leah to Kaelen and Kaelen got the impression that she saw more than the average person, much like Nalla. But she wasn't ready to admit any other realizations to people she'd only just met, even if they were more found family and trusted by Leah. Lucky for her, conversation was neutral and she enjoyed the ride since Maddy also possessed an electric vehicle.

"How do you like working for Lockheed? Mom and Leah have nothing but amazing things to say about you."

Kaelen sat in the back of the car, but she could see Maddy's eyes in the small mirror. "I enjoy it immensely. My entire life's purpose was to contribute to society in a meaningful way and we are doing good work at the SPL."

Maddy's eyes narrowed when Kaelen met her gaze. "And do you think the nanobots will be able to restore spinal cord function? Because I'm telling you right now, Kaelen Ra-Evon, I don't want my sister to get her hopes up only for them to fall again. She's…Leah is amazing, and kind, and has already gone through so much."

Kaelen wasn't sure how to answer Maddy but the warning contained within her words was clear. "I—"

"Babe, Leah isn't the only one who has experienced loss. Both of our fathers died, but none of it compares to an entire planet." Tasha turned slightly in her seat to look at Kaelen. "Don't mind Maddy, she's being an overprotective big sister. She also knows there are no guarantees in science."

"I respect Maddy's need to protect Leah because she is a precious resource to the Earth people. But more than that, she's an amazing person who deserves to bathe in the light of Vos. But Tasha, there are guarantees in science if it's done correctly. The nano technology will work, even using such primitive tools as found on this planet. It may take a little longer, but our science is sound. So, it's not a matter of if nerve damage can be repaired, but rather when.”

"Holy shit.”

"Maddy,” Tasha cautioned.

Maddy looked at Kaelen in the mirror, then spared a brief glance toward Tasha before focusing her eyes back on the city streets. "Do you know what this means for the medical community? This is amazing!” She paused again and Kaelen could see Maddy briefly chew her lip. "Thank you, Kaelen.”

That she understood. "It's my pleasure and honor to help the people of my new home, especially my friends.”

A few minutes later they pulled up in front of Kaelen's apartment. Tasha glanced out her window, then turned in her seat to look back at Kaelen. "Uh, you live here?”

"Yes, is something wrong with my apartment building?”

"You do know that crime is incredibly high in this area, not to mention—”

Maddy turned to stare at her as well, wearing a look of disgust. "Kaelen, this place is a shit hole.”

"There's no excrement—”

Tasha gently interrupted. "It's a saying, Kaelen. What Maddy means is that it's not a good home, perhaps not safe, and certainly not pleasant. Are you struggling financially?” She looked at Maddy with concern. "Doesn't Leah pay her people top grade?”

"She does. Why do you live here, Kaelen?”

Kaelen shrugged. "It was the first place Wex found in the internet listings that met my price parameters. I don't need much in the way of physical comfort, nor do I have any belongings. This apartment was inexpensive and already had furniture inside. I also believe that people are allowed to have pets because I occasionally hear them in the walls. It's comforting because there weren't many personal pets approved on Argon.”

"In the walls?” She nodded.

Both women grimaced and their looks could be best described as horrified. Tasha muttered, "Oh my God.”

Maddy was more of a problem solver. "Kaelen, you can't stay in an apartment that has rats!”

"But the lab has rats—"

"These aren't pets! The ones in your building are most likely vermin infested rodents who are not supposed to be living in the walls. We can help find another place if you need it."

Kaelen looked down. "I don't want to be a burden to anyone. I can utilize Wex to begin the search for another apartment, one that doesn't contain wild wall pets."

"Babe, what about your place?"

Maddy suddenly struck her forehead with the palm of her hand. "Duh!" She smiled back at Kaelen. "I recently moved in with Tasha and the lease on my apartment is up at the end of the month. I'm sure I can talk the owner of the building into renting it to you instead. You know what, I'll text her tonight so it should be immediately available."

Kaelen looked back and forth between them. "That is a kind offer. I'll still need to shop for furnishings if I move."

"Actually, I was going to sell or donate most of my furniture. It's not like we need two sets living at Tasha's place and her stuff is a lot nicer. So, you should be good, especially if you don't have much in the way of belongings, as you said."

"How long is your lease, Kaelen?"

"You mean contract for inhabitation?"

"Uh, yes. That."

"I pay weekly in cash."

Maddy snorted. "Well, that explains a lot." Tasha rolled her eyes. "We both have tomorrow off. Why don't we help you move first thing in the morning?"

Kaelen contemplated removing her communicators from the satchel and asking Wex for advice but quickly discounted the idea. Much like getting control of her hearing, she needed to adapt and make decisions for herself. "I'd like that a lot."

"Do you need to give notice to your landlord? How much stuff do you have? If it's a lot, we can probably help you hire a truck first thing in the morning."

"I've already paid through Sunday and if I don't leave money under the door by Monday morning, I was informed my locks would be changed. And I only have my satchel."

Tasha shook her head. "No, I mean what else do you have, furniture, clothes, stuff like that?"

"Yes, only my satchel. I stopped purchasing the ration bars of CLIF when Leah showed me how to order takeaway from restaurants. And once I figured out how to manipulate the nanofibers of my ship suit, I simply change its form every day to replicate Earth clothing. My Argonian biology means that I never need the toiletries created for humans."

"Fucking hell, could you be more of a perfect specimen?"

"Maddy!"

Maddy grimaced. "Sorry, Kaelen. I just meant that— " She shook her head. "You know what, never mind. I'm clearly being an ass. How about we come pick you up first thing in the morning at say…" she glanced at Tasha. "Eight?"

Tasha smirked. "Nine. It's our free day."

"Free day? Oh! Is tomorrow the day you two bang like bunnies? I don't want to interrupt your personal day of noise making together."

"Wait, what?"

"Where did you hear that? Did Leah tell you?"

Kaelen shook her head. "I overheard you speaking about it in her office months ago." She took note of the expression of discomfort on both Maddy and Tasha's faces. "Sorry, I probably shouldn't have listened to your private conversation with Leah and Ellie. Sometimes it is hard to dampen my hearing when Leah's heart rate speeds with delight or distress."

Maddy rubbed her temples. "It's too late to unpack all that, but rest assured we'll have a conversation about your extra normal hearing and potentially stalking my sister tomorrow when we pick you up at nine."

"Wait, Maddy." Tasha looked back at Kaelen. "What did you mean when you said noise making?"

Kaelen grew confused. "Isn't that the meaning of banging?"

Maddy and Tasha looked at each other then started giggling. It was Maddy who explained. "Banging like bunnies is a euphemism. It basically means having a lot of sex."

"Oh." Kaelen paused to contemplate Maddy's words. "Oh! I'm sorry for interrupting your coitus then."

Maddy winked at her. "It's fine. I'm sure Tasha and I will have plenty of time later in the day for pleasurable activities." Tasha slapped her shoulder, but Kaelen could see playful intent.

"Okay. You've both given me invaluable assistance and advice. I look forward to seeing you tomorrow." Kaelen made Argonian motions of respect and possession while Maddy and Tasha remained twisted in the front seats, watching. "I now claim you as my people."

"Uh…"

"Claim us?"

"Yes, Einstein says that we are found family and that people can claim each other as such, to protect, nurture, and respect. I want to claim you as part of my found family."

Tasha smiled at her then Maddy. "Aww, that's the sweetest thing I've ever heard."

It was Maddy's turn to roll her eyes. "Accepted. Now, it's late and I'd like to make some noise with my girlfriend before we hit the sack. Uh, that means sleep." She made a shooing motion toward Kaelen. "We'll be here tomorrow at nine. We'll even take you to breakfast first."

Kaelen nodded. "Thank you. Food is always appreciated." She quickly exited the vehicle, not wishing to delay them further. They waved goodbye and Kaelen watched for a few minutes then walked toward the front door of the building.

A yell pierced the night air before she could open it. Kaelen quickly retrieved her communicators from the satchel and placed them in her ears. "Wex, someone is screaming nearby."

"Kaelen Ra-Evon, it would be unwise to involve yourself in human affairs."

The scream came again, followed by a much quieter "Help!" as though the person's mouth were muffled in some way. "I can't stand by and do nothing!"

"I would recommend concealing your identity if you wish to inspect the disturbance."

Kaelen's clothing reformed back into that of her ship suit with its glowing House of Ra symbol on the chest. Her ship suit was nearly at capacity for fabric cover but she had an idea. Following Wex's suggestion, Kaelen caressed her collar and the nanotech moved up the sides of her face to form an eye mask. "Wex, dim the beacon please." The symbol darkened to give off a faint luminance.

Hearing the heart rate increase nearby, Kaelen sped around the corner behind her apartment building where she found two men restraining a woman. "Wex, what is the force needed to render a human unconscious without permanent damage?"

"Medical texts in my database indicate that as little as ten Newtons, or around one kilogram of force, can render the average adult human male unconscious if you hit precisely on the point of their chin."

"Thank you." Armed with that knowledge, Kaelen rushed forward and delivered the appropriate blows required, then caught the woman before she fell to the ground. "Are you uninjured?"

She appeared fearful but answered anyway. "Pretty much, thanks to you."

"Will you be safe now? I want to take these men to the local police station before they wake."

"I live nearby. I'll keep my pepper spray handy all the way to my door. Thanks."

Her mention of food seasoning was odd, but Kaelen nodded. "Go now then, I'll listen to be sure you arrive safely. Whisper the word 'home' and I'll hear you." The woman's mouth dropped open and Kaelen grabbed each man by the back of their pants and lifted off the ground until she hovered a few yards above.

"Who are you?"

Kaelen hesitated, floating in place for a moment. She was unsure how to answer. Wex cautioned, *"You should not give them your full identity. It would be unwise."*

"I am the last scion of Ra."

She began to lift again as the woman glanced at the crest on Kaelen's chest then called out, "Thank you, Scion!"

Kaelen didn't sleep much that night, her mind racing with what she'd done. She'd always assumed her greatest accomplishments to society would come from the scientific knowledge engineered within her mind. But the yellow sun powers gifted to her on this new world opened up possibilities Kaelen had never imagined. She wasn't sure if she liked the implications of it all.

Chapter Seven

The next morning, Kaelen made sure all her belongings were stowed safely in her Argonian satchel then knocked on the landlord's door. She didn't expect him to answer as he wasn't particularly interested in maintaining the upkeep of the apartments within the building, or interacting with the tenants.

"Who the hell is banging on the door this early?" The door abruptly opened and he sneered at Kaelen. "You could have waited 'til a little later in the day to give me next week's rent."

Kaelen wrinkled her nose at the scent emanating from the slovenly form in front of her. "I'm sorry, Mister Gregg, but I will no longer require my apartment. I'm here to return the key."

He jabbed his finger at her. "You can't do that, you bitch! You have to give me a month's notice to move out!"

"You're wrong. I pay you weekly for rent and according to housing paperwork I signed when I moved in, I only need to give you the key before the next week begins to cancel the agreement." She held out the key and her landlord's face turned a strange shade of red. His heart rate pounded in her ears, and she observed the blood vessels near his temples expand and throb. Sweat formed along his forehead and Mr. Gregg curled his hands into fists. He displayed all the usual signs of rage, which was an extreme reaction to a tenant moving out.

"Kaelen Ra-Evon, his physical positioning and overall demeanor indicates that he intends violence. He will damage himself if he strikes you. Perhaps you could try giving him some of your US dollars."

He didn't accept her key. Instead, he took a step forward in an aggressive manner. "I'll take that key and shove it right up your ass, you snooty bitch! You too good for this place, or what?"

Kaelen remained calm and smiled. She moved forward so fast she assumed it looked as though she simply appeared right in front of him. Kaelen held up the key, then reached into her satchel with the other hand and withdrew the first bill of paper currency she found. Once Kaelen was certain of his attention, she leaned to the right with the one hundred-dollar-bill against the trim and pushed the key through the bill into the wood, like she would push in a thumbtack.

His eyes widened as he looked from Kaelen to the key, then at Kaelen again. He swallowed and took a step back. Kaelen gave him a penetrating stare. "Will this sufficiently compensate you for the trouble experienced from my abrupt departure?"

"Um, yes. That's cool…you're cool." He held up his hands and stepped back again, nearly tripping on an empty liquor bottle, and quickly slammed the door. He didn't even bother taking the key or the money. Kaelen shook her head and moved toward the exit.

Outside, the sunshine made her skin tingle, and she turned her face toward the eastern sky. A minute later a horn blared, and Kaelen smiled to see Leah's van. She hurried to the passenger door where the window was open. "Leah, hi. It's a wonderful coincidence that you happen to visit at the same time I was outside waiting for Maddy and Tasha to pick me up."

Leah snickered. "It's not a coincidence, I'm your ride. Maddy and Tasha are meeting us at The Bean Bag. I volunteered to pick you up when I found out you were moving into Maddy's old apartment today."

"Why would they tell you that I was moving?" Kaelen got into the van and fastened the safety belt.

Leah answered as she pulled away from the curb. "I found out Maddy's plan because she had to text the owner of the building last night. Obviously, I said yes."

"You are the owner of the building that Maddy used to live in?" Leah nodded. "That's great! How much is my rental charge? If it is too high, I will need to go to the international bank and take out more US currency for purchase."

"You were paying for your old place in cash?" Kaelen nodded and

Leah sighed. "I'm sorry, Kaelen. If I'd known the place was such a dump when I dropped you off months ago, I would have helped you find a different place to live. As for rent, most places take check or electronic payment. Maddy only paid for utilities on the apartment so you'll be responsible for the same." She turned to Kaelen at a stoplight and winked. "Family discount."

"Why would Maddy move in with Tasha if she were paying less in one of your buildings?"

"Because, uh…" Leah clearly struggled with explaining Maddy's reasoning.

"Should I ask her myself?"

"Maybe."

Kaelen squirmed a bit in her seat. "I don't want to make her uncomfortable like I did last night when I asked them about banging like bunnies when they mentioned that today was one of their free days."

Leah burst out laughing. "You did not!"

"I assure you that I did." Kaelen rubbed the back of her neck.

Leah shook her head as they pulled into a parking spot on the street near their favorite café. "I'm assuming you overheard that conversation when Ellie was asking them to visit her?"

Kaelen looked down, not wishing to disappoint Leah in any way. "I didn't mean to. But as I told Maddy and Tasha last night, sometimes it's hard to tune you out when I hear your heart rate increase, or hear your laughter. Maddy said I was stalking."

"Kaelen Ra-Evon, California's wiretapping law is a 'two-party consent' law. California makes it a crime to record or eavesdrop on any confidential communication, including a private conversation or telephone call, without the consent of all parties to the conversation." Kaelen gasped at Wex's explanation. Her mouth dropped open in horror as she looked at Leah.

Leah tilted her head curiously. "What's wrong?"

"Wex said that I broke the law by listening to you. California wiretapping law clearly states—" She stopped talking when soft fingers covered her lips. Leah had leaned toward her, closing the distance between them.

"It's fine, Kaelen. You didn't mean any harm by it, and I know your special hearing isn't something you can control well. The day we stop learning is the day progress dies."

Kaelen nodded at Leah's wisdom. "That's true. Even before coming to Earth, I would strive to learn something new every day."

"Good, now that the issue of your eavesdropping has been settled, let's grab some breakfast. I'm starving." Without waiting for a response, Leah's door split and she smoothly exited the van. Kaelen scrambled out her own door. She heard the distinctive chirp of the van's locks engaging then followed Leah to the front of the café. Remembering that she was going to socialize and not work, Kaelen removed her communicators and stowed them in a separate pocket within the satchel. There was no real need for Wex during breakfast.

She rushed forward to open the door for someone who was exiting with a drink in each of his hands. He gave her a polite nod and Kaelen continued to hold it open for Leah.

"Thank you."

"Hey, it's about time you got here!" Maddy called from the corner of the café.

Kaelen could see her and Tasha sitting at a four-person table and waved. Everyone hugged when they got to the corner and Kaelen reveled in the physical sensation. She'd always been tactile when she was a child growing up on Argon. But it seemed that she'd become desperate for physical affection since landing on Earth.

"Sorry, but I was delayed when the landlord got angry because I was leaving."

"Are you okay? You didn't say anything when I picked you up."

Kaelen shrugged. "I was fine. I left him the key plus a one-hundred-dollar bill." She didn't add the part about intimidating the man because it would hint at powers that she'd have to explain to Maddy and Tasha.

It didn't take long for the four of them to order, eat their breakfast, and arrive back at Maddy's old apartment. It was farther from work than her previous residence. Kaelen read aloud the engraved name on the building. "Rembrandt Tower." She turned to the other three women. "It sounds very, regal. Like something we would have on Argon though—" She glanced back up at the worn brick face "not nearly as soaring or pristine." She smiled. "My home was in Kypl City and we were known for our architecture, specifically the decorative spires at the top of many structures."

"It sounds beautiful, Kaelen. Shall we go look at your new place?" Leah rested her hand on Kaelen's forearm.

Maddy pulled out her keys and led the way into the building. "It's apartment 6A. You need a key to get in the front door, plus one for your apartment. If someone wants to visit you, they'll have to push the button for your apartment on the intercom."

Kaelen nodded. "Significantly more secure than my other place."

"Kaelen, I think a cardboard box would have been more secure… and maybe cleaner." Tasha shook her head as they all made their way inside to the elevator. "I've seen a lot of bad neighborhoods in my line of work, and where you were living was one of the worst."

"It's true. But this is a great location. I know it's a lot farther away than your old place downtown, but the city has numerous modes of public transportation available such as tram, bus, or taxi."

"Could I ride a bicycle or scooter?"

Maddy shrugged. "I mean, you could but it's a little over ten miles so it would be quite a ride. This building is on the corner of Duquesne Avenue and Culver Boulevard. If you follow Duquesne a little past Ballona Creek, you see the Culver City Park. Tasha and I used to have picnics there on our mutual days off when we first started dating. And if you go a few miles southwest along Culver Boulevard, you'll eventually see the ocean and beach."

Kaelen considered her Earth vocabulary to come up with a meaning for the word she hadn't used before. "You don't picnic anymore?"

Leah snorted. "I suspect they're too busy fucking like bunnies on their days off now."

"Dammit Leah, I'm telling Mom you keep bringing that up!"

"Babe, where did that even come from?"

Maddy explained, "I took lunch to Mom and Leah one of the days I had off but you were working. Mom was pressing me to bring you over for dinner and when I tried to explain that we are busy and don't have many days off together, someone," she glared at a grinning Leah, "told Mom that we were too busy having sex to come for dinner on our days off."

"Ah, well that explains Kaelen's 'banging like bunnies' comment last night." Tasha laughed and covered her eyes while they rode the elevator up. "Maddy, we can make time for dinner with Ellie. I love that woman like a second mother. It's no hardship."

Kaelen gazed at the three women as they spoke, but she lingered longest on Leah. She liked the dimples on Leah's cheeks when she smiled.

The new apartment was spacious compared to her old one, but it similarly didn't have a separate bedroom. Instead, it was separated from the main room by curtains. While it wasn't as large as Leah's penthouse, it was significantly larger than the first two places she'd lived in on Earth.

Maddy gestured around. "Nice, right? The kitchen has a new fridge and dishwasher. The washer and dryer are only a few years old." She made a face. "Not that you need those, apparently."

Leah moved to the large floor-to-ceiling windows. "I love this view and I'm glad someone else I know is moving in here. What does Maddy mean that you won't need the washer and dryer?"

"I don't wear Earth clothing. My ship suit is made of nanofibers and infused with nanotechnology. I can alter the shape, color, texture, and any number of other things related to aesthetics. It is self-cleaning, self-healing, and also keeps my person clean, though I have learned to use Earth's toilet facilities. The paper is primitive and wasteful, though it does the job of cleaning well enough."

Maddy snorted and Leah wore a familiar look, one that indicated she was hungry for knowledge and would probably ask many questions later. Tasha simply looped her arm in Kaelen's. "Let's go look at the rest of the apartment, shall we?"

It didn't take long to see the entire floor plan and investigate the furniture left behind. Maddy apologized. "Sorry, Kaelen, but I took my sheets and bedding with me, as well as the pillows. So, you'll have to buy some of your own. I also took my cookware set and throw blankets. The kitchen appliances will all remain though, as will the silverware."

"I don't use a kitchen. I've been ordering takeout for my meals. Are there many restaurants near here, close enough to walk home with food and not have it lose heat?"

Tasha gave her a wide-eyed stare. "You don't cook?"

"No."

"Uh, I could probably teach you how. Maddy loves my Spaghetti Bolognese." She held up a hand to block her mouth from Maddy's view, though her words were loud enough for all to hear. "If you ask me, that's the meal that made her realize she wanted to date me exclusively."

"You keep telling yourself that, babe. You totally wanted to date me exclusively first."

Kaelen looked at Leah. "Are they always like this?"

"If you mean sickeningly in love, then yes." She turned so she could see everyone. "If you two are finished with your verbal foreplay, Kaelen clearly still needs some stuff to make this place a home. Since there was nothing to actually move, Maddy you can probably hand over your keys and I'll be sure the paperwork gets signed. After that I'll take her shopping."

"Sounds good to me." Maddy threw the keys across the room to Leah, but Kaelen's quick reflexes got them first. Maddy blinked at her in shock. "Okaaay, they were going to go to you anyway. All right kids, we're heading out. Call if you need anything, Leah."

Maddy and Tasha hugged the other two, saying their goodbyes. Tasha walked out the door first. As Maddy was following her, Leah called out, "Have fun banging, sis!" She got a middle finger in return.

Kaelen looked from the closed apartment door back to Leah. "Was she waving? I haven't seen that one before but then, it looks like American sign language and I've yet to study that."

"It's sign language of a sort, though not specifically for those who are hearing disabled. It's a hand gesture that means fuck you."

The information was a little shocking. "From a sibling?"

"It's not a proposition, darling. Remember when we discussed the versatility of that particular bit of profanity?" Kaelen nodded. "Well, when someone is angry, or fake angry in Maddy's case, they will say things like fuck you, or go fuck yourself."

"Oh."

"Mrs. Wegman is the building supervisor. We can head down to her apartment so you can sign your rental agreement, then we'll go to the mall. That sound good?" Not all of it made sense but Kaelen trusted Leah so she nodded.

Leah's phone rang before she could exit the parking garage. She looked at the screen and sighed. "Can you give me a minute to take this call? L-I is getting ready to pay out yearly bonuses and payroll was working overtime today to audit all the employee's accounts to determine distribution."

"I'm in no hurry." Kaelen looked around the neighborhood from her place in the passenger seat of the sleek van. She used her x-ray vision and her telescopic vision to look through the lower corner of the apartment building so she could see the park that Maddy had been talking about.

"What?"

Kaelen's attention was drawn to Leah after the exclamation but Wex's warning about California laws and the rules of propriety prevented her from eavesdropping.

Leah looked at Kaelen, eyebrows raised with disbelief. "Kaelen, why haven't you cashed any of your payroll checks? It's been about six months since you received your first one and the audit team says none of the checks cut to you have processed."

"Am I required to take them to a bank?"

"You can't hold a payroll check more than a hundred and eighty days or they'll be invalid."

"But you're already helping me find the location of the Argonian beacon, and I enjoy the work I do at the SPL. I didn't think it was honorable to take money from you."

Leah blinked at her a few times, then spoke into the phone. "I'll call you back." Once she'd ended the call, she turned a bit in her chair so she could see Kaelen better. "When you work here on Earth, you are entitled to compensation for your efforts. Not only that, but you also signed paperwork for medical insurance." She held up a hand when Kaelen opened her mouth. "I'm well aware that you don't need such insurance because of your Argonian biology. However, you should accept the paychecks."

"Why?"

"For starters, you will need to purchase items for your new home. Not only that, but despite the deal Maddy was getting, I'd wager the utilities for your new place will be significantly more expensive than the total cost for the last one." She paused. "Perhaps you could discover a hobby or other activity that fascinates you. Earth is a lot more than language, food, and science."

Kaelen didn't want Leah to worry about her, so she began to explain her finances. "I have money in an international bank here in this city, one that is also located in Vancouver, where I have something called a lockbox."

"Lockbox?"

"Yes. My parents prepared me as much as possible for life here. They sent along a collection of ordinary and unique minerals from Argon that are in actuality precious gems here on Earth. I placed those in the lockbox, as well as some of the malleable metal that is atomic number seventy-nine. I put five pounds of that in storage and cashed in the other five pounds. I have been living on that money, though I will admit it will eventually run out. I should perhaps be a little more frugal with my restaurant expenses."

Leah didn't speak for nearly a minute and Kaelen grew concerned that she'd done or said something wrong. Before she could ask, Leah sputtered, "You have ten pounds of gold?"

"Well, I only have five pounds now."

"Kaelen, that's over two hundred thousand dollars!"

"Yes."

Leah sighed. "I'm going to make some suggestions for you, but you don't have to do any of them, okay?"

"I trust you."

"Do you still have those checks you received from Lockheed?" Kaelen opened her satchel and reached into a smaller compartment, then withdrew a handful of checks with the company logo on the corner. Leah shook her head and continued. "I think you should deposit those checks." She looked at her watch. "Banks are still open for another hour. You should also set up direct deposit so your future checks will go right into your bank account."

"No more paper money promissory notes?"

Leah smiled. Kaelen had been vocal about her dislike of paper throughout their friendship. "All digital. And first thing Monday morning, I want you to send an email to Ana. If you remember, she's our chief financial officer but she's also a genius with financial planning.

She's given me a lot of good advice over the years. She'll explain things like proper ways to either save or invest large amounts of money to best prepare for the future."

Kaelen frowned. "I can do that. But what about all the resources you've allotted in the search for the beacon? You've scheduled satellite time for the project and Wex says that is expensive by Earth standards. Should I pay you for that work, the way you pay me for mine?"

"I'm helping you as a friend. You don't need to compensate me for it. If you feel bad that you're not contributing in some way, you can always donate some of your money every month to one of the local non-profit organizations. Los Angeles has many. You can even specifically give your money to aid the alien refugee population."

The idea had a lot of merit and Kaelen appreciated the suggestion. "I would like that."

"My last bit of advice is for you to buy a smart phone. They aren't only for communication purposes, like the desk phones in the lab. I noticed that you don't always wear your communicators when you're out with friends. Think of your cell phone as a pocket computer."

"We had those on Argon. The ones on Earth are," Kaelen frowned, "significantly lacking. Computational power is one of the issues that slows progress on our project."

Leah rolled her eyes. "Yes, well, that is to be expected given the disparity between your technology and ours. But a cell has many more purposes, even if they are fairly simple ones. You can order takeout via an app and have it delivered to you."

Kaelen's mouth dropped open. "They'll bring the food to me?" She'd assumed you had to have special permission for things like lunches brought to the company, or for Leah's game nights. Kaelen had no idea ordinary citizens could order food.

"Yes. Usually, it's customary to tip the delivery person, the same way I showed you to leave a tip in the restaurant. Though that rule changes once you're outside the United States. You can also hire transportation in case you need to go someplace that is too far away to walk, check your finances, listen to music, watch videos, play games, and so much more. With—"

Kaelen held up a hand to stop her friend. "I'm convinced. You've made a valid point about the convenience and necessity of a smart phone. Will we be able to visit a store that sells such things?"

"The mall has everything you could want, Kaelen. But we need to make the trip to the bank first while they're still open."

They pulled into the mall parking lot an hour and a half later. Kaelen took in the sprawling structure. "This is a retail storehouse?"

"This is many stores under one roof. They have pretty much everything you could need here. Bedding, clothing, housewares, electronics, phones, shoes, and all the rest." After the van was locked, Kaelen walked alongside Leah, still in awe of the size of the building.

They spent the afternoon in the mall and made enough purchases that Kaelen had to take items out to the van three times after Leah said, "Just a warning, I don't mind transporting all your purchases in my van, but I refuse to carry them out for you. I'm no pack mule."

Kaelen grinned at her. "I'm fully capable of carrying everything myself. But it should be noted that you're too attractive to be a beast of burden." She observed the color rise on Leah's cheeks as they entered through a large grouping of doors. While she didn't understand the full nature of the reaction, Leah's heartbeat indicated it was positive.

By late afternoon, Leah and Kaelen sat side by side on Maddy's old couch. Kaelen had already put away all the housewares. Leah even convinced her to buy a television. At least half their time post shopping spree was spent programming the smart TV and the cell phone. Leah made sure the major food ordering apps were downloaded and showed Kaelen how to use everything.

"You know, you should consider investing in a computer as well."

"Do I have to buy it fully-constructed like I did the other items or can I purchase components? Your computers are fairly basic and I'm certain I could create something significantly more powerful on my own."

Leah shook her head and smiled. "Many people build their own computers. You should ask Einstein on Monday. He built his desktop computer and laptop. I've teased him many times about computers building computers. For that matter, my friend Gabe has been building his own gaming computers since he was in high school."

Kaelen looked down at the phone in her hand, then lifted it with a smile. "Or, I could text Einstein now. That way he'll have my phone number."

"Good idea. He'll pass it on to Nalla as well if you like. Ask him."

If Leah noticed that Kaelen's thumbs were a blur on the keyboard, she didn't say anything. Kaelen had grown comfortable enough with her friend that she no longer wished to hide all those things about her Argonian biology that made her unique. After she finished texting Einstein, she also sent messages to the rest of the people she'd met at Leah's game night. As she sent the last one, her stomach gave a mighty rumble. She clutched it and looked at Leah with dismay.

"Apparently, my food court pizza didn't last long. I, would you—"

Leah gave her a concerned look. "Darling, what is it?"

"If you are not tired of my company, would you like to have dinner with me?" Rather than rejection, Kaelen got a bright smile.

"I've never yet tired of your company. I don't think it's even possible. Would you like to go someplace to eat like we did before, or order in?"

"You've provided invaluable assistance for no other reason than kindness. I trust your recommendations for dinner."

"Hmm…" Leah looked down at her casual jeans and designer zip hoodie. "How about this, I know a little Mexican hole in the wall nearby that is amazing. It's not fancy or well-known but it's some of the best food in Los Angeles. Even better, we don't need to dress up or make reservations. Does that sound good?"

"This hole is large enough to serve food?"

"It's slang for a restaurant that is out of the way, or not many people have heard of. Not fancy."

"Oh. In that case, everything sounds good with you."

When they finished with their dinner at the restaurant, Leah removed the napkin from her lap and placed it on the table. "What are you going to do with the rest of your night?"

Kaelen gave the question serious thought. "I'd normally be working at the lab since my old apartment had nothing with entertainment potential. But I'll admit I haven't stopped thinking about Earth's motion pictures since we saw all the boxes lined up in the store."

"A movie."

"Yes, movie. The one about the dragon looks like it takes place on Tamar. They were lush with flora and fauna and featured a lot of water… much like Earth, actually. Now that you've shown me how to sign up for the Disney company, that's what I wish to do."

Leah had barely taken a sip of her sparkling water when Kaelen answered and she abruptly pulled the glass away. "Oh, I've been wanting to see that one for a while now. I usually only watch Disney movies when I'm feeling depressed. They always cheer me up."

"You suffer from depression?"

"Every year on the anniversary of my family's death, and sometimes around the holidays. It's hard to stay sad with the Tucks. I know Maddy has also battled depression around the holidays too, since that is the anniversary of when Charlie died. She's the one who introduced me to Disney movies." Leah paused when the server came around to place the bill on the table. She wasn't fast enough to grab it. Before she could blink, Kaelen had money tucked inside.

"You were telling me about Maddy and Disney movies."

Leah wagged a finger at her. "Sneaky! I know you used your pinky swear powers to steal that bill!" Kaelen smiled innocently. She was finally getting the hang of some of Earth's normal social interactions. Leah continued, "Anyway, I loved my first family, the Lockheeds, but because both Maddox and I tested as geniuses early in our development, there was a lot of pressure put on us from a young age. That means I didn't have what you would consider a normal childhood for the first thirteen years of my life." She shrugged. "I've been called weird too many times to count."

Leah began fidgeting with her napkin and Kaelen reached across to take her hand. "I don't think there is any one way for a childhood to be. I myself didn't have anything similar to an Earth experience but I was happy and educated. Even though I was still technically a minor in Argonian society, once I inducted into the Thinker Guild, I was supposed to begin contributing to the greater good of my people. I'd only been doing my adult work for a few weeks when I was sent away."

Dark brows lifted with shock. "Really?"

The server picked up the bill with Kaelen's cash and smiled at them. "Do you need change?"

"No, you can have the extra as a tip. Thank you for your service." Once he was gone, Kaelen answered Leah as honestly as possible. "Yes. I'd gone beyond typical Argonian education, and the rest of my learning would have been done via the medium of life experience and my fellow scientists."

"You're right, that is different. And yet, you seem intelligent, well-adjusted, and happy…all things considered."

For the first time since they'd met, Kaelen let a glimpse of her hidden pain come to the surface. "Yes, well I too have dark thoughts that keep me up at night. Sometimes they're triggered by the sounds of the city, sometimes by nothing. I think about my family and my planet."

"I'm sorry, Kaelen. I can't even imagine what that must be like."

Kaelen sighed and looked away from Leah's expressive eyes. She'd previously told Leah about the events that led to her planet's destruction so her friend knew that family was a touchy subject. "I think the knowledge that my parents lied to me for so long hurts more than all the rest. And here I am, now on a strange planet, far from anything I've ever known and unable to perform the primary task that was bestowed upon me. How can I contribute to society here when I'm mired in the past, fixated on the hope that the mystery beacon could belong to one of my immediate family? The knowledge that I may be the last of my people puts pressure on me that I'm not sure I can handle. All this strength and I falter under the weight of expectation."

Leah turned her hand over so they rested palm to palm. "Darling, you *do* contribute to society. You've proven instrumental in our current nano project progress, which will help countless people live a better life. But, I'm always here if you want to talk. Or you can do like I do and find yourself a good therapist. They help. Mental health is an important part of our lives, and I'm a huge advocate for proper treatment and therapy when needed."

Kaelen laughed but it reflected her sadness more than joy. "It's okay. I was assured by Wex that I had plenty of what humans call therapy while sleeping through ten years of my life." She decided not to say more on the topic and Leah didn't press. They made their way out of the restaurant and were nearly to the van when Kaelen asked, "Would you like to watch the dragon movie with me?"

Leah paused and glanced at her watch then met Kaelen's gaze. "I don't want to overstay my welcome."

"That's impossible because you're my favorite person. I enjoy your company more than anyone I've ever met."

"You're quite the charmer, aren't you?"

Even though the sun was low enough to cast a reddish orange glow across the city, Kaelen could make out the pink of Leah's cheeks. "Charmer…charming, you mean to say I'm charismatic? I don't think anyone has ever told me that before. Back on Argon I was friendly, courteous, curious, and driven."

Leah shook her head and lifted her chair enough to wrap an arm around Kaelen's waist and pull her into a one-armed hug. "Whomever you were on your original planet as a child, on this one you are delightfully appealing. Take the compliment, Kaelen."

Kaelen carefully hugged her back. "Thank you." A sound suddenly caught Kaelen's attention and she froze while scanning around the lot for other people nearby.

"What's wrong?"

Kaelen whispered, "Someone is hiding over there." She pointed toward a car where a man squatted low beside an SUV. "He has a machine in his hand that was making a rapid clicking sound."

Leah frowned. She raised her voice loud enough for the man to hear her. "Please get in the van. He's a vulture looking for a story from the reclusive Lockheed gimp."

She wasn't sure what was going on but Kaelen obeyed. She knew she could exit quickly enough to prevent harm if Leah looked to be in danger. Rather than engage with the hidden person, Leah also entered the van and drove them out of the parking lot.

Once they were on the street headed back toward Kaelen's apartment, Leah spoke. "There is something you probably don't realize, would never have known about Earth. People here that have a lot of money become pseudo-celebrities. Despite staying out of the public eye, I'm still the head of one of the richest companies in the world, making me one of the richest people. I have private security that follow me around to keep me safe."

Kaelen craned her neck around then looked back at Leah. "I've never noticed such a thing."

"You wouldn't. They're trained to keep their distance, to blend in with the people in the background. I also send them home when I know I'll be in your company. I feel quite secure with you."

"You are safe with me." Kaelen said it like the words were a vow, one that she meant with every cell of her being.

Leah patted her hand. "I know, darling. I'm trying to explain that I've been harassed by reporters and photographers for a long time. They're constantly looking for the next big story about the disabled Lockheed girl."

Kaelen frowned. "I don't understand why you speak so negatively about yourself. You're one of the most capable people I've ever met."

"Yes, well you see the world differently than everyone else. To most humans, I'm incapable of independence, powerless, and inadequate. I've been fighting stereotypes my whole life, and there are many."

"Is that why you strive to repair your spinal cord, because of how you think people see you?"

"No!" Kaelen was surprised by the adamant response, but she stayed quiet because she knew Leah would explain. "If anything, that's the one reason I would stay exactly as I am. If only to remind people of everything I've accomplished in life with a disability. I made changes to Lockheed's business model that added a third more revenue in the past five years. Not only that, but in the same amount of time I've also been personally responsible for sixteen patents."

"Proving my point that you are eminently capable."

"As you see, I have succeeded in life with my paraplegia. If blind or deaf, I'd want to find a way to restore those senses as well. One of Lockheed's main foci is in the biomedical industry, to make people's lives better. If we can repair the damage to my spine, we can repair the damage to anyone's. How many children out there want to run again? How many adults?"

They traveled in silence. Leah pulled into the parking garage and shut off the van before hazarding a glance toward the passenger seat. Kaelen reached out to carefully take Leah's hand in both of hers.

"Leah Lockheed-Tuck, I appreciate your passion and devotion to the betterment of everyone's lives. Your company's dedication and mission are the main reasons I wanted to work there."

With an insecure look, Leah asked, "I'm not too much?"

"I think you are just enough. As I've previously mentioned, you are my favorite person of all, on this planet or others. When you feel low remember how many lives you've touched, and how many people you helped with your company, or personally, like you have with me. You are appreciated."

A sigh whispered out in the quiet cab of the van. "Thank you."

"Do you still want to watch the movie with me?"

Leah laughed and Kaelen delighted in the way her eyes wrinkled with joy. "I would love that."

Chapter Eight

Leah sat at her desk going over reports when her computer chimed with an alert. She looked at her calendar and knew exactly what it was. She opened the report and copied the coordinates into her browser. From there she was able to find the address of the beacon's location. It appeared to be a large barn on a parcel of property located just outside Zeeland Michigan.

"Let's see who you belong to, *hmm*?" Leah had plenty of resources when it came to digging for information. She had to backtrack a few times because of missing data, which made her suspect government involvement. It was strange that the beacon would still be transmitting from such an out of the way location if that were the case.

The property belonged to Paul and Shelly Miller. On further investigation she found that the couple had one twenty-one-year-old son attending the School of the Art Institute of Chicago, and another eleven-year-old son in public school. Leah scrolled through the couple's social media accounts, but none of them looked like Kaelen.

Leah sat back in her chair and contemplated what she should do. Kaelen was going to want to meet the couple in an effort to discover the truth of the Argonian beacon emanating from their property. But a selfish part of Leah didn't want to lose her new friend as they'd grown immeasurably close over the past ten months. Not only that, but they'd cleared the last government hurdle and were scheduled to begin human trials in one week. Losing Kaelen from the project would certainly push it back.

Leah groaned and thumped her head on the desk. "Stop being such a selfish git, Lockheed!" Chastisement finished, Leah picked up her desk phone and punched in the extension for the SPL. It rang three times before Ellie answered.

"Good afternoon, Leah."

"Hi Ellie, is Kaelen available? I need to speak with her."

There was silence for a few seconds before Ellie answered again. "Is it urgent? She's finishing up a different replication code for the nanobot trial. It shouldn't take her more than ten minutes at the speed she's typing. I know I've said it before, but that woman amazes me."

Leah smiled. "Yeah, same. Despite complaining about how primitive our technology is here on Earth, Kaelen is still learning and growing as a scientist. Some of the theories she's shared with me over our dinners are simply mind-boggling."

"Is there anything wrong? You don't normally call anyone up to your office in the middle of the day."

Ellie had always been intuitive. "No, nothing's wrong. It's just that—"

"Wait, today's scan day. You found it, didn't you?"

Intuitive and smart. Leah sighed. "Yes."

"Well done, sweetheart. I'll send Kaelen up as soon as—oh, she's finished and gone already. Well, shoot."

Leah should have known Kaelen would hear. "No worries, Ellie. She'll be here soon. Thanks anyway."

Less than five minutes after Leah hung up the phone, Kaelen pushed open the door to her office, Jenna hot on her heels. "I'm sorry, Miss Lockheed. I tried to stop her but she's too fast." Jenna huffed and glared at Kaelen.

"It's okay, Jenna. You can put Kaelen Ra-Evon on the all-access sheet along with Maddy, Ellie, and Ana. Anytime, okay?"

Jenna scowled but acknowledged the order. "Yes, Miss Lockheed." Then she narrowed her eyes at Kaelen before turning and striding from the room. Kaelen herself remained oblivious to Jenna's ire. Instead, all her attention was focused on Leah.

"You found the location?"

"You were careful around the cameras, right?" Leah referred to the abundance of security cameras that would pick up her too-fast speed upstairs.

"I took the elevator to the first floor, then ran up the stairs the rest of the way. There are no cameras in the stairwells, only on the exits and entrances to the floors and in the main room of the SPL."

"Good, I'm glad you're being careful." Leah waved her around the desk and didn't mention the way her friend seemed to blur then appear right next to her. "Careful-ish." With a couple clicks of the mouse, Leah brought up the satellite findings, then showed Kaelen the location on the map and pictures of the family she'd saved.

Kaelen shook her head. "None of them look familiar but there is something about the youngest boy…I don't know."

"He was adopted two years ago but records of him go back ten years. Given his age," Leah shrugged. "Perhaps Einstein's theory of a dark matter spatial anomaly holds merit."

"I certainly wouldn't discount it."

"But no one in the Miller family are members of your house?"

"No. But Wex was very clear about Argonian law. If this boy is one of my people, I have a duty to take him into my house and raise him."

"Kaelen…" Leah hated to be the one to break what would certainly be bad news. "The boy was legally adopted by Paul and Shelly Miller and records show that he's been living with them for a decade. That would have made him little more than a babe when his ship landed. Darling, even if he is Argonian, they're the only family he's ever known."

Stricken blue eyes turned from the screen to Leah. "If I uphold my duty, I will be taking him away from his Earth family."

Leah nodded. Kaelen tilted her head and her gaze grew unfocused, indicating to Leah that she was probably listening to Wex. "What is it?"

"Wex says that an Argonian should not remain with humans if there is another house capable of taking him in. It says that because I'm the only remaining Argonian who has been inducted into a guild, that I am the last scion of Ra. That means I'm the remaining heir to my house and duty bound to raise him as Argonian culture dictates."

Leah grasped Kaelen's hand. "There has to be a compromise, something that will allow you to uphold your duties and still let him grow up happy, healthy, and safe."

Kaelen was quiet for a few seconds then shook her head with a sigh. "I will have to investigate Argonian law for an alternative. This may be a case where I forge my own path because I am under unique circumstances never faced by one of my race."

"All this postulation could be for nothing. He may not be one of your people at all."

"The beacon is still Argonian and I need to know more about that ship."

Leah sighed. "Based on some of the data I found, it appears as though the government is aware of this location. It may be under active surveillance by an agency like the CORP."

Kaelen looked back at her with wide blue eyes. "Can they prevent me from retrieving the pod?"

Leah nodded. Kaelen tilted her head, obviously listening to Wex again. "What is it?"

"Wex told me that the personal craft is Argonian property and it is my duty to claim it as the last of my people. And if the adopted boy is the one who arrived in the pod, I need to know that as well."

Leah grasped Kaelen's hand. "Even if it means endangering yourself, or exposing your existence on this planet?"

"I don't know but Wex is most insistent."

"I'm sorry."

Kaelen stretched out her hand to caress the city Leah highlighted on the screen. She was quiet for a few seconds then shook her head with a sigh. "I am at a loss but will accept suggestions as to my path forward." Kaelen paused again and frowned. Leah was surprised by the next words from her friend's mouth. "Leah is fully capable of intelligent reasoning, Wex. Shut your face." Then Kaelen turned off her communicators and looked at Leah. "What?"

"Darling, I think Maddy is a bad influence on you."

She got a shrug and smile. "I like Earth slang. Sometimes it fits my mood much better than standard vocabulary. Besides, I may have appreciated Wex's information and guidance when I was still a child but as an adult living on a new world, I find the constant warnings and instruction to be fuckingly annoying."

Leah snickered. "It's fucking annoying, and I imagine that you would." Leah clicked out of the report and brought up her project calendar. "If you like, I can book you a flight to Michigan, and a private vehicle once you arrive that will take you to Zeeland. It looks like their address is less than an hour from the nearest major airport."

"I don't understand what I should do when I get there. I can't exactly come out and admit that I know they're holding a ship from my planet. Won't that, uh, 'out' me to the authorities?"

Leah tapped her bottom lip. "You have a point."

"Not to mention, I can leave work to do this? What about the nano project?"

Leah winked at her. "It's Friday and I think that under the circumstances the boss will let you leave early." She paused to consider Kaelen's other question, the one she'd been contemplating before calling down to the lab. "You could simply ask questions about the boy, explaining that you have reason to believe he may be one of your family members. They don't have to know the exact details. I don't anticipate this first visit taking long. You'll either confirm that he is or isn't Argonian on the trip. If we, or you more specifically, are delayed then we'll push the trials back a week." Kaelen caught her bottom lip between her teeth in a familiar look of anxiety. "What's wrong?"

"I'm afraid."

"Of meeting the Millers?"

Kaelen looked away. "Of going alone."

Leah turned slightly in her chair so she could lean into Kaelen's side. "Hey, look at me." Kaelen complied and Leah squeezed her hand. "Do you want me to come with you?"

"I, um…I didn't want to ask. I know you're busy, very important to the company—"

"I'll be there for you, Kaelen. Anytime, anyplace. Okay?"

"You're sure?

"Yes, darling. I'm sure. We're friends."

Kaelen gave her a relieved smile. "Thank you."

Leah was already typing, setting up the private jet for a flight out early the next morning. "No thanks necessary. We'll leave first thing tomorrow, that way we'll have time to meet with them during normal daylight hours." Kaelen looked as if she wanted to disagree, but Leah reassured her. "It's best this way, trust me. It's too late in the day now."

"I trust you. I'll always trust you." Kaelen straightened and walked around the desk to the visitor side. "I should return to work."

Leah glanced down at her watch. "Actually, it's after four. I'm instructing the pilot that I want to leave at seven a.m." Leah typed in an internet search, then did a quick calculation in her head for distance and time to Michigan. "We'll have to fly in to Grand Rapids because that's the nearest airport. The flight should be around three hours, give or take, but we'll lose three more due to the time change. Why don't you head out for the day?"

"Why would I do that?"

"So, you can go home and pack—" Leah laughed. "Never mind. I forgot about the suit thing. What do you sleep in? Tell me it's not still the suit."

Kaelen shook her head. "Of course not. That would be pointless. I enjoy the tactile sensation of the sheets you purchased for me, so I sleep nude."

Leah did her level best to ignore the mental image of that particular statement. She was extremely attracted to Kaelen but never felt right acknowledging the pull. And despite Kaelen's words from the game night months before, Leah hadn't seen anything to indicate Kaelen was interested in a relationship beyond that of friends. But the main reason Leah hadn't 'made a move' as Ana put it, was because Kaelen had become her closest friend. She was loathe to upset that balance and lose what they'd built.

"Hmm, I was planning on having my driver pick me up early, then pick you up before heading to the airport. Why don't you come over to my place for movie night and stay in my spare room?"

Kaelen grinned. "*Mulan*?"

"Yes, we can watch *Mulan*. I know that was next on your list."

"And?"

Leah rolled her eyes fondly. "And if we have time, we can watch *Moana* too."

"Excelsior!"

"You're ridiculous and you need to stop copying Einstein's nerdy exclamations!"

• • •

Hours later they'd both eaten enough pot stickers to feed an army, well mostly Kaelen. The closing credits for *Moana* scrolled up the large screen and Leah yawned, feeling relaxed. She looked over at Kaelen who seemed equally as relaxed. "I'm ready for bed, how about you?" Kaelen had convinced Leah to sit on the couch with her, so they were pressed tightly together. Something that did not help Leah's heart or libido. Those worked perfectly well.

"I'm not sure."

Using arms that had been strengthened by years of regular exercise, Leah shifted herself away from Kaelen on the couch so she could see her better. Kaelen's face was pensive. "Are you feeling overwhelmed about tomorrow?"

Kaelen met her gaze and whispered, "Yes."

"Darling, it's going to be okay. Let's take things one step at a time, all right?"

"You are wise, and a very good friend."

Leah plucked at her sleeve. "Come on. You mentioned how much you love my guest shower the last time you stayed over. Take a long hot one and I think you'll find your mind more at ease when you're done. If not, come see me."

"Will you take your own shower? I wouldn't want to disturb you."

"I meant after. I've got to complete my nightly routine before I can go to bed. That involves bathroom maintenance, shower, and the like."

Kaelen looked confused. "You've never mentioned bathroom maintenance before. Is your lavatory in need of repairs?"

Leah's face grew warm when she realized that she'd never explained all that was required to stay healthy with a spinal cord injury. She was used to speaking frankly with her family and Ana. She didn't want to explain it to Kaelen because the thought of it was mortifying. But she also didn't want to ignore the question either. "Why don't you look up D-I-L and bowel management on your phone while I get ready for bed?"

"I can do that."

Leah pressed a button on the arm of the couch on the end farthest from Kaelen and slid herself along the length of it until she was right at the edge. She called her hoverchair with the touch of a button on a customized watch app. The transfer from couch to chair was smooth and familiar. Leah called out before zipping up the stairs to her room. "Have a nice night, Kaelen. Knock on my door if you need anything."

She didn't recognize the look on Kaelen's face at that moment, but Kaelen nodded. "I will. Thank you for everything." She had a familiar wrinkle between her brows.

"I know you'd do the same for me." Then Leah left her sitting there deep in thought.

Nearly two hours later, Leah woke to tapping on her door. She hadn't been asleep long, having stayed up to read for a bit after her own shower. "Yes?"

"May I come in?"

Leah called out, "Sure. Lights, twenty percent." The lights came up to the desired level showing Kaelen's hesitant form in the doorway as she pushed through. Instead of being nude, or even wearing normal clothing, Kaelen was in the same black suit with the glowing symbol on the front that Leah saw briefly during her interview. "Is something wrong?"

Kaelen approached the bed and stood with her arms straight down at her sides, fists clenching and unclenching as she shifted from foot to foot. "I'm feeling too many things to say no, but I don't know if I can say yes either."

"Are you worried about tomorrow?" Kaelen nodded. Leah patted the empty side of the bed. "Dim the glow and come lie with me." The symbol faded to a dark metallic gray with a light brush against the center of the suit collar. Then Kaelen made her way around the bed and crawled on top of the covers, lying on her side to face Leah. "Good. Now tell me what you're afraid of."

"I fear what will happen when I meet them tomorrow. What if that adopted boy is one of my people? He doesn't know anything about Argon, about his family or mine. Vos lives on in us, but that child will know nothing of our history."

"You could teach him."

Kaelen sighed and she was near enough to Leah that her breath caressed the wisps of her hair on the pillow. "Tell me something…do you consider yourself more of a Tuck or a Lockheed?"

Leah sucked in a breath, not expecting that question. "I…I guess I never thought about it."

"You made a good point when you said the Millers were the only family he's ever known. What if he doesn't want anything to do with his Argonian heritage, with me?" She paused then met Leah's gaze in the low light. "You asked me what I fear regarding this child. I'm afraid to act and at the same time I'm afraid not to act. If he stays with that family, the Millers, then I'll have failed my people. But if I take him with me as the only member of his race and he's emotionally miserable because he misses what he sees as his real family, then I will also have failed in my duties. I have no good path forward."

Leah could sense something in Kaelen's gaze and rough breathing. "What else?"

Kaelen took in a shuddering breath and she physically hunched her shoulders while lying on the bed. "I'm riddled with longing for connection to my people and my past, but I'm also devastated that he's not one of my house. How can I be so angry at my parents and elders for the lies and yet feel equal anger that this child isn't them? The feelings are illogical and fill me with guilt."

"I, too, was mad at my family for a long time."

Eyes widened across from her. "Why?"

"For leaving me." Leah brought up a finger to still Kaelen's question. "I know they didn't choose too. As you pointed out, the feelings tied up with grief and loss aren't rational. My therapist at the time said I suffered from survivor's guilt. It got better as time went on. As an adult I understand a lot of things that I didn't before."

"Such as?"

Leah frowned. "I know now that my father wasn't the most morally upright person. He was very focused on the business of making money and made a lot of gray decisions. I think that's one of the reasons I've dedicated my life to improving the lives of others. I don't want money to be my main reason for living."

"I've never understood that particular human trait."

"What I'm trying to say is that you should give yourself time. You're allowed to feel all the feelings, to be disappointed, hopeful, hurt, and joyous. If we meet this family tomorrow and realize the boy isn't a misplaced Argonian, then we pivot and move on to uncovering the mystery of the beacon."

"And if he is?"

Leah cupped Kaelen's cheek and caressed it with her thumb. "Let's just see what his situation is and move forward from there. If he's one of your people, there will be plenty you can teach him, should he wish to learn."

"That brings us back to my Argonian duty."

While Leah wasn't on the same caliber as Einstein or Kaelen, she was still a genius. She wracked her brain trying to come up with a solution and was certainly more familiar with human emotion and social situations. "I take it Argon didn't have anything like adoption?"

Kaelen shook her head causing a *shoosh-shoosh* sound against the pillow. "Taking in another family's child would never happen while a member of the house still lived."

"What about something like fostering or boarding?" She realized Kaelen may not know what that was and rushed to explain. "That's where one family will send a child to an instructional institution or to another family so they can learn, whether it's to further their education or to be apprenticed in a particular craft. I went to boarding school for a few years when I was younger."

"Oh!"

Leah gave her a curious look. "Did you think of something?"

The pensive look washed away and Kaelen's smile grew wide. "*Kuz ashum*. It roughly translates to 'learn away from.' Occasionally children would travel to another place, usually on Argon, to learn a specific skillset. It would last anywhere from one to ten years. It typically occurred with other members of the house or in some circumstances, a different house in their intended guild. But I don't know his guild."

"As you mentioned, you're operating within a unique set of circumstances, being here on Earth and as the last of your kind. In the event this boy is Argonian, perhaps he could live with the Millers under the guidelines you listed. Will that satisfy your dedication to duty and honor?"

"Yes, I think it will. You are a brilliant woman and I'm eternally grateful that you're in my life."

Leah squeezed Kaelen's hand where it rested on the bed next to her own. "I feel the same way. Do you think you can sleep now?" Another strange look washed across Kaelen's face and the wrinkle returned. "Is something else the matter?"

"I…" Kaelen swallowed and closed her eyes. "I don't want to burden you."

"You're never a burden, I've told you that a thousand times."

Riveting blue eyes opened and Kaelen gave her the tiniest of smiles. "You've definitely not told me that often. I don't like admitting to vulnerability when I'm so strong on this planet."

"Darling, everyone is weak sometimes. What's wrong? You can tell me. I promise I won't judge you."

Her words came out as a whisper. "I'm lonely for my family. I really hoped my parents had kept their word."

Leah saw a single tear roll down Kaelen's cheek and her heart ached for her. "Oh, sweetheart. It's going to be okay. You can stay in here with me tonight if you like. Slide beneath the covers." Kaelen complied and looked a bit stiff when she turned onto her back. "Is this a new feeling?" Kaelen shook her head. "What do you normally do when you feel this way?"

Kaelen took a deep breath and let it out slowly. "I don't sleep. Instead, I listen for your heartbeat, matching my breathing to yours to calm myself."

Leah wasn't surprised because she'd heard the same admission before from Kaelen. And part of her knew there was something deeper connecting them, more than simple friendship could allow for. "Does that help?"

"Sometimes."

"What do you do when it doesn't?"

Kaelen's gaze was firm and her expression one of loss and heartbreak. "I remain lonely."

Decision made, Leah grabbed hold of Kaelen's wrist and tugged. "Not tonight you won't. Come here and cuddle with me. Maybe we can chase each other's demons away."

At first Kaelen resisted. "What if I harm you in my sleep? I told you I'm remarkably strong."

"You won't."

"But how do you know?"

Leah smiled at her, refusing to back down once she'd made up her mind. Heart and libido be damned. They'd have to go on hiatus for the night because her best friend needed her. "Because I trust you, too." With those words, Kaelen slid closer and cuddled into Leah's side.

"Thank you, *zhee*."

Leah didn't ask what it meant but filed the term away for later. "Good night, Kaelen. Sweet dreams, darling."

The Lockheed private jet landed at the Gerald R. Ford International Airport outside Grand Rapids, Michigan a few minutes before one local time. Leah had arranged for a driver and van that could accommodate her hoverchair the night before. She'd even made the driver and company representative sign non-disclosure forms so she could protect Kaelen's and the Millers' privacy as much as possible.

It took more than an hour to make a forty-five-minute drive to Zeeland with road construction along the highway keeping their speed slower. Luckily, Leah had anticipated their boredom and brought her laptop loaded with simulations from another one of her eco projects. Given how anxious Kaelen had been the night before, Leah assumed it was best if she could keep her friend distracted.

"Wait, you're saying that humans don't have a way to make the ocean water potable on Earth? This is one of the most bountiful planets I've ever visited and yet people here suffer from water scarcity all over the world." Kaelen scowled. "That is untenable and disastrous for the future needs of the citizens."

Leah explained, "It's not that we can't do it. But as you know, the chemical bonds between water and salt are some of the strongest and it requires a lot of energy to fuel the desalination process. The cost varies wildly from place to place, with many factors involved with its determination."

"Factors?"

"Yes. Labor, energy cost, land prices, financial agreements…even the salt content of the water itself. The report I commissioned stated final cost was anywhere from one dollar to well over two dollars per cubic foot. That's not feasible for a struggling nation, or many third world countries. I want my company to solve this problem for the good of the world."

Kaelen appeared thoughtful. "But it will cost significant capital to create a project of this magnitude. How will Lockheed fund such a thing? I'm assuming you don't want to sell it to those countries, or even their governments."

Leah sighed. "It's true that my board of investors wouldn't touch this with a ten-foot pole if I present it to them as a philanthropic endeavor. However, I would have to prove out the technology on a larger scale anyway. My goal is to market it to major seaboard cities as they're always piping water in from far away—mountain reservoirs, and the like. The cost of the system would be size and income based for the region. The persistent droughts on the west coast alone make it a viable region for test and marketing and frankly they have the money to afford it. Once we can prove that the system will pay for itself within x number of years, I plan to market a design for smaller case types like farms, villages, towns, and personal use."

"Have you considered that many of the places lacking fresh water and suffering from drought also benefit from an overabundance of sunlight? Perhaps solar power generation is what you need."

Leah considered it and shook her head. "While I agree with you in theory, not even Lockheed's solar technology is efficient enough for something of this magnitude."

Kaelen grinned. "It is a good thing you have me at your disposal then. I believe the problem can be solved in two possible ways. First, we could make it easier to break the bond between dihydrogen monoxide and sodium chloride, thus making current technology feasible for the job. Second, we create more efficient solar photovoltaic cells and better batteries for power storage. Perhaps one or more of those tasks can be on the project list for SPL."

Despite working with Kaelen for over a year, there were instances of sheer brilliance that caught her off guard.

"What are you thinking?" Kaelen asked.

"You know, it's strange. I've never considered myself particularly religious. But every day I'm in your company, being treated to the miracle of your intellect, is another day on Earth that I question the existence of a higher power. Your mind is…indescribable." She shook her head and snorted. "Ana questions why I assert that I'm sapiosexual…she clearly hasn't spent enough time around intelligent people."

"Sapiosexual. That is a thing? I haven't come across that word before."

"Didn't you tell me you read the three most popular English dictionaries?"

"Yes—oh. According to the English shoe school dictionary, it is a person who finds intelligence sexually attractive or arousing." Kaelen swallowed as understanding washed across her face.

"Was that okay for me to admit?"

Kaelen visibly shuddered and she wet her lips. "While I'd never heard of the word before, it describes my thoughts and feelings about intelligence in addition to the more physical expression of desire."

Leah froze and time seemed as though it slowed. The air grew thick between them. It was the first moment that Leah felt like Kaelen may share in her hunger for something more physical between them. She considered that even if Kaelen didn't find her physically attractive, perhaps the mental one was enough.

Then Kaelen blinked and the moment was lost. "I, uh, I…" She cleared her throat. The new knowledge about Leah's intellectual preference had clearly left her unnerved. "The desalinization project—"

Rather than poke at the strange thing between them, Leah took pity and allowed her friend to change the topic. The entire point of the conversation was to keep Kaelen distracted. "Let's take care of the nano project first. Once the technology is proven, I'll arrange for a handoff to another lab for advanced marketing and testing, then SPL can start my next pie in the sky project."

"Pie in the sky? I'm not familiar with that particular saying."

Leah giggled. "You look like a curious puppy when you tilt your head like that. "The phrase refers to something that is wanted but unattainable, or not easy to attain."

"I like pie. Especially the peach fruit pie Ellie brought into the lab."

Leah laughed and patted her leg. "I know you do, darling."

Their conversation was interrupted by the driver. "Miss Lockheed, GPS says we're about ten minutes away. I apologize for the bumps but this road is a bit rough."

Leah had been so focused on the laptop and the idea of a new project that she didn't realize they'd turned off the paved road onto one made from gravel. Kaelen twisted to look out the rear window of the van and Leah did the same. She noted the excessive amount of dust kicked up behind them. The side windows only showed rows of some low, green crop that Leah couldn't identify. It was late August and, given the region, probably lettuce or potatoes.

"Okay, thanks David. And when we get there, you're okay to wait in the van? I'm not sure how long it will take."

He grinned at them through the rearview mirror. "I've got AC and a book. I'll be fine."

"What is that—oh, it's you." Leah placed her hand on Kaelen's thigh and the jiggling limb stilled. She met Kaelen's gaze. "Nervous?"

Kaelen cleared her throat. "How can you tell?"

"Well, barring this," Leah squeezed the leg beneath her left hand, doing her best to ignore the defined musculature, then reached across her body to smooth the right forefinger between Kaelen's eyes, "your worry line is back. Let's see how the Millers are, hmm?"

Kaelen took in a slow breath and released it gradually. Leah watched as the tense set to her shoulders disappeared. "Okay."

The van slowed and David turned up a long driveway. The mailbox near the road was battered, it's red flag down but not enough to hide the block letters spelling MILLER across the side. The driveway ended at a single-story ranch home with a good-sized porch. The two-car garage was unattached. Leah peered between the house and the garage and saw large barn farther back near the tree line. She gestured toward it and whispered to Kaelen, "That's where the beacon is coming from."

Kaelen followed her pointing finger and squinted. "My enhanced sight confirms the existence of something the shape of an Argonian pod in a lower level." When she turned back to Leah, they fell into each other's gaze.

David broke their intense eye contact. "I'll go around and fetch your chair, Miss Lockheed."

Leah spoke before he could exit the van. "You only need to open the back and side doors. I'll call the chair to me."

He nodded, as if such technology were commonplace, or he'd seen everything the world had to offer during his stint as a hired driver. Maybe both were true. A few minutes later, the side door opened, and Leah pushed a button on her watch which brought up a touch surface she could use as a remote control. The chair powered up and Leah maneuvered it out the back of the van, then followed the perimeter of the vehicle until it sat near the side door.

"Do you want me to lift you into it?" Kaelen asked.

"The offer is sweet but unnecessary. As I've said many times before, I haven't gotten so far in life by depending on others. Watch." The small footprint conveyance easily fit in places something bulkier would never reach. Leah raised the hoverchair until it was level with her seat, then slowly moved it toward her. The arm rest of the bench seat easily folded up, and much like she did on their movie nights, the side of the chair slid down. After that it was a matter of swinging her body from the bench seat into the chair and raising the side of the chair again.

Kaelen shook her head. "You are far and above the average human. While your intellect is beyond most, I also admire your agility and independence."

"She's right, miss. And that hoverchair is fairly genius. I'd heard those were handy like that, but we can never seem to get insurance to pay for one."

Leah blushed at the praise. "It was actually my adoptive father's design. If you don't mind me asking, David, who do you know in a chair?"

"It's my mama. The diabetes took her legs last year. We couldn't afford a different house that was all one level, and one of them stair lifts was too expensive. It's been a struggle with her having to sleep in the converted dining room.”

“Well, this one is actually a prototype but I tell you what, you give me your address and I’ll have one shipped to you with a more conventional remote. One on the chair, and one you can use separate. We even have an app if your mother is savvy with a phone.”

He grimaced. “She’s not, but I think a regular remote will be fine. Strangely enough she likes to fly the boys’ drone around. It’s got a camera and it gives her something to do and see now that she can’t walk.”

She smiled at him, intending to provide more than what was asked for. “Consider it done.”

“Isn’t that expensive though?”

Leah winked at him. “We’ll call it an extended prototype testing session. I won’t tell if you won’t.”

“Miss Lockheed, I don’t know what to say other than thanks from the bottom of my heart.”

“It’s really my pleasure. I like helping people.”

David nodded then shut the doors to the van after Kaelen exited. He got back inside as they turned to face the Miller home. The porch was about ten yards away from where the driveway ended at the garage. It was still close enough that the Millers should have heard their vehicle pull up. “I’m surprised they haven’t come outside to investigate. I don’t think we’re too far out in the country, but we didn’t pass any other cars on the road here so, they probably don’t get a lot of visitors.”

She watched as Kaelen closed her eyes and frowned. “I hear loud, twangy music playing inside and the adults are discussing financial issues.”

Leah didn’t call her out on the eavesdropping. “Oh?”

“Yes. The man is talking about taxes and them having to take out a third mortgage on the house because of the cost of Tate’s tuition. They’re worried about losing the house.”

“Tate is their son who is attending university in Chicago.”

Kaelen turned away from the house and met Leah’s eyes. “That’s not right. They shouldn’t lose their home over education costs.”

“Sadly, it happens all the time.”

“If that beacon is coming from an Argonian ship, it’s possible there is something worth trading inside—oh.”

"What is it?"

Kaelen checked her ever-present satchel, but she didn't bring Wex's nanobot drone with her. "There was a vial of regenerative serum in my pod, but it—" She glanced at the van. David had the windows up and engine running, so Leah thought it unlikely he'd be able to hear them. "It, um, had been irradiated during interstellar travel and became harmful to me. Neither my natural resistance to radiation, nor my suit, were protection against something with no recorded existence in Argon archives."

Leah rested her fingers on Kaelen's forearm. "What did it do?"

Kaelen frowned. "It felt like broken shards in my veins. I don't know if there is an AI installed but the regenerative serum is standard in the medical kit of all Argonian craft, even the personal pods. Wex says the ship probably shut down all systems but the locator beacon to preserve power. That would make sense if it has been here for many Earth years."

"How about we see what they have first, and we'll deal with any altered serum when the time comes."

Kaelen nodded then stood a little straighter. "I'm ready."

Chapter Nine

The steps creaked beneath Kaelen's feet. The home appeared quite sturdy, despite peeling paint on the shutters and railings. There was a swing hanging from thick eye bolts and an abundance of plants lovingly tended on a table near one corner of the porch. She reached for the handle of the outer door, then paused.

"Go ahead."

She nodded, grateful for Leah's presence and her continued encouragement. Kaelen knocked and heard the woman inside say, "Are we expecting someone?" before the music quieted and footsteps made their way to the door. It was pulled open to reveal the same man she'd seen in the photos in Leah's office. The woman from the photos stood slightly behind him.

With a steadying breath, Kaelen spoke. "Mr. and Mrs. Miller? My name is Kaelen Ra-Evon and I believe you may be raising a member of my family." While she knew the young boy couldn't actually be a member of her house, she told what Leah explained was a white lie to avoid giving herself away.

Shelly Miller gasped and placed a hand on the center of her chest. The middle-aged couple made eye contact, and Kaelen could see from their body language that they were going to send her away. Before they could, a boy near eleven years old clattered up a nearby set of stairs. "Mom, Dad, there's a van in the driveway—oh."

He stopped when he got to the top, a mere two yards from where Kaelen stood in the doorway. He didn't look familiar but there was an energy about him that resonated with Kaelen. "By Vos…"

He certainly wasn't shy around the strange women. The boy walked right up to stand between the Millers. "Hi. My name is Michael. Who or what's a vos?"

Kaelen looked at Leah in shock. "He's not a member of my house but there is something about this boy that leads me to believe he's Argonian." She grew silent, feeling more than a little overwhelmed.

Leah pushed forward in her hoverchair. "My name is Leah Lockheed-Tuck and I'm a friend of Kaelen's. I think we all need to talk."

"Wow!" The boy's mouth formed an "o" and he looked from Leah to his parents. "The owner of Lockheed International is visiting us. That's cool!"

The woman smiled and ruffled his dark mop-like hair. "He's always been bright, our Michael. He loves science and follows all the big news. Though he likes writing fantastical stories too." Kaelen watched as Shelly and Paul Miller appeared to communicate without saying a word. Shelly stared at him and hitched her shoulders. Then he blew out a breath and nodded. It was fascinating. The woman interrupted her character study. "Won't you both come in? I made pies yesterday and we put on a pot of coffee about fifteen minutes ago."

Kaelen nodded and held open the storm door for Leah, which earned her a smile that appeared both polite and wary. "Thank you, Mrs. Miller," then Kaelen nodded toward the man. "Mr. Miller."

That got the man to uncross his arms and open his posture. "Nonsense, none of that. Mister Miller was my dad. You can just call us Paul and Shelly."

The Millers led the way into an open kitchen with a table surrounded by six chairs. There was a strange split down the middle and Kaelen guessed it was for expansion purposes. Paul moved one of the chairs out of the way and Leah lowered her hoverchair so it would fit beneath.

"That's so cool. Did you build that? Lockheed is famous for all the neat stuff it makes. Do you make it all yourself or do you have scientists working for you?" He smacked his forehead. "I'm so dumb. Of course, you have lots of people working for you."

Shelly was busy at the counter, running water in the sink and pulling plates from the cupboard. Paul took his own seat at the table and folded his hands together. "Michael, you're not dumb and stop pestering Miss Lockheed-Tuck.”

Leah waggled a finger at him. “If I’m calling you both Paul and Shelly, then you can refer to us as Leah and Kaelen.”

That seemed to remind the boy of their other guest, and he stared at Kaelen curiously even as she stared back at him. “Are you a scientist too? Like Miss Leah?”

“I am. I’ve been a scientist since I was not much older than you.”

His mouth dropped open with awe as he whispered, “Really?”

She nodded and smiled at him. “Yes, really. I’m from a planet called Argon, specifically from the house of—I mean a family where many of us were thinkers of the highest order. My father and grandfather were scientists as well.”

“What about your mother, dear?” Shelly placed a carafe on a trivet in the center of the table and set coffee mugs out for anyone that wanted some. There was already creamer and sugar in place. She left the table again and returned a moment later with a pitcher of water and a stack of plastic cups.

Kaelen met Shelly’s kind eyes. “My mother was a judiciary…um, I think it would be something between a judge and lawmaker in Earth terms.”

Paul looked from Kaelen to Shelly, then from Shelly to Michael. “Should we send him down to his room?”

“What would be the purpose of that? Not only does this discussion directly involve him, but he’d still be able to hear us, wouldn’t he?”

More eye contact between Shelly and Paul, then Paul answered Kaelen. “I don’t know what you mean. Michael is an ordinary eleven-year-old boy. He wouldn’t be able to hear our conversation from his room, right Michael?”

All eyes turned to the boy in question, and he swallowed hard. Kaelen placed a hand atop his. “You don’t have to lie. That goes against one of the founding principles of our people.” Even as she said the words, Kaelen’s stomach burned at the untruths perpetuated by her own kin. She pushed away thoughts of the past to focus on the present and turned to Shelly and Paul. “You were discussing financial matters when we arrived, but had your music turned up too loud for it to be enjoyable or easy to have a conversation. This led me to believe that young Michael has already developed one of the many powers he will have here on Earth.”

“We have no idea what you’re talking about.”

“Is he not the one who arrived in the small ship located in the barn out back?”

Kaelen was grateful for Leah’s presence. She hadn’t anticipated how unwilling the Millers would be to admitting the truth. She heard the slightest sound and turned to see Michael leaning away from them in his chair, his face gone pale. Leah spoke before she could. “Is something wrong?”

He answered in a quiet, fearful voice. “Is she going to take me away?”

Leah responded in the same tone she used whenever Kaelen was fearful or anxious. “What makes you say that?”

“Mom and Dad,” he cast a worried glance toward them, “told me when I was adopted that I wasn’t from Earth. They said if people found out I was different they’d take me away from them. The CORP would come back and get me.”

That was the confirmation Kaelen needed. But, as soon as his eyes welled up with tears, she knew she would be going back to Los Angeles empty handed. With a reassuring nod toward the Millers, she held out her hand to shake with his. “No one is ever going to force you to leave your family. But Michael, you and I are the last of our people, of our planet.”

“The last?”

“Yes. I don’t know how you got here but Argon was destroyed right after my parents sent me away.” She caressed the collar of her clothing and the black suit appeared with its glowing symbol of their house. All three Millers gasped.

Shelly said, “That looks like some of the symbols that were on his ship!”

Michael grinned. “And my blanket!”

Kaelen remembered that horrific day and shook her head before breathing deeply to steady herself.

“Are you okay?”

The memory of leaving her home and seeing it explode behind

her brought tears to Kaelen's eyes. She wiped them as discretely as possible and felt Leah's hand rub her back. "I'm sorry, but the memory of watching the destruction of my planet is still difficult."

"You actually saw it happen?" Shelly looked horrified.

"Yes. My ship left mere minutes before the explosion. There was no time for anyone else," She glanced at Michael. "Or so I thought." She wondered about the boy's origins, whether or not he had come from Argon like her. If so, what of his parents? Strangers who had done the same as her own by sending their child away. The difference was hers knew of their impending doom and kept it a secret rather than warning everyone. She'd already decided they were nothing like the saviors they should have been. Ra was the head of the Thinker Guild and valuable leaders of their people. They should have led the fight for a solution, not searched for ways to hide the problem.

Kaelen continued, "Argon exploded as I was flying away. I need to know if you came from our planet and not an interstellar vessel."

Paul shifted in his chair. "I don't mean to be blunt, but does that change anything? Michael's been here ten years already."

"Ten years." She glanced at Leah who shrugged. "We suspected but…" Kaelen shook her head. "If he came from a larger vessel then I can only hope there are more Argonians out there. But if he came from Argon the same as I, then we are truly the last." She looked at Michael. "Somehow you landed many years before me and grew up here with your found family."

"Do you know who my birth parents were?"

"Not without access to your ship."

Leah cleared her throat. "Speaking of the ship, when I was researching your family and property, I discovered evidence of CORP involvement. My satellites didn't detect any digital monitoring before our arrival but I need to be sure of my friend's safety."

Paul and Shelly met each other's gaze. Shelly nodded and Paul gave a grunt before turning to answer Leah's question. "Truth be told, part of our fostering agreement was to send them quarterly updates, and report if anyone comes looking for Michael or the ship."

"We were supposed to report if he displayed any powers too." Shelly added.

"But you didn't."

Shelly shook her head. "No, we didn't."

"We don't owe them anything! They said they'd give us a stipend for Michael's care until he reached the age of eighteen or we adopted him."

Leah held out her hand. "I saw that you adopted Michael two years ago. I assumed that's when the stipend ended?"

Paul didn't meet their eyes when he answered. "Yeah. Then I got laid off right after that and Tate went away to school." He drew in a deep breath and let it out slow as he looked at his hands. Shelly told them what he couldn't.

"Tate is a good boy. He offered to stay home and work to help out but Paul and I couldn't have that. That fancy art school had been his dream forever."

Paul finally chuckled. "It's true. I swear sometimes that boy came out with a pencil in hand."

Leah winced and Shelly made a face. "Definitely not. I'm sure I would have felt that." Everyone laughed. "Anyway, we sent him off to school and Paul found work around here but it wasn't as good as his job at the furniture factory."

"It's true. I hurt my back driving hi-lo for so many years. Couldn't sit or stand for long periods of time and a lot of factories around here that pay worth a spit require it. Without college, wasn't much I could do."

"So, you've been mortgaging the house."

"Seemed to be our only option. Shelly's job managing the resale store pays okay but it's just not enough anymore."

Kaelen glanced over at Michael. He appeared stricken with tears shining in his eyes. "It's because of me, isn't it?"

"What? No, never. Son…it's complicated."

"But mom says I eat enough for five boys. I'm hungry a lot but I can try to eat less if that helps. Maybe I can pick up cans and bottles after school, or—"

"You'll do no such thing." Shelly's voice was firm but kind. "What you'll do is be a boy, go to school, play, have fun, and grow up. That's all we want for you."

Kaelen had heard enough. "I think I may have a solution for you. If

Michael really is Argonian, then I owe you a debt for taking him in and raising him."

"You don't owe—"

She interrupted Paul's protest. "I'm sorry, but Argonian law is very clear and I have an obligation to my race. No matter who his family is, I'm the last living adult so would absorb Michael into my house, thus making him kin of a sort." Kaelen moved her gaze to take in all three of the Millers. "Michael, I know you have a home here and adoptive parents who love you a lot. But as the last of my people, and because you will be coming into many more powers that are difficult to control, I'd like to get to know you so I can help." Then she focused specifically on Shelly and Paul. "Would that be okay with you?"

Shelly had tears in her eyes. "We always worried the day would come when someone would knock on our door. You swear you don't want to take him away?"

Kaelen met everyone's gaze around the table, fixing on Leah's eyes for longer than the others, then looked back at Shelly. "I've only been on Earth a little less than a year, but I've met some incredible people here. Leah is my best friend and she's taught me the importance of found family. You're Michael's family and no one will change that if I have any say. But," Paul bristled and she rushed to explain her idea, "Argonian society is quite different from Earth. My laws and rules of the house demand that I raise and care for him. However, we have something called *kuz ashum*."

Paul shook his head and grunted. "I'm not even gonna try to pronounce that. What does it mean?"

"It means if I consider you a foster family of good standing, I could leave him here with you for anywhere from one to ten years. It was a common enough practice on my planet."

"Ten years, you say?" Paul's look was calculating, and she could see that Shelly understood as well.

"Yes. All I ask is that you sign a document stating your intentions to educate, train, and care for him as you would for someone of your own house. Let's call it the House of Miller. As the head of my house, I'll also provide compensation for his care." She shrugged. "I'm sorry, but it's the only solution I could find since I'm duty-bound."

Shelly smiled. "We understand, Kaelen."

Paul was more pragmatic. Skepticism fairly radiated from him across his stern facial features and in his body language. "How do we know we can trust you, that you're even one of his people like you say? Can you prove any of what you've told us?"

Leah responded, and Kaelen recognized the angry tone from one she'd heard before when speaking on the phone. "You admitted that the symbol she's wearing is one of many that were on your son's ship—"

"I'm sorry Miss Lockheed-Tuck, but you can never be too sure. And Michael is our son, I'd do anything to protect him. It's one of the reasons we didn't call the CORP when he first showed signs of super hearing."

Kaelen reached into her satchel and removed the holocube she'd brought with her, as well as her cell phone. She slid the cube across the table toward the small family. "Wex, access all stored photos of Argon, specifically an image of the personal craft I arrived in."

"Yes, Kaelen Ra-Evon."

"Push the pod and other images to the cube." Even Leah moved forward to see the images flickering across every surface. The most telling one was that of a gleaming silver craft.

"Gosh!" The boy was easily impressed and seemed to love all things scientific. He would have enjoyed Argon.

"Oh. That's identical to the ship that landed in our field." Shelly glanced at Paul and he nodded. Michael remained fascinated by the cube while Shelly asked, "What did you mean when you said he would be coming into many more powers? He hasn't done much out of the ordinary, other than the hearing thing."

Kaelen looked over at Michael, who suddenly stilled. His eyes held fear and guilt in abundance as his heart began to race. "You've not told them everything, have you?" He shook his head.

"Told us what?"

"It's scary."

She whispered so low that there was no way any of the humans in the room could hear her. "Michael, how fast can you run?"

He answered right away, though everyone else looked confused. "I can run faster than everyone else. Why?"

She winked at him. "I'll race you to the road and back."

He jumped up. "Deal!" Then he was off. Kaelen waved at the Millers' and disappeared from their sight to follow him. He was fast, certainly a lot faster than any human. But he wasn't up to full speed yet. She easily passed him, picked some wildflowers growing by the mailbox and was sitting back in her seat when he appeared in the kitchen seconds later. She showed him the bouquet then set it on the table. "You did well and with time, you'll become faster."

Shelly covered her mouth and Paul uttered a curse beneath his breath. "How can we help him with something like that? He'll have to hide it around here."

Kaelen nodded. "I know too well how much he'll have to hide and it's safest if he does. But while he's growing, I can help him learn control. We could use video chat, phone calls, I can visit Michael, and he can visit me in Los Angeles."

His eyes lit up. "Really?"

"Really, as long as Paul and Shelly say it's okay. It's only a three-hour flight."

He grinned excitedly. "So cool!"

Shelly patted him on the head. "I think summers when school is out would be as good a time as any, right Paul?"

He nodded. "That would probably be best. Now, how about I show you the ship?"

"It's below the barn, right?"

"How did you know?"

"Multiple-spectrum vision, including x-rays, is another Argonian power here on Earth that he'll eventually develop." Seeing the fear on their faces, she changed the topic back to the *kuz ashum*. "If you have a piece of unlined paper, I can write the contract before we head outside."

"Will printer paper do?" Kaelen nodded and Shelly turned to Michael. "Can you grab a pen and a few sheets from my craft room?"

He grinned, "Sure!" then sped away only to return again a few seconds later. Once he placed the items on the table, Kaelen began writing out what she thought the contract should cover in her small, precise handwriting. She used maximal speed to create two copies in less than a minute then set them aside so the ink could dry.

Paul looked thoughtful as he read the text. "Is there anything we gotta do to prove our worth as this House of Miller?" He made a face. "Though I wouldn't exactly call ours a 'house of good standing' at the moment."

Paul picked up the top sheet and held it out so Shelly could see. She chuckled. "It's easier to read your contract than the instruction manual for that universal remote." She gave Kaelen a knowing look. "And it just so happens to cover from now until Michael is grown. That's very kind of you."

"No, it's kind of you. Michael landed as not more than a babe and you took him in and raised him as your own. I'd say that's as strong a bond as any before, up to, and including the family that sent him away. *Dolem*-Ra," she amended her words, realizing they wouldn't know the Argonian phrase. "I'm from the House of Ra, which is now Michael's house with the absence of his Argonian parents. My people owe you a debt."

Paul grumbled, "Let's not talk about any more debt today."

Leah spoke up. "If you're in urgent need, I can transfer—"

Paul cut her off. "Not that we don't appreciate it but save your money for people who are worse off. We Millers…we always find a way."

Kaelen pushed the pen toward Paul and Shelly. "As I said, Argon owes you a debt and that's my responsibility. I already told you that I will compensate you for his care. If Michael's parents sent anything of value in the pod, you can use that as you see fit. Otherwise, I'll split equally the items provided by my own parents."

"What did—"

"Sign the contracts and I'll explain."

A few minutes later, both pages held all three of their signatures. Kaelen reached into her satchel again and removed a ring with the symbol of her house on the flat surface.

Leah gave her a curious look. "What is that?"

Kaelen caressed the side of the ring and watched the surface heat, then she pressed it onto the paper. A puff of smoke curled off before she pulled the ring away and repeated the action on the other copy. The ring cooled within seconds, and she put it back in the satchel.

"That's so cool!" Michael looked up at Kaelen. "Do you think the ship will have rad stuff like your ring?"

His question was alarming. "I hope there is nothing irradiated, but it's possible—"

Leah snickered and cut her off. "Darling, rad is slang for cool or awesome."

Kaelen felt her face heat. "Oh. Okay. Uh, maybe?"

Everyone stood and Leah backed away from the table. Shelly shooed them out the door. "Go on and see that ship. I'll plate up some pie for when you come back in."

Michael ran over to Shelly and hugged her around the middle. "Thanks, Mom. You're the best! Then he kissed her cheek and raced out the front door.

"No running in the house, Michael!"

Kaelen laughed and held up her hands. "Sorry, I should have asked permission before encouraging him to a race that started inside."

"It's quite all right, Kaelen. I think you'll be a wonderful influence on him over the next few years." Kaelen nodded but didn't respond. Instead, she pushed the wildflowers toward Shelly then turned and followed Leah where she trailed behind Paul.

Out in the barn, Paul pointed toward the ceiling where there was a hook and pulley. "I'll have to lower that down to lift the floor out of the way."

Leah raised a dark eyebrow. "Is there no security? I thought for sure the CORP would have this place locked down."

"Well, they were supposed to. The initial group helped stow it away then honestly, I think they forgot."

"Interesting. Sounds like typical government bureaucracy."

Kaelen scanned the wooden boards where he indicated. "Is it all one piece?"

"Only the section over the ship. It's hinged in the back. I think someone used to keep a still down there during prohibition. This whole place was a farm a few generations ago until it was split up and sold to multiple landowners. I'm glad we snapped it up when we did because prices in the area have shot up over the past two decades."

Kaelen was unfamiliar with Earth land prices. He pointed out the seams, then to a steel ring set in the wood. "Step back, please."

Paul, Leah, and Michael all moved back, and Kaelen casually

grabbed the loop that was placed by the nearest seam. She lifted it easily, walking along the edge of the door until she had the section of flooring open all the way and leaning against the back wall of the barn. Below them was a space large enough to house a ship exactly like her own, though it was covered in dust. There was plenty of room in the opening, but she wasn't sure how much of a drop Leah's chair could handle. She floated the eight feet down, then raised her hand. "Paul and Michael, I'd like you both to come down here."

He moved his gaze from the large wooden trap door to Kaelen. "It's safe, right?"

"Yes. I'm going to see if I can activate the ship and I want to show you how to open it."

"Okay." Michael jumped over the edge similar to Kaelen, landing lightly on his feet with no trouble. Paul turned and climbed down the ladder bolted to one wall.

Kaelen was relieved to hear a low hum as she showed Paul and Michael the correct keypad sequence to open the door. Unlike after she'd landed on Earth, there was no pressurization inside, so the clear lid lifted silently. "Did it close on its own after you removed Michael from the ship?" Paul nodded. "It's possible there was an AI on board that would have seen to his education for the long journey."

"AI?"

"An artificially intelligent computer."

"Is it like your Wex?" Leah peered down at them over the arm of her chair.

"Maybe not as advanced, but AI was standard for most craft. They would be very similar, minus the data mine has gathered since landing on Earth." Kaelen pushed a few buttons on the console inside and it powered up.

"Ceresh bom, Kaelen Ra-Evon"

"Use Earth English, North American standard. What is your moniker?"

"Yes, Kaelen Ra-Evon. I am Tuk, as this ship is a standard pod assigned to the Tuk platform orbiting Argon."

Kaelen paused to consider Tuk's statement. "Who was your passenger?"

"Kai Xe, son of Nov Xe and Tale Ce-Bek."

"Guild?"

"Both parents were members of the Thinker Guild and stationed on Tuk for one vosan."

She translated for everyone. "The closest equivalent to one vosan is an Earth year." Michael leaned nearer to the ship, mouth open and dark eyes wide with awe. Kaelen spared him a glance then asked the hard question. "Tuk sensors would have been the last in operation, acquiring data up to the moment the platform was destroyed."

"Yes, Kaelen Ra-Evon."

"Were there any other survivors besides Kai Xe? And how did this ship coordinate to Earth? I thought standard procedure for platform craft was planetary destination?"

"Only two personal craft escaped the secondary and tertiary blast effects. Tuk pod registered no safe planetary destinations. In the absence of planetary destination, pods are programmed to follow the leading Argonian ship. Wex communicated destination coordinates to Tuk but a spatial anomaly prevented this pod from following the same course."

"Wow. I traveled through a spatial anomaly?"

Paul ruffled the top of his curly hair. "Looks like it, kid."

Kaelen gestured toward Paul. "Tuk, this is Paul Miller, from the House of Miller. Because of the anomaly, Kai Xe landed many years before my own. I agreed to *kuz ashum* with the House of Miller for Kai Xe's education and care."

"My database indicates zero Argonian education for Kai Xe. Has he received any since arriving on Earth?"

"No, Tuk."

"According to Argonian law, Kai Xe will not be able to take his rightful place as a lineal scion within Dolem-Xe until he receives full Argonian guild induction. Having inducted before leaving Argon, you are the only legal heir to your own house and only living Argonian guildmember. It is your responsibility to take Kai Xe into your house."

Kaelen frowned and she pressed her lips together, hating that Tuk was reminding her of all she'd lost in such a dispassionate and impersonal manner. "I'm well aware of Argonian law, Tuk. Do not mention it again to me."

"As you wish, Kaelen Ra-Evon. I have updated my records on the status of Kai Xe."

She glanced at Paul then added, "Please add Kai Xe's Earth name to your database as well."

"It is highly unorthodox—"

In a bit of arrogant temper, Kaelen asked, "What is my title, Tuk?"

"Kaelen Ra-Evon, as the only remaining guild member of Argon and eldest of your house, you are now the last scion of Ra."

"And my title?"

"You are Ra in its entirety."

"As Ra, I am also the head of the Thinker guild. Is there anyone of higher status according to Argonian law given there are no other existing guilds?

"No, Kaelen Ra-Evon. I am programmed to accommodate your wishes."

She saw Paul and Michael watching her with wide eyes. "Thank you. My order is for you to update your records with Kai Xe's Earth name which is," she turned to the awed boy and he answered for her.

"Michael Allen Miller."

"Acknowledged, Kaelen Ra-Evon."

She nodded. "I wish for you to guide Michael and teach him about Argon. I will also sync my Wex with your system so you can help him learn to control his powers as they develop, the way my Wex helped me when I first landed. All the data from our experiments is well-documented."

"Do you have a data puck?"

"No, I have my ship communicators." Kaelen reached into the shielded pocket of her satchel and removed a single earpiece. Then she opened a slot on the ship's main console, removed one of the communicators there, and replaced it with her own.

"Please stand by, synching data now."

Kaelen looked at Paul. "The communicators are powerful and will work for a great distance, even below the barn since you're on a hill here. However, they won't go through any major curvature of the earth. You should be fine for a few miles, but you won't have the kind of distance that I benefit from with my Wex because of the unique placement of my ship."

"Where is your ship, Kaelen? You've never mentioned."

She grinned up at Leah. "On a mountain in Canada."

Leah covered her eyes and shook her head. "I'm not even going to ask."

"Synching with Wex is complete. You may remove your communicator, Kaelen Ra-Evon."

Kaelen removed her device, then took the other one as well and presented Michael with his pair. "Try them."

He put one in each ear and his mouth dropped open.

"Hey, his voice is talking to me now."

She shook her head. "Remember, Tuk isn't masculine or feminine. Tuk is an AI created to aid Argonians, specifically the families on the platform where your parents were stationed. While Tuk will be good at educating and guiding, you must eventually learn to make your own decisions. If Tuk can't answer a question, you only need to contact me, and I'll try my best to help you."

He took the communicators out and suddenly looked serious, perhaps too serious for someone so young. "Are we really the last of our families where we come from?"

"Our entire planet is gone, and I don't know if anyone was off-world at the time of its destruction. As far as I know, we are the last of everyone."

Perhaps he'd learned to be intuitive from Shelly Miller, or maybe it was something he was born with. But Michael reached out to take Kaelen's hand. "I'm sorry I don't remember it like you do, that I was too young when we left."

"It's okay. It's probably best that you don't. No one needs to carry that level of grief."

Paul rested his hand on Michael's curly dark hair. "You carry it though."

She nodded. "I'm strong. I'm the remaining scion of *Dolem*-Ra, and I can shoulder that weight for both of us." Kaelen could hear Leah's heartbeat where it sped above them. She took comfort in the sound and continued with her duty. "Two more things: I wish for Michael to learn about the history of Argon, as well as the language. Tuk will help with this. Perhaps you can set up a schedule that doesn't interfere with your family life or his Earth schooling."

Paul nodded. "That seems fair."

"Second, I'd like to investigate his ship to see if it was sent with items that would aid the passenger once they reached their destination." She pointed to the insulated compartment at the front of the padded cradle. "My own pod contained a selection of ordinary Argonian elements, some of which are in fact quite rare on Earth. But my parents also had more time to prepare and used a private vessel, not one assigned to a work station as this was."

"Sure, if you think it will help."

She turned back to the ship. "Tuk, are your storage holds empty or full."

"Full, Kaelen Ra-Evon."

She moved toward the open hatch as Leah called out from above, "Be careful."

Kaelen smiled up at her. "The back compartment would be personal items. The front compartment will contain a medical kit with items like the regenerative serum."

"Okay."

She pulled her gaze away from Leah's worried stare and opened the compartment. There was a satchel containing an Argonian holocube and a heavy, sealed container no larger than a book. Leah called down, "What is it?"

"It's a *palda*. Uh, a container that can hold a variety of different things, from science implements to personal trinkets." She released the clasps on each end and opened the lid. "Interesting. The items inside appear similar to the minerals sent in my own pod. I don't recognize a few of them, probably something they were investigating in their lab when the platform sensors alerted crew to the danger."

"Nov Xe and Tale Ce-Bek were tasked to investigate minerals and elements discovered within an asteroid on far orbit around Vos. It was suspected the materials could be used to improve Argonian processes and equipment."

"I wonder if my parents got some of my elements from the same source." Kaelen had to physically shake herself to keep from going down the black hole of her parents' motivations and plans. "Either way, the items are yours to use as needed."

Paul looked taken aback and lifted his hands in protest. "I don't think—"

"Paul Miller, from the House of Miller, I will remind you of my obligation to your family. They are yours to use for Michael's safety, his home, his education, and his happiness."

"I understand."

"Tuk, is this craft equipped with Argonian regenerative serum?"

"Yes, Kaelen Ra-Evon."

She sighed and glanced up at Leah then spoke to Paul and Michael. "Unfortunately for both myself and Michael, his serum was most likely altered on the journey the way my own was. The radiation it emits is especially strong, affecting even our specialized constitution. Now that I see Tuk is operational, I'll have it send a drone to remove the flask."

"Kaelen Ra-Evon, I hold the records from your previous experience with the irradiated serum and can confirm the sample in the medical kit emits the same frequency. If you all leave the vicinity of the ship, I will dispatch the drone for removal."

Paul and Michael climbed out of the sub-level while Kaelen flew out and stood next to Leah. "Wow, will I fly too someday?"

"I don't see why you wouldn't."

Leah nudged her arm. "If this altered serum gives off radiation, will lead seal it enough to make it safe?"

"Perhaps. What are you thinking?"

Leah frowned. "I'm thinking that if my best friend says something feels like broken shards running through her bloodstream, I'd like to find a way to protect her from that."

"It's unlikely that we'll ever see such a substance again here on Earth. After all, there are no more facilities to manufacture it, not to mention it would have to travel through certain portions of space to be affected. But we can try to collect it safely if you want to study the substance. The base formula may aid Earth science in the future."

Kaelen was also curious about the irradiated liquid but didn't want to put herself or anyone else at risk. She turned to Paul. "Do you have enough lead to make a container that could shield something the size of an Earth medical syringe?"

He rubbed his whiskered chin in thought, then snapped his fingers. "I've got some old lead pipe from when we had the water lines replaced years ago before we moved into the house. Not sure why it wasn't replaced before that since everyone knows it's harmful to folks. I'll go see if I can find a short piece with threads still on it."

"Don't worry about the threads. I can seal it once the flask is in."

Leah looked concerned. "Won't it hurt you though until the pipe is sealed?"

"Yes."

Paul turned to leave the barn, but Michael sped back inside, already holding a length of pipe about six inches long. "Will this work? It was in the plastic bin around back."

Kaelen took it with a smile and ruffled his hair the way she'd seen the Millers do. "That's perfect. Thank you, Michael. You should go back to the house with Shelly. I don't want you to feel what this substance can do, okay?"

"I can handle it, I'm strong."

"I know you are, but you don't have to be strong for this." She stared at him until he relented. As soon as she heard him enter the house, she called out to Tuk, "Please proceed." The compartment opened automatically then Kai's ship drone entered and came out carrying an Argonian medical kit. Kaelen quickly squeezed the end of the pipe shut, the soft lead turning malleable within her strong hands. She set the pipe down and waved Leah and Paul back. "Tuk, dump the contents onto the ground near the pipe, then place the serum flask inside."

"Yes, Kaelen Ra-Evon."

Despite being two yards away from the drone, weakness stole over her at the same time pain sliced through her entire body. Kaelen grunted and staggered. "Please hurry, Tuk."

"Affirmative."

They watched as the drone upended the capsule. Leah and Paul's mouths dropped open when a variety of strange implements and flasks tumbled onto the wood. Kaelen sucked in a breath when a flask containing glowing orange liquid landed on the wood next to the rest. She was relieved to see only one. The drone grasped the serum and placed it into the lead pipe. Kaelen immediately felt better. Before she could overthink it, she sped to the pipe and squeezed it closed. For added safety to prevent radiation leakage, she hit it with a small burst of her laser vision to be sure it was properly sealed, then stuffed it into the satchel at her side.

Kaelen shoved the other items back into the capsule and returned it to the storage compartment near the front of the pod. "These can stay in the pod since there is nothing here that Michael will need for the foreseeable future, if ever. Tuk, recall the drone and close the ship. You have instructions to only open it for five people."

"Who do you wish to grant access, Kaelen Ra-Evon?"

"Paul Miller, Shelly Miller, Michael Miller, myself, and Leah Lockheed-Tuck. She is the other human near me. Record their biometric readings. You'll find Shelly's near your communicators with Michael."

"All readings are complete and locked within my database. Ship access is limited to three humans and two Argonians, Kaelen Ra-Evon."

Kaelen watched the ship close, then rushed to lower the floorboards back into place. She held the satchel out to Paul. "This is yours. Use it wisely, Paul Miller." He didn't say anything, but she could see the tears in his eyes and knew he was thinking about their financial trouble. Even though there were no large cubes of gold, she recognized enough precious Earth gems that they would no longer need to worry about the house, their other son's education, or the future. The Millers were safe, which meant Michael would be safe.

His voice was a gruff whisper. "Thank you, Miss Ra-Evon."

"It's Kaelen, and thank you for taking care of him." She looked around the barn, then back at Paul and Leah. "Shelly said something about pie? As a warning, Argonians eat a lot."

Paul chuckled and led the way back toward the house. "Tell me something we don't already know."

Chapter Ten

It was late by the time the jet touched down in Los Angeles. They stayed and ate an early dinner with the Millers, who even invited David inside to dine with them. Leah explained that David wasn't allowed to divulge anything he saw while in their company. A fact that made Shelly and Paul feel a lot more comfortable having the stranger at their dinner table.

Because David had been such a good sport about sitting for hours in the van before being invited in for refreshments, Leah gave him a large tip when he dropped them off at the airport. She also got his address and phone number, promising a hoverchair would arrive within two weeks, along with a technician that could show them how to use it.

Leah glanced at her watch as the weekend driver arrived to pick them up. She yawned. "I'm exhausted. Jaunting back and forth across multiple time zones in one day is for young people."

Kaelen remarked, "You are young by Earth standards."

Leah patted her hairline where quite a few loose hairs floated around after dozing on the plane ride back. "I'm sure I look awful." She called out to the driver, "You can take Miss Ra-Evon home first and drop me off last, Dan."

"Yes, Miss Lockheed."

"I thought I told you to call me Leah?"

Dan's eyes crinkled in the rearview mirror of the custom van, indicating mirth that he tried to hide. "You have, Miss Lockheed."

Kaelen snickered. "Let me reiterate that you're not old, Leah. And you look quite nice, the opposite of awful."

They were suddenly thrown forward as the van came to a screeching halt in the middle of the empty street. A flash lit the darkness outside and Dan yelled. "It's a Chromodec, get down!"

Nothing hit the van but Kaelen and Leah could see something ahead of them that was luminous enough to light up the buildings on either side of the street. Kaelen chanced a look around the front seat and saw a woman glowing white with power, standing a few hundred feet down the road, right in the middle of the lanes. A ball of something equally bright floated between her hands. With a wave, she sent it toward them. It struck the road right in front of the van. The attack sprayed asphalt everywhere and left behind a large, smoldering hole.

Leah called out quietly, "Sit tight everyone. I don't know what she's tossing, but the metal cage surrounding the passenger compartment will protect us if she hits the van with electricity, as long as you don't touch anything metal."

Kaelen whispered back, "It looks more like plasma. Who is that?"

"I don't know."

"And are we supposed to sit here, helpless?" Kaelen followed the dangerous woman's movements intently.

"With any luck, agents from the CORP will arrive to deal with the threat. They're pretty good about a fast response, especially since I helped design SIMoN's updated power tracking system that lets them know when levels are fluctuating somewhere in the city."

"Simon?"

"Synthetic Intelligence Monitoring Network. It's the heart and soul of the CORP, tracking and controlling information from all over the world. Everything from the HUD in the agents' helmets to the defense protocol for the CORP facilities in each city are tied to SIMoN. Not a true AI, but close."

Kaelen had read all about the CORP when she first moved to Los Angeles. The organization and their activities sounded noble. They were Earth's version of a special police force for both aliens and Chromodecs. Wex warned her that one of the reasons she needed to keep her powers hidden was so she didn't come to their attention. While the CORP was a force for good, Wex counseled her to be cautious for her own protection.

Car alarms up and down the block went off as the woman hurled another ball of plasma toward a parked car ahead of them, causing it to explode. Kaelen looked at Leah with concern. "Should I go out there?"

Leah gripped her arm. "No!"

"I could give assistance." Kaelen remembered the woman outside her old apartment and the men who had attacked her. She knew she would be able to help with this threat and was uncomfortable remaining inactive. "She is a danger to the people and property here."

"The woman is also a danger to you. Please, stay here with me and let the CORP handle this."

"She's right, Miss Ra-Evon. Even if you're strong, it's illegal to interfere unless you're an agent or have special clearance from the government."

Another ball of energy took out a transformer close to the van. "What? Why can't people help when help is needed? That is ridiculous."

"Hey, look at me." Kaelen turned to meet Leah's gaze. "Vigilantism is illegal everywhere in the United States. The government doesn't want someone running around halfcocked creating as much damage and danger as they are trying to prevent. This is for trained agents, not an average person with an above average need for justice. Those kinds of people are more likely to get hurt and are nothing but a lawsuit waiting to happen."

Kaelen could understand the rationale behind such a law, but something caught her attention outside. She pointed toward the strange woman. "She is clearly here for us because she's been watching the van the entire time. I may not have a choice but to take action."

They were all startled when the woman yelled, "Leah Lockheed, it's on you to pay for the sins of your family!"

"Are you sure you don't know her?"

Leah shot Kaelen a worried look. "I have no idea who or what she's talking about. But watch, it takes her nearly two minutes to form each new plasma ball."

The woman walked in their direction with her hands held out in front of her, another glowing ball of plasma grew between her palms. Before she could throw it, someone appeared right behind her in a flash of light as multiple black vehicles careened around their van to block the woman's forward progress. She tossed the ready-made ball at one of the trucks, but it must have been armored because the vehicle only rocked in place. The black side smoldered though, so Kaelen assumed that whatever the balls were comprised of was extremely hot. Definitely plasma of some sort.

Dan's calm voice cut through the tense atmosphere in the van. "Calvary's here! As long as she doesn't hit us, we should be able to get underway soon."

The first figure in black wrapped the woman in a bear hug, disrupting her building concentration. "That's Portis." Leah gave a sigh of relief.

Kaelen had never heard that name before. "Who is that?"

"One of the Chromodec agents stationed at LA's CORP facility. She can teleport anywhere she has a line of sight."

Dan and Leah both jumped when someone in black knocked on the driver's window of the van. Kaelen had heard the woman approach. Dan rolled the window down and the woman looked in to see the other passengers. "Everyone okay in here?"

"Yeah. She didn't hit us but she took out a few cars and some electric poles farther down."

Leah said, "Rodriguez, is that you?"

The agent leaned in a little farther and gave a nod. "Hey, Miss Lockheed-Tuck. Glad to see none of you were hurt. Your tracking system worked beautifully."

Leah smiled. "Excellent! Thanks for your hard work, Agent. All of Los Angeles appreciates what the CORP does."

Yelling drew everyone's attention. They all watched the mysterious woman disappear and reappear ten yards down the street. Then she disappeared and another flash of light came from the top of a nearby building. "Holy shit!" Rodriguez shot the passengers of the van an astonished look. "Sorry, folks, but it looks like she got away. I've never seen a Chromodec or alien with multiple high-level powers like that. I bet the SAIC is gonna call in the big dogs for a consult."

Leah's concern was obvious with her racing heart. Kaelen asked the strange agent. "What does this mean for Leah? The woman specifically called her out and said she needed to pay for the sins of her family."

"She said that, exactly?" Leah, Dan, and Kaelen all nodded. "Well damn. I'll let Jove know. We'll set up a grid around your corporate office building and your apartment building for the next few weeks to monitor for more energy spikes like the one tonight."

"Okay, thank you, Spark."

Agent Rodriguez, aka Spark, nodded and gave a little salute. Electricity arced from her fingertip to the open shield of her helmet before she backed away from the van. Most of the agents returned to their armored carriers. Some stayed behind, presumably to assess damage. Another agent waved Dan forward. "Ready to go home, ladies?"

Leah grumbled back, "I'm not even going to dignify that with an answer. I'm so exhausted I feel like a zombie at this point. Let's get out of here before another Chromodec arrives to wreak havoc. I'm too tired to deal with death threats today."

"Will do, Miss Lockheed."

"It's Leah!"

"Mmm hmm."

Kaelen heard him chuckle quietly and accepted that such strange attacks occurred often enough that they'd become commonplace to the regular residents of Los Angeles. She'd seen it on the television news but had never witnessed an attack in person. Kaelen was extremely concerned that someone was specifically targeting Leah.

Even though neither of them admitted it, Kaelen heard Dan and Leah's hearts race during the confrontation. She feared for both, but definitely more for Leah. Kaelen's attraction to her friend grew stronger every day but she remained silent. What would she say, anyway? That she'd been drawn to Leah since the moment they'd met in that interview room? Kaelen was conscious of their interactions after that first game night conversation about sexuality and attraction. Leah never spoke of Kaelen's admission, so Kaelen assumed her own interest was one-sided.

Instead, she spent a lot of time studying the relationships in her new friend group. Maddy and Tasha seemed well-balanced, each working together with their individual strengths and weaknesses.

Nalla and Einstein were an unusual couple, but despite having a nearly dichotomous viewpoint on the world around them, they also appeared quite stable and happy. She'd heard the saying opposites attract from one of the engineers in Lab 5 and thought it was certainly true in her lab partner's case.

Tasha and Nalla remained two of the more observant and intuitive members of the group. She thought it had to do with the former's profession as a therapist, and the psychic power of the latter. Kaelen had a habit of unintentionally focusing on Leah whenever she was in her presence and her interest wasn't as discrete as she would like. She caught Tasha looking back and forth between her and Leah more than once, but in the end, Maddy's girlfriend never said anything.

Nalla confronted her about it when they had lunch together. She said that Kaelen's pining was a downer and that she should make a move before someone else came along and did. Kaelen was still trying to decipher that advice.

Her thoughts were interrupted by yet another yawn and she offered a solution. "Why don't you have Dan drop you off first? Humans are extremely dependent on achieving the required number of REM cycles per night, so it is imperative that you sleep. I can walk home or use the Uber."

"It's just called Uber, and you've had as long a day as I have. Not to mention it must feel quite overwhelming to suddenly discover another Argonian after what, a little less than a year on this planet?"

Kaelen nodded. "Yes. I'm still not sure how I feel. About finding Kai Xe—Michael. and my decision to leave him behind again. Did I do the right thing?"

"For your duty? I don't know. For Michael? I think you did."

"The other thing weighing on my heart is that no matter how much I tried to temper my hope, there was a large part of me that wished the pod belonged to a member of my house. As soon as I saw Michael, I resented his survival over that of my own family…then felt guilty over that resentment. Does that make me a bad person?" She turned to look at her best friend. Leah's face was illuminated in flashes under the passing streetlights in the dark van. More golden hued than the white flashes from the plasma woman.

"Why don't you stay with me again tonight? I've got that ice cream you like if you're hungry. Otherwise, we can talk until I crash, okay? I'm not going to send you home alone with all this on your shoulders and no one to talk to."

"I have Wex."

Leah rolled her eyes, a gesture that Kaelen had begun to find cute.

"No offense, but Wex seems like kind of a dick."

"Wex is an AI, it cannot have a personality."

Her response elicited a snort. "Trust me, I knew a few people back at MIT with the same personality as your Wex…they were all dicks. So, you'll stay over?"

It wasn't as if Kaelen could deny any request Leah made. "Yes." She hesitated, then admitted, "I would like someone to speak with. And I'd feel better knowing I was there to protect you in case the woman finds out where you live."

"I trust the CORP to watch out for me and my business." Leah patted her hand then called out to Dan. "Change of plans, drop us both at my place before you put the van away for the night."

"Yes, Miss Lockheed."

"Damn it, Dan!"

Kaelen laughed, feeling lighter than she had all day.

A half hour later, they sat on the couch in Leah's living room. Leah sat on one end of the couch with her legs stretched out resting on the cushioned surface. Kaelen had folded her legs and faced Leah while eating directly from a carton of ice cream. She swallowed another spoonful, unfazed by the size of the bite or the temperature.

Kaelen paused mid-chew as she realized that it was long after Leah's normal nighttime schedule for personal care. "Do you need to, uh, perform your daily health maintenance?" She picked up the phone that lay on her thigh then looked back at Leah, alarmed.

"It's fine. I'm prepared whenever I travel and was able to drain my bladder on the plane, as well as perform my other bathroom routine. One of the main reasons I want the nanobot trial to succeed is to have control of my bodily functions again."

Kaelen wanted to make Leah's dream a reality immediately. Success was a certainty but they still needed to run the human trials. Nearly all the test rats had regained full function, but it took many months. Something the size of a human would take significantly longer unless they could cascade the production of the specialized nanobots so they could introduce more into the system with the first injection. The process worked, but it took a long time to assemble enough to effect rapid measurable change with Earth's current technology.

"Are you still thinking about Michael?" She looked up to see Leah watching her intently. Kaelen shifted in her seat and remembered the half-eaten ice cream that had begun to melt. She lifted the container so it was closer to her face while meeting Leah's curious gaze, then exhaled a quick burst of her freeze breath to solidify the creamy treat.

Leah's mouth dropped open. "Is that…did you—?"

Kaelen used her distraction to speed the dessert back to the freezer and returned before Leah could formulate a real question. "Yes. It is another one of my yellow sun abilities."

Leah shook her head. "It seems as though every day I learn something new about you, and yet I'm still curious. What were you thinking about before your little party trick?"

"I was actually thinking about the trials that are slated to begin next week. I wish we had a way to cascade the assembly at a higher rate so the bots would replicate faster once injected into the subject."

"In all the simulations you and Einstein ran, what is the predicted timeline for partial nerve repair and the beginning of returned feeling for humans?"

Kaelen considered their previous trials. "If you remember, it took Krigh nearly two months to achieve full nerve function and begin to walk. Sleepy still isn't there yet, but he's moving all four limbs. All the others that came after are still in various stages, but Krigh is our proven model."

Leah smirked. "I'm well aware that he's your favorite, darling."

"No, you're my favorite." Kaelen did something Nalla called finger guns to see what Leah's response would be. She wasn't disappointed.

Leah threw her head back and laughed, and Kaelen's eyes were drawn to two freckles dotting the pale skin of her neck. Kaelen's stomach clenched with *want*. The unfamiliar and distracting emotion surged through her, and she curled her fingers into fists and willed them under control. When her gaze moved upward, Leah had covered her face with one hand and was shaking her head.

"You have lunch too often with Nalla at The Bean Bag."

Kaelen was honest. "She makes me laugh and reminds me a little of a friend I had on Argon. We were both slated for the Thinker Guild, though I was the only one who made it in the end." She took a shuddering breath and looked down at her fists, her emotions taking another, equally overwhelming direction. "I failed my people. I am inadequate for the position I now hold."

"Darling, no. Look at me." Kaelen bravely met Leah's gaze, conditioned to obey those she respected. "You didn't fail anyone, nor are you failing your duty as the last of *Dolem*-Ra."

"But Wex explained Argonian laws and I knew it was my duty to raise and protect Kai Xe in absence of any other Argonians. Yet I left him behind."

Leah took her hand. "You were naught more than a girl when you were sent away but you've adapted to this planet remarkably. As a matter of fact, you told me yourself that there has never been a situation like the one you're in now."

"You mean regarding me being the last of my house?"

"The last of your people. I highly doubt any of your written laws dealt with the exact set of circumstances you find yourself in. Frankly, I admire how you were able to take a bad situation and come up with the best solution that would satisfy all needs on the table. Few could do that but you did. Michael is loved, he's happy, and he's being educated about Earth, exactly as what would have happened if he had traveled as long as you did. He's also getting the Argonian education he needs."

"But I left him alone. I didn't keep him at my side as dictated by guild law, instead making up excuses not to take him with me."

"You wouldn't have devised that solution if you didn't believe it followed Argonian laws. Michael is a boy growing up with the only two people he remembers from childhood, three if you count his brother, Tate. The Millers will teach him about love, life, and family. But he'll also have you to learn about his people, his house, and honor. Trust yourself, love."

Kaelen shook her head. "You think highly of me when I have no patents or other significant achievements to my name yet on this planet. I was naught but a girl when I left, and now I'm nothing more than... what was that book Nalla mentioned at the last game night? A stranger in a strange land on Earth. I want to do good work for you, for all the people here. But I fear my journey has only just begun."

"I beg to differ. Your journey began the moment you saw your planet die. I don't care how many therapy sessions that AI implanted in your head with your Argonian science, it's not the same as speaking with someone about your loss and fears. You are good, honest, noble, and so full of hope that I can't help but feel the same way when I'm around you."

Kaelen sucked in a breath and focused on Leah's heart. The beat was steady and true, but she still had to ask. "Do you mean that?"

"Which part?"

"All of it."

Leah smiled. "Absolutely. Don't tell Maddy, but you're my favorite person too."

Kaelen's heart hammered in her chest to be the recipient of Leah's intense gaze, at her friend's passionate faith. "Thank you. If you believe in me that much, then as someone who respects your intellect and honesty, I'll believe in myself." Kaelen sighed as she remembered the original topic of conversation. "As for the performance algorithms for human trials, it's exactly as expected based on the differences between human and rat subjects. The size and complexity of the human nervous systems when compared to a standard rat means that it could take more than a year before we see full recovery."

Leah was silent for a minute, staring toward the fireplace. Kaelen remained quiet, knowing Leah would say what was on her mind eventually. "I want to be in on the first trial."

Kaelen had already expected this. Einstein hypothesized that Leah would want to be in either the first or second human trial. "Are you sure? As you are well aware, there is always risk with any medical procedure. The spinal cord damage could be worse than expected when we run baseline scans, or your muscles and other nerves could be so atrophied that it will take significantly longer to see any progress."

"I'm well aware of the risks, and my damaged spinal cord remains the same as it has been for the past eleven years. But I trust you, Kaelen. If you tell me to wait then I will."

Kaelen placed her hand on the back of the couch to rest atop Leah's. "Our science is accurate and safe. I don't want you to get your hopes up when the technology is so slow. It could still take a long time." She contemplated other alternatives. "I wish we had a way to speed the process. If only my Argonian regenerative serum weren't damaged—holy Vos!"

"What?"

"The serum! The regulatory T-cell serum created by lab twelve. It's still in testing, correct?"

Leah nodded slowly. "It was proven to effect repair on nerves and surrounding tissue. However, it is a slower process than NRN. Why?"

"What if we combine the two methods. Inject NRN at the same time as the serum?"

They stared at one another for nearly a minute. Leah frowned. "But what if NRN reads the serum as something to be repaired or eradicated. It would take even longer because the bots would waste their time dealing with the lab twelve serum."

"No, they won't. As long as I have a sample, I can program the nanobots with the chemical structure to treat the serum as friendly. I only need to scan the molecular makeup into the NRN program and tailor the base code."

"You think that will work without serious complications?"

Kaelen's stomach clenched at the thought of any harm coming to Leah. "I would never risk you. Never. I'm not promising this will do anything more than give the NRN a small amount of assistance. But it could, and I want to stress the word could, significantly increase the process."

Leah took a deep breath and slowly released it. "Like I said, I believe in you and I'm willing to try both. And if it still takes a long time to see any measurable results…well, it's a good thing I've got my high-tech mobility and a strong friend around when I need her." She suddenly yawned again, stretching her arms above her head. "Now, I don't know about Argonians who are hopped up on sugar, but the human in the room is well past her bedtime."

"Okay. Thank you for the talk. I appreciate your compassion and understanding."

Leah swung her legs around using her arms and upper body inertia and transferred to the chair. "You never have to thank me for that. It's a pleasure to call you friend." She paused and met Kaelen's gaze with an oddly serious expression. "Actually, I learned a long time ago that life is too short not to be honest with yourself and the people around you. That's why I'm going to tell you now that you're precious to me and I like you the way you are."

Kaelen felt an unfamiliar sensation that she didn't recognize. It was like she'd missed a verbal cue. But the look in Leah's eyes made her feel a strange mix of emotions, and an oddly thrumming pressure in her chest. She swallowed and tried to will the tight feeling away. "Thank you."

"Now, I'm going to bid you good night. You know where everything is in the other suite. You don't need me to hold your hand."

Kaelen stood as Leah began to ascend the stairs. Feeling brave after Leah's admission, she called out, "What if I do?"

Leah turned the hoverchair so she was facing Kaelen with her back toward the stairs and paused her ascent. "What?"

"What if I need you to hold my hand. Would you? I mean…is that something you would like?"

Leah wore an odd expression and her heart raced faster than normal. Kaelen didn't know how to interpret the reaction. She feared she had made Leah uncomfortable. "Never mind. You should go to bed now."

"No. Say what you want to say."

Kaelen sighed. "I don't know how to say what I want."

"Fine. Then ask me again."

"Ask you—oh! What if I need you to hold my hand, would you like that?"

Leah smiled and it was as if the sun shone down from high above. "I would be ecstatic." Kaelen took a step forward but Leah held up her hand. "However, neither one of us has had much sleep and you've gone through a major emotional upheaval today. If you still feel the same way in the morning, you should ask me again."

Kaelen spoke with certainty. "The question won't change."

"Well then…I'll look forward to hearing it in the morning. Good night, Kaelen."

Then she turned and continued up the stairs while Kaelen watched with two parts elation and one part fear.

Kaelen whispered back, "Good night."

• • •

The next morning Leah woke later than normal but it was Sunday and she had no set plans. Maddy texted her about brunch at eleven while they were in Michigan the day before, but she explained that she was out of town and wasn't sure when she'd be back. Leah rubbed the sleep from her eyes and glanced over at the clock, surprised to note it was after nine-thirty. Clearly, she'd been exhausted. She wondered if Kaelen was awake yet, then suddenly remembered the last words spoken between them right before she came upstairs.

"Oh." Leah glanced at the door to her suite and contemplated if the memory was real or a dream. Or worse yet, if the words spoken were simply born of Kaelen's loneliness and insecurity. Lying abed wasn't an option so she decided she may as well find out from the woman herself. If there was one thing she'd learned from the Tucks, it was how to face things head on.

It took Leah half an hour to ready herself for the day. She was dressed casually in a soft MIT hoodie and leggings with her hair pulled back in a French braid. She didn't see Kaelen by the time she went downstairs, and Leah feared her friend had gone back to her own apartment. Then Leah noticed movement out on the balcony. Kaelen stood there in her strange black suit, looking like a goddess.

She took a deep breath and made her way outside. Despite her fears, Leah's worry proved unnecessary. Kaelen turned and stepped directly in front of her.

"Leah Lockheed-Tuck, would you be interested in a courtship with the last scion of Ra?" Kaelen clenched and unclenched her fists as she shifted her weight back and forth on each foot.

Leah smiled and shook her head, then held up a hand when Kaelen frowned. "No, but I would like to pursue a romance with Kaelen Ra-Evon because she is a brilliant scientist, compassionate woman, and my friend."

Kaelen released the breath she'd been holding, and Leah felt the chill of it caress her cheek. "Thank you." Kaelen ducked her head shyly. "I know I don't have much in the way of experience with romance and, technically, you're of a much higher standing here on Earth. Despite all that, I'll try my hardest to make you happy."

"You do make me happy and I didn't fal—grow to care for a status or rank. I grew to care for you. The real question is why you'd be interested in a woman with a disability who may remain this way, despite our best efforts." Leah's heart raced with her near-confession. She also worried about Kaelen's response, unsure if she had considered all the complications involved with a potential relationship.

Kaelen's mouth opened, and then closed again. When she spoke, she was indignant. "Leah! I've often asserted that nothing about you is a detriment. Your injury doesn't determine who you are as a person unless you let it. I was drawn to your mind the moment I read about your company and accomplishments. In addition, I was attracted to you the second you came through the doorway the day of my interview. I may not have realized what it was at first, but I've come to consider you my…what does Nalla call it?"

Leah snickered. "Bestie."

"Yes, my bestie! The success or failure of the nano trial has no bearing on my interest in you. All I want is your happiness, and to be part of that happiness if you let me." She paused and glanced out across the city. When Kaelen turned back, a look of fear had replaced all the other emotions on her expressive face. "But there are other, larger, hurdles between us that have no connection to your injury and everything to do with who I am, an Argonian. I know many if not most humans seek physical intimacy. You and some of your friends have discussed this topic on game nights and I know what you prefer in a relationship."

"If you don't wish to—"

"I do! That's not the problem. The problem is my abilities, my strength. I don't want to hurt anyone, especially not someone I care for the way I do you." She whispered, "I don't want to hurt you, *zhee*."

Leah recognized the word. She'd heard Kaelen whisper it to her before. "Will you tell me what that means?"

Kaelen pursed her lips and shook her head. "Not yet."

Leah let it go. "Why don't we take things slowly? I have my own fears about a physical relationship. I've had a few but clearly none that lasted. I have to be careful who I trust with my heart and my body." Leah paused to think about what more she was willing to admit.

"What is it?"

"I suppose if there was ever a person or time to speak of my own insecurities, it would be with you here and now. I don't have a lot of physical experience myself. I've got my less-than-sexy routines, and to put it bluntly, my sexual response is different from most people. That's not even mentioning the scars from the accident and subsequent surgeries. Taking off my clothing is hard for me because of the way I look."

Kaelen met her gaze. "I think you are beautiful no matter what you're wearing, not wearing, scars, or no scars. Your mind is like no other. I carry your smile right here," Kaelen's hand touched the center of her chest, "and it makes me less afraid on the darkest days. A single hug from you leaves me tingling more than hours under the yellow sun. In case you forgot, I left Argon when I was thirteen. I haven't so much as kissed another person let alone done anything more…involved."

Leah hadn't considered that, and Kaelen made good points. Then her brain caught on the last part and she smiled. "Would you like to kiss someone now, Kaelen?"

"You?"

Leah rolled her eyes and laughed. "Yes, who else would I be referring to? You, darling, are brilliantly stupid sometimes. Then again, Maddy has told me the same thing often enough. I think we deserve each other, hmm?" Her eyes moved to Kaelen's lips without her permission. Leah struggled to control her breathing at the thought of caressing such softness with her own, a fantasy she'd had many times over the past few months.

Kaelen licked her lips and whispered, "Yes. But what if I hurt you?"

Leah lifted her finger and crooked it to indicate Kaelen should come closer. "You can lean in and let me kiss you. Respond in whatever way makes you feel most comfortable, the same as you would when we hug. If I recall, it didn't take you long at all to get good at that."

Kaelen leaned against the hoverchair. Her lips were soft but firm during the short kiss. Leah backed away slightly and opened her eyes almost as if she could sense Kaelen's gaze. They stared at one another intently. Seconds later, Leah kissed her again. The second kiss lasted a lot longer, and Leah coaxed Kaelen's mouth open with her tongue. When their lips parted, Leah wasted no time exploring further.

They eventually pulled apart and Kaelen's gorgeous blue eyes fluttered open as an expression of wonder washed across her face. Leah had been worried she wouldn't like it. Emotions surged within her. Wonder, curiosity, arousal, and fondness. Happiness stole her breath but she found it again to say, "Was that okay?"

"Okay? Kissing is better than ice cream! Is that why Maddy and Tasha always want their alone time?"

"One of the reasons, yes. And it gets so much better…but we'll work up to that."

Kaelen grinned at her and took her hand. "I will work up to whatever you want. Does this mean you are my…uh, girlfriend, partner? Lover? Are we dating? What is the best term for us?"

"Well, we'd have to go on dates to be dating." Leah reached over to caress between Kaelen's brows. "Wrinkle."

"Dating: to interact socially with someone as a romantic couple. We haven't done that."

Leah continued. "We also haven't had sex, or made love as people who are romantically inclined toward one another call it. If you want a monogamous romantic pairing, we could be girlfriends."

"Do you practice monogamy?" Leah nodded. "Good, I want that too. I don't want a courtship with anyone else. Can we tell our friends and the rest of the world? Should I announce that your house has accepted mine and that we are courting?"

Her rapid-fire speech was a lot for anyone to take before coffee and breakfast, but Leah didn't mind in the least. "You're adorable. And, darling, we can tell whomever you want—"

No sooner had she said the words when Kaelen left her side and rushed over to the balcony wall. She yelled out to the city below, "Leah Lockheed-Tuck has accepted Kaelen Ra-Evon as a potential match!"

Leah laughed at her antics but was happy to see the blue eyes twinkling with pleasure when Kaelen turned around again. Of course, she was happy for herself too. Happy and scared. She hadn't let someone close to her in a long time. There were a lot of obstacles for them to overcome to make a relationship work, but Leah had never met anyone like Kaelen before.

"What is it?" She blurred to Leah's side.

Leah's heart eased at the sincere concern. "It's nothing serious, darling. I've just…" She shook her head. "You give me hope for so many things. My best friend has admitted to having feelings for me when I thought my emotions were one-sided. It's like a romance novel come to life. I'm only twenty-four and I'd practically given up ever finding someone who wanted to be with me for the right reasons."

"But now we're girlfriends. Still friends, true, but with the potential for something exponentially greater." Kaelen paused and gently clasped Leah's hand. "I like you more than I can adequately express, but I'll try. The light of Vos was made dim by your brilliance in my life. People who don't understand how precious you are could never be worthy of your heart."

Tears welled up in Leah's eyes at Kaelen's declaration. "I know exactly what you mean and feel the same way." Leah glanced at her watch then back to Kaelen. "Are you hungry—what am I saying? You're always hungry. Maddy invited me to brunch at eleven today, but I told her I might be busy because I didn't know when we'd be back from Zeeland. Why don't I text her and let her know we'll both be there?"

"Since we're officially girlfriends and we'll be interacting socially together over a meal, would this be a date? Our first date?"

Leah considered all the ways she could romance someone she cared about. She could afford nearly anything a heart would desire. Fancy candle-lit dinners, concerts, plays…her thoughts rambled to a halt when she looked up to see Kaelen's joyous face. All that mattered was that they were together and felt something beyond simple friendship.

She didn't need a fancy first date and knew Kaelen well enough that she wouldn't expect something like that. She returned Kaelen's soft smile. "Yes. This would be our first date." Seconds later, she was the recipient of their first kiss initiated by Kaelen. The kiss may have been oh-so gentle, but the weight of it was immense.

Chapter Eleven

Maddy waited until food was in front of them before moving her gaze back and forth between Leah and Kaelen. "You refused to say where you went yesterday, but I put it together so, spill. How was Michigan?" Then she paused and winced. "Oh shit, sorry, Kaelen. I'm guessing if you're here alone you struck out."

Leah gave her a cross look. "How did you even discover where we went anyway?"

"Mom." Maddy stuffed a large bite of omelet in her mouth when Leah looked like she was going to ask another question.

"Of course, she did." Leah put her hand on Kaelen's arm. "Darling, I know it's probably still hard to come to terms with it all. You don't have to explain to anyone if you don't want to." She noticed Maddy's raised eyebrow though her sister didn't say anything. Yet. Leah was reveling in the fact that she was able to touch Kaelen as much as she liked, rather than constantly worry she was sending the wrong signals.

Kaelen sat with a large stack of pancakes in front of her, and she appeared to be torn between answering Maddy, answering Leah, or eating. She grumbled and set down the fork before addressing Maddy. "It's okay. You are part of my Earth family, and I don't mind if you know. We did find the ship and the young boy who came to Earth in it. His Argonian parents were stationed on the orbiting platform and they put him in a pod before it's destruction. His ship navigation system synched with mine but due to a spatial anomaly, he arrived ten years ago."

"Holy shit."

"Michael, his adoptive name, has been living with the Millers this entire time. They were his family and there was no way I could bring him back to Los Angeles. To satisfy my guardian duties as head of *Dolem*-Ra and thus the Thinker Guild, I created a *kuz ashum* between our houses." At Maddy's confused look, Kaelen explained, "You would call it a fostering contract. That will allow him to stay with the Millers until adulthood."

Maddy paused her eating and stared for a moment. Then she moved her hand across the table to grasp Kaelen's and gave it a squeeze. "It must have been hard to leave the last of your people behind with strangers."

"Yes. It was hard but the truth is, Michael is also a stranger. While he may physically be Argonian, he is a child of Earth in both mind and heart. I showed them how to use the AI sent with his ship. He will begin receiving the education of our people from his Tuk. As for the rest… with no more guilds or way to induct into one, he will never be an heir to the House of Xe or a registered adult of Argon. I am the last."

"I'm sorry, hon." Maddy gave the hand another squeeze before retreating to her side of the table. "I wish Tasha could have been here today. She's a lot better at knowing what to say with this stuff."

"Stuff?" Kaelen looked from Maddy to Leah.

Leah rolled her eyes, understanding her sister quite well. "She means feelings. Brilliant though Maddy is, I think she was emotionally stunted at birth."

"Says you."

"Says the girl who met you when she came to live with the Tucks, newly-orphaned." Leah knew she could say it because they'd come to terms with their rocky start ages ago.

Maddy lifted a finger, ready to protest, then put it down again and gave a nod instead. "Okay, fair enough. I was a total asshole back then." She cut off another bite as Kaelen started in on her pancakes.

Leah noticed her eating significantly faster than a normal person and put her hand beneath the table to rub Kaelen's firm thigh. Her new girlfriend tensed, then choked at the caress, but managed to slow her eating once she recovered. It wasn't that no other aliens or Chromodecs existed in the world. But Kaelen was adamant about hiding how special she was from the general populace and Leah respected her wishes.

Kaelen suddenly looked at her and smiled when they locked eyes.

"Is this acceptable?"

Leah knew exactly what she meant and felt an upspring of emotion. Sweet Kaelen was worried that it wasn't a good enough first date for courting when, little did she know, Leah would have been happy to sit through a courtroom deposition as long as it were Kaelen by her side. She leaned over and kissed Kaelen on the cheek, then took her hand, keeping them clasped together above the table. "It's perfect, darling." She knew exactly what she was doing and mentally counted the seconds in her head until—

A fork clanked across the table and Maddy interrupted their private communication. "Okay, you two…what's going on?" She pointed at their hands, then at Kaelen's cheek.

Kaelen answered for the both of them, proudly proclaiming, "This is our first date. The House of Lockheed has accepted *Dolem*-Ra as a potential match."

Maddy gaped at them. "Really?"

Leah studied her sister carefully. "Yes, really."

"Is—" Kaelen turned to Leah, then looked back at Maddy. "I don't know Earth protocol. Were we supposed to consult with your family first?" She turned a worried gaze toward Maddy. "Is this okay with you?"

"Okay with me?" Maddy's voice rose on the last syllable.

"Do you have something to say, Maddy?" Leah wasn't sure how Maddy felt about Kaelen in regards to that sort of relationship. She'd only spoken with Ellie about her feelings for Kaelen on a few occasions. Ellie was supportive but Maddy had always been a bit overprotective. A lot overprotective.

She shouldn't have worried. Maddy snorted and grinned. "The only thing I have to say is it's about time! We were all—whoops, ignore that last part." She abruptly pressed her lips together.

Leah narrowed her eyes at her sister. "Who is we, and what were you all doing?"

"Uh, we as in the entire found family, as Kaelen calls us. We've been watching you two pining for each other separately for months. Nalla was going to take drastic measures. She said she even spoke with you about it, Kaelen."

Kaelen's brows wrinkled with worry or confusion, and Leah wanted to reach across the space between them and smooth it. "Nalla did speak with me. We had a strange conversation about Leah. But she told me to make a move and I was confused. I thought she liked me and I've grown fond of Los Angeles so I didn't take her advice."

Maddy burst out laughing and Leah bit her bottom lip so she didn't do the same. Maddy got control of her mirth to explain. "She was telling you to make a move— uh, ask Leah out on a date. You'd been going nowhere in regards to a relationship, so in that context make a move was not about moving away, but about—"

"Active pursuit of romantic connection."

"Uh, yeah. That."

Leah took a sip of her cooling coffee. "So is Mom in on this too?"

"Who do you think started the betting—shit, this is why Tasha doesn't let me leave the house by myself."

"Betting pool! Madison Shiloh Tuck, you better not have a spreadsheet going about when we would get together. You know I'm not a fan of that level of scrutiny on my private romantic life. I'm pretty sure you learned the hard way that speculation leads to hurt feelings, right?"

Maddy held up her hands. "Yeah, sure. I remember. And for the record, I don't have a spreadsheet." She muttered beneath her breath, too quiet for Leah to hear.

Kaelen quickly tattled. "She said that Nalla has the spreadsheet."

Leah pointed at her big sister. "You better not spill the details to everyone until we can tell them together."

"Of course not." She smirked. "Now, who asked who first?"

Kaelen grinned. "I confessed my feelings last night, but Leah told me to wait a day and ask again in the morning when I'd had sufficient sleep. She was concerned that my interest could be mistaken for emotional overload. We agreed to be girlfriends this morning before meeting you." Kaelen suddenly realized that Maddy had begun texting during her happy explanation and Leah watched with glee as she narrowed her eyes. "Excuse me, Maddy, but did you ignore what Leah said sixty seconds ago?"

Maddy abruptly stopped texting. "Uh, what did she say?"

"Hey, Kaelen," Kaelen turned her gaze to Leah. "Since we are courting, and Maddy is my sister, would you like to let her in on the pinky swear?" Beneath her breath, where she knew Maddy wouldn't hear, she added, "We can mess with Maddy a bit if you tell her your secret. Is there something discrete you can do that would seem intimidating to an ordinary human?"

"Hey, what are you mumbling over there?" Kaelen nodded and Maddy said, "What pinky swear?"

"You remember when we were kids? Every time we told each other a secret we'd pinky swear on it."

"Yes."

"I have a secret I shared with Leah and she pinky swore that she wouldn't tell another without my permission. I like you, Maddy and I think you are safe to share this with." Kaelen paused. "I think Ellie would be acceptable too."

Maddy leaned forward. "So, what is this secret?"

"First you must swear." Kaelen held up her hand, with the pinky raised.

Maddy groaned but curled her pinky around Kaelen's. "Fine. I swear not to tell anyone about your secret unless you give me permission."

"Thank you. I'm not like ordinary humans."

Maddy snorted. "No shit."

"I have powers that are beyond anything else on this planet."

"What?" She glanced at Leah, who nodded. "How is that even possible when Earth is full of Chromodecs and aliens already?"

Kaelen carefully reached across the table to pick up Maddy's butter knife. She rolled the thick metal utensil until it resembled a silver cinnamon roll and placed it on the table again with a thunk.

"Uh…"

"I also have extranormal hearing, as you already know, and…many other powers."

Leah added, "She has x-ray vision, oh, and she's very protective of me too." She narrowed her eyes at Maddy. "Very protective. Even more than you."

Maddy looked as though she were torn between fascination and intimidation. Her gaze darted from the knife, to Kaelen, then down to where Leah and Kaelen's hands were once again clasped together on the table. She swallowed and looked up at Kaelen. "Really?" Kaelen nodded. "Which arm did I break as a child? There will be a bump where the—"

"Bone fused together. Yes, I can see it clearly on your left humorous, above the elbow joint. That must have hurt immensely."

"Holy shit! Oh, and yes it did. Have you ever broken anything? I see the scar next to your eyebrow."

Kaelen closed her eyes, perhaps to bring up the memory of the event. "I fell during a science expedition to Thanjee when I was ten. We weren't near any of the shuttles, so it healed for a week with only basic medical aid. My father offered to have it repaired with a regenerative serum when we returned to Argon, but I liked the reminder of the trip so I kept it."

Maddy nodded. "Given how careful you are around everyone, I doubt you've so much as stubbed a toe here on Earth."

"Actually, I can't be injured on Earth."

Maddy sprayed a mouthful of water to the side. Luckily there was nobody nearby when she did it. "What?"

Leah smirked to see her so rattled, though honestly, she didn't know that particular detail about Kaelen either. "What about the Argonian regenerative serum?"

Kaelen conceded, "That's only because it absorbed galactic cosmic radiation and the two flasks were the last in existence." She paused and added, "I'm also susceptible to high decibel sound because of my enhanced hearing. Regarding the rest, Wex says I have a nearfield of invulnerability. I'm also extremely strong." She pointed at the butter knife. "That is the real reason I'm so careful. I don't want to accidentally hurt anyone."

"Oh, fuck. I'm sorry Kaelen," Maddy said. Leah could see the wheels turning in Maddy's head. "That must be hard."

"It is, but I enjoy the hugs others give me. A lot."

A loud scraping sound echoed through The Bean Bag as Maddy slid her chair back. She circled the table and threw her arms around Kaelen. "Welcome to the family, kid. You can always count on a Tuck to dole out hugs."

Kaelen's eyes fluttered shut and Leah's heart swelled to see it. That was the sister she'd grown to love over the years. "Thanks, Maddy.

You're the best."

Maddy straightened again and returned to her seat. She gave Leah finger guns. "I know." Leah rolled her eyes but delighted that the news had gone so well.

The following Monday, near mid-morning, Leah, Einstein, Kaelen, and Ellie were all downstairs in the SPL. Because of the experimental and somewhat invasive nature of the nerve regeneration nanobots, or NRN as they'd been calling them, and the emotional damage it could cause if they failed, Leah made an executive decision to be the first person injected during the phase one trial. She reasoned that as soon as they began to see results, they'd go forward with the rest of the vetted volunteers.

"Honey, are you sure about this? No matter what previous tests have shown, the human immune system may react differently with the NRN."

"Yes, I know and I'm absolutely sure that this first needs to be me. I've already explained about the emotional risks and depression associated with giving false hope to people who expect full recovery—"

"But aren't you also someone who would risk depression? If this doesn't work on a larger scale…I would hate to see my friend suffer." Einstein was lining up the syringes they'd use for the injections when he interrupted Leah's explanation.

Leah turned to Kaelen, who was checking the controller program one last time. "Kaelen?"

Kaelen was listening to the conversation but wanted to make sure everything was perfect for the test. She looked up to see the other three watching her. "Yes, *zhee*?"

"You've been on the program for nearly a year with us and I trust you implicitly. Will this work?"

Kaelen met the gaze of each one, then nodded. "This will work," she held up her hand to forestall any other comments, "but, I must caution you all that full success could take much longer than it did with the rats, even with the additional lab twelve serum injection. It will take at least a week before we can establish an estimated timeline of repair and recovery."

"See," Leah waved toward Kaelen and smiled triumphantly. "she says it will work but we can't prove it to the world unless someone is fully recovered. I'm ready." She shrugged and gave them all a wry grin. "If for some reason it doesn't work, I've had plenty of therapy for dealing with depression."

Ellie conceded. "Okay. Let's position you on the table."

They'd done one final round of tests and thorough scans first thing that morning. They had a baseline before starting phase one. The two injections didn't take long but they were painful. Kaelen snapped the stylus she'd been holding when Leah gritted her teeth through the discomfort. Einstein carefully removed the tablet from her other hand.

Leah was on her stomach because they determined the injections would work fastest if done at the last point of sensation, closest to the original injury. There wasn't much else to do afterward except go about their day.

Ellie fussed over Leah once she was fully dressed and back in her chair. "Remember to log your stats every two hours during the day, as well as right before sleep and right after waking. If you feel anything out of the ordinary, even if you think you ate some bad pot stickers—"

"There's no such thing." Leah was adamant about her favorite food.

"Then I want you to log it and call me for a more thorough physical."

Leah sighed. "Yes, Ellie. I promise you'll be the first to know. Well, actually, Kaelen will probably be the first to know, but you'll be a close second."

Ellie smiled fondly at her. Kaelen always appreciated the interaction between the two women. It was different from what she'd shared with her own mother. She loved Clovi Ze-Est a lot, but she was much less approachable. Kaelen was never sure if that's why she spent so much time with her father, or if following in his footsteps is what pushed her mother away. It was a question she'd never learn the answer to.

"Are you sure you still want to fly to New York the week after next? You know I can lead the shareholder meeting in your stead if you like. We'll tell them you're under the weather."

Leah scoffed. "And let those pompous old vultures speculate that I'm suddenly unable to perform my duties? I don't think so. Jenna scheduled the smallest company jet for that Monday night, the other one is already booked. I'll send you the finalized itinerary and flight plan when I get back upstairs."

One of the many things Kaelen admired about Leah was her drive and brilliance. But she knew that Leah's intense focus on work wasn't always a positive or healthy one. They'd shared many conversations and Leah admitted one evening that she constantly felt the need to prove herself, to show the board, the investors, and the world, that she could do anything regardless of whether or not she had a disability. Unfortunately, she was prone to overworking herself when there was a problem to be solved.

"Leah," Kaelen said. Ellie had already gone back to her office and Einstein ran upstairs in search of sustenance for his organics, so they were alone in the lab.

"You better not lecture me either. I won't push myself, but I'm also not going to wrap my body in cotton while I wait for results."

Kaelen moved so she was next to Leah. "I was merely going to request permission to listen to your heartbeat as an added measure of monitoring while you participate in the trial. However, I'm aware that you may not appreciate such an invasion of privacy."

Leah tilted her head and stared back at her. Kaelen wasn't sure if she should have made the request. She'd taken out the communicators the previous week. Instead of always having Wex's voice in her ears, she created a custom app for her smart phone that would allow her to stay in contact with the AI. Wex offered to reprogram the entire device to run more efficiently, and Kaelen agreed for the sake of expediency.

"And if I asked you not to?"

Kaelen frowned at the question. "I would obey to the best of my abilities. We've spoken before about times when your heart races and something in my automatic reflex tunes in. It's not intentional but I think a part of me is reassured by your heartbeat and instinctively listens anyway."

"I appreciate your honesty. I don't feel comfortable at this time having you consciously monitoring my heart rate. I'll simply trust in your instincts, you know, in case something bad happens."

Kaelen was disappointed but she also understood about autonomy and privacy. "Fair enough. To broach another subject, how long will you and Ellie be in New York?"

Leah looked at her watch then nodded toward the door. "Why don't you follow me up to my office and we can order lunch. Do you need to log out of the workstation or clean up first?"

"The workstation logs out automatically after ten minutes and all the syringes are empty. I'll drop them in the biowaste receptacle on the way out."

Kaelen watched as Leah texted Jenna to call in their usual order as they rode the elevator up to the top floor. Back in her office, Leah logged in to her own computer. "I'm going to send the itinerary for the trip to Ellie then I want to show you something."

"Okay."

Three minutes and a few clicks of the mouse later, the large screen on one wall of Leah's office powered on and displayed a set of prototype designs. Kaelen moved closer to the screen, taking in all the parts. "Is this the desalinization machine that you were telling me about on the way to Zeeland?"

"It is."

"But we still need to work out the power and battery efficiency, correct?"

"Yes. I'm going to email the designs for our most current solar arrays and electric batteries later today. While we are waiting for results on the NRN, I want you and Einstein to look into the next project. If you'd rather focus on one side or the other, I can always assign half the project to lab ten, they're wrapping up the underwater breather and sending it off to R&D for mass-market testing."

"Lab ten!" Kaelen sneered. "Einstein says lab ten is full of unevolved fungus and not fit to design paper bags."

Leah burst into laughter. "Oh, come on. Do you think Lockheed would employ minds like that? Einstein has been biased against lab ten since the donut incident."

Kaelen was unsure why such a delicious treat would embitter her friend against an entire lab of scientists. "Donuts?"

"Yes. I think it was about two years ago. Einstein's motorcycle was in the shop for a few weeks. Nalla gave him a ride to and from work each day. On the second day of her waiting down in the lobby for him, one of the engineers from lab ten, Chad Gant, decided to bring the pretty woman a donut and ask her out on a date. He had no idea that she and Einstein were a couple."

"She didn't agree to the date, did she?"

"Of course not. But Einstein was pretty irritated when he found out that night. He went up to lab ten and challenged Chad to a duel of wits for his disrespect. He set it for first thing the next morning. Chad agreed and said Nalla was a beautiful woman who deserved better than some 'sparkly robotic freak' which obviously didn't set well with our friend, Mister Trog. If I remember correctly, they called lab eight down to bring the most difficult questions they could think of, as well as moderate."

Kaelen raised her brows with disbelief. "Clevna Trog is a twelfth caliber intellect. It wouldn't be a fair contest in any capacity. Nor is it polite to ridicule someone for their physical makeup or atypical mannerisms."

"Yes, well, in the end none of it mattered. Chad didn't know that Einstein was an alien android. He was calling names based on rumors he'd heard. He lost the challenge so badly that he actually grabbed one of the laptops nearby and hurled it across the lab."

"What? Surely that level of volatility wouldn't go unpunished."

"Of course, it didn't. He was fired immediately. Last I heard, he went to work for Guardian Technologies."

Kaelen scoffed. "I had Wex research that company. It was less than reputable."

"That's one word for Donald Guardian."

"Hmm, may I use your desk phone?" Leah gave her a curious look but waved Kaelen toward it. Kaelen hit the button for speaker phone and dialed the SPL.

"SPL, Clevna Trog speaking."

"Hi, Einstein. Leah and I are discussing her desalinization project. Do we want to work on improving the battery, or increasing the solar power efficiency?"

"Curious. Could we not work on both? I believe that in this instance, we have an advantage between our two cultures. Donbothians are known for mobile power storage and Argon used a lot of sun-based energy. It stands to reason that if your people can make solar power efficient and workable with such a low energy red sun, you could do wonders with our yellow one."

Leah tapped the desktop with a single manicured nail. "You make an excellent point. I told Kaelen I'd send the rudimentary schematics down to SPL. I want you to split the project. Einstein, you see if you can improve battery storage. Kaelen, I want you to look into more efficient solar conversion."

While Einstein wasn't particularly emotional, nearly the opposite of Nalla or even Maddy, Kaelen had learned the inflections in his voice after nearly a year of working together and could tell he was excited about this next project. "Stellar! I shall look forward to your email after lunch." He hung up before Kaelen or Leah could say any more.

Leah turned her gaze toward Kaelen and smirked. "What should we do with ourselves while we wait for the food to arrive, hmm?"

On one hand, Leah's words indicated a wish for further work. On the other hand, her expression and overall demeanor led Kaelen to believe she was seeking less serious pursuits until the Thai Guys delivery arrived. Instead of assuming one way or another, Kaelen had learned that it was always best to ask. "What would you like to do?"

"I would like to go out on the balcony with my girlfriend." She pointed toward the reinforced glass doors leading to a large, enclosed space very similar to the one she had at her home. "Then I'd like to kiss her while enjoying the beautiful day."

Kaelen grinned. "I would never say no to kisses."

"Really? Any kisses, any time?"

Leah's words filled her with doubt about her inflexible declaration. "Uh…"

"Any place?"

Kaelen swallowed. "Perhaps I spoke too soon. What I meant to say is that under normal circumstances and in the place of our choosing, I would never turn down kisses from you specifically."

Leah smirked. "Better answer. Let's go kill some time."

Even thinking about kissing her love made Kaelen's heart race and stomach flutter. She suspected that her reactions were hard to control because they were tied to emotions. When it came to Leah Lockheed-

Tuck, her feelings were like a tidal wave battering her heart. "As you wish, *zhee*."

"Mmm hmm. Come along, darling." Then Leah backed away from the desk and zipped over to the balcony door, clearly expecting Kaelen to follow.

Chapter Twelve

By the end of the week, everyone was tired but elated. Leah hosted another game night at her penthouse, promising plenty to eat and a new game. Kaelen was the first to arrive but frowned when the elevator doors opened and she didn't smell any food. "You promised we would have pizza. Is the delivery late?"

"You're early, give it a little more time." Leah moved back so Kaelen could exit the car into the penthouse proper. Then she tapped her lips, giving Kaelen a little pout. Kaelen was happy to oblige since kissing Leah was her new favorite activity.

They pulled apart and she felt that familiar flutter in her stomach. It was as though she had butterflies trapped inside her, similar to the one she'd first seen the day she landed on Earth. Kaelen had studied many sources of Earth and Argonian data on the subject of attraction and sexuality since they began dating. None of them accurately described what it was like for Leah to caress her neck while they kissed, or the insistent tingling she experienced in all her erogenous zones.

When Kaelen informed Wex that she and Leah were courting, the AI warned her to be wary of making close alliances with humans without verifying their worthiness. In response, Kaelen tasked Wex to look up all past data about Leah Lockheed-Tuck, including her work, her inventions, the charities, and every other contribution the brilliant woman had made to the world. It took less than twenty-four hours for Wex to come back with a determination that Leah Lockheed-Tuck of Earth was indeed worthy of *Dolem*-Ra.

One cloud in Kaelen's sky was the fear she felt whenever they kissed or caressed each other for too long. The feelings invoked were both wonderful and nerve-wracking. Unfortunately, Kaelen was always the one to end their make out sessions because she was still afraid of what could happen if she forgot herself in a moment of pleasure. She grew more confident by the day, but it was a slow process.

Rather than dwell on things they couldn't change in that moment, Kaelen took note of Leah's flushed cheeks and beautiful smile as the other woman's eyes fluttered open. "What is the new game?"

Leah gestured for Kaelen to follow her down the hall to the game room. Leah's cell rang before they could go more than a few feet.

"Yes? Okay, send her up." She hung up and looked at Kaelen. "Want to help me set up the pizza? The delivery person is heading up." Kaelen nodded and followed when Leah spun around and made her way back down the hall.

There was an accent table next to the elevator doors and Leah removed a wallet containing an abundance of spare cash that she used specifically to tip for food delivery. Leah was rich by Earth standards but she wasn't greedy. She appeared to enjoy giving back to the community in a variety of ways. Leah glanced at Kaelen and bypassed the smaller bills to remove a fifty.

Kaelen looked at her with surprise. "How much did you order?"

Leah took out another fifty. "We've got a few extra people coming tonight. You remember Devon, Tasha's brother." Kaelen nodded. "He's back in town after traveling through Thailand on a photography trip. Gabe Murphy, he's a friend of ours that used to work for Lockheed and was actually poached by the Los Angeles division of the CORP."

"He left Lockheed on purpose?"

Leah rolled her eyes. "I know, right? Gabe though, he's brilliant and innovative, as well as a hacker. He wanted something a little more challenging and when my adopted dad's old boss approached him to become an agent, well…Gabe couldn't turn down the opportunity to be a badass and a tech geek."

Kaelen contemplated the information that Leah had given her. They'd spoken about the CORP before, and she'd already witnessed the agents in action the night of the Chromodec attack. She was also conscious of the warning Leah and Dan had given her about the illegality of vigilantism. "Will Ana be here?"

"She's got a date tonight. That woman is perpetually looking for mister or misses right."

"Who—?"

The elevator dinged before Kaelen could finish her question. The doors slid open to reveal an androgynous young woman sporting purple hair and combat boots that clashed with her company polo shirt. She carried a massive stack of boxes in her arms that were over her head. Kaelen rushed forward faster than wise and quickly relieved her of the boxes. She recognized the woman that had been the delivery person on a few of their game nights. "Hi, Tay. Thanks for bringing these up. I'm starving!"

"Anytime, that's my job, right?" Once unloaded of the delivery, she wiped her forehead with her sleeve. "Whew, thanks! Are you feeding an army tonight or what? That's more than you normally get."

"No armies, merely a few extra people and my girlfriend, the bottomless pit." Leah pointed her thumb toward Kaelen over her shoulder.

Tay grinned at Leah, then Kaelen. "Congrats. I'm pretty sure you called her your friend the last time I was here."

Leah nodded. "I did. I'm surprised you remembered."

Tay blushed. "Yeah, well you two are in the local gossip mags a lot." Leah frowned but Tay kept going. "Not that I like that stuff but I gotta admit that me and my friends talk about it cuz we don't have a lot of high-profile role models, you know? We've been shipping you pretty hard."

Kaelen had no idea what Tay meant about shipping but Leah nodded. "Yeah, I know exactly what you mean. We could definitely use more LGBTQIA plus representation on TV, in business, and just…across the board really."

"Anyway, we took a vote, me and my friends and all the people at Coast Pizza."

"A vote?" Kaelen looked at her curiously.

Tay nodded. "We all decided that you two look cute together and everyone else should go fu—uh, leave you alone."

Leah snickered but Kaelen was confused. "We are the topic of conversation amongst your friends and coworkers?"

"Darling," Leah took Kaelen's hand to pull her closer. "I'm rich-famous. Remember the photographer after dinner that night? That was the first time we made the gossip section."

Kaelen frowned. "You never told me."

"Because I don't care about them. Yes, I value my privacy, but I value you more. I'm sure plenty of people have opinions about me, whom I'm seen with, and any number of other things that I consider part of my private life. I've always hated the attention, but," she gave Tay a smile, "if my being in the spotlight with someone I care for can inspire people to be true to themselves, then I suppose I'm okay with it."

Tay beamed at them both. "Yeah, you're super cool. Oh, and I forgot to tell you that my friends and I also have game nights, though they're usually during the week when none of us is working. Anyway, if you like cooperative games, you should try Pandemic."

Leah had already paid for the pizzas online. When she handed over one hundred dollars as Tay's tip, her eyes widened comically. "I'll keep that in mind. We're always looking for new games."

Tay focused on the bills. She suddenly straightened and swallowed before meeting Leah's eyes. "I'm sorry Miss Lockheed-Tuck, but this is too much."

"Nonsense. If you feel that badly about it, you can buy your friends pizza the next time you have your own game night."

Kaelen chimed in, "Or pot stickers! Those are the best."

"Thai Guys, right? Now that is the place I should have applied for. I would love a discount at Thai Guys."

"Food is discounted if you work at Thai Guys?" Leah and Tay both nodded. "Does that apply to all food places?"

Tay shrugged. "Usually. It's a perk for having such a low paying job. Though honestly, I deliver so much I rarely want to look at pizza, let alone eat it."

Kaelen smiled at Leah, amazed at the new information. "You mean I could work for my favorite restaurant and pay less for the food?"

"You're a scientist, Kaelen." Kaelen nodded at Leah's matter of fact observation. "You're a very good scientist."

"Yes, but I would be a great delivery person. I'm extremely fast."

Leah covered her eyes and shook her head, even as Tay giggled. "But, darling, you would do the world a disservice if you weren't a scientist anymore. Your mind is best suited to that which you're already doing."

Kaelen considered the statement, her mind wandering back to the night she helped the woman with her sun-given powers. But she knew that wasn't her greatest contribution to humanity. "Hmm, you make an excellent point. I suppose I will need to keep paying full price for my food deliveries."

"You two are the cutest. Wait 'til I tell my friends— uh, can I talk to my friends about this Miss Lockheed-Tuck?"

"You can call me Leah, and sure, why not. HR is always telling me I need to be more open and approachable."

Tay grinned. "Seriously though, you folks are dope." Kaelen heard a buzzing sound and Tay pulled a cell phone from her pocket. "Oh, shoot. I gotta get back to the shop. Thanks again, Miss—uh, Leah." She moved her gaze toward Kaelen. "Can I call you Kaelen too?"

Kaelen smiled, finding the younger woman's grin particularly infectious. "I would like that."

"Done! Catch you on the flip side, or the next game night. Have fun." Tay waved and stepped into the elevator, presumably to return for her next delivery.

Kaelen looked from the closed elevator doors to Leah. "She was… vivacious. And I suspect an alien."

"Really? How do you know that?"

"She had little tufts at the tips of her ears, mostly covered by the purple hair. Her pulse was twenty percent faster than that of average humans, and she had a nictating membrane that occasionally covered her eyes. To be fair, you wouldn't have noticed because it moved faster than humans are capable of seeing." Kaelen shrugged. "I didn't even notice it until today. This is the first time Tay has said more than a few words to us."

"Fascinating."

Even though Kaelen was hungry, she wanted to see the new game that Leah mentioned earlier. "What is the new game called?"

Leah looked from Kaelen to the tower of pizza boxes, then back again. "Will your stomach hold out for five minutes?"

"My stomach is not the master of my actions." A sudden, loud, growl followed Kaelen's declaration and she winced. "Maybe only five minutes, no more."

"Done." Leah and Kaelen moved side-by-side down the hall. "I discovered it after you told me how much you like to draw."

"Is it an art game, like Pictionary?"

"Something like that. It's called Telestrations."

Kaelen grew excited at the prospect of a new challenge that involved drawing, a skill she discovered only after landing on Earth. "I look forward to learning."

A few hours later, most of the partiers had stuffed themselves with pizza and all but Kaelen held an alcoholic drink in their hand. Maddy had already collected money from everyone for the bet, which annoyed Leah to no end. She called her on it in front of the group.

"What, so you won the bet on when we would get together? I can't believe you'd do something like that to your own sister." Leah pointed at her. "I'm telling Ellie."

Everyone burst into laughter and Kaelen frowned, unhappy that their friends appeared to be laughing at her beloved. "What's so funny?"

Leah quickly covered Kaelen's fist where it rested over her thigh and Kaelen relaxed. She looked around the group. "Yes, care to let us in on the little joke?"

"Uh, Leah…" Gabe covered his face with his hands and peeked at them from between his fingers. "Please don't shoot the messenger! But you haven't seen the spreadsheet, have you?"

"No." Leah narrowed her eyes and glared at Maddy. "Why?"

"Well, the truth is…Ellie actually came the closest and won. Ana was in second place."

"Are you kidding me?"

Kaelen merely patted the top of Leah's hand. "I like Ellie. She is worthy of winning, unlike the rest of our friends. They are duplicitous and meddlesome."

"Duplic—meddlesome—what kind of language is that? Who are you and what have you done with our friend? I've been training you so hard in Earth slang, young Padawan." Nalla pointed a finger at her.

Kaelen had no idea what a padawan was.

Einstein took a drink from his glass and raised a single eyebrow. "I don't know, I found her words to be perfectly acceptable."

He was an excellent scientist but also a true comrade. "Thank you. As for where I got the phrase, it was Einstein himself who said it two days ago when we were discussing the man running for mayor of Los Angeles."

Nalla snorted. "Of course, he did."

Tasha curled her lip with disgust. "Trent Davidson. Ugh, he's the worst one of all the candidates."

Gabe waved his hand to get their attention. "Garen says they're running a trace on his campaign funds. But even if that turns up nil, they've got a lot of back-alley chatter about some of his campaign methods. Spoiler, they're less than above board." He turned to Leah. "Speaking of the CORP, they've had a net around Lockheed and this building but your attacker hasn't returned. I tracked the initial energy signal until it changed that night. Then I tracked the new one, and the signature disappeared entirely. Garen's conclusion is that the woman is either a Chromodec with a rare multiple power signature, or an alien species that we've never seen before."

"Garen. Is that the head of Los Angeles's CORP and your boss?"

Leah turned to Kaelen, then tilted her head back slightly. "Oh, that's right, I forgot that this is your first night meeting Gabe. Yes, Agent Garen Grath is in charge of the CORP here, and the one that recruited Gabe."

"He occasionally does field work but wouldn't have come out for something like the Chromodec that attacked your van on the west side of town last weekend."

"What the hell are you all talking about? Someone attacked Leah?" Maddy stood from her chair, bristling with an odd mix of anger and dismay.

Leah slumped a bit. "I'm sorry, Maddy. I honestly forgot about it because of other stuff that happened right after that."

"What kind of other stuff," Maddy made quotes with her fingers, "makes you forget about an assassination attempt?"

"Kaelen admitting her feelings for me and our first kiss. Need I go on?"

The room was tense, with everyone watching the exchange between the sisters. Maddy blew out a breath and crossed the space between them in three strides. She pulled Leah into a hug. "Please tell us about these things in the future, okay? I worry about you."

"Maddy, you know this stuff happens on occasion. Ellie didn't even mention the incidents that she dealt with until we were both over eighteen. I've got security, and the CORP is on top of all the folks with power. I'll be all right. Garen runs a tight ship over there. I mean, he keeps Gabe in line."

"Fine." Maddy resumed her seat, then took a drink and addressed no one in particular. "You know, Garen also tried to recruit me for the CORP, two years into medical school."

Leah's mouth dropped open, but Tasha beat her to the punch. "Babe, you never told me that."

"Yeah, well, obviously it didn't happen. I think it was right after the previous SAIC, Lingua, retired."

"Who is Lingua?" Kaelen asked. All the names were a bit confusing, but especially in regards to their CORP. Leah explained that CORP agents had multiple, their real name and their codename for when they were active.

Gabe excitedly answered Kaelen's question. "Sara King, or Lingua, was the previous special agent in charge of LA. The city was sad to see her go since she was one of the main heroes that helped end the Chromodec uprising. But she's also one of the few humans within the CORP so I suppose us regular folks gotta slow down eventually." He sighed dreamily and Nalla punched his shoulder.

"Don't mind Gabe, he's a total fanboy. I have no idea how he's able to do any work the way he drools over the field agents."

"Puhlease! Have you seen the mag twins in their suits?" The entire group laughed, with the exception of Kaelen. She didn't know the local heroes like everyone else did so had no opinion about how they looked in their suits.

Maddy raised her voice to finish what she was saying over the trailing laughter. "Anyway, Jove apparently looked up Dad's records which led to me and my ASVAB scores. It wasn't the first time the government tried to recruit me but it was the last. I was dead set on being a doctor and helping the community, so I didn't see a reason to join some shadowy government organization filled with hackers and heroes."

"Hey," Gabe protested. "I resemble that comment." Chuckles went around the group and he turned to Kaelen. "Garen is an alien from a planet in the Proxima Centauri system and goes by the codename Jove. You may recognize that name from the news."

Nalla coughed and muttered, "A bit of an egotistical name if you ask me."

"Jove is familiar from the television. I find it enlightening the way so many heroes and agencies work to protect the people of Earth. It's inspiring."

Leah smiled at her. "Is this what you want to do now? What happened to delivering for Thai Guys?"

"What?" The group began talking at once, asking for Kaelen or Leah to explain the comment.

Kaelen huffed. "I don't want to work for Thai Guys. I was merely speculating about the convenience of receiving a discount for the food of any place you're employed."

Devon tipped up his beer bottle to finish it off, then set it on a coaster. "I mean, I can see your point, Kaelen. But you'd have to eat out a whole lot to make it worth the salary cut." Everyone laughed since they all knew how much Lockheed paid, which was well above market standard. "How much do you actually eat out?"

Maddy muttered, "soon to be a lot more," beneath her breath but Kaelen had no idea how to interpret the obviously private statement. Instead, she answered Devon's question. "Every day, why?"

Gabe leaned forward in his chair. "Like, lunch? Or do you sometimes order dinner?"

Kaelen looked back and forth between the two men. "All the days, all the meals. Unless Leah cooks for me. I don't know how to put Earth foods together, nor do I have an interest in learning."

"Wow, okay. I see why you're interested in an employee discount."

Gabe gasped. "Wait, Earth foods. You're an alien?"

Nalla snorted, "Dude, you're so clueless."

"Gabe." Leah's voice was a low warning."

He glanced at her and swallowed. "How does someone with a body like that survive solely on takeout?"

"Gabe! You're such an idiot." Nalla threw a pretzel at his head because Leah had already admitted to everyone that they were dating.

He held up his hands. "Sorry, I wasn't looking, I swear! But damn, girl."

Leah turned to Kaelen. "Darling, as long as you keep working in the SPL, I'll buy all your meals."

Einstein lifted a single finger. "Question: does that offer stand for everyone currently working in the SPL?"

Nalla swatted him on the head with a pillow. "She's not dating you!"

"You seem full of violence tonight but," Nalla glared and aimed a throw pillow at her boyfriend, and he rushed to finish his statement, "you also have a good point. I see now why the offer was made."

Kaelen felt a wash of warmth flow through her at the thought that Leah cared so much about her well-being. "I could never leave you. We do good work together and will only improve the longer we have."

"We do, don't we?" Leah smirked at her and someone yelled, "kiss already" from their circle of friends. Kaelen wasn't sure who it was because she was too busy gazing into Leah's eyes.

"Should we give them what they want?" Leah licked her lips and Kaelen wasn't going to wait for a second offer.

"Eww, gross! That's my sister, Ra-Evon!"

Nalla was a little more supportive. "Yeah, get it girl!"

No sooner had they begun to kiss when Leah stiffened and Kaelen heard her heart racing. She immediately pulled away. "What is it?"

Leah spoke through gritted teeth. "Pain in my lower back. Not something I've felt before."

Maddy rushed around the table. "Where does it hurt? Have you done anything to exacerbate the old injury?"

"She received the trial injections on Monday. Perhaps this is a side effect?"

"Trial injections?" Maddy gave Einstein a piercing look. "She's taking part in the study on your nanobots?"

"Lockheed International's nanobots and yes, though the study was expanded to include the nerve regeneration serum in addition to the NRN. Kaelen suggested that they could work significantly faster in combination, and medical data from the first round of testing indicated the same. Ellie gave Leah the injections on Monday." Einstein squatted down on the opposite side of Leah's hoverchair, across from Kaelen, while Maddy knelt in front of Leah.

"*Nnngh*! This is worse than the shots!" Leah writhed a bit in her chair. She gasped then suddenly exhaled in relief.

Kaelen exhaled with her and addressed Maddy. "The pain has stopped."

"How do you know?"

"Her heart rate has slowed and the muscle fibers throughout her body are unclenched."

Leah scowled as she opened her eyes. "I'm right here. You could ask me."

"Sorry, sis. How are you feeling now?"

"The pain is gone so, significantly better. That was unexpected and unpleasant."

Maddy looked between Einstein and Kaelen with concern then focused on Leah. "Can you describe the pain?"

"It started as an ache that quickly turned into a cramp. Then it was a sharp pain that lasted a few seconds before it disappeared."

"We should get you to the lab."

"We should get you to the hospital."

Einstein and Maddy spoke at the same time, then looked at each other. Kaelen ignored them and gently grasped Leah's wrist. "What would you like to do? Should we call Ellie?"

Leah shook her head. "She's home for the night in Sello Bay and I don't want to bother her." She held up a hand to forestall whatever Maddy had taken a deep breath to say. "The pain is gone now. If it comes back, I'll call her and come in for testing." She met Kaelen's gaze from a few inches away. "What do you think happened? Is this a setback?"

Somewhere in the background, Kaelen noted that the music had stopped. She assumed Nalla was responsible for it since the woman declared herself the official DJ of the evening and used her phone to play songs through Leah's speaker system. Kaelen contemplated the project and Leah's sudden reaction at the injection site. "I have a theory. Please give me a minute to check historical medical data on wound healing."

"A minute? Excuse me, I went to school for years—"

"Maddy, trust her."

Kaelen pulled out her cell phone, conscious of everyone watching her. She typed a quick search into a custom form she'd programmed with the help of Wex. Essentially it was a super search function that was boosted by the AI. She scanned pages and pages of documents in seconds, the screen a blur to most people nearby. When she was finished, she turned off the screen and stuffed the phone back in her pocket. "As I suspected, sharp, shooting pains can be common in a wound area."

Maddy snapped her fingers. "They can be a sign that sensation is returning in the nerves."

"Yes, exactly that. One thing that surprises me is that this is occurring so relatively soon after the initial injections. We haven't even completed the first post injection tests."

Einstein expanded on Kaelen's explanation and addressed everyone. "Leah underwent the procedure on Monday, and we decided to do weekly scans to set a timeline for nerve regeneration progress."

"But what if something went wrong?" Tasha stood next to Maddy and put her hand on her shoulder. "Sweetie, maybe you should let Maddy check you out, just in case."

Kaelen listened intently for a moment, then did a quick scan with her x-ray vision, reasoning that it wasn't so much an invasion of privacy as it was a quick checkup to reassure Leah. "All her vitals appear stable. Heart rate, blood pressure, and respiration are within acceptable limits for a human. She has no internal bleeding that I can detect."

"Dude, whoa! Who are you, Svengali, or something?"

Kaelen turned to look at Gabe. "Who is Svengali? Are they an alien?"

"He was—you know what, never mind. That's not the point. You can tell all that by simply standing near her?"

"I felt her wrist to detect blood pressure. The rest was visual and aural observation."

Gabe looked around the group then back at Kaelen. "Who the hell are you? I don't know of any aliens that can do all that. Speed reading, super smart, looking inside someone…maybe Garen would know."

Suddenly Leah straightened in her chair. "First, I want everyone to step away from me. I'm fine, the pain is gone. Second," she pointed at Gabe, "not a word about Kaelen gets to your boss, you hear me?"

"But, but…it's literally my job to monitor the Chromodec and alien presence in the region. What's the big deal if he knows?"

"The big deal is that I'm asking you to keep her abilities private and within this small group. You don't tell your bosses, other friends, or hookups. You don't write about it at Meta News Network, and you don't speculate on her abilities at the hospital water cooler."

Devon shrugged. "I mean, whatever you need, I'll go along. I've learned to respect people's privacy over the years. Sometimes building trust is more important than getting the next greatest shot." He met Kaelen's eyes. "I won't say a word, promise." Everyone else in the group verbally agreed as well. Even Gabe mumbled "fine" before stalking off to grab another beer.

"Great, now that I'm mortified to have been the center of attention over something so insignificant, can we finish this game?"

Einstein raised one silver eyebrow ridge and steepled his fingers together. "Are you sure we should not head to the SPL and run the next set of tests tonight, or first thing tomorrow?"

Leah met his challenge with her own. "At eleven thirty? No way. We're all going to enjoy our evening and when you leave, I'm going to cuddle with my girlfriend."

Nalla snickered. "Is that what you kids are calling it these days?"

Leah raised her middle finger toward Nalla, and Kaelen remembered the gesture from when Maddy did it at her apartment. "When she waves like that it means to fuck you." The rest of the group burst into laughter and Kaelen wasn't sure why. She looked at Leah. "Did I say something wrong?"

Leah smiled at her fondly. "Not at all, darling. Now, I want you to sit next to me and I'll show you how to beat Maddy at poker."

"Oh, that's the next game? Nope, I'm out. The last time you and Maddy played, the two of you took all our money and Maddy still flipped the table."

"It was one time! You are all a bunch of drama queens." Maddy threw her hands up in the air and stalked off for a refill on her own drink. Jeers and catcalls followed her down the hall toward the kitchen.

"Lies!"

"You've flipped the table on every game we've ever played, Tuck, even Uno!"

Kaelen looked at Leah. "Are they always so contentious?"

"It's in good fun, I promise. We like to tease each other but don't hesitate to speak up if something makes you uncomfortable, okay?"

"Okay." Kaelen paused for a moment then whispered, "Thank you for helping me keep my secret. I'm afraid that I'm not good at it. Even though I've only had these powers a short time, they're part of me and hard to avoid or hide."

"You never have to worry about me, Kaelen. I've always got your back." Leah looked around the room but kept her voice equally quiet. "Do you think the pain was a sign that sensation is returning?"

Kaelen nodded. "I am close to certain but I'll feel less anxious after you go in for your next round of tests. Are you sure you don't want to do that tomorrow?"

Leah squeezed her hand. "We've got tickets to the Los Angeles Zoo with the special behind the scenes otter encounter, then the planetarium later. I want to have a leisurely weekend with my best friend and girlfriend. So, no. I promise we'll begin the scans first thing Monday morning." She leaned toward Kaelen slightly and pleaded, "Trust me to know my body and the scientific process."

"I trust you and I can't wait to see the otters in person. They look like wet, thick-bottomed cats in the videos I've watched."

Leah shook her head and grinned. "You're not wrong."

Kaelen loved the otter encounter, as did Leah. At one point, Leah had two otters in her lap in the hoverchair before they scampered off to play. They arrived back at the penthouse with Leah slightly damp and smelling of fish. Kaelen's suit was self-cleaning and had no lingering odor, a fact that Leah grumbled about. Leah changed and took care of a few other personal tasks, while Kaelen altered the outward appearance of her suit to something more appropriate for the rest of their evening.

Later at the planetarium, they sat next to each other watching the show as stars and entire galaxies spun above them. Leah glanced to the side and saw tears glittering on Kaelen's cheek. Concerned, she leaned close and whispered so they wouldn't disturb anyone else. "What's wrong?"

Kaelen swallowed thickly and turned to meet Leah's gaze. Her pale blue eyes were visible in the low light, as was the heartbreak within them. "I used to love visiting new worlds with my father. There is so much life out there to see, so many types of people and experiences. When I view all this," she discretely indicated that star filled black expanse above them, "from this safe place on Earth, I'm reminded of how much is out there…and of what is now missing. Argon left a hole in the universe with its disappearance. I feel very alone whenever I touch on that thought."

"Your sun, Vos, is still there?"

"Yes." Kaelen gave her a curious look.

Leah gently wiped the tears tracking down Kaelen's cheek. "And you are here, right?"

"With you, always."

A wave of emotion filled Leah and she wanted to take away all Kaelen's pain. She moved the hand that was damp from tears up to the center of Kaelen's chest, right where she knew the symbol of Ra was located on her suit. "Your planet may no longer be orbiting around Vos, but it will always live right here. Argon is inside you, as is the knowledge of your people, your culture, and your house. They will continue with you, and eventually Michael. You are Ra and you're not alone."

Kaelen whispered as a smile curled upon her lips. "I'm not alone."

"No, darling. And with you, neither am I."

"I—I feel a great depth of emotion that I've never felt for another."

Leah held her breath, wondering if Kaelen were going to admit something she herself had felt for quite a while. "Do you know what it is?"

"Yes."

"And?"

Kaelen looked around then leaned over until her lips were inches from Leah's. "I love you. That is what I've been feeling, the emotion that has been building for many months. It doesn't matter if we have yet to be physical with one another because I always feel the passion rise to the surface every time we kiss. I love your mind, your compassion, and your dedication to helping the human race. You say that I'm full of hope, but I only shine with the light that is around me. You, Leah Lockheed-Tuck, are my light."

Leah surged forward and poured every bit of how she felt into the kiss they'd teetered on the precipice of throughout Kaelen's declaration. When they pulled back for air, Leah whispered, "I love you too. So very much."

"I told you we would make a good match."

Leah blew out a breath and leaned back in her chair, not wanting to give the other patrons more of a show than perhaps they'd already done. "So, you did." She kept hold of Kaelen's hand until they left for the penthouse. While the evening didn't end with them breaching the barrier of physical passion, Leah fell asleep safe within the comfort of Kaelen's arms.

Chapter Thirteen

Exactly as promised, they performed the second round of scans and blood tests on Leah first thing Monday morning. She went back upstairs immediately after for a meeting with Ellie and an investment group, but Kaelen promised that she and Einstein would analyze the data and inform them of their findings later in the day.

Einstein stood over one of the computers displaying results from their tissue and blood flow scan. "Quark! She is already showing a twenty percent increase in blood flow, not only to the injury site but to her entire lower body."

Kaelen looked up from her own printout. "Was there anything on the EMG?"

He switched screens and opened the results. "Electromyography and the nerve conduction study both show marked improvement over baseline." Einstein smiled at her. "This is working!"

"Of course. We are the creators, and two twelfth caliber intellects would never fail an endeavor such as this."

Einstein nodded in acknowledgement of their combined capability. "Did she have any more pain after the party Friday night?"

"She experienced three more mild incidents of cramping followed by fast, sharp pain. None escalated beyond the first incident, and I had a high percentage of certainty that it was because of the rapid healing, centered on the place of original spinal cord compression." Kaelen waved the paper she held. "I'm even more certain after seeing these results. Knowledgeable though I am, even I didn't predict the rapidity of regeneration when combining the Lab twelve serum with the nanobots.

This fantastic discovery could change the face of human medicine." Kaelen frowned.

"What is it?"

She met Einstein's curious gaze. "Are we changing too much, too fast? I was cautioned against such things by my parents. It was one of their objectives for me."

Einstein tilted his head in thought, perhaps considering all the angles to their possible dilemma. "I don't believe so. We have not introduced something new to Earth. All we did was give the current technology a more focused direction. This was the next step for them, Kaelen Ra-Evon. Let us enjoy the success."

"Okay. I trust you."

"Good. I shall make a call upstairs and ask Jenna to send Leah and Ellie down as soon as they're finished. I'm sure they'll want to hear the good news as well."

Kaelen tucked the printouts back into the file they'd secured for the phase one trials. "While we're waiting, would you like to see my design suggestions for Lockheed's current photovoltaic cells?"

"Absolutely."

It was another hour before Leah and Ellie made it downstairs. Leah seemed weary and the way Ellie squinted indicated she was suffering from a headache.

Kaelen looked back and forth between them. "Is something the matter?"

Leah answered. "I got a call from the hanger where the private jet is stored. Apparently, it failed the most recent inspection. It needs a part that is on backorder due to a safety recall and will probably take months to arrive."

"What does that mean?"

"It means that my lovely adopted daughter and I will be flying first class via Atpac Airlines on a direct flight from here to New York next Monday evening because Lockheed's other private jet was booked months ago."

Einstein looked back and forth between them. "First class passage is most acceptable."

Leah sighed. "Yes, but still not convenient when I'm using this hoverchair. Either way, it can't be helped. We have to attend this meeting, so I'll do what I can to prepare for the more than five-hour trip. I'm also not looking forward to three time zones difference there and back."

"Try it when you hit your sixties then talk to me about it." Ellie snorted, but the tightness around both their eyes remained. However, their expressions quickly changed when Kaelen and Einstein gave them the results from Leah's newest scans.

Leah sat in shock before saying, "There must be some mistake."

"We've made no mistakes. Kaelen and I crosschecked each other's results to be certain. She thinks the faster-than-expected activity is a direct result of the combined treatment vectors."

"Yes. Rather than add the two predicted nerve function return probabilities to extrapolate a new one for the dual test, it appears as though simultaneous use of the serum and nanobots has prompted an exponential increase in healing speed."

"How much faster?"

Kaelen shrugged. "For that, we'll need another round of tests. Hopefully we'll have a better idea next Monday morning. It is advantageous that you don't fly out until evening."

Ellie tapped her lip, something she often did when she was deep in thought. "And you're certain this isn't dangerous to Leah?"

Einstein nodded. "We have determined that while she may continue to experience mild to sharp pain and discomfort, it will not actually be harmful to her. They are merely symptoms of the accelerated healing process." He glanced at Leah. "Obviously you should continue to monitor your vitals and record the incidents when they happen."

"I do."

"Good!" Einstein clapped his hands together, seemingly satisfied that all was well. "Now, if you need me, I shall be in the shielded room taking apart one of our high-capacity battery cells."

Leah raised her hand to stop Einstein but he was already walking away. "Be sure to wear proper safety equipment, Trog! You remember what happened last time you took something apart back there."

He stopped and turned on his heel to face the three women. "Unlike a certain CEO that I know, I always wear my safety equipment in the lab." Then he spun again and continued toward the door that led into the smaller specialty labs of the SPL.

Kaelen found his comment curious. "What did he mean? Do you not always wear the proper equipment?"

Leah rolled her eyes as Ellie laughed. "It was one time and he never lets me forget!"

"Honey, you literally chastised him for not wearing an apron when he was getting ready to start the ferric chloride etching experiment and you weren't even wearing goggles."

"Fine, you're right. But it was still more than two years ago. You all should let it go."

Kaelen put her hand on Leah's shoulder. "Don't worry, *zhee*. I don't think you would make such a mistake again."

"Thank you!" She turned to Ellie. "See, Kaelen has faith in me."

Kaelen elaborated. "Yes, even Earth primates have the ability to learn from their errors and not repeat foolish actions a second time." Leah huffed and Kaelen smiled back at her while Ellie laughed at them both.

A week later, the third set of tests showed even more improvement in Leah's nerve function. To celebrate, Einstein talked Kaelen into coming out to dinner with him and Nalla. Leah and Ellie said their goodbyes then a driver picked them up from L-I and took them to the airport. Nearly two hours had gone by since they left, but Kaelen missed Leah immensely. While they didn't spend every evening in each other's company, they easily spent half their week together, so she wasn't looking forward to the upcoming days of separation.

Kaelen enjoyed the evening with her friends. The three of them were having drinks in a sports bar near Kaelen's apartment since Nalla and Einstein didn't live far away from her. They were in the middle of a trivia game when Kaelen suddenly dropped the controller, certain that something was wrong. She froze in her seat and listened intently in an effort to discern what had changed to cause such a reaction. Kaelen focused her hearing outward, and the sound of a racing heart assailed her ears. Then screams.

Nalla snapped her fingers in front of Kaelen's face. "Hey. I called your name three times. Is something wrong?"

Before Kaelen could answer, a beeping alert garnered everyone's attention, and a banner scrolled across the screens displayed around the restaurant. Most of the sports bar, including the three of them, paused what they were doing to watch. Someone nearby yelled for the bartender to turn it up.

"If you're just joining us, Atpac Airlines Flight 327 bound for New York began experiencing loss of altitude shortly after takeoff. The pilot appears to be circling the city after an apparent engine failure."

Einstein sucked in a breath. "327. That's Leah and Ellie's plane!"

Suddenly, one of the anchors covered an ear, exactly as Kaelen used to do with Wex. He stared at the camera with a grim look upon his face. "This just in, we have reports that Flight 327 has now lost two of its engines and officials are concerned that they won't make it back to the airport. The 787 is carrying 336 passengers and is currently heading toward downtown Los Angeles."

"I have to do something."

Nalla gave her an odd look. "What can you do? I only hope the CORP has something or someone that can help."

Einstein grimaced. "I'm pretty sure even the CORP doesn't have the ability to stop a plane crash."

The heart that had become more precious to Kaelen than her own raced with frantic speed and in that moment, she didn't care at all about hiding. She looked at Nalla and Einstein and said, "I need to go," then she was out the door in a blur. Kaelen touched the edge of her collar as soon as she arrived in the alley next to the bar. Her clothing changed back to that of her ship suit with the glowing white House of Ra symbol on the front. Pavement cracked below Kaelen's feet when she jumped into the sky, arriving at the location of the disabled plane in seconds.

Kaelen knew right away that lifting something so immense while it was under thrust would be significantly more challenging than her small ship. She wished she'd grabbed her communicators from her bag before she left the bar. Instead, she was only in possession of her thoughts and fears. Kaelen floated far ahead of the jet and calculated the velocity and lift needed to compensate for the loss of two engines.

Once she had the numbers in her head, she flew toward the plane, angling below it to match speed. Another engine caught fire and Kaelen blew it out as she heard the pilot onboard tell the flight attendants to brace for impact. She took immediate action and flew up so she was beneath the wing, supporting it. Kaelen had a view of the forward most window in the passenger cabin and saw Leah look out at her. Leah's face was a study of shock and fear.

When lifting the wing proved to be ineffective, she flew beneath the belly of the plane, giving the entire aircraft a ride on her back. Unfortunately, the plane was directly over the downtown area, the skyscrapers and bustling streets below providing no space to bring down such a massive plane. Lights were shining off in the distance and she enhanced her vision enough to see a large green space.

The remaining engine gave out as Kaelen flew in that direction which put all the lift and navigation solely in her hands. When she arrived at her destination it became obvious that the field was a sports complex of some kind and in use. People in uniform were on the dirt and grass, and tens of thousands of watchers were seated in the surrounding stadium seats. Kaelen lowered herself and the plane toward the center of the open space. No one saw or pointed and she assumed they were focused on the game. A crack sounded and she watched as a small white object sailed toward her, only to bounce off her invulnerable forehead.

"Sprock."

That's when the screams started. She lowered the plane slowly, giving the players time to evacuate the field. Her position beneath the plane made the landing awkward. Luckily, the pilot had the foresight to put down the landing gear. The jetliner hadn't lost power, just thrust.

The sheer number of people in the stands gave her pause and Kaelen thought it prudent to make an attempt at hiding her identity, especially given the number of cameras she saw on her initial approach.

Kaelen stood below the belly of the plane, watching to make sure it was stable. Just as she did before, Kaelen caressed her collar and the nanotech moved up the sides of her face to form an eye mask. Once in place, she floated to the top of the wing and gazed toward the front of the plane where she knew her beloved sat.

Leah stared out the window right where Kaelen stood, bathed in the lights of the stadium and news helicopters circling above. Then slowly, Leah's face was lost from view as she pulled herself upright. It lasted only a second or two before Leah collapsed back into her seat again. Kaelen didn't have long to be amazed because a loudspeaker cut through the night.

"Unidentified vigilante, place your hands on your head and await the authorities." Kaelen looked toward the edge of the field and saw familiar black vehicles coming through a large service door. They were followed by a handful of emergency vehicles. She caught a glow in the night sky rapidly approaching and realized it was another powered individual, probably one of the CORP agents. Rather than wait around to be apprehended, she jumped into the sky faster than any of them could see or follow.

An hour later, Kaelen sat in her apartment watching the continuing news coverage of the incident. Wex spoke through the speaker system she'd installed a few months before. *"Kaelen Ra-Evon, it may have been unwise to show yourself in such a public manner. Your efforts broke multiple laws tonight and you've been deemed a vigilante by local law enforcement and the media."*

"Wex, I saved more than three hundred people, including my future mate and her mother. I could do no less."

"You must be careful in the future. It appears as though the brightness of your house symbol worked in conjunction with the mask and made your face unidentifiable on all the video footage taken. Your identity remains safe, but you may not be so fortuitous if you show yourself again."

She sighed. "Yes, I know." Something on the television caught Kaelen's attention and she unmuted the volume.

"We have a caller on the line who says she recognizes that symbol. Hello, ma'am? You're live on the air with WNLA. You said you have a name of the person who saved Flight 327?"

A woman's voice came on and Kaelen recognized it from the night in the alley by her old apartment building. "Yeah, that lady is a hero. She saved my life when two men attacked me on my way home from work a few months ago."

The news anchor prompted, "The video footage is unable to make out the person's face. How do you know this is the woman who saved you?"

"She had the same mask and black suit with the crazy white glowing backward Z or S-lookin' thing on the front. Said she was uh, the last Scion or something, whatever that means. I've been calling her Scion when I tell people about what happened. What else would the letter stand for?"

The image cut back to the recorded video of the plane again, showing Kaelen looking like a masked shadow in her ship suit, standing on the wing with the symbol of her house glowing for the whole world to see. The newscaster's voice overlaid that of the helicopter footage.

"There you have it, folks. One eyewitness states this woman has played hero at least one other time before. The Chromodec Office of Restraint and Protection has issued a statement declaring that the woman is a rogue and should turn herself in for questioning. But until that happens, the identity of Scion remains a mystery. Who is she and where does she come from? More importantly," the image changed back to that of the newscaster with his professional demeanor. He tilted his head forward slightly to draw the viewer in. "Will Scion be seen again?"

Then the camera angle abruptly changed as he looked in a different direction and said, "Well folks, it looks like the Dodger's will hit the road until their stadium can be repaired. What will this mean for their winning streak?" She didn't understand the dramatization of human news.

Kaelen curled her lip. "They're calling me Scion?"

"Kaelen Ra-Evon, this world seems to prefer their powered individuals with some sort of codename. If they think your house symbol represents one of their English letters, it makes sense they'd deduce that was your identity from what you told the woman. Perhaps it is for the best. Especially if the alternative is that they discover your real name and arrest you."

"I suppose" Kaelen grumbled.

"I would advise you to make a greater effort to disguise your identity in the event you choose to rescue more people of Earth."

"How would I do that?"

There was nearly a minute of silence before Wex spoke again. *"After analyzing the video footage from the news agency, it is obvious the mask was sufficient to hide your features. The symbol on the chest of your suit also has flash reflective properties so nighttime photo imaging would be unable to capture your face in normal night circumstances."*

"I didn't like the mask. It was distracting and obstructed my vision just enough to be annoying."

"Unfortunately, without a mask or something similar, daytime imaging would create a problem. There would be no shadows to hide your identity."

Kaelen ran her hand through her longish hair in frustration and realized she was overdue for another cut. "Maybe this will help." She used her maximal speed to rush into her bathroom and performed the routine styling using two mirrors and her laser vision. Then ran the exhaust fan to clear out the acrid smell. Kaelen continued to contemplate the problem of identity when she returned to the living room. "I think shortening my hair will help."

"I concur, Kaelen Ra-Evon."

"Unfortunately, I don't have anything I can attach to my ship suit that would work in conjunction with the existing nanotechnology responsible for altering my every day Earth clothing program. Perhaps I could—wait, I have the cloak gifted by my *zodha* and *ghun* after my induction ceremony!"

Kaelen sped over to the dresser where she kept a few of her personal belongings. She didn't own much because she didn't need much. The fabric was heavy, greater than standard Earth clothing. It moved with a sentience not found in anything else on the planet. The cloak contained the same technology and nanofibers that existed in her ship suit. It was reversible, with shimmering silver on one side, and the deepest black on the other.

"Kaelen Ra-Evon, you should be able to synch the cloak with your ship suit."

"I'm well aware, Wex." She quickly reversed it so the shimmering silver side faced her back. Kaelen swiped a few complicated patterns on the collar of her ship suit and the symbol flared brighter for a second then faded. She pulled the deep hood up and turned toward one of the cameras she'd installed in her apartment. "Wex, check for identifying characteristics."

"Checking…complete. There are not enough viewable feature points for effective facial recognition."

Kaelen touched the collar and the *Dolem*-Ra symbol returned to its normal brightness. "Check again, please."

"Checking…complete. While viewable feature points increased by fifteen percent, there are still not enough for Earth's most advanced facial recognition software. The hood is effective despite the brightness of Earth's sun."

"Thank you, Wex. I will be sure to use the cloak if I undertake another endeavor."

Kaelen pushed through the curtain separating the living room from her sleeping chamber. She stood in front of the full-length mirror, turning one way then the other to see how the cloak looked with the suit. She hadn't worn it since she was thirteen and still living on Argon. It had been ankle length then, but now it only hung down to mid-calf.

The buzzer to her apartment rang before Kaelen could dwell on it further. She activated the Earth clothing randomizer and the cape and ship suit disappeared into one of the two dozen clothing profiles she'd programmed. She didn't need to ask who was downstairs because she easily heard Leah's heartbeat strong and steady. Kaelen sped to the panel and buzzed her up. She opened the door to her apartment when she heard the elevator ding on her floor.

Relief washed through her as soon as Leah exited the lift. However, she wasn't alone. Both Ellie and Maddy accompanied her. Kaelen was afraid of the look on their faces. Each one held worry and consternation. Rather than speak, she backed inside the apartment and gave the Tuck women room to enter.

Kaelen sped to Leah's side once the door was closed and leaned down to look her in the eyes. "Are you okay?" Then she glanced at Ellie. "Are either of you injured?"

Ellie smiled kindly. "We're both fine, honey. Just a little banged up."

"Where is Tasha?"

"She stayed home. I rushed to the stadium as soon as I got Leah's call saying they were both okay and unharmed. I had a feeling it was you, Kaelen." Maddy ran a shaking hand through her hair.

Kaelen nodded, then realized for the first time that Leah was in the same chair she'd been in on the plane. "How were you able to remove your hoverchair from the plane?"

Ellie was the one who answered. "One of the CORP agents is able to make portals—"

"Portis, I remember."

"Yes, anyway, some people went down the emergency slide and she helped evacuate the rest from the plane safely and quickly."

"Kaelen," she moved her gaze back to Leah. "I recognized your ship suit and symbol."

Maddy added, "Ship suit? I mean, I thought but—it really was you in the black suit that saved their plane."

Kaelen wasn't sure how to feel, didn't know why the others were so solemn after such a wondrous event. "I…I, um, yes. And I would do it again if it meant saving all those people." She closed her eyes and swallowed, then looked directly at Leah. "If it meant saving you. I don't care if the news is calling me a vigilante or a rogue."

Maddy sighed. "You'll care if the CORP finds out who you are."

Kaelen snapped back, "It was the right thing to do! My found family was in mortal peril, other innocent people and children were going to die. How is that wrong?"

Maddy clasped her shoulder and squeezed it. "It wasn't, at least not in my book. You saved my mom and my sister and," Maddy's eyes watered as she drew in a shuddering breath. "I can never thank you for that." She pulled Kaelen into a quick hug.

"You don't have to thank me, Maddy. You three are as much my family now as anyone I left behind on Argon. Will you stay for a bit? I've restocked the refrigerator for guests."

Maddy said, "I'm going to grab a beer, if you don't mind." Kaelen nodded and Maddy went into the kitchenette to fetch herself a drink before taking it into the living room. She took a swig from the bottle, then placed it on a coaster and collapsed onto the couch. It was something she'd obviously done many times before since the couch used to be hers.

Ellie looked back and forth between Leah and Kaelen, then pointed to the kitchen. "I'm going to get some water."

That left Kaelen and Leah by themselves near the front door to her apartment while the news replayed coverage of the crash in the background. Kaelen swallowed. "Can I hug you?"

In response, Leah raised her arms. Kaelen held her as tight as was safe. "I was so worried. I was sitting in the sports bar—oh no! I left Einstein and Nalla sitting there when I rushed out. I hope they have my satchel. It would go poorly for me if that were to be claimed by the wrong person. I should call them." She made to pull away but Leah didn't let her go.

"Kaelen, stop."

Leah wore a strange look and Kaelen grew concerned. "Did I do something wrong? Are you angry with me?"

"No, darling. I'm not angry with you in the slightest. But Kaelen, they know you exist now. I'm terrified for you."

Kaelen leaned back. "For me? I wasn't the one who nearly died in a plane crash tonight."

"It was reckless to reveal yourself the way you did. What if someone takes you away?"

"You were going to die!" Kaelen took a shuddering breath. "I can't lose my world again. Don't you understand?"

"Your world? Kaelen, Earth isn't going anywhere."

"No." Kaelen swallowed and looked down at their joined hands, hoping Leah could understand. "You are my world. You're my person, the one my heart loves above all others. I couldn't let something happen to you. No one will take me away, I promise."

Leah was silent after Kaelen's admission, and Kaelen grew afraid that the depth of her emotion was not matched, despite their mutual declarations of love. Leah sighed and used her fingertips to raise Kaelen's chin until they could look at one another. "I can see the fear in your eyes. You don't have to worry about how much I care. My feelings are the same as yours. I think that's why I'm so afraid."

Maddy called out from where she sat next to Ellie on the couch. "Between the mask and the weird glare her suit gives off under the lights, they don't know who she is. My guess is they're not likely to figure it out either, even with the technology employed by the CORP. As long as Gabe keeps his yap shut, we should be okay."

"How would he know who saved the plane?"

Maddy shook her head. "He may be an idiot sometimes, but that guy is brilliant and a trained agent. He'll put it together eventually."

Kaelen gave the hand she held a little tug. "Come into the living room. Do you need anything?"

"I'd like some water too, please."

"Go be by Maddy and Ellie and I'll join you in a few seconds."

Kaelen blurred into the kitchen to fetch water as Leah zipped her hoverchair farther into the apartment and stopped next to Kaelen's favorite seat. Kaelen handed the glass of water to Leah seconds later. Ellie turned away from the television. "They're calling you Scion."

Kaelen frowned. "I saw."

"What's this about a woman that called in saying you saved her from two attackers months ago?" Maddy took another swig of her beer and leveled a stern look toward Kaelen.

"I, she was…I heard screaming outside my old apartment. It was the night you and Tasha dropped me off. I saw two men assaulting a lone woman when I went into the alley to investigate. She was crying for help, Maddy. What was I to do?"

"What exactly did you do, anyway?"

Kaelen answered Leah's question. "I delivered impacts of exactly one kilogram of force to each of the attacker's chins, rendering them unconscious. When I lifted both into the air—"

"Into the air, like, above your head?"

"No. I flew into the air, carrying each of the men by the back of their pants. It seemed the sturdiest method. I was about to leave the alley to drop the men off at the local police station when the woman asked who I was. Wex cautioned me not to reveal too much so I told her I was the last scion of Ra."

"Wait, you can fly?"

"Maddy, how the hell do you think she saved our plane?" Ellie rarely used Earth expletives and Kaelen suspected she was still upset about the accident.

Maddy flushed. "Sorry, Mom. Forgot for a second."

"Yes, I can fly on top of all the other abilities."

Ellie looked from Maddy to Leah, then back at Kaelen. "You have other abilities?"

Kaelen nodded but Leah answered for her. "Do you trust Ellie?"

"I trust you three more than anyone else. We can tell her."

Maddy snorted. "Tell her? You still haven't told me everything yet."

Leah spoke quietly. "I didn't know either, Maddy."

Kaelen's stomach clenched with guilt, and she realized the error of entering into a relationship without disclosing her abilities in full. She feared that keeping the rest of her powers a secret may have driven a wedge between them. "I'm sorry. I didn't mean to keep it from you. But I don't use many of the powers here in Los Angeles so I didn't think of it. My only goal has been to assimilate and fit in here on Earth, to do good work. I don't want you to be angry with me."

"Oh, darling, I'm not mad at you. You do good work, the best."

Kaelen blew out a sigh of relief.

"We're only worried about you and want you to be safe. But we can't help unless you share with us the things you can do."

Everyone except Kaelen jumped when Wex's voice came out of the surround sound speakers. *"Kaelen Ra-Evon, it may be beneficial to have others aware of the full scope of your powers. The women from the House of Lockheed and the House of Tuck have proven their loyalty to Ra."*

She scowled toward the nearest camera. "Now you want me to tell someone? What happen to the precious directives you lecture me about?"

"Kaelen Ra-Evon, I do not lecture and they are not my directives—"

"I don't need your permission, Wex. Please remain silent while guests are here unless I ask for your assistance."

"As you wish, Kaelen Ra-Evon."

Maddy tipped her bottle up to finish it off. "That thing is creepy."

"It's pretentious." Leah made a face toward one of the cameras.

Kaelen laughed. "It's neither of those things. Wex is an AI whose only purpose is to aid *Dolem*-Ra. But this is not an Argonian matter, it's an Earth matter."

"Ain't that the truth!"

"Maddy, hush. Why don't you have a seat, Kaelen?"

"Actually," Leah interrupted. "Can I see your ship suit again?"

Kaelen reached up to caress the collar of her shirt and it rapidly shifted to that of her ship suit, the new version that was merged with the hood and cape.

"That doesn't look like what you were wearing on the news. And you cut your hair. What does the backward Z mean?" Maddy pointed toward the image of Kaelen standing on the wing of the plane in the helicopter spotlight.

"Yes, well," Kaelen pulled up the deep hood so her face was cast in shadow. "Wex suggested that I make it harder to identify my face while wearing the ship suit and performing illegal activities. I remembered the cloak given to me by my grandparents and integrated it into the suit's technology. The symbol is not an English letter, despite speculation otherwise. It merely represents the symbol of my house, *Dolem*-Ra. It stands for an Argonian phrase that means *Kymeth Sal ne Ra*—"

"I remember that from your interview. With intellect we overcome, right?"

Kaelen smiled to hear her house creed spoken aloud by Leah. "Yes, that is the approximate translation to English."

Leah reached out to feel the fabric of the cape. "This is beautiful and strange." She lifted it. "It's heavier than I assumed."

Maddy looked her up and down. "It's also effective at hiding your identity. Will the hood stay up while you're, uh, flying?"

Kaelen touched the opposite side of her collar and suddenly the hood tightened around her head, completely covering her face. It left her eyes and mouth uncovered. "Will this suffice?"

Maddy snickered. "Now you look like you walked out of a fancy S & M club."

"Madison Tuck!" Ellie swatted Maddy's arm then turned to her with a kind smile, but conceded, "She does have a point. You may want to cover your entire face unless the fabric isn't breathable enough. Or maybe you can turn it into a cowl while in flight, like The Staffman in Chicago."

"Or Flashlite. Hell, even the CORP has helmets they wear when going up against super-powered people wreaking havoc."

Kaelen had seen pictures of the two superheroes on the news often enough, though they rarely left their own cities. She scoffed, "How is it that Man Staff and Flasher are allowed to save people when they are not part of this CORP organization?"

Maddy nearly spit her beer. Kaelen gave her a questioning look and she explained. "It's the Staffman and Flashlite. One is, uh, some broody baddass that cleans up the streets of the third largest city and the other converts vibration to light beams. Your names make them sound like B-grade porn stars."

"What's porn?"

Leah raised her voice to be heard over Maddy's hysterical laughter. "Moving on, certain heroes work with the CORP as…I guess you can call them special consultants. It's not in a legal capacity but they don't kill anyone. They prevent civilian casualties and keep property damage to a minimum, so the CORP turns a blind eye to their activities. At least that's what Gabe told us."

Maddy snorted. "And nobody knows who they are so…there's that."

Kaelen thought of the various ways she could cover her face. "The cowl idea seems…constrictive. I disliked the mask I created after saving the plane because of altered peripheral vision. Perhaps I could do it only when I'm flying at maximal speed, and only use the hood for average wear in the ship suit." The nanotechnology in the suit held some of the same function as the nanotech in her ship. She could link with it mentally to visualize what shape she wanted the fiber to take. It was the same way Kaelen's ship could link with her mind to educate her on the long journey from Argon.

She caressed the collar one more time and the hood shifted so that her lower face and jaw were left bare. The black fabric came down the bridge of her nose, leaving the base of the nose clear as well as the lips and cheeks below. She also dimmed the symbol on the front to that of a metallic gray, as she'd done on other occasions. Kaelen looked back at Maddy, who'd been the most vocal about the appearance of her suit. "And now?"

"Perfect. As long as you can see well out of those eye holes."

"Of course."

Kaelen returned her clothing to a standard human pattern and took a seat next to Leah.

Ellie smiled at her. "Now that we've gotten that figured out, the scientist in me is dying to know what all these powers are. Will you tell us?"

Kaelen looked around the small group, her found family. "Our houses are linked now and I trust you. Our motto isn't only for those of Ra."

Leah took her hand. "Thank you."

"You want to know about my powers. Wex and I ran tests when I first landed on Earth in someplace called the Northwest Territories of Canada. This is what we learned…" Kaelen told them about each power she had discovered through their testing, as well as the ones she'd discovered by accident since that time.

Eventually, Maddy and Ellie called it a night. Maddy said she'd drop Ellie off at her mother's apartment in the city on her way back home. Kaelen offered to let Leah stay over, which she'd done on a few other occasions. That meant she had some necessary items there, like she used to have at Maddy's apartment before Maddy moved in with Tasha.

When Leah was finished with her evening routine, she moved over by the bed and Kaelen blurred to her side. "Please, *zhee*. May I?"

Leah pressed her lips together and Kaelen recognized the look. Leah despised having things done for her. After some hesitation, she gave a weary nod. Kaelen turned back the covers and lifted Leah to the bed. She covered her and caressed Leah's dark brow with her lips. Then, in deference to her guest, Kaelen took a soft set of pajamas into the bathroom to change. Leah's gaze stayed on her when she returned, eyes never leaving Kaelen's face as she came around the bed to slide beneath the covers on the other side.

Kaelen moved closer until she could caress Leah's face. "Are you okay? You weren't harmed?"

"I promise that I'm fine. And I'm definitely better now that I'm with you."

"I will always be here. I won't let anything happen to you."

Leah moved closer until her head was on Kaelen's chest and her hand rested on Kaelen's stomach. Kaelen listened as Leah's breath hitched, then hitched again and she broke down. "I was so scared. I was afraid that I'd never see you or anyone else again."

Kaelen held her while she cried, stroking her dark hair, and whispered words of comfort. "I'm not going anywhere. You're safe with me."

"I know." Leah took a shuddering breath, then repeated it again quieter. "I know." Shortly after, she fell asleep. Kaelen stayed awake, listening to Leah's heart beating in the dark.

Chapter Fourteen

Kaelen jerked awake. The night had been filled with strange dreams that replayed her actions the evening before. Each instance in the dream had a different outcome. One time she didn't save the plane and everyone died. Another time she saved the plane but was captured by the CORP. The last dream she remembered before waking featured Leah pulling herself up and pointing at Kaelen through the window, yelling that she was too alien and their houses would never make a good match.

Eyes wide open in the dim light of morning, Kaelen tried to control her breathing. She turned her head to see Leah sleeping soundly next to her, lying on her back with their arms touching beneath the blankets. Then Kaelen's dream caught up with her and she gasped. With all the activity and explanations of power the night before, she'd completely forgotten what she'd witnessed through the plane window. She turned onto her side and gently shook Leah awake.

Leah moaned, "For the love of God, Kaelen. I know you don't need as much sleep as a human, but I was literally in a plane crash less than twelve hours ago and could desperately use more rest."

"Do you remember your actions on the plane last night?"

Leah opened her eyes. It was more of a squint really, but at least they were open. "What?"

The bed trembled with Kaelen's excitement. "You stood! I watched you pull yourself up after I climbed onto the wing of the plane."

Leah searched Kaelen's face, perhaps suspecting a joke. Then she closed her eyes in a familiar action of deep thought. She sucked in a breath and opened her eyes again to stare at Kaelen in shock. "I did.

I'd completely forgotten but remember now. I'm guessing it was an adrenaline response but…"

"Adrenaline or no, you wouldn't have been able to do it unless at least partial nerve and muscle function has returned."

A slow smile spread across Leah's lips. "It's working."

It was a curious statement to make considering they'd shown Leah the results of her tests before she left for New York. "But Einstein and I gave you proof of your healing progress when we went over the EMG scores with you yesterday morning."

Leah shook her head but didn't lose her wide smile. "Darling, it's one thing to hear that your spinal cord, nerves, and muscles are healing, it's another to actually stand after being unable for more than ten years." She looked down at her legs where they were hidden beneath the blankets. "Is it too early to begin physical therapy? How soon do you think before I can walk unassisted?"

"I don't know. As we explained yesterday, your recovery is proceeding faster than expected. The more that is repaired by the nanobots, the less is left to repair, meaning that more nanobots will be devoted to the task which exponentially increases the time to completion."

"I'm so close, Kaelen!"

Kaelen interlaced their fingers. "I know. But patience may be extremely important here. Not because I'm concerned about permanent damage, but rather, you need to let the nanobots and serum do their job. If you hurt yourself by beginning physical therapy or any other exercises before the nerves and muscles are ready, you will create more tissue that requires repair, thus extending your recovery time."

"Patience isn't exactly my strong suit."

"You're a scientist, thus fully capable of patience. You only need to wait a bit longer for the treatment to complete."

Leah squeezed Kaelen's fingers. "I'm well aware of the scientific process. The difference between all those other times and now is that my dream is at my fingertips. I've been working for years to assemble the right people and technology that can reverse the damage done to my spine in that car. I can never bring back my birth family, but I'd like to walk again."

Kaelen understood. They were similar with their loss. Leah didn't lose an entire world, her people, and her culture. But that didn't make her loss any less significant. Both of them were left permanently changed by the experience. All things considered; Kaelen felt like her own life was easier after her loss. She couldn't comprehend how she would feel if everything had changed so completely and abruptly the same way that Leah's did. "You will and I'll be by your side when you do. After all, people across every galaxy in the universe dream of better worlds, what is science if not a way to make dreams come true?"

Leah pulled Kaelen into a kiss that lasted significantly longer than their normal connection. When they separated so Leah could breathe, Kaelen kept their foreheads pressed together. "I love you, *zhee*."

Leah opened her eyes and settled into the pillow. "I love you too, so much." She reached up to caress Kaelen's cheek, then trailed her fingers down her neck. Kaelen shivered at the delicate touch, sensitive despite her nearfield invulnerability. Leah moved her fingers up through Kaelen's hair and caressed along the outer edge of her ear, and down her neck again to rest upon the collarbone showing through the opening of the sleep shirt.

Kaelen sucked in a breath and met Leah's intense gaze. "What are you doing?"

Leah rubbed her finger along her collarbone and across the top of Kaelen's chest. "Is this okay?"

"I…it feels—" She gasped when Leah's hand moved around to the back of her neck and tangled in the hairs at the base of her head. "It feels?"

Kaelen moved forward again and claimed Leah's lips. She explored her mouth until Leah was panting. Leah moaned and pulled back. Her pupils were dilated with arousal, one of the signs Kaelen had previously read about. "Are you okay?"

Leah smirked. "You can touch me too." She wasn't sure what emotion Leah must have seen on her face that made her frown. "Unless you don't want to."

"I do! I'm just—I'm afraid of hurting you."

Leah moved her roving left hand to grasp Kaelen's right. She brought it up to rest on her own cheek. "It's okay to explore, I trust you to be gentle."

Her words were a gift. Even knowing Kaelen could lift entire planes with her strength, she still trusted Kaelen to touch her body with soft reverence. At first, Kaelen's touch mirrored what Leah had done. Cheeks, neck, collarbone, hair, and ear. Then she grew bolder and moved along Leah's arms and back up her sides, outside the sleep shirt. Leah's breathing grew heavier and Kaelen stopped. "Are you well? Does it hurt?"

"No, it feels amazing." She squeezed their clasped hands. "You don't have to stop if you don't want."

"I don't, but what about you?" Kaelen contemplated the direction they were headed. "I've no wish to harm you and I don't know what level of pleasure you're able to achieve. There are no expectations from me. We should only move forward if it's something you truly want."

"Darling, I definitely want. I have what the doctors call residual pelvic innervation. I've had sex before and masturbate regularly. Women and men are capable of orgasm with SCI because it's not necessarily tied to brain input, though we definitely have to be in the right mindset. I'm ready to take this step with you, if you're also ready."

It was new information for Kaelen. She'd researched human sexuality plenty but admittedly didn't know much about how that was different for someone with spinal cord injury. "I want to show my love for you intimately, to connect with you in a way we haven't yet tried. But I also want to make sure you feel as much pleasure as possible. Will you show me what to do?"

"I would love to. First keep touching me and let me touch you. There is a lot of heightened stimulation for the rest of my body, intellectually, and emotionally. All my erogenous zones above the injury are more sensitive. Prolonged foreplay is more important for someone with my type of injury."

Eager to please, Kaelen asked, "Are there things I need to avoid?"

"Because I lack sensation, I have to be careful of intense friction and lack of lubrication so I don't suffer from injury that I can't feel. Being intimate takes preparation so I can make sure I won't lose control of other bodily functions. Having to take extra time has not always gone well in past relationships." Leah frowned, perhaps at some memory of a past lover. "But I'll need a little time to prepare for anything further between us."

Kaelen felt as if Leah's words and actions didn't match. "I'm more than willing to be intimate with you. You are worth any accommodations that need to be made for sexual connection. But I don't want you to rush this because you think I'll disparage the time and necessary precautions. What do we need to do?"

Leah suddenly pulled her down into another kiss and Kaelen didn't protest. When their lips trailed apart, she saw tears in Leah's eyes. "You are one of a kind, Kaelen Ra-Evon."

"I'm only me and I feel desire that I suspect matches yours. But, just as there are things to consider with the function of your body in regards to sexual response, there will also be details about how I react that are directly related to my yellow sun powers. We'll learn about each other together."

Leah gave her a blinding smile. "Yes, we will."

Unsure after such a serious talk, Kaelen asked, "Do you want to proceed now, or should we wait? I think, what does Nalla say? I think the 'moment' has passed."

"Hmm, perhaps. There are some essential body things I would need to do before sex. You're right in that I was perhaps rushing a bit just now because of my own fears. I also have a few aids that will make things better for me, more intense."

"Like?" Kaelen had read about sexual aids but wasn't sure what someone with spinal injury would use.

A red flush worked its way up Leah's neck to stain her pale cheeks. "Well, I have a clitoral vacuum suction, uh, gadget called an Eros device. While I didn't date anyone often, I certainly wasn't dead."

"And that helps?"

Leah snickered. "That's putting it mildly. But we don't need to use that our first time. We could use something like a dildo instead." She paused for a few seconds before speaking again. "Okay, let's consider the rest of the day. I sent an email to Jenna last night to postpone the board meeting in New York, as well as make an official Lockheed International press release about the accident. I also told her to let Einstein know that you, I, and Ellie wouldn't be in the office for a few days."

"Not go to work on a workday?"

"I own the company, Kaelen."

Kaelen contemplated the rationale then decided she wanted to stay with Leah after the scare from the night before. She could do good work later in the week. "But why send this press release?"

"Stockholders and board members tend to be reassured by open communication. The press release is an official statement to let them know that while Ellie and I were both on the plane, we are unharmed. It's to thank all the emergency personnel for their efforts in treating everyone, and the CORP for getting people off the plane." She smirked. "I also told her to mention the mystery woman that actually saved the plane from crashing."

Kaelen tilted her head. "To what end?"

"Because it mattered, Kaelen. It was important. Despite what the law says and regardless what name the CORP or news brands you… hundreds, if not thousands of lives were saved by your actions last night. If that plane had crashed in downtown Los Angeles—" Leah shuddered at the thought and Kaelen drew her close for a hug.

"I wouldn't have let that happen."

Leah patted her arm. "I know, darling. What do you think of us spending the day together? We can go back to my penthouse to cuddle on the couch and watch movies. Then later we can go out for a nice dinner before retiring for the evening. Perhaps we'll explore the last unknown between us. Is that a satisfactory plan?"

There was an immense pressure within Kaelen's head and heart that she realized was her love for Leah. She gave her another, longer embrace. "I think that sounds perfect."

The rest of the day was easy and relaxed, exactly as proposed by Leah. Rather than take Kaelen to a fancy high-end restaurant that served notoriously tiny portions, she made reservations at the Asian restaurant Kaelen had first eaten at. They dined there regularly and were delighted to see Xiuying working that day. Kaelen found out that Leah and Xiuying met at university, the same year Leah had met Ana. Xiuying eventually took over her family's restaurant. She and the rest of her family took turns in the various roles of running it. That was why she wasn't often working when Leah ate there.

Xiuying laughed when she saw Kaelen, then pointed at her

accusingly. "You!" She turned to Leah. "Did you know she orders so much food that she runs us out of many items some nights?" She looked back at Kaelen.

"How many people are you feeding?"

Kaelen shrugged and answered her in Mandarin. *"Only me. I have a large appetite."*

Leah spoke at the same time. "She's feeding herself. Kaelen has a massive appetite."

"That's exactly what she just said. How have you been, Leah? Did you hear about the plane that came down in Dodger Stadium yesterday? It's all over the news. It's crazy to think how many people would have died if not for that rogue vigilante. Our restaurant was in the flight path drawn out by WNLA."

Leah frowned. "Ellie and I were on Flight 327 heading for a board meeting in New York. I'm thankful not to be a casualty."

"Truth. So many lives would have been lost if it had come down any place but the baseball field. I don't care what the CORP says, I'm grateful for that Scion, whomever she is." Then she shook herself and pulled out a pad of paper. "What can I get for the two of you?"

"Since when do you need to write out an order?"

Xiuying pointed at Kaelen. "Since I found out how much this one eats. It's best to write it down so I don't forget the entire list. I hope you pay her well for all the food your girlfriend orders."

Kaelen looked at her with surprise. "How did you know that Leah and I were dating? We've been circumspect."

Xiuying indicated their clasped hands with her pen, then pointed it back and forth between their faces. "I've been watching the way you two look at each other since that first time Leah brought you in. After a while I saw how you'd hold hands and knew that you two had figured it out."

"You are intelligent. I appreciate that."

Xiuying rolled her eyes and looked at Leah. "Intelligent she says. The last time you were in you let it drop that you speak ten languages fluently."

"Oh, I speak more than ten. Wex says those are the most common here on E—"

"Aren't you hungry, Kaelen? We should probably order, hmm?"

Kaelen's stomach chose that moment to growl loudly. "Oh, yes. I'm ravenous." She looked back at Xiuying. "Sorry, but Leah is right. We should probably order now."

Xiuying stared at Leah intently and Leah wasn't looking away. Kaelen wondered what sort of non-verbal communication they were using but eventually Xiuying nodded and turned back to Kaelen. "What will you have?"

Both Kaelen and Leah gave her their orders and Xiuying left to put in their ticket. Leah lowered her voice. "You need to be more careful now, Kaelen. At one time you were adamant about hiding your powers, but you've never been particularly good at it. It's even more critical that you maintain a certain level of discretion concerning your identity and full capabilities on this planet."

Her words made Kaelen extremely uncomfortable but they were sensible. "I understand and will try to be conscious of what I say to people who are not part of my found family."

Leah reached across the table. "You know I love every part of who you are and what you can do. I worry about what will happen if law enforcement or the CORP discover that you're Scion. I can't lose you."

"I'll be more careful." She held up her hand and smiled at Leah. "I pinky swear." Leah laughed and hooked their pinkies together.

"Thank you."

Kaelen wandered around Leah's condo looking at pictures and paintings on the walls. Leah had disappeared upstairs to shower off the day's sweat and prepare herself for an evening of intimacy. She was concerned that Kaelen's suit wouldn't clean all native Earth germs and bacteria that could enter into her urethra or vagina, so she asked Kaelen to shower as well. Kaelen learned that cleanliness was important for human sexual health, especially for someone with SCI. Earth bacteria couldn't affect her own biology but she could easily spread it to a lover.

Leah said she'd call when she was ready, and Kaelen assumed it would be soon since she heard the water turn off a few minutes before.

She'd already washed herself and stood around waiting in the sleep clothing she kept at Leah's penthouse. Kaelen was as nervous as she'd been the first time that she ran her own experiment under her father's direction back on Argon. It was an important one, but also dangerous, and she'd been entrusted to see it through to completion.

Sexual intimacy was no experiment but the nerves didn't abate. Kaelen wanted positive results no matter what task she performed. In the lab, she wanted to do good work, to contribute exactly as she'd been designed, trained, and taught. But with Leah, she simply wanted to please her. She wanted Leah to feel as much pleasure and happiness as possible.

"Kaelen." Leah spoke at normal volume but she easily heard her name as well as the slightly increased heart rate from her beloved. It was time.

Rather than speed up the stairs to the second level the way she wanted, Kaelen kept to a human pace. The door to Leah's suite of rooms was left open and a flickering glow spilled out. Kaelen pushed inside and took note of the tiny flames softly glowing around the room. Leah herself was reclined on the bed beneath the covers. Her damp hair splayed out on the pillow like a dark corona around her head.

"You're beautiful." Kaelen closed the door behind her and moved slowly toward the bed. "You are more radiant than the light of Vos." She stopped near the foot and twisted her hands together. "Kaelen?"

"Yes?"

"Come to bed. I want to love you."

Kaelen still hesitated. "What if I can't please you?" Then she whispered, "What if I hurt you?"

"Darling, you already please me. And trust that we won't hurt each other, okay? We should be fine as long as we communicate with each other throughout." She patted the bed again, and Kaelen was called to her side by the love shining in Leah's eyes.

Once beneath the covers, she felt Leah's bare skin against her arm. "Are you nude?"

"I am."

Kaelen was worried she'd already done something wrong. "Should I be nude as well?"

A warm smile assuaged her fears. "If you'd like."

"Okay." Kaelen exited the bed and began removing the Earth garments. She didn't wear underclothing as it was wholly unnecessary for her. Leah's heart rate sped again, and Kaelen looked up to see Leah lick her lips.

"Do you find me appealing?"

Laughter met her question and Leah crooked a finger at her. "You're like a goddess made flesh. But if you come back here, I'll show you exactly how appealing I find you."

With such a promise given, Kaelen didn't need to be told twice. She rushed beneath the covers. The second time they touched, the sensation of Leah's bare skin was heightened where it rubbed against her own. A moan resonated at the base of her throat when Leah caressed her side, running her hand along her rib cage upward to skirt along the side of Kaelen's breast.

"How does that feel?"

Kaelen's skin tingled and her body felt warm all over. "I've never experienced anything like it. I didn't know my body could be so sensitive."

"Perhaps you weren't being touched the right way, then."

"I've only touched myself."

"Let's change that right now."

Leah moved her hand to caress beneath Kaelen's right breast, then up between them to lay on the center of her chest where the house symbol would normally rest. Kaelen's breath hitched. "I didn't do anything like that. I'd like to make you feel tingly too. Texts I studied mentioned that humans have individual tastes when it comes to sexual pleasure and that you should ask your lover questions about their preference."

"My entire upper body is extremely sensitive, especially my breasts, neck, and transition zone where I go from full sensation to none. Use your hands or your lips, both feel nice."

"Lips?"

Leah smiled. "Yes, like this." She pulled Kaelen toward her with the hand she'd been using to caress the back of Kaelen's neck. Instead of kissing her on the lips as Kaelen expected, Leah started at her jaw and worked her way down Kaelen's neck, occasionally nipping the skin with her teeth.

Kaelen sucked in a breath. "Oh! That is, uh, very precise pressure. And titillating."

The kissing stopped and Leah pulled back to meet her eyes. "Kaelen."

"Yes?"

"Less talk, more action."

Kaelen brought her hands up to begin caressing Leah the way she'd had done to her. "Is there any place you don't want to be touched?"

"I emptied my bowels earlier today and bladder before I came out of the bathroom. Touch me wherever you're comfortable touching. But I…I have scars from the accident."

Leah started to look away but Kaelen cupped her cheek. "Every part of you is beautiful and unique. Your mind, your heart, your body. I will love it all if you let me. If you want me."

Strong hands pulled Kaelen down for another kiss and Leah mumbled through it, "Love me then."

They spent the next two hours learning each other's bodies, talking, caressing, and cuddling in the candlelight. They pleased each other multiple times before cleaning themselves thoroughly and settling in to blissful slumber. Kaelen never felt so connected to another being, nor had she ever loved someone so deeply or fully. There was nothing she wouldn't do for Leah.

Despite Kaelen's reluctance to miss work, she appreciated the days she got Leah all to herself. Both of them returned to work on Thursday, three days after the plane crash. Rather than die down, the accident and Kaelen remained regular topics on the news. The CORP had run ads asking for any tips on the vigilante known as Scion. Pundits debated who Kaelen could be and what she may do next. Throughout it all, Kaelen pondered the wisdom of being so bold the day she saved the plane.

She rode with Leah to work on Thursday morning and espoused her concerns. "Should I have tried to hide myself better that night? Perhaps I could have dimmed my house symbol, or flown out of sight as soon as I saw that you were safe."

Leah glanced her way for a second before turning the van into the parking garage attached to the office building. "It would have been hard to hide yourself in the bright lights of the stadium. But why didn't you?"

Kaelen sighed. "I think there were multiple reasons. One, I was a bit drained. It's not like I have many opportunities to fully exercise my powers. Not to mention, I'm stronger under the light of the yellow sun than I am at night. I was also happy that I saved the plane and nobody died. I saw you through the window and watched as you stood. It wasn't until I heard the voice speaking to me and the CORP showed up that I realized I should leave."

"Well, darling, if you hadn't been watching me through the window, I may not have even remembered standing."

They exited the van and it gave a double chirp as the doors locked. "Will you come downstairs for more testing?" Kaelen paced next to Leah's chair as they made their way to the parking garage elevator.

"Unfortunately, cancelling my trip means we'll be holding the meeting virtually from Los Angeles. I'll be tied up all day with Ellie."

Kaelen stopped walking when the sound of another thundering heartbeat hit her ears. Leah paused with her and gave her a curious look. A mechanical clicking sound hit Kaelen's ears a fraction of a second before a boom echoed through the underground structure. Kaelen's reflexes kicked in and she caught the bullet seconds before it struck Leah in the chest. Anger infused her in the time it took to drop the bullet. Leah looked at her in shock.

"Was that…"

Tires squealed at the farthest end, close to the entrance of the garage. Kaelen intensified her vision and saw a car break through the barricade across the exit. She focused on her hearing and recognized the heartbeat she'd heard before the gun went off. The shooter was getting away. She turned to Leah. "I have to go after them."

"What if there are more?"

Kaelen scanned the garage with her hearing and x-ray vision as the car got farther away. "You're safe, no one else is here. Head inside where security is better. I'll be back."

"Wait! I need to call the police. You should let them handle this."

"Leah, the attacker is getting away!" Then before Leah could say another word, Kaelen activated her suit and flew out of the garage. She was so concerned about catching up with the fleeing car that Kaelen didn't temper her flight acceleration. Her speed on the straightaways was so fast she was supersonic before the car hit the highway leading out of downtown.

At least she had the foresight to activate the cowl feature since it was broad daylight. It was still rush-hour in Los Angeles and Kaelen lost the car with all the others of similar model and color in the heavy expressway traffic. She paused briefly, floating in the air while she honed in on that heartbeat. Direction set, she took off again and rapidly caught up with it. Kaelen could see the male driver through the front window. He was going faster than safe and weaving in and out of traffic.

She didn't want to take a chance that he'd cause an accident so Kaelen swooped down and lifted the entire vehicle from the road. He began screaming from inside, "What's going on? Put me down, you bitch!"

At first, she'd dug her fingers into the roof of the car but quickly realized that wasn't a sturdy enough place and that the vehicle was in danger of tearing free from her grasp as the metal began to bend away. Unconcerned for the terrified attacker inside, she gave the car a short toss and quickly flew beneath it where she held it by the frame over her head. She floated high above Los Angeles for a few minutes, contemplating what to do with him.

He tried to hurt Leah and part of her wanted to drop the car from the highest height she could fly. But Kaelen wasn't a killer, wasn't even violent by nature and Leah remained unharmed. Perhaps if the bullet were retrieved from the garage, then the man could be handed over to the authorities.

Kaelen's thought process was interrupted by multiple heartbeats approaching her location. She glanced around and saw a flying person that looked half like the flame of a rocket. That was the one she remembered from the night she saved the plane. She also saw two more people in black that had no obvious sign of propulsion. All three wore full black helmets with face shields.

Kaelen couldn't fly away too fast or risk harming the human inside.

"Scion, you are under arrest for crimes committed within Los Angeles."

She called out to the nearest CORP agent, a woman from the fit of her suit. "Crimes?"

"Property damage, vigilantism, and—"

"Abduction or would it be grand—"

"Theft auto?"

The man shrugged at the woman who had originally started speaking. "Eh—"

The woman finished. "Maybe both?" The two that were most similar and didn't have any flame capability spoke symbiotically, something Kaelen had never seen before. She suspected they may be related in some way.

Screaming started again from inside the car. "Get me out of here, this bitch is crazy!"

Kaelen addressed the agents. "I would like to hand this man over to the proper authorities. He is not good."

"Not good?"

"He attempted to murder a citizen using the gun that is in the vehicle with him. There is a single bullet in a parking garage downtown that was aimed at the CEO of Lockheed International."

"And how do you—"

"—know that?"

The way they shared their sentences was confusing. "I heard the click of the weapon and the gunshot. Then I raced to stop the bullet before it could cause injury. While the CEO appeared shaken, she was unharmed. If you contact that person, you will find the evidence of the bullet I caught."

"And how do you know the CEO of Lockheed?"

"I have seen her on the news. Barring the exact resemblance, the woman in the parking garage was also in a mobility chair."

The flaming agent called out, "Yup, that's Leah."

Before Kaelen could explain further, the man in the car yelled. "Fuck you! That woman is crazy, I don't even know where this came from." Kaelen watched as the gun sailed away from the car, obviously having been thrown out the window above her head.

"Oh no you don't!" The female agent raised a hand and the gun froze midair.

Kaelen tilted her head at her. "Are you an alien?"

The non-flaming man answered. "She's an agent, like the rest of us. And you are under arrest."

"Gauss, can it for a minute." She pointed at the agent who was floating farther away. "Not a word out of you either, Afterburn. Give me a minute here." She turned back to Kaelen. "Listen, my name is Sinter. You realize that you've broken the law, right? You can't just…pick up cars with bad people and fly them away. We have proper procedures for this sort of thing—"

"Procedures?" Kaelen grew irritated and suspected they were merely stalling for other agents to arrive. They were probably the only ones that could fly under their own power. "Your stupid Earth procedure would have let a jet full of hundreds of passengers crash in the middle of Los Angeles."

Sinter looked at the two men, then swung back toward Kaelen. "We know that and we're grateful. But rules are important for any functioning society."

Kaelen could hear approaching jets and knew her time was running out. She switched her vision to look at the three flyers. The propulsion from the one called Afterburn was obvious. Not so for the other two. "Let's assume I were going to come with you. What would you have me do with the vehicle?"

Sinter waved toward the agent closest to her. "Gauss can take it. If you let it go, he'll make sure the car gets back to the ground safely, and that the man inside is apprehended until guilt or innocence can be ascertained."

Kaelen was skeptical. "He can lift this vehicle? It is nearly two tons."

Gauss answered confidently, "I have the power of magnetism."

"Fascinating." Kaelen put the clues together and realized they were the Mag Twins that Gabe had mentioned during one of the game nights. She supposed they fit their suits well enough. And while she did find their power interesting, she didn't have time to contemplate it. Her maximal hearing picked up the communicators within the agents' helmets. A tiny voice could be heard from whomever was controlling them. "Keep her busy a little longer." It was Gabe's voice. Time was running out so Kaelen nodded once. "Good. I suggest he take it now then."

She couldn't see facial expression with the shiny, black, full-face helmets but she definitely heard worry in Sinter's voice. "Why? Are you afraid you'll drop it?" Sinter waved toward Gauss and Kaelen let go of the car. It continued to float in place.

The approaching jet caught her eye and she smiled. "No, but I need to go now. I have good work to do. Thank you for apprehending this man for me." Before any of them could react, Kaelen shot straight up, higher than she'd gone before. Then, concerned the CORP could track her using Earth's technology, Kaelen circled the world multiple times before returning to Los Angeles, flying low, skimming the ocean surface. She'd been reading about various ways to stay hidden. All she could say for certain when she returned was that the car was gone from the skyline and it was time for her to go to work.

Chapter Fifteen

Kaelen found a discreet alley to change her suit back into one of the programmed Earth outfits, then made her way around to the main entrance. She assumed that Leah would be concerned for her wellbeing, so she went upstairs to the top floor first. Kaelen made eye contact with Jenna as soon as she stepped off the elevator. "Is she in her meeting yet?"

Jenna looked at her watch then scowled back at Kaelen. "She's in conference room eight and you have six minutes."

A minute later Kaelen was down the hall in the executive wing. She poked her head inside the correct room. "This room has been booked—oh, it's you!" Leah sped her hoverchair around the table as Ellie stood from her seat. Leah raised her chair as soon as she drew next to Kaelen and pulled her into a hug. "I was so worried about you."

"I am fine. Did the authorities come to your parking garage?"

"Yes. They asked a lot of questions and I pointed at the bullet that lay on the ground, then showed them where the car had been parked. They found a spent casing there and asked if I knew the identities of the shooter or Scion. Of course, I said no. I also had the foresight to delete the parking garage security footage from the elevator cam. The others picked up the car leaving and your black blur, but they have no evidence of the rest."

"I hadn't thought of that. Thank you. My only concern was keeping you alive and preventing the guilty party from escaping to try again."

"Sadly, it's not the first time I've been targeted."

Kaelen froze. "What?"

"Kaelen, I told you before that I have security with me wherever I go. If I'm driving, they're usually following."

"Why weren't they with you today?"

Leah pursed her lips. "Because I've been spending so much time with you and I thought I'd be okay, that I'd be safe with you."

"I—oh, Vos. You put your trust in me and I failed you!"

"On the contrary, darling, you did save me. There will always be someone out there with an axe to grind or a grudge. Plenty of folks don't like the way Lockheed used to do business years ago, people who don't think my family paid their full dues in regards to a few terrible events. I've tried to make it a force for good but the memory of tragedy is long-lived."

"It is, truly."

Leah loosened her grip. "My main concern is for you. I don't want you to be found out, especially if you're seen helping me."

Kaelen gently cradled Leah's hand between both of hers. "Please don't worry. I told them I heard a gun round chambering, and the gunshot. I mentioned that I'd saved the CEO of Lockheed International, whom I recognized from the television because of your mobility chair. I indicated that not only wasn't I nearby when it happened, but that I didn't know anything about you or the company. Then I let them take the car I'd been carrying and flew around the world a few times to avoid tracking."

A quiet sound came from Ellie and Kaelen looked at her for the first time since entering the conference room. "You…you flew around the world a few times? You told us you could fly, but you never said how fast."

"Yes. My speed is exceptional."

Leah rubbed the space between her brows with the first two fingers of her right hand. She glanced down at the watch on her slim wrist. "As much as I'd like to discuss the events that occurred before walking into work, our conference call begins in a minute. I'll be down later when I've got some time between meetings, okay?"

"Fine, and I'm happy that you're safe."

"Oh, me too. A bullet would have made the week so much worse. First a plane crash, then some sort of hit man… I'm starting to think that someone wants me dead."

After the first attack by Mimic, Leah had explained her suspicion that the woman was targeting her because of the previous Lockheed business model, and the horrific events that unfolded more than a decade before. Kaelen asked Wex to bring up all the articles about the mass shooting involving David Roger Coleman, as well as anything written about the company, and the Lockheeds in particular. By all accounts the family was as brilliant as they were rich, but they didn't always make their money in ways that could benefit society. It was something that Leah felt guilty for, despite the fact that she was as much a Tuck as she ever was a Lockheed.

"Honey, don't even joke about that! I know that we've struggled with your family's public image for years, but this company isn't the same as it was then, and you don't deserve to be targeted."

Kaelen agreed with Ellie. "She's right. Your death is not a laughing matter."

Leah sighed. "I'm sorry. I have a dark sense of humor sometimes, as I've explained before. Go on now, some of us have work to do."

The fact that Leah had been attacked before concerned Kaelen. "What if something like this happens again?"

"Number one, I trust you. Number two, I'll call the head of my security team and have them beef it up for a bit. Okay?" Kaelen hesitated. "Even if you're with me."

"Thank you."

"Sorry again about the poor taste joke." A face suddenly appeared on the large screen that covered most of the far wall of the conference room. Leah sighed and muttered beneath her breath. "Speaking of jokes…" Kaelen took that as her cue to leave and made her way out of the room and to the elevator.

Einstein was bent over a circuit board when she scanned into the lab. He looked up and gave her a broad smile. "Welcome back to work. Have you had sufficient time to recover from your heroics?"

"I…" Kaelen had been cautioned not to confirm or even speak of her identity as the vigilante known as Scion by all three Tuck women. Leah assured her that their found family were all trustworthy but that telling them of her identity could cause problems if she were later discovered or captured by the CORP. She mentioned something about plausible deniability. "Uh, I stayed with Leah to help her recover from the harrowing plane accident."

He tilted his head one way, then the other. Einstein squinted at her, closed one eye, then opened both wide again. "You are indeed the one they are calling Scion. You are the last heir of your kind, and you have a variety of powers I don't recall Argonians possessing. I speculate they are a product of your travel here, or something on Earth has initiated a cellular change. Perhaps it is because of the unique radiation output of Sol? Of course, we knew some of your abilities, but it seems you had more that we were not aware of."

"Who is we?"

He smiled. "Nalla calls us Leah's Squad. Though to be fair, I've only spoken of my speculation to Nalla, and she would never disclose such dangerous knowledge about one of our group." He held out his hand toward her. "I hope you know that, Kaelen Ra-Evon."

She hesitated, then admitted, "How did you know?"

"Know?"

"About me?"

Einstein tapped his temple. "Twelfth caliber intellect. Also, I recognized the suit and symbol from your interview."

"Oh, that's right. I'm afraid that the attack on Leah has me rattled and not thinking clearly."

A strange look washed over his face and he added, "Even without that, I'm always watching the world around me. It's something I learned from the Tau."

She knew he was referring to his job as a Watcher and contemplated the details of his past before coming to Earth. Kaelen sighed. Having genius friends certainly made it more difficult to hide portions of her life, especially if they knew her well from working together daily. "I was cautioned not to say anything to anyone."

Einstein nodded and steepled his fingers together. "Wise. Well, if we are not speaking of the thing that shall not be named, I would say instead that I'm glad you had to leave our trivia night early. I brought your satchel with me today. It's in your drawer." He nodded toward the cabinet along one wall.

"Thank you, Clevna Trog. You're a true friend and valued scientist. I'm glad to do good work with you."

"As am I. Now, if I may change the subject somewhat…what would you do if you needed to exit this lab in a hurry? How would you go about it?"

Kaelen glanced around the large main lab, noticing the security cameras in each corner. A single door on the south wall led to a long hallway containing doors to eight rooms. One side housed four smaller labs, each one shielded, fully-vented, and dedicated to various long-term and short-term experiments. The four rooms on the opposite side of the hall were all devoted to different sub-specialties of science and filled with expensive and highly-tailored equipment for each of those specialties. The SPL was the only lab in the building that didn't have to share such equipment or test spaces. That's why only the best scientists were placed downstairs and why the main lab had multiple security cameras.

Unfortunately, only two levels existed below theirs. The next one down housed the company servers, and the one below that held all the maintenance and mechanical operations for the skyscraper. Being so deep beneath the ground in a highly secured lab meant she would find it impossible to reach the surface in a stealthy manner. And while she could do it rapidly by simply blasting her way upward, it would cause millions of dollars of property damage, as well as setting back countless experiments from the above labs that were years in the making.

She sighed in defeat. "I don't know. I can't see a way without causing structural damage, setting off alarms, or being caught by security personnel." The more she thought about Einstein's questions, the more it bothered her. "What if Leah were in trouble upstairs and I couldn't arrive in time to prevent harm?"

"Leah isn't typically in danger of physical harm on the corporate level. Corporate attacks, especially on a personal level, are exceedingly rare."

"You didn't hear about the incident this morning?"

Einstein came around the center work bench and took a seat at the stool. He pointed at the screen in the corner with the news replaying footage of Kaelen carrying the gunman's car over her head. "Does it have something to do with that?"

Kaelen moved closer and took her own seat. She clasped her hands tightly together, hoping to stay the unease she felt at the thought of someone trying to harm her beloved. "The man in that vehicle fired a bullet at Leah as we moved from the van to the parking garage elevator."

"Quark! Did he miss?"

"No, I—" Einstein was another alien with an intellect to match her own. She needed help if she were going to keep Leah safe. "I can tell you if you pinky swear that none of what I say leaves this lab." She held out her hand, pinky up, and Einstein quickly hooked them together.

"I will honor your pledge, Kaelen Ra-Evon."

"Good. I caught the bullet."

Despite never wearing his image changer while working in the lab with her, Einstein's face was incredibly expressive. His metallic brows lifted with surprise. "To do so you'd need either extreme speed, or precognitive abilities, as well as some sort of invulnerability."

She ticked off her yellow sun powers on her fingers. "To date, I've discovered that I possess: maximal speed along with the accompanying reflexes and reaction time, flight, maximal strength, a near-field of invulnerability, extraordinary stamina, ice breath, maximal hearing, and a variety of enhanced radiation emitting visions, including, but not limited to, laser vision and x-ray vision."

"That is…impressive. I'm not sure if anyone in the CORP or Earth could match the sheer number of your powers. Perhaps the only ones on or near your level would be Jove, here in LA, or T'ala and Nova up in Seattle."

"Who are T'ala and Nova?"

"T'ala is the special agent in charge of the CORP office in Washington, like Jove is for LA. Nova works in the CORP science division there. They did an interview about a decade ago admitting that they both came to Earth as babies from the planets Reyna and Tora, and were born as soul mates. Nineteen years ago, Nova absorbed the explosion from an arsenal of bombs that leveled about thirty square miles of land in Guantanamo Bay, when she took out the rogue Chromodec responsible for the Uprising. Their powers are also impressive."

Even Kaelen wasn't sure she could survive such a blast. Perhaps the arrogance she'd gained since discovering her special abilities was unearned. "Oh."

"Do you have any weaknesses?"

She trusted Einstein. "I am susceptible to high decibel sound because of my enhanced hearing. And we discovered that my flask of Argonian regenerative serum absorbed galactic cosmic radiation during the journey to Earth and had an agonizing effect on my body."

"I was taught that Argonians are genetically engineered to be immune to radiation in all forms."

"I was as well, but my people had clearly never encountered this, or possibly it is unique to when that particular element absorbs the radiation and reacts to my changed cells here on Earth. Luckily, there were only two flasks, one sent in each Argonian ship as part of the standard medical kit. Wex disposed of one in northern Canada and Leah has the other sample."

"While your powers are excellent, none of them can move you from one place to the next undetected—"

She held up a finger. "I'm fast enough that the average human wouldn't detect me."

"Yes, but your speed gives no advantage while in a secured underground lab that is highly monitored by state-of-the-art cameras. We are accessible via elevator and emergency use stairwell only, all under observation."

"Leah says there are cameras on every level below ground and that an alarm will sound if the doors to the stairwell are opened without it being an emergency. Only the stairwells above the main floor are freely accessible." Einstein nodded. Kaelen slumped a bit in her stool and picked up a six-inch bar of metal they'd been using as a paperweight. She pinched it flat, working the metal into another shape in an effort to expel her nerves. "Do you have any suggestions?"

He nodded. "I can think of a few. It would take a lot of time and money to construct a secret bolt-hole leading from the lab to the surface, not to mention it would potentially expose the company to a security breach from the outside. Another idea is less risky but still potentially disastrous. That would be for you to utilize the hatch in the top of the elevator and fly up the shaft to the roof. But if the elevator were in motion,

full, or there were no extra room in the shaft for you to move through…"
He made an explosive sound while expanding his hands outward.

"Those aren't good ideas."

"They are not. But there is one other option if we can gain clearance from Leah to work on it."

Curious, Kaelen dropped the bar onto the table with a thunk and leaned forward slightly, resting her elbows on the matte black top. "And that is?"

"What do you know about portals?"

"Scientifically? Not much. It wasn't a technology that existed on Argon, though I saw it once or twice on other worlds. If I remember my history correctly, it was outlawed by the High Council to prevent foreign threat from gaining access to the surface. The Thinker Guild even developed technology that could block portals from being used to or from the planet. It happened during the height of the war with Hogath. I also know that some Chromodecs here on earth possess the ability."

"Yes, though it is exceedingly rare. I have the schematics for a portal creator in my memory banks, but there is one problem."

Kaelen frowned. "Would this be advancing human science too far? I thought that was against the Tau Ceti rules?"

"I know well every Tau rule in existence and it doesn't. I've seen previous sketches that Leah uploaded to SPL's private server that were originally started by Charlie years ago. He was close. No, the real problem is converting the schematics over to use materials and a power source available on Earth. I think it can be done but we need time and financial allocation to work on it."

"This could be a valuable tool for science. Even if it couldn't be used by everyone on Earth, it may come in handy for other things. We should present it to Leah together and see if she will give approval. Perhaps we could merge her father's plans with the ones stored in your database. From what I've discovered, many materials are common across the universe. We merely need to research the molecular structure to determine what they are called here."

"I suspect you are right about merging and common materials. I also predict that Leah herself will want to work on this project with us."

"Leah mentioned that she'd stop in later today after her meetings with the board. We can ask her then."

"Superb. In the meantime, I will upload my schematics to the SPL private server." Einstein held his hand out to the computer and images flickered across the screen in rapid succession. Being an organic alien android, he was able to send layer after layer of schematic drawings and specifications remotely into the device.

It was nearly six by the time Leah made her way downstairs. She looked exhausted and Kaelen gently rubbed the back of her neck and shoulders to alleviate the tension. "You've had a long day."

Leah laughed. "It was even longer for those folks on the east coast where the rest of the board was located."

"You like science so maybe this will make your day better." Kaelen turned to Einstein, who showed Leah his schematics for the portal generator, and compared the base points side by side with the one Leah had in the Lockheed project file.

She smiled fondly as she picked up the printed sheet. "You know this was created by Charlie. He never could get the power source worked out. Everything he tried fluctuated too wildly to be safe for regular use."

Einstein cleared his throat. "Well, I'm ninety-nine point-nine percent positive that we can work out the power fluctuations as well as solve the material conversion. The real challenge would be in finding a stable and compact power source."

Leah held her left arm across her middle while the right hand pressed against her chin as she tapped her top lip in thought. It was something that Kaelen had seen Ellie do on occasion. After less than a minute of internal debate, Leah nodded. "Table the desalination project and make this one a priority. You can pivot the battery work you've already done into the portal generator." She moved her gaze back and forth between Kaelen and Einstein. "Give me an estimated timeline and submit the materials to special requisitions. I'll sign off, but try to be mindful of cost, okay?"

Einstein grinned at her. "Yes, ma'am." He closed his eyes for a brief second then addressed the other two. "It is past time for me to return home. Nalla said she's cooking something new for dinner tonight and I am looking forward to the meal."

"What is she making?" Kaelen was genuinely curious about the art of cooking. It appeared to be a lot like science, but of a type she didn't wish to learn. Not when so many wonderful establishments existed all around the city that could make delicious food in quantities to satisfy her.

He shrugged. "She did not tell me what, only that it would be a culinary adventure. It sounds most fascinating."

Leah snickered. "Good luck with that."

He packed his bag and gave a quick wave as he exited the lab. They watched him make his way down the hall through the clear windowed walls. Kaelen walked to the bench and picked up the original portal design sheet to study. She held it up and moved to meet Leah's gaze. "From everything you've told me, and what I've seen of his old designs, your adoptive father was a brilliant scientist."

Leah sighed. "He was also a good dad. We lost him too soon. Maddy and Ellie lost him too soon."

"Loss has no interest in age or intent and not everyone feels loss in the same way."

"How do you mean?"

"It's a hole inside. Some people are large and the hole is small in comparison, leaving them able to navigate life efficiently and without too much pain. Other times they are small and the hole feels immense."

Perhaps Leah could sense that Kaelen referred to more than the loss of Charlie Tuck. "What happens then, if the hole is too large? How do you navigate life full of sadness?"

"Only two ways I can think of. A person can minimize the hole and make the loss less significant."

"That's pretty impossible last time I checked."

Kaelen nodded. "True."

"And the other thing?" Leah moved her hoverchair so she was right next to Kaelen, then took her hand.

"You make yourself larger. Fill your life with so many new things, people, emotions, and experiences that the loss seems small when compared to all that you've gained."

Leah sucked in a breath and her heart rate sped slightly. "And have you done that? Made yourself large in comparison to the loss of your planet and people?"

"I've begun to."

Leah smiled at her. "Yeah?"

"I have you, Leah Lockheed-Tuck. There is no greater gain in my life. No loss can compare with having you in my heart."

"I don't know what to say."

Kaelen thought about their conversation and all the ways she'd changed since arriving on her new planet. She also contemplated all the ways she would continue to change. "Say you understand."

"Understand?" Leah tilted her head in confusion.

"I'm still growing here on Earth. I continue to learn about all I can do as well as explore my boundaries. After the events this morning, I realize that I cannot remain idle as harm comes to people around me, to those I love, and do nothing. I'll try to be careful, but I will continue to do as my conscience dictates when using my abilities in a manner that vilifies me as a vigilante. I understand if keeping me employed at Lockheed is too much of a risk with the law, or—" Kaelen stopped speaking, unable to say the next part. Her eyes watered and chest felt heavy. She looked away.

Leah squeezed her hand. "Or?"

Kaelen hastily wiped the tear away. "Or if you no longer wish to remain in a courtship with my house." She added, "With me," in a whisper.

"Kaelen," she was afraid to see the look in Leah's eyes and refused to turn her head. A soft hand came up to caress Kaelen's cheek and pulled her face gently to the left. "Please, *zhee. Nep gahn i zhetinao.*"

Kaelen gaped at her. "You used my language. You know my words. But how?"

"I only know a few. Remember the laptop that you installed a modified version of Wex on for me?" Kaelen nodded. "I've been asking it for lessons in Argonian. Your words are incredibly difficult to say, worse than German."

"German is a beautiful language."

Leah rolled her eyes, but the smile remained. "What I'm trying to say, darling, is that I'm with you. You are my love and I'm not going anywhere. Promise you'll let me help you and you won't give up on us without open communication. Okay? Don't be self-sacrificing because you fill a hole in me as much as I fill the one in you. We are stronger as a team."

Kaelen pulled her into a hug, careful with her strength while she was so emotionally overwhelmed. "Thank you."

"No, thank you for giving me your heart. I cherish it." When they pulled back from the embrace, Leah's face was slightly flushed. "I know you're probably sick of my company, but would you like to have dinner tonight?"

"I could never grow tired of you."

Leah laughed. "Okay, in that case, dine in or carry out?"

"Will we be eating at your home or mine?"

"Wherever you prefer, darling. I know it's been days since you've been to your apartment. I can come to yours if you need to go home for something."

Kaelen shrugged. "I have nothing of real value at my home save a couple of mementoes taken from Argon." She paused for a few seconds before admitting, "My memories are lonely after a while."

"Yes, they can be." Leah conceded. "Why don't we order takeout and go back to my place and watch *Lilo and Stitch*?"

"That is another animated movie, correct?"

"Yes, and it's one we haven't seen yet. Well, I've seen it but I know you haven't. I think you'll like this one."

Kaelen's chest felt tight in a rush of emotion. She'd grown so much since meeting Leah and happiness filled her, despite no longer living within the light of Vos. "I would like that a lot. Nalla has been educating me about Earth movies and television. She says when you go to someone else's house for entertainment it's called Netflix and chill."

Leah choked and burst into laughter. "Kaelen, no. That is an old euphemism. It's a way of saying you want to come over for the express purpose of sex, without saying you want to come over for sex."

Kaelen blinked at the unexpected information. "Oh." Then she made a face at Leah. "And you say my language is difficult! Earth English is complicated on so many levels that I don't think I'll ever become used to all the slang words and phrases."

"Scroll through Urban Dictionary for a few hours and you might." Leah gestured toward the exit and followed Kaelen out into the hall.

The lights in the lab were programmed to shut off if no movement was detected for more than ten minutes. It was annoying if you were sitting still while working for too long, but it did save energy, which Kaelen found satisfying. "Is this Urban Dictionary an official reference source?"

Leah snickered as they approached the elevator. "It most certainly is not. It will either help you learn Earth slang…or scar you for life."

"That sounds unpleasant."

A snort met her comment. "So is being tricked into looking up what a lemon party is."

"Uh, I think I'll avoid that one." The elevator dinged when they reached the parking garage, but Kaelen blocked Leah's path. "Please let me check for other people." Leah swallowed and nodded.

Kaelen left the elevator car, listening intently for any sound of life in the garage besides their own. She focused her x-ray vision on the van, checking the entire thing for parts that didn't belong or ones that gave off a signal that was abnormal for the machine. Once she was certain that everything was clear and safe, she moved out of Leah's way so her girlfriend could exit.

"All good?"

"Yes, this level is empty and it doesn't appear as though your vehicle has been tampered with."

"Excellent. And in case you wondered, I made a call to Hans earlier today and he's increasing my security team starting tomorrow." Leah hit the remote to unlock the doors. "I also texted Thai Guys with my order while you were doing your inspection. We can swing by the place near my penthouse and pick up dinner on the way."

Once they were both safely in the van, Kaelen asked, "What is *Lilo and Stitch* about?"

Leah explained as they made their way up the slight ramp of the parking garage to the exit. "It's about a lonely alien who learns what *ohana* is from the love of a little girl. It means extended family."

Kaelen sucked in a breath and turned to look at Leah. She sounded out the foreign word. "*Ohana*. I think I'm going to like this film a lot."

"Me too, love. Me too."

* * * *

Later, after the movie, they lay together on Leah's couch. They'd reached a point where Leah trusted Kaelen enough to lay fully atop her body. The sound of Kaelen's heart was strong beneath her ear, and the feel of gentle stroking threatened to lull her to sleep.

Suddenly, one of the strange cramps hit her lower back, which quickly turned into sharp pain. Leah stiffened and cried out, "Ah, shit!"

The stroking stopped and Kaelen tensed beneath her. "What can I do, is this the same pain?"

Leah spoke through gritted teeth. "Yes, but it's not subsiding. It feels like…I don't know what it feels like but it's not pleasant."

Kaelen gasped. "Leah, the muscles in your legs are flexing."

"What?" Leah breathed through the pain and twisted far enough to see her legs where they lay pressed along the length of Kaelen's. She focused all her energy and kicked one foot, then the other. "I did it! Did you feel that?"

Kaelen beamed at her. "You're moving your legs. Did you do that on purpose or is it a pain response?"

"On purpose. I only wish—oh, thank fuck. Sorry, Kaelen, but that one lasted way too long."

"I don't like when you're in pain. I can sit you upright the easy way."

"What is the easy way?"

Kaelen floated off the couch with Leah on top of her body. Then she slowly tilted their joined bodies upright while holding Leah firmly against her. Once vertical, Kaelen placed Leah in the middle of the couch. "Would you like to try it again while sitting?" Leah nodded enthusiastically. "Okay, I'm going to hold my hand an inch from your ankle, randomly alternating between legs. Ready?"

"Yes." Every time Kaelen's hand moved in front of one of her legs, Leah succeeded in giving it an unaided kick.

After trying it a few times, Kaelen put her hand against one of the shins. "Now I want you to push as hard as you can. They did that a few times on each leg. "Your strength is definitely returning. What's truly amazing isn't the level of force displayed so soon into your recovery.

It is the level of fine motor control you have in choosing which side to kick. I predict that it won't be long before the nanobots and serum will have completed their task."

Leah was silent for a few seconds. "I know we decided that the nanobots were safe enough to leave in the human body once their primary task was complete. But it's a shame they couldn't be repurposed or reprogrammed for another task. Like an overall health boost, perhaps."

Kaelen shrugged. "It can be done. It would require injecting another dose of nanobots to boost the existing ones, along with a newly reprogrammed queen that can alter the original nerve regeneration focus to another helpful repair function. Is that something you're interested in?"

"I think now that we've proven the technology, it's in our best interest to see how far it can take us. Think of the possibilities, not only for nerve regeneration but tumor removal, surgeries, even cutting out malignant cancerous tissue. The nanobots could detect and remove exactly the amount needed. This will change the world!"

"Leah, you're already doing that. But I'll gladly do good work to help you achieve even more for the people of Earth."

Leah smiled at her. "I knew I could count on you, darling."

Chapter Sixteen

The following Monday, funding and their acquisitions requests for the portal project were easily approved. That meant Kaelen and Einstein were busy on their new tasks down in the SPL. Leah instructed Einstein to begin translating the alien materials to their Earth equivalent, while Kaelen worked on the program for the supplemental nanobots and queen they would inject once Leah's spinal cord and muscles were returned to 100% function.

Leah wasn't able to come down for her weekly trial tests until later in the day. Ellie joined her in the SPL for the discussion regarding the reprogramming injection. "Are you sure about this, honey?"

"Ellie, the science is sound and I've made huge strides already. I've got an appointment with a private physical therapist at noon tomorrow. It makes sense to repurpose the bots that will be hanging out once the primary task has been performed."

"NDAs for the therapist?"

Leah smirked. "Of course. I don't want news of my recovery to leak before we unveil the project at CES."

"What is CES?" There was much about Earth that Kaelen still didn't understand and half the things she did were made even more confusing by the prevalence of acronyms within the English language. She hypothesized that it was some sort of conference.

"That is an aggressive timeline to run through phase one and phase two trials." Einstein turned to Kaelen. "CES is an acronym that stands for Consumer Electronics Show. It is the most influential tech event in the world, and Leah was invited to speak at the upcoming one in January."

Leah moved her gaze around the group. "It runs from Tuesday the third to Friday the sixth, and I speak on the opening day. Can we do it? Phase one officially began with the rest of the volunteers two weeks ago. Everyone involved with the project has signed iron clad agreements not to disclose the results, and all the volunteers agreed to continue using assistance in public no matter their progress."

"I heard from Doctor Vaughn that each one has responded exactly the same way as Leah."

Ellie tapped her top lip. "From a medical standpoint, it is incredibly aggressive, but I can't deny the results. When you stood for a minute earlier—well you saw my tears so I don't need words to say how I feel. I'm so happy we've reached this point for you and everyone else with a spinal cord injury. We will have to move swiftly if we want this to be the presentation you make. But it is possible. I'll have a marketing team put something together, similar to what they do for our other sensitive launches."

"Is there a reason you are pushing to unveil the NeReNaSe at this event?"

All three of them gave Kaelen a curious look. Einstein asked, "Nee-reh-nah-say?"

She shrugged. "You have yet to officially name it, so I shortened it for casual reference. Nerve regenerative nanobot serum."

Leah answered Kaelen's question with another. "What is the thing that CES is best known for?"

"The wide range of fantastic technologies?" Einstein suggested.

Ellie suddenly grinned. "A show. The flashier the technology the bigger the audience."

Leah pointed at her. "Exactly! Wellness sciences aren't usually a huge draw, but I want Lockheed International to be the absolute talk of the conference. Think of what this will do for our stock. If profits go up then we can put more guilt-free money into R&D on things like the desalinization project."

Her passion was contagious and Kaelen appreciated that Leah's reason for doing it wasn't to make more money for the sake of profits alone. She was doing it to be free to spend on those technologies that could help less fortunate countries solve major problems, such as making sustainable agriculture possible in dry climates to help cure world hunger. "Think of what this will do for Earth when people learn what's possible."

"It's true. This will fuel medical breakthroughs for decades."

Ellie rubbed Leah's shoulder. "I know it will. Patents?"

"You didn't raise me to be a fool. Utility patent applications were filed for all relevant processes and tech involved, for both the serum and the nanobots."

"Fantastic!"

"Once word gets out of your full recovery and Lockheed's new technology, I predict you will be inundated with interview requests."

Leah scowled. "You know I don't talk to reporters, Einstein. I have never given a private interview and I'm not about to start now."

He held up a placating hand. "But think on this. You wish for the news to spread far and wide, but you will want to control the narrative, yes?" She nodded. "What if we bring Nalla in for the interview?"

"Doesn't she usually write about human interest topics?"

"She covers a variety from what I've gathered, and this definitely has a human-interest angle by giving the world technology to help people walk again. But Nalla is also talented, and I am not saying this as her significant other. It could be beneficial for you to interview with a friend rather than someone looking to score a win against the Lockheed who has refused all one-on-one interviews."

"He's right."

"Not you too, Ellie. You know I hate this sort of thing."

"I know, dear. But I think this will be good for both you and the company. Either way, you have plenty of time to think about it as you won't be asked until after the unveiling."

Leah sighed. "True. Okay, I'll consider the idea. Give Nalla a heads up that I may personally tap her for an interview, but don't tell her the details of my recovery yet."

He grinned at her. "Stellar, and I won't. If we're finished here, I would like to continue my translations." Leah waved him off and he wandered back to his desk.

Ellie beamed with happiness. "Today's results were so incredible that I look forward to next Monday's scans."

* * * *

A few days later, Ellie walked into the lab while Kaelen, Leah, and Einstein were hard at work. It was near the end of the work day but Kaelen was intently focused on her nanobot queen project while Leah and Einstein were talking about Charlie's portal design. "Look at you three, solving the world's problems down here."

"Hi Ellie," Kaelen said brightly.

Ellie addressed her and Leah. "Are you two busy tonight? I thought it was time I got to know Kaelen a little better since the fact that you are dating won me a fair amount of money."

Leah rolled her eyes. "How much?"

"Everyone bet fifty."

A bark of laughter echoed through the lab. "Maybe you should treat us then."

Kaelen disagreed. "I don't think that's a good idea. I eat more than what is considered polite."

"Darling, I'm kidding. And you eat as much as you need. Let me leave a message for Maddy to see if she and Tasha are off tonight." Leah retrieved her cell phone from the special holder on her hoverchair and pushed the speaker button before dialing Maddy.

All three of them were surprised when Maddy answered after the first ring. "Hey, Leah! You calling for pointers with your new girlfriend?"

Leah snorted. "Like you didn't learn everything you know from the internet."

"Oh, fu—"

"Hello, Madison. Nice to know my daughters treat each other with such love and respect."

Silence followed Ellie's comment, though Kaelen could hear Maddy's heart rate increase through the phone. "Uh, hi Mom. Sorry. I didn't realize that you'd be there or that Leah would put us on speakerphone."

"I am, and she did. Are you and Tasha free tonight? I know it's a Thursday but I'd like a family dinner with all five of us."

Clothing rustled on the other end of the line. Kaelen could hear

Tasha whisper, "We should get dressed," before Maddy spoke again. "Actually, today is our day off so we're free for dinner. Where would you like to meet? Forewarning though, we're not really, uh, presentable for upscale dining."

Kaelen suggested, "Leah and I both enjoy Thai Guys."

"I'm drawing the line at Asian food, that's all you two ever want!" Maddy complained.

Kaelen clearly heard Tasha say, "Babe, I could totally go for some Pad Thai." She called Maddy out on the lie. "Tasha disagrees with you. She likes Asian food and would eat at Thai Guys."

"Dammit, Kaelen! Stop listening to private conversations."

"Sorry, Maddy."

Leah turned to Ellie. "What about you, Mom, anything in particular you'd like?"

"You know what I've been craving?"

"*Walker, Texas Ranger* reruns?"

Even Leah laughed at Maddy's answer. Ellie sighed and shook her head. "I could go for a burger and fries."

"Beast Burger," Leah offered.

"Yes, that's exactly what I'm craving. Something terrible for me." She looked at Kaelen and winked. "It's one of my guilty pleasures."

Maddy responded a few seconds later. "That's good for us. How about the location on the corner of Locust and Main, will that work for everyone?"

"What is Beast Burger?" Kaelen had tried many restaurants all over the city, but for some reason, despite its prevalence, she hadn't eaten at that one.

Silence reigned for a few moments until Maddy spoke with obvious disbelief. "You mean to tell me that you've been on this planet for…uh, how long have you been on Earth, Kaelen?"

Kaelen looked back and forth between Ellie and Leah's astonished faces. "I landed exactly one year ago today."

"What? Kaelen, why didn't you tell me?"

She looked at Leah. "I didn't realize it was significant."

Leah took her hand. "Darling, you mentioned the other night that you didn't celebrate birthdays because of the multistep, artificial Argonian birthing process. I think since you didn't have an official date, we should make the date that you landed on our planet your rebirthday."

Maddy laughed. "Re-birthday, that's great."

Tasha interrupted Maddy's laughter. "And because today is the day, we should celebrate your birthday as part of our family dinner."

"Okay, change of plans." Leah smoothly took over. "Mom, Maddy, and Tasha, if you don't mind, let's eat at my place. We'll play some games and see if I can order a cake to be delivered. I'm afraid options will be limited this late in the day so it will most likely be pre-made."

Kaelen was uncomfortable that they'd go through so much trouble for her. She never wanted to be a burden. "You don't need to do all that. I already feel more than welcome with your family and on this planet." She paused. "With the exception of the CORP agency that wants to incarcerate me."

Maddy's sure voice brooked no arguments. "Nope, we're doing this, Ra-Evon. You are part of the family now so you better get used to it. We'll meet you all at Leah's in an hour. You want us to pick up the burgers?" Leah smirked at Kaelen. "No, send me your order. I'm going to have it delivered by Fleet Eats. I want Kaelen to try one of everything from the menu so she can never again say she doesn't know what Beast Burger is."

"One of everything?" Maddy said with disbelief.

"She's an alien, remember?"

"Fair enough. Okay, sis. We'll see you within the hour."

Leah hung up then looked at the time. She called across the room. "Hey Einstein, it's after five, why are you still here?"

"I started late today and was hoping to make up some ground. Leaving early doesn't set a good example for the other labs—"

"Einstein,"

"Yes?"

"I'd say you've stayed enough late nights on the nano project to earn a few early days. Say hi to Nalla for us."

He nodded once. "That's an astute observation and a wonderful gift. Nalla should be finished covering the fall equinox festival at Grand Park for MNN by now. I shall surprise her with Thai Guys for dinner." He shrugged when all three of them stared at him. "Your conversation incited a powerful craving that only their pot stickers can satisfy."

Leah laughed. "I knew I liked you for a reason."

Kaelen found the comment strange. "His sense of humor and twelfth caliber intellect wasn't enough of a reason?"

"More than enough." Leah said to Ellie, "You want to ride with us?"

"No, I'll take my car. That way I can go straight to my city apartment and not have to come back here after. I may be a little late because I've got to make a stop on the way."

Hearing that they were all leaving, Kaelen rushed around the lab and shut down various machines and other equipment. Einstein took care of the rest, and the group made their way to the elevator together. Once in the parking garage, Kaelen insisted that she scan their level to make sure no one was around before letting any of them leave the elevator. Ellie deposited a kiss on Leah's cheek then surprised Kaelen by giving her the same. "See you girls shortly. Leah, you already know my order."

"Of course. Bye, Ellie, see you in a bit."

An hour and a half later, the five women sat around Leah's dining room table. Maddy stared at Kaelen with an expression that wavered between disgust and amazement. "I don't know whether to be jealous you're able to eat like that, or feel nauseated."

Kaelen had already eaten half of what Leah ordered. At least one of the burgers was listed as "wild style" on the wrapper. She grinned at Maddy. "It tastes amazing. And you say this food is unhealthy for humans?"

Tasha snorted. "All fast-food is."

"That's unfortunate for you then. Beast Burger is warm, salty, savory, sweet, and packed with protein. I especially like their fried Frenches."

Maddy snickered. "French fries."

"Yes, those."

Luckily for Kaelen, she ate significantly faster than the rest, else she'd still be eating after Maddy, Tasha, and Ellie went home. "This food, our dinner tonight…it makes me feel—" She stopped because she was unsure how to form words from her emotions.

"What is it, darling? How does it make you feel?" Leah reached out to lay her fingers across Kaelen's left wrist.

Kaelen met her gaze, then looked around the table at the other three women and sighed. "It makes me feel happy, as happy as when I was a child on Argon. Like I belong and that my found family is now my real family."

"Kid, we are your real family now and don't let anyone tell you different," Maddy said.

Tears threatened but not ones of loss. They were a sign of how large she'd grown compared to the past she left behind on that long trip away from Vos. "Thank you, Maddy."

"Anytime, kid—"

Leah's phone rang and she pointed at Kaelen. "No listening."

Kaelen nodded and focused her hearing on the loudest sound near their location in the city. She was vaguely aware of Leah's responses over the phone but was unable to hear the other side of the conversation with her attention split.

Leah hung up and smiled at the group around the table. "Two minutes."

Ellie prompted, "Until?"

"Until we sing."

"Ah, gotcha."

Confusion brought Kaelen's concentration back to the room. "Sing? Like the music I was listening to?"

"Music? What are you talking about?"

Kaelen elaborated. "I can hear a show playing music somewhere in LA. A woman is singing with other instruments in the background and people cheering."

"Holy shit! Are you talking about 'Resurrection'? They're performing at El Rey Theater tonight. I tried to score me and Tasha tickets but the show was sold out within minutes. I'm so jealous that you can just," Maddy wiggled her fingers, "tune in like that whenever you want."

"It is nice when it's something I want to hear. But more often than not I wish for silence. For instance, I can hear every conversation in the building if I choose. I can listen and hear every siren across Los Angeles, as well as every cry, laugh, or shout of anger. It's more overwhelming than beneficial."

"Oh, Kaelen. I'm so sorry." Tasha gave her a look of compassion.

"How do you cope with it all?"

"Wex taught me how to control my hearing before I moved from Vancouver to Los Angeles. Until that point, I'd been relying on the filtering program in my communicators. Sometimes, when things seem especially loud or I feel vulnerable, I'll put the communicators back in and ask Wex to filter for me."

Her gaze was drawn to Leah, who in turn looked thoughtful. "You also mentioned that high decibel frequencies were a weakness. Perhaps we can find a better way to help muffle the ambient sounds for you. I'll make a note to dive into the topic later this week."

"Thanks, *zhee*."

The elevator gave a ding and broke up the heavy moment. Everyone turned to look, then Ellie, Maddy, and Kaelen all stood from the table when the doors opened to reveal a woman pushing a cart loaded with three boxes. Leah turned around and waved the woman forward. "Hi Val. Can you set it up over there? And thanks again for the late request. You're a life saver."

"It's no problem, really." Val pushed the cart across the apartment to the large kitchen island.

Maddy said to Leah, "I can't believe you scored LA Cakery on such short notice. Kaelen, you're in for a real treat."

A sweet scent perfumed the air as the five of them watched Val carefully assemble the dark pink frosted layers of cake on the cleared surface. When the three layers were stacked, Val removed multiple bags of frosting from a cooler and touched up the edges around the base of each cake. She finished it off by adding fresh raspberries.

"The smell reminds me of donuts. Does cake taste similar?"

"Oh, for the love of fu—"

"Madison," Ellie gave her a stern look.

"Uh, fudge." She looked at Leah. "She hasn't had cake yet either?"

Leah shrugged. "Apparently not. She had pie at The Bean Bag, and donuts from nearly every donut shop in Los Angeles."

"Kaelen," Tasha said, "you'll like cake. Trust me."

Once the cake was assembled with the decorative touches added, Leah removed the wallet from her special drawer and gave Val a few hundred dollars tip. "Thanks for the last-minute setup. I wanted Kaelen's birthday to be special, but we didn't know about it until a little while ago."

Val smiled at her and pocketed the cash. "You're lucky I had the layers already made up in the cooler."

Leah gave her a worried look. "This isn't going to cause trouble with another order, is it?"

"No, I was working ahead. I'll make more tomorrow morning when I open the shop. It's all good. Pleasure doing business with you, Leah." Val pushed her cart back into the elevator and called out to Kaelen, "And happy birthday!"

Kaelen smiled and waved back. "Thank you." Then the doors closed, leaving them with a three-tier cake, fully iced and ready for someone to cut. Kaelen moved nearer to the beautiful creation. "That smells delicious. What flavor is it?"

"Double chocolate cake with raspberry buttercream frosting."

Maddy groaned and turned to Tasha. "Babe, we are so taking some of that home with us."

Leah smirked at her. "You're assuming there will be any left."

"Why wouldn't there—" Maddy stopped speaking and glanced down at the pile of empty burger wrappers in front of Kaelen. "Dammit."

Ellie spoke to Maddy. "You don't even know if Kaelen will like it."

"Sure. Pull the other one, Jan."

Ellie snickered. "You're too young for that show. Heck, *I'm* too young for that show since it was your grandma's favorite when she was growing up. And you never know about Kaelen's tastes, stranger things have happened."

"Mom," Maddy groaned. "Kaelen is like a garbage disposal, or like…some kind of eating machine." Kaelen was finishing the rest of Leah's fries when Maddy gestured toward her. "She's a human version of a Labrador retriever, with the appetite to match."

Tasha smiled at her. "More like a golden retriever."

"While you have an excellent point about my girlfriend, can we stop comparing her to dogs?"

Kaelen perked up. "I love dogs. I have a lot of pictures of dogs from around Los Angeles in my phone. I can show you later if you like—"

Leah covered her lips with a slim finger. "Later, love. Right now, we have a song to sing." She moved her chair into the kitchen and sorted through one drawer until she came up with two boxes. Leah pulled out two tiny candles from one of them and pushed them into the top layer. Then she opened the other box, removed a small wooden stick, and scraped it along the side until it produced a flame. She lit the candles and smiled at Kaelen.

"Why are you putting romance flames on the cake?"

Maddy and Tasha snickered as Leah gestured for Kaelen to come closer. "Darling, candles are a way to make celebrations more festive."

"Oh, like the night we—"

Maddy clapped her hands over her ears. "La, la, la, I don't want to hear about any bedroom stuff between you and my sister!"

"You're such a child, Maddy. And Kaelen, it's part of the birthday celebration. As for why two, I chose one candle to represent Argon, and one for Earth because you are a woman of both."

"Well said, Leah."

Leah smiled at Tasha. "Next, we'll sing you a song, then you make a silent wish in your head, and carefully blow out the candles. We don't need you to freeze the cake."

Kaelen looked around the assembled members of her Earth family. "You know that wishes are highly illogical, right? It wasn't something that was encouraged within members of the Thinker Guild. When I discussed the topic with Einstein, he said his people felt the same and any wish coming true would be a simple mathematical configuration of probability odds combined with the inclination of nature to repeat itself."

Maddy burst out laughing. "That sounds exactly like something Einstein would say."

Leah shook her head and gave Kaelen the smile that always made Kaelen's stomach flutter. "Apparently Argonians and Donbothians are alike in that way. Must be the twelfth caliber intellect thing." She winked. "Illogical or no, you should still make a wish. It doesn't have to come true, make sense, or even be possible. Wish for what the heart wants."

Maddy suggested, "You could wish for money."

"Or wish for love." Tasha gave Maddy a pointed look.

Ellie added, "You can even wish for health and happiness."

Kaelen looked at them all, surprised that Leah hadn't called out her own suggestion. "But I already have what I would wish for, the thing I want most on this world."

"What's that?"

Kaelen moved her gaze to the person she referred to. "Leah. Her health, happiness, and affection are my only wish."

"Aww, that is so cute!"

"Dammit, Kaelen! You're making me look bad in front of my girlfriend."

Kaelen shrugged, feeling as if she kept getting in trouble with Leah's older sister. "Sorry again, Maddy. But it's the truth."

"Fine then, let's sing and you can wish for her or something else. Either way, let's do this so I can put a piece of that cake into my face hole."

What happened next was a first for Kaelen. As one, all four of the other women began singing a simplistic song with a repetitive tune. They looked at her expectantly when it was over, and she took that as her cue to blow out the candles. She was careful not to strip it of frosting or freeze the cake. They all clapped and Leah removed the candles and dropped them onto the counter.

Kaelen looked around the small gathering. "While I love the ceremony and thought behind this tradition, that was the most unimaginative Earth song I've ever heard."

Even Ellie chuckled. "She's not wrong."

"Kaelen," she glanced at Leah, who gestured toward the small top tier of cake. It was about six inches in height and six inches in diameter. "Remove this for me and you can take the entire thing as your piece. We should have plenty left to send home with Ellie, Maddy and Tasha."

Leah cut the second layer and placed slices on saucers while the rest of them cleaned off the fast-food debris from the table. Despite Maddy's seeming desperation to eat her piece, they all waited so they could watch Kaelen eat her first bite.

She stabbed her fork down the tall layer and removed a long strip, counting six separate dark layers with more dark pink frosting between each one. Kaelen managed to cram the entire forkful into her mouth and moaned as the rich mix of flavors hit her tongue. She savored the explosion of sweetness. "This is the most amazing thing I've tasted since I landed on Earth."

Maddy laughed and pointed a fork at her. "I told you so."

Once everyone was finished with their cake, Leah packed two containers for when the others left and had Kaelen put the rest in the refrigerator. Kaelen made mental plans to eat more after they were gone. At first, Kaelen didn't understand why Ellie handed her a decoratively wrapped package. Then Tasha and Maddy handed her an envelope. Maddy added, "You're hard to choose a gift for, especially on such short notice."

"You didn't have to give me a gift."

"It's birthday tradition, Kaelen. Of course, we did."

Kaelen's face grew warm. "Your company and the wonderful cake were more than enough."

Maddy shrugged. "Even so, you're still getting gifts so deal with it."

Kaelen opened the envelope first. Inside were two tickets to the Los Angeles Museum of Science and Industry. She looked at Maddy and Tasha, delighted. "Leah and I were talking about going here soon. Thank you."

Tasha laughed. "Where do you think we got the idea?"

Ellie's gift was next. Inside the box, Kaelen found a folded double frame. When she opened it, there was a photo on each side. One of her and Leah on the left, and the one on the right was a selfie that Leah had taken during their first group lunch in the Special Projects Lab. Leah, Einstein, Ellie, and Kaelen were all smiling at the camera. She looked up at Ellie, unsure what to say.

Ellie said, "You didn't seem to have much in the way of personal items at your apartment. I thought that might look nice on the table closest to the TV."

Kaelen cradled the frame to her chest, more than a little overwhelmed at the gesture. "Thank you. That's exactly where I'll put it when I get home. Is—is it okay if I give you a hug?"

"Oh, Kaelen. You never have to ask." Ellie came around the table, meeting Kaelen as she stood as well.

When they pulled back from the hug, Kaelen wiped the tears from her eyes. "Ellie Tuck, you're nothing like my *liu*. But if I had to pick a mother here on Earth, it would certainly be you."

Leah let the emotional moment play out for a minute before she spoke. "I have something for you as well, Kaelen, but I'll give it to you later."

"I bet you will."

"Madison!"

"Maddy!" Tasha slapped Maddy's arm.

"Okay, I get it. Jeez, why is Leah everyone's favorite? I came along first."

"Stop picking on your sister."

Maddy sighed. "Fine."

Leah snickered. "Get your mind out of the gutter. I'll tell you now since Maddy is incapable of controlling her curiosity. I planned to take you and Einstein, as well as the team in Lab twelve, with me to CES at the beginning of January. After all, it's the fruit of your labor that has worked in conjunction to make this project possible."

"Blah, blah, blah, work stuff. Is that really all you're giving her?"

"Ellie, will you close your eyes for a second?" Ellie smirked but complied, allowing Leah to wave her middle finger at Maddy, prompting a lot of grumbling from across the table. Tasha and Kaelen locked eyes and giggled at the Tuck sisters' antics. "But to answer your question, no, that's not all I'm giving her. I've also arranged for the two of us to go a few days early to celebrate New Year's Eve and attend some of the shows in Vegas."

Maddy looked back and forth between Leah and Kaelen. "Will she even like Vegas shows? No offense, Kaelen, but you're very… science-y."

"That's not a word, Maddy."

"Says you."

Kaelen interrupted what was sure to be another debate between them. "I like anything as long as I'm with Leah."

"Aww, babe!"

Maddy grumbled, "Dammit, Kaelen."

Leah laughed and took Kaelen's hand. "You'll have to program a few formal Earth outfits into that suit of yours." She must have picked up on Kaelen's confusion because she added, "I'll show you some examples later. It's only the fall equinox, we have a few months still."

"Okay."

They played a variety of games for the next few hours until everyone agreed to call it a night. Kaelen and Leah exited the game room with the other three and made sure they got their containers of leftover cake. Hugs were given then Maddy, Ellie, and Tasha were lost to sight as the elevator doors closed. Leah and Kaelen turned to face each other and Leah asked, "Well, what did you think?"

"I've had many good days since coming to Earth, specifically when I'm with you. But I have to say that today is my new favorite."

Leah raised her chair and pulled Kaelen into a hug. "Oh yeah? Well, you're my favorite."

Kaelen sank into the embrace. "Thank you for everything."

"Vrildif, nes gahv i zhetinao imolaht."

That earned Leah another squeeze. "Always? And if anyone is a lovely scientist, it's definitely you. I never expected the one I courted to be so physically appealing. It is certainly a bonus. I wonder if the bonding program would have matched us if you'd been Argonian?" Leah's cheeks grew pink and Kaelen delighted at the sight.

"I could only hope. Come along, darling. Let's get ready for bed. I assume you're staying?"

"Of course. I always sleep better with you."

"Really?" Kaelen nodded. "And why is that?"

"Because Wex usually wakes me with the rising sun, explaining that a proper Argonian starts the day early as it's the most efficient way to guarantee good work. It was a common practice where I'm from."

"I've said it before, and I'll say it again, Wex is a dick."

Kaelen began to protest, intent on explaining, yet again, that Wex was an inanimate AI, then stopped. She contemplated each time the AI had woken her from a pleasant night's dream. "You're right. Wex is a dick."

Leah paused long enough to pat Kaelen's cheek, then directed her hoverchair up the stairs, calling over her shoulder, "Of course I am. And I already know you'll eat more cake while I'm in the shower, but don't be too long."

Kaelen grinned even as she raced into the kitchen to cut another large slice. She called after Leah as she retrieved a clean fork. "I won't."

Chapter Seventeen

The weeks passed swiftly after Kaelen's birthday. She was happy with her life on Earth and in her relationship with Leah. She'd been good about not going out as Scion since the day of the parking garage attack. One thing that Kaelen wasn't happy about was the fact that the police had not determined who hired the man that shot at Leah. The news said that he'd been sentenced for attempted murder and a number of other outstanding criminal offenses, but the real culprit was still out there.

Leah's physical therapy progressed enough that she'd begun walking on her own in the privacy of one or the other's home. First with a cane, then eventually without. Kaelen kept careful watch on her to make sure Leah's legs didn't give out. By the end of October, about two months after the first injections, her scans no longer showed any damage to the spinal cord or surrounding nerve clusters. The muscles continued to improve and strengthen during their accelerated growth period, which still caused the occasional cramp. However, the pain associated with the return of nerve function had disappeared.

It was Friday, three days before Halloween, and Kaelen and Einstein had spent most of the day trying to assemble a prototype for the transmatter portal generator. "Everything is perfect but we don't have access to a power source that is small enough to fit in this." He held up the large, titanium watch case he'd converted to hold the portal actuator.

Kaelen's mind raced with ideas as she studied the schematics again. "What if we don't need to put the full power source within the case?"

"How else would the portal have the energy to open?"

"This would be simpler if we were creating the portal in a frame that could provide the necessary power. But theoretically that would only be needed for a large portal, which draws power at an exponential rate as surface area is increased. However, for something the size of one or two people, you wouldn't need much at all to rip open one end. The other exit portal will open on its own reactively, homing in on the origination point. The majority of the near portal will draw ambient energy from charged atoms around it."

"That still leaves the beginning boost of power."

"Where are you with your battery research for the desalination project?"

Einstein frowned. "I've been testing various metals to replace the steel, with the hope of increasing power absorption and return without significant discharge or capacity loss over time."

"You'd want stability as well, especially in high heat if this is working in conjunction with solar charging."

"Precisely."

Kaelen contemplated all the metals existing on Earth. She picked up the cube-shaped paperweight that Leah had purchased to replace the chromium one Kaelen had destroyed when she was fidgety. The new one was made of terzenite. Leah found it delightful that Kaelen couldn't break or malform the cube no matter how hard she tried.

"Archimedes' eureka!" She held up the weight and turned to Einstein with a smile. "We've had the answer right under our noses this entire time!"

"Quark, you're right! Terzenite is a hyper conductive metal native to Terzen. Expensive, yes, but I'm sure Leah wouldn't mind using a bit for the project. This material will allow us to create a battery on nearly a microscopic level that will hold the same charge as something significantly larger."

"I've actually been to Terzen with my father. Did you know terzenite is rumored to have a variety of beneficial properties?"

"I did. Besides being the strongest metal discovered, it is supposed to negate gravity, speed healing, increase strength, and protect one from extremes in temperature." They both glanced down at the block of metal that was clearly affected by Earth's gravity. "Maybe it works in conjunction with something else to achieve such fantastical properties."

He looked thoughtfully toward the block. "Perhaps I can make that my personal side project."

Kaelen shrugged. "Maybe. Until then, we'll need to determine how to form it into useful pieces. It is obviously mined and manipulated somehow, but I don't know the heat requirements for processing."

"I know that magic can be used to melt and shape it."

"The official stance of Argon's Thinker Guild was that magic didn't exist, though there were some houses that insisted they could manipulate such energies. That means I know nothing of magic. Any other suggestions?"

"Pity." He grumbled. "When all else fails, go directly to the local source of alien knowledge." Kaelen found his statement a bit confusing. "I'll text Gabe. The CORP would certainly have the information within their database." He sent a message on his phone then placed it back on the bench. "If it's within the heat range of one of our lasers, we'll need to book time in the optics lab. They have the only high-powered machine. It's the one thing we couldn't have of our own down in the SPL."

Kaelen shrugged. "It hardly seems worth complaint since we have everything else we could need."

"True." Einstein's phone vibrated on the table, and he smiled when he saw the message. "Gabe says the melting point of terzenite is 4,275 degrees Fahrenheit. I'll check the calendar to see when they've got a machine free."

He spun the trackball on his mouse and Kaelen called out, "Wait."

"Yes?"

"Maybe I can cut it."

Einstein appeared perplexed as he moved his gaze between Kaelen and the block of metal. "We already established that your strength isn't enough, nor well suited, for this type of work."

"I have, uh, laser vision. Sometimes it is merely ambient radiation, other times I can focus to shoot beams of light from my eyes."

He was obviously fascinated by the new information. Einstein stood and announced, "That makes logical sense given that your other optical powers utilize varying forms of radiation. We should test this laser vision immediately. We can use the last lab down the hall. It's insulated to absorb heat and light energy."

A few minutes later Einstein had gathered a variety of metal samples and placed them out from lowest melting point to highest. They were on a table made from heat tiles commonly found on old Earth spacecraft. Kaelen used her laser vision on the first sample, easily melting the titanium into slag.

"That was good, but the beam is too wide for anything practical like cutting. Can you focus more?"

She shrugged. "I can try." With eyes narrowed slightly, Kaelen focused her vision on the next metal, which was chromium. While the laser cut easily through the plate, it was still too wide.

Einstein rubbed his chin. "An observation: chromium has a 2,180 degrees Kelvin melting point and your laser vision appears deep red. If we're comparing it to actual laser light, red penetrates more into the target material and is diffused." He pointed at the first two plates. "Notice the de-focused spots here, here, and here. You mentioned your power was a form of radiation output. Would it be possible for you to shift your laser vision on the light spectrum to blue? And do you know the maximum temperature you're capable of?"

Kaelen frowned as she contemplated his suggestion. "Blue laser produces a small, focused point on the surface which would result in a cleaner, precise cut." She huffed. "Honestly, I don't know. I haven't had much call to use this particular power since arriving on Earth."

"It cannot hurt to try. Visualize the laser you emit and attempt to shorten the wavelength to shift it further down the light spectrum."

The next metal plate was a bit of iridium which required more than 4,000 degrees. Kaelen took a few deep breaths then focused intently on the plate while she relaxed the muscles in her eyes that kept the power in check. Fine blue beams shot out and merged to neatly bisect the plate. The laser vision cut off and she turned to Einstein with a smile. "I did it!"

"Phenomenal. Okay, one plate left. Tungsten." He pointed at the last one he'd taken from the cabinet.

Kaelen used the same tight focus from before and the twin beams shot out to hit the metal. It glowed brightly as she made multiple cuts then the plate split into even pieces. "Do we have anything stronger? What is the melting point of tungsten?"

Einstein rattled off the answer. "Approximately 3,695 Kelvin. I've got a gauge that we can use to check the limits of your power. I'll be right back."

He left the lab and Kaelen picked up the small metal plates that was still glowing. She used her freeze breath to cool it then returned it to the tile table. Einstein came through the door holding a large cylinder with a long cable wrapped around his arm.

"What is that?"

"It's a pyrometer." He unwound the cord and plugged it into an outlet on one wall. "Focus on the tungsten again with as much heat as you're capable of producing. Don't worry about it cutting through. I'll take a temperature reading while you do that."

Kaelen complied until the largest metal plate glowed with heat and sliced neatly in half. Then she began cutting through the tiles below and abruptly stopped. "I'm sure I can go hotter, but something is holding me back. Probably for the best."

Einstein looked at her with a raised brow. "That test produced an impressive amount of heat. 9,978 Kelvin. That is hotter than the sun! And if you're able to produce even more..." The magnitude of her power was staggering.

"I suppose that makes sense since I'm powered by the yellow sun. Perhaps my body stores the energy in my cells like a battery. By focusing the projected power I'm able to achieve an even greater temperature."

"Astute. Let's try the terzenite blo—" Kaelen rushed out of the smaller lab and returned with the paperweight before Einstein could finish his sentence. "—ock. Place it on the table please, then slice the thinnest section possible."

Kaelen repeated the process, focusing more than the previous times. She used her laser vision in conjunction with her microscopic sight, which was one of the most difficult tasks she'd performed with her powers since their discovery in the wilds of Canada. The thinnest square of metal pealed from the block, deformed slightly from the high heat. She picked up the tiny slice, then blew on it to cool it down. It was thin enough that she was able to flatten it out again before placing it in Einstein's open hand. "Will this work?"

"It's a start. I'll need a series of tiny disks to assemble the battery for testing. But you can do that later if you're tired." He turned to her with a smile. "It has been invigorating working with you, Kaelen Ra-Evon. I find your abilities truly fascinating."

"I've enjoyed exploring my powers. Especially since we're also doing good work. Thank you for your help." Rather than wait until a different time. Kaelen plucked the thin square from Einstein's fingers and lay it on the tile table. She brought both beams together into a single focal point. With a precise application of her laser vision, Kaelen cut a series of small circles. Once complete, she carefully blew cold air across the table.

"There, now you don't have to wait."

"Perhaps you are impatient."

She held up her hands and shrugged. "Guilty. I want to see that portal work."

Further discussion was interrupted by Leah. "There you are." She wasn't using her hoverchair and walked into the lab. "What's going on?"

"Kaelen was testing the limits of her laser vision."

Leah gave Kaelen a sharp look. "He knows?"

"Einstein is as intelligent as I am. He easily figured it out."

"I see." She moved her gaze to Einstein, who shook his head.

"I will not tell anyone of Kaelen's abilities or her other identity."

"See that you don't."

Kaelen stepped close enough to give Leah a hug. "Did you need me for something?"

"I did, actually. Maddy texted me and said she wants to go out tomorrow night to celebrate Halloween."

She found Leah's statement confusing. "I thought the Earth Halloween holiday was on the last day of the month?"

"It is, but many bars will celebrate on the weekend before because people don't want to go out if they have to work the next day."

The explanation made sense. "Is this a well-regarded holiday?"

Einstein chuckled. "From what I've observed, it is an excuse for children to receive candy and for adults to drink alcohol and dress like children."

Kaelen was confused about his explanation. "So, is it a good thing or bad thing?"

"It's a blast if you're with the right people. And speaking of the right people, Maddy decided last minute that she and Tasha, along with the rest of us, will go to the Halloween bash at Szot's bar tomorrow. She suggested dinner first at Farro's at seven, but she wants numbers so she can make a reservation." Leah smiled at Einstein. "The invite extends to you and Nalla."

He pulled out his phone and began texting. A few seconds later he looked up with a smile. "Nalla said she's in. Please let Maddy know. Will there be a contest?"

"There always is." Leah looked down at her own phone. "You know what? It's Friday. Why don't you go home. That way you can get a head start on your costume for tomorrow. I expect something amazing, Mr. Trog."

He rubbed his chin in contemplation. "Hmm, it is short notice but I think I have an idea. I've got a few spare parts at home that Nalla has threatened to throw in the trash. Those should work perfectly for my costume."

Leah laughed. "What, no protest about me sending you home at three in the afternoon on a workday?"

Einstein gave her a serious look. "Not when there is a contest to be won! Now, if you'll both excuse me, I have blueprints to draw up." He gathered the terzenite disks then looked at the demolished metal samples remaining on the table.

Kaelen waved him off. "I'll clean. I want to see a fantastic costume tomorrow. This will be my first time participating in a Halloween celebration." He nodded and exited the lab, leaving Kaelen and Leah facing each other.

The corners of Leah's eyes wrinkled slightly with her smile. "Hi, love." She pulled Kaelen close and kissed her tenderly.

Kaelen savored the taste of Leah's lips and went back for another. "*Mmm*, unprofessional though it may be, I enjoy getting visits from my girlfriend at work."

"Even though I'm technically your boss's boss?"

"Maybe especially."

Leah laughed and shook her finger at Kaelen. "You have come a long way from that quirky alien who solved the Collatz Conjecture a year ago."

Kaelen smiled at her as she used her maximal speed to clean up the disfigured plates and deposit them into the appropriate bins of scrap metal for potential use at a later date. Then she returned to Leah's side and took her hand. "Will I like this Szot's bar?"

"Wait, you haven't been to Szot's with us? I know it's been a few months but…oh, right. You refused to meet with everyone until fairly recently. Well, I think you'll enjoy Szot's, though you may want to bring the lead core earplugs in case it gets too loud."

Leah scowled when they approached the end of the hall housing the specialty labs. But camera placement inside the main lab, as well as the glass walls lining the hallway that led to the elevator meant she couldn't risk walking around beyond that point. The only ones who actually knew she'd been walking were the four of them that worked in SPL, plus Leah's physical therapist. They hadn't even told Maddy yet and Einstein said he'd not mentioned it to Nalla. It was one of the best kept secrets in LA, better, apparently, than Kaelen's other identity. Leah sighed and sat in the chair, then maneuvered it into the main room.

"Leah, what will you wear to the costume party, and will I need to dress in alternative clothing as well?"

Leah gave her a secretive smile. "That is going to be our first stop once we leave work. I've got some ideas that I hope you'll like."

"I am open to anything with you."

Leah's lips turned up at the corner. "Oh really?"

Kaelen recognized the flirtatious look. "I've said as much many times. But you know my limits remain due to lingering reservations about my strength."

"I know, darling. I'm only teasing you. Let's sign off for the day and head to the costume shop, shall we? It's a specialty place for folks that have a lot of money."

"Can I program my suit for something?"

"You could, but where is the fun in that?"

Leah's heart beat a rapid pace as she and Kaelen stood outside the restaurant the next evening. Maddy informed them that their group was in a private dining room in back. "Are you sure you're ready? This is a big step…uh, I mean—"

Leah laughed and took her hand. "Relax, I know what you meant and it literally is a big step."

"If you're worried about your secret, I don't think anyone will know it's you. All but your mouth is hidden beneath the cowl, your hair color is different, and, well, you're walking. None of those things would be associated with CEO, Leah Lockheed."

"I know, I know. I'm mostly worried about Maddy."

"Really? She will be ecstatic when she learns of your recovery."

Leah sighed and pulled them farther from the restaurant entryway where they wouldn't be overheard. "She's always taken care of me, you know? What if she sees me differently now? I'm no longer the little sister that she remembers."

"I've observed Maddy for nearly as long as I've known you. The Tuck women are a fiercely close-knit family, and extremely protective. Maddy adores you and nothing will change that." Leah pursed her lips, but Kaelen could hear Leah's reaction to her words without a verbal response at all. Hearts never lied. Each beat unique, every one reactive to humans' moods. Kaelen had learned to interpret it all over the past thirteen months on the planet.

"You know, you've gotten good at this."

"What?"

"Being human."

Kaelen grinned at her. "Thank you. But right now, I'm not human. I'm the—" she made quotes with her fingers. "CORP approved vigilante known as Bolt." She tugged the fabric of the deep blue suit and frowned at the symbol on her chest, unfamiliar to what she'd normally see. It was a purple lightning bolt crossing diagonally over a white oval. Rather than a full cowl with a built-in wig like the one Leah wore as Alley Cat, she had a half cowl that allowed the dark wig hair to flow free above. She also wore lavender-tinted wraparound glasses and a waist-length white jacket.

Leah grabbed the hand that was pulling the bottom of the jacket. "Stop fidgeting, you look amazing." To prove her words, Leah moved her gaze from Kaelen's head to her feet and licked her lips. Kaelen recognized that look too. It was one Leah wore often when they were alone once her recovery reached a point where they no longer needed excessive prep time for sexual activity.

"You mentioned this Bolt is a speedster? Someone who runs fast?"

"Yes, why?"

Kaelen huffed. "A jacket made from Earth materials would be highly impractical for such things. It's clearly for aesthetics. It's a wonder these special consultants manage to help at all."

Leah snickered. "Remember that this is just a replica of Bolt's outfit and not the actual one she wears. I'm sure the heroes all have better quality material for their uniforms. Also, don't be bitter, darling. The fervor over Scion in the media has already died down with no sightings of you for so long."

"Gabe says they're still trying to find her though. He was suspicious at the last game night but was wise enough not to bring it up."

"I warned you that he'd figure it out but he's also loyal. Gabe won't say anything, and Garen can't mind scan without skin-to-skin contact, which helps."

"Mind scan?"

"Yes. The SAIC of LA has formidable powers. He can shape shift and is telepathic."

"Fascinating. It's too bad we are on opposite sides of this CORP conflict. Your Jove sounds like he'd be an interesting person to speak with. But it's reassuring to know that Gabe can prevent interference from his boss. Now, I am extremely hungry and you promised me as much pasta as I could eat. Are you ready to astound your friends?"

Leah suddenly pulled Kaelen into an embrace. "Our friends, and yes."

Inside, Leah gave Maddy's name to the hostess and they were brought through the restaurant to the private dining room. Kaelen easily guessed each of their friends inside based on their heartbeats, despite the fact that they all wore costumes. Per their plan, Kaelen entered first and quickly garnered everyone's attention.

Maddy was dressed like Adora, from the show She-Ra and the Princesses of Power. Tasha wore furry ears and a tail to resemble Catra.

Kaelen watched the show on Maddy's recommendation and knew it was a favorite of the other couple.

Maddy called out, "Holy shit, Kaelen! Tell me that suit is padded and you're not that ripped."

Nalla fanned herself. "Nope, she's that ripped. Hello, haven't you seen the video they posted of, uh—" She looked around the room. "I mean, I've seen her in shorts. She's like a goddess. It's disgusting, really."

Maddy rolled her eyes while the rest of the group laughed. "Anyway, it's about time you got here." She craned her head to see around Kaelen, most likely looking for the hoverchair. "Where is my sister?"

Kaelen grinned. "Actually, I made a new friend when someone thought I was the real Bolt." Kaelen turned to wave Leah forward from where she stood out of view of the others in the room. "Come meet my friends."

Leah moved into the room to stand next to Kaelen and gave a little wave to her squad. She pressed the button on her belt that activated the voice modulator and said, "Hey." Kaelen carefully closed the door to prevent anyone from seeing in or listening.

Wary faces gazed back at them, all except Gabe. He appeared a little star struck as he pointed at Leah then the whip coiled on her hip. "Is that really…"

Maddy cuffed him on the back of the head. "Obviously not. This is Halloween."

"Uh, babe…who is it then?"

That earned a befuddled look from Maddy that made Kaelen fight to hold back her laughter. Maddy looked back at Leah. "What she said, who are you?"

"Someone who ate homemade cookies with you every time you came home from school."

"Oh my God." Maddy slid her chair back and stood, frozen in place.

Tasha stood as well and put a hand on Maddy's arm. "Babe, what's wrong."

"No fucking way!"

Leah glanced at Kaelen, and Kaelen gave a little nod. It meant Kaelen would watch her to make sure she didn't stumble or fall. The suit was a little heavier than everyday clothes, and Leah hadn't been walking for that long on her own without a cane. Her muscles were still getting stronger but not yet at one hundred percent. That was all it took for Leah to make her way around the table and draw Maddy into a hug. Both had tears in their eyes when they pulled apart again.

The rest of the group caught on one by one. "Fuck yes! I knew you'd do it!" Nalla took her own opportunity to hug Leah, then turned to Einstein and swatted his arm. "You didn't tell me!"

He sat there in his gray coveralls and shrugged. "I was not at liberty to say."

Leah hugged everyone then made her way back around the table to take a seat across from Maddy. "He's still not at liberty to say. Neither are the rest of you. This has to be the closest secret you've ever held because I want to unveil the treatment and our success at CES on January third when I give my presentation." She looked around the table as Kaelen opened the door to the private room then took her own seat at Leah's right, across from Tasha. "Not a word to anyone, got it?"

"Leah," she looked at Gabe. "This is huge. I mean, this is game changing for the medical industry."

She smirked at him. "I'm counting on it."

Maddy shook her head, smile not fading in the slightest. "I can't believe you and Mom kept this quiet. How long have you been walking?"

"A few weeks. I'm still building strength in my legs and relearning what I'd forgotten after so long. I started with a cane but was able to get rid of it after the first week because of the increased strength from the rapid muscle growth. The chair is for show as much as it gives me a needed break throughout the day. But tonight, when we're all unrecognizable…I wanted to walk around and feel free."

Tasha smiled at her. "We get it, Leah. None of us will say a word."

Kaelen looked around the group, then leaned closer to Leah. "You should make them pinky swear. A serious secret requires a binding verbal agreement."

Gabe scoffed, "That's not how—ow! Why did you kick me?" He scowled at Nalla who smiled sweetly back. She held her own pinky from her spot next to Leah.

"Bring 'em in, people. Not a word gets out about the results, or anything else we happen to see tonight. Agreed?" Maddy, always the protective older sister, glared at the people around the table. Even Kaelen and Leah, which Kaelen found funny. They all put their pinkies together and Leah hooked them as best she could. At least she'd taken the heavy gloves off and left them next to her plate on the table. No sooner had they returned to their seats when a server entered and stood at the head of the table, the spot between Kaelen and Tasha where no one was sitting.

"Oh, get a load of this group. These are great!" She pointed at each person, naming their costume as she went starting to her right. "Let's see, Catra and Adora, Indiana Jones?" Gabe nodded. "A ghostbuster," Einstein grinned. Kaelen could see a complicated looking backpack leaning against the wall in the corner. "And the Warrior Princess herself," she said, nodding at Nalla. She looked at Leah and Kaelen. "Alley Cat and Bolt. If it weren't Halloween, I'd say you two were the real thing! I hope y'all are going to a party later because these are too good to waste on dinner alone."

Nalla laughed. "Szot's bar is having a costume contest."

"You're gonna do great. Can I start you off with some drinks and appetizers?"

They got their orders quickly despite the fact that it was a Saturday night. Leah shifted a few times during dinner and Kaelen grew concerned. She whispered in Leah's ear, "What's wrong?"

Leah's lips twisted. "My hoverchair is a lot more comfortable."

Kaelen laughed quietly. "I'm sorry, *zhee*. I'll massage your back and legs later."

Greenish blue eyes twinkled back at her. "And more?"

Even after months of dating, Kaelen was amazed at the depth of her attraction for Leah. It was odd considering she had no experience with the notion of it until she came to Earth. She licked her lips, already thinking of the things they could try later. "Yes."

"Hey, Kaelen," Maddy called across the table. She looked away from Leah to meet Maddy's gaze. "Szot's has Karaoke."

"Karaoke?"

Leah reached up and smoothed the skin between her eyes and explained. "It's singing popular songs in front of people. A machine provides the background music and the lyrics on a little screen. You only need to sing along, pretending to be the lead singer."

Joy filled Kaelen. "I like to sing!"

"We know. Why do you think I told you?"

"But I've never done this Karaoke. I don't know a lot of Earth music."

Nalla asked, "Who are you listening to now, Kaelen?"

"An upbeat artist called Brittney Spears from the classic pop section. I've listened to about seventy-five percent of her work."

Maddy made a face. "I'll leave you to that. Let me know when you want to try some real music."

"I like Miss Spears," Kaelen said defensively.

"Fine, then. I'll give you fifty dollars if you sing a Brittney song at Karaoke tonight."

Kaelen shrugged. "I'm not sure why it would be worth money but I'll do it. I already said I like to sing."

Nalla raised a hand. "I bet Kaelen blows the crowd away."

Gabe looked from Maddy, to Kaelen, then to Nalla. "Really?"

Nalla snorted. "It's Brittney, bitch!"

The entire table laughed uncontrollably after that, except Kaelen. She assumed it was a pop culture reference that she wasn't familiar with.

Once the bill was paid, everyone piled out of the restaurant onto the sidewalk. Szot's bar was only a few blocks away from Farro's, so the entire group decided to walk there. Leah looked around, then addressed Maddy. "Where's your car?"

Maddy gestured toward her and Tasha. "We took an Uber so we wouldn't have to worry about driving home after."

Nalla replied, "Same."

Gabe looked back at everyone. "I took a cab."

"My van was customized specifically for the hoverchair and doesn't actually have pedals. I also gave my driver the night off so Kaelen and I took an Uber as well."

Kaelen held up her phone and nodded. "The app is handy, though not as good as Fleet Eats."

The group groaned and Maddy tried to shove Kaelen's shoulder, then grunted when Kaelen didn't budge. "Only you would say that!

You're a walking stomach."

"Yeah, yeah… Kaelen eats, Maddy is grumpy, and I hate snakes. Can we get this show on the road now? Those shots at Szot's aren't going to drink themselves."

Leah whispered to Kaelen, "Gabe's in a real mood tonight. I predict he's going to have a hangover tomorrow."

Kaelen responded, "What's a hangover?"

Maddy spun around from where she'd been walking in front of them. "Really? You suck!" Then she stalked forward again, making her way down the street after Gabe.

Kaelen looked after her with concern. "Is she angry at me?"

Leah squeezed her hand. "Not at all. She's irritated that you won't suffer from a very human side effect of drinking too much alcohol."

"Oh."

"Are you having fun, darling?"

Kaelen beamed back at her. "I am."

"Well, the night's just getting started so hopefully it will be even better once we get to Szot's."

Kaelen shook her head. "You're all I need to have the best night. The rest is…" She waved her hand around in the air. Gesturing vaguely in front of them. "Frosting on the cake."

Leah sighed and snuggled close. "That it is."

Chapter Eighteen

Szot's bar was dark and crowded when they paid the entry fee and pushed inside. It was still early so none of the Halloween events had started yet. Leah told Kaelen that many wouldn't arrive until closer to ten, when the contest was set to begin. Maddy and Nalla made a beeline for the bar while the rest of them found the big wraparound booth near the pool tables Maddy had reserved for them. The opposite end of the large space held a stage and various pieces of sound equipment. There was a younger guy singing something heavy and grating and Kaelen cringed.

She'd taken the outside end of the half circle bench, next to Leah. On Leah's other side were Einstein and Gabe, leaving Tasha in the end seat on the opposite side of the table. She looked around at her friends incredulously. "That is not pleasant."

Gabe also made a face. "It gets better…and worse, and better. That's the nature of Karaoke. No one here is a professional, they sing because they like it."

"That's why I sing, but I don't usually hurt my own ears."

"You know, Kaelen, Gabe here is a pretty good musician too. Perhaps you can sing a duet if you find a song you both know."

Tasha's comment brought a smile to Gabe's face. He gave her an inquiring look. "Do you know any musicals?"

"I know Disney songs." Kaelen looked at Gabe. "Those are musicals, right?"

He huffed. "I suppose that would do."

Einstein helpfully commented, "Gabe has concerns about projecting an alpha male aura and singing Disney songs are more of a beta male pastime."

"Dude, can you not?" He looked at Kaelen with brows squished together. "*Pssh*, what does he know anyway? I'm not concerned about people seeing me sing Disney songs. That's crazy talk."

Kaelen listened to his heartbeat and nodded with understanding, then turned to Leah. "He's definitely lying. I trust Einstein's assessment."

"Well, that's just rude."

Einstein laughed. "Rude but accurate."

One thing Kaelen noticed was that Einstein turned off the hologram inducer before they got to the bar. "Aren't you concerned about your alien status out in public?"

He shook his head. "Szot's is considered a safe space among the alien and Chromodec communities. It's one of the best kept secrets in Los Angeles."

She looked around and saw the truth of his statement.

"I quite enjoy my time here because I can be me, Clevna Trog. Or better, I can be Einstein. It doesn't matter the makeup of my skin or where I come from. Nobody cares about my people or past, only that we're all having a fun evening." He leaned a little closer to Kaelen. "Also, Nalla says she thinks my shimmery android skin is sexy. I try to oblige whenever I can." He winked at Kaelen then straightened.

Two trays hit the large table nearly in unison causing beer to slop over the edge of the pint glasses on one of them. Maddy passed around full-size drinks, while Nalla's tray contained small glasses. Gabe called out, "What's the shot of the night?"

"Oatmeal cookie, because the holidays are coming."

Groans went around the table with at least one call of, "Too soon, it's only Halloween!"

Kaelen eyed the glasses of creamy liquid skeptically. "That doesn't look like a cookie. Is it injectable?"

"Inject—oh, not that kind of shot, Kaelen. A shot in this context is a small portion of very strong liquor, either mixed with other flavors or straight. This particular shot is called an oatmeal cookie because that's what it tastes like."

"I see." Kaelen lifted the tiny glass and sniffed. "Cinnamon, cream, and something else. I've had a lot of different cookies. I can understand the naming analogy."

Nalla grinned at Kaelen after passing Tasha her shot. "Yup. Now, if you two could slide out for a sec so I can sit by my man, that would be great."

Tasha moved over and let Maddy have the end. Once everyone was seated, Maddy lifted her shot glass and addressed Kaelen. "Since you're new to Szot's, and bars in general, this is our tradition. We all lift our glasses and gently clink them together in a toast."

"Ah, a salutation or words of congratulation. That's cold—uh… cool." She looked at Nalla and her friend nodded to indicate she'd used the right slang.

Leah lifted her own shot glass, followed by the rest of the group. "We usually go around the table and say what we're toasting to. Maybe it's something great that happened that week, or news that we're thankful for. It doesn't have to be excessive or long. Once we've all gone around the table, we gently tap our glasses together then throw the shot back, drinking it all in one swallow."

One thing Kaelen had discovered that she enjoyed about Earth, and humans in particular, were the traditions they had. Individual, unique, and heartfelt, she liked that even in the most troubling times, humans came together as a group to celebrate the things they loved. It was an odd dichotomy when compared to Argonians with their intellectual and fairly emotionless society. Argon lacked the basic human passion that she'd come to associate with her new planet.

"I'll start." Maddy looked around the table. "My toast is for Leah's success, and to Einstein and Kaelen for helping my sister achieve her dreams."

The toasts continued around the table, with each person saying something they were excited about or thankful for. When it got to Leah, she glanced at everyone in the group, meeting Maddy and Kaelen's eyes last. "I want to toast to every one of my friends here tonight, and those who couldn't be here to celebrate my first night out after recovery."

That left Kaelen to look around the table at the faces that had become so beautifully familiar over the past year. "I would like to toast to my friends who have become my found family here on Earth." She raised her little glass slightly higher. *"Zhetinao ne Ra Vesh."*

Maddy asked, "What does that mean?"

Leah leaned in for everyone to tap glasses. "It means heart and intellect unite or united, I'm not certain which."

Kaelen nodded, pleased. "United. It is a state of being in this usage."

Gabe called out, "Cheers," then they all drank down their shots.

"Oh, that's delicious!"

Nalla laughed at Kaelen's response. "I knew you'd like it."

Maddy grumbled beneath her breath, then reached into her pocket and handed Nalla a ten-dollar bill. "You were right." She looked at Kaelen and shrugged. "You never drink at game nights or any other time that I've seen. That's why I got you a glass of water."

Gabe made a face. "Do you hate her? Why would you bring her Szot's tap water?"

"Earth has a problem with pollution and its lack of biodegradable packaging materials. I would rather drink tap water than use something wasteful like a polyethylene terephthalate plastic water bottle." She paused and added, "It's commonly referred to as PET on Earth."

He scoffed. "I know what it is. So, we have yet another tree hugger in the group. Einstein and Leah weren't enough?"

"I've never hugged a tree."

"Darling, it's slang. It means someone who highly values and cares about the environment."

Kaelen had never heard the term but found it fitting. "Oh, in that case I'm an unabashed tree hugger. I like that term. And concerning alcohol, it's not that I don't wish to drink. But it doesn't make sense to waste alcohol on me when the majority tastes bad and it doesn't have the effect for which alcohol is intended."

"You mean you can't get drunk?"

"No."

Gabe nodded. "Well, that makes sense. Given how much you eat, I'd wager your metabolism is through the roof."

Leah snickered. "Among other things."

Maddy plugged her ears. "I don't want to hear about my sister's kinky sex life."

Kaelen understood her protest. "Noted. While we haven't yet

explored the notion of sexual kink, I'll be sure to keep the results of our activity private so we don't damage your sisterly bond."

The table roared with laughter. Once they calmed down again, Nalla clapped her hands to get everyone's attention. "Okay people. Who is going to sing?" Kaelen watched Nalla, Einstein, and Gabe raise their hands so she put hers up as well. "If you know what you want to sing, tell me and I'll enter the songs for you when I go up. Kaelen, do you want to come with me and look through the music selection?"

"Yes."

"Great."

Kaelen stood and let Leah and Nalla out of the booth, then Leah slid back in. Gabe called out, "Put me in for Bruno Mars 'Grenade,' and a duet with Kaelen."

"You already know what I wish to sing."

Nalla nodded at Einstein. "Yup. Anyone else?" Maddy, Tasha, and Leah all shook their heads. Nalla looped her arms with Kaelen's and pulled her through the crowded bar toward the stage. She called back over her shoulder. "Don't wait up, kids. We're gonna get Miss Bolt here a drink that will get her buzzed on our way back. Tarynn is working tonight and I'm sure she will know of something with enough kick."

The noise grew louder the closer to the stage they got, and Kaelen regretted not getting the earplugs from Leah before leaving the table. Unlike her own costume of Bolt, Alley Cat had many utility pouches. Not that she'd have had any place to put the earplugs if she'd been in her own ship suit, though she could program some pockets in.

"Okay, this is the DJ table." Nalla interrupted Kaelen's thoughts, then pointed at a touch screen. "All the songs are in this system. Sort by title or artist. Once you have what you want, touch the song to select it, then enter your name when prompted." Nalla indeed knew exactly what she wanted and entered her own song to demonstrate the process. "Okay, your turn."

The DJ watched them curiously while a tall woman belted out a song that was vaguely familiar. Kaelen assumed she'd heard it in the periphery at some point. She sorted the screen by artist then rapidly pressed the page turn button to look for a song she was familiar with.

"Holy shit! Are you really her?"

Kaelen looked up at the DJ. "Her?"

"Bolt. I just watched your hand move so fast that it blurred. Are you here on a mission?"

"Oh, I'm not—"

"Allowed to work while drinking. She's here to have fun and unwind for the night." Nalla quickly broke in with a wink at Kaelen.

"Sweet!" The DJ stood and held out a hand. "I'm Sparrow. My pronouns are they/them." Kaelen shook their hand and Sparrow smiled at Nalla. "I recognize you and your boyfriend. I haven't seen your crew here in a while."

Nalla nodded. "Work's been crazy lately, you know?"

"Girl, I know. I'm working toward my Master's, and my brain is ready to explode." Sparrow held their hands around their head and made an explosion sound.

"This isn't your primary job?"

"It is because I own the business. I went back to school so I could grow it into a franchise. Maybe even branch out. Say, if you're The Bolt, can you prove it to me?"

"What, you saw her hand blur with speed. What more proof do you need?"

Sparrow huffed. "Well, I mean plenty of aliens and Chromodecs have powers, including speed. It's also Halloween." They smirked. "Do the phase thing."

Kaelen looked back and forth between Sparrow and Nalla. "The phase thing?"

"I'm not sure what the real name for it is. Here, I'll show you. Check out this footage from the bank robbery last week in Detroit. Apparently, the CORP and other heroes have been trying to reduce property damage lately during rogue encounters." Sparrow held up their cell phone to show video of a woman wearing the same outfit that Kaelen sported. She walked up to the glass doors of the bank then began vibrating so fast her entire body was a blur. Bolt moved forward through the door to the inside of the bank and stopped vibrating. The glass remained unbroken.

"So cool." Nalla's mouth was open, then she looked at Kaelen and shrugged. "Whoops, looks like the gig is up."

Kaelen was unsure what a gig was in regards to their current conversation. "Practical theory states that vibrating one's molecules at an atomic level would allow you to pass through solid objects." She looked at her hand curiously, then began to vibrate. The change was subtle but Kaelen felt the shift when it happened and moved her hand toward a nearby support column. Nalla and Sparrow's mouths dropped open when her hand passed through the beam, leaving both unscathed. She stopped vibrating. "Is that what you were looking for?"

"Hell yes! Can I have a picture with you?"

The request was odd and Kaelen was uncomfortable misrepresenting herself, but Nalla stepped close to her. "She would love that. I'll even take the picture for you."

"Sweet."

As they walked away a few minutes later, Kaelen leaned close to Nalla's ear and said, "I don't think I could have done that with more than my hand. It was incredibly difficult."

Nalla laughed. "Difficult or no, it was hella impressive." She led them through the crowded space and up to the bar. "Tarynn, Kaelen here would like something sweet to drink but with enough kick it can affect her unique physiology. She's extremely uh, hardy."

Something about Tarynn's physical appearance seemed off to Kaelen. "You appear human but your heart beats in a strange location. Is that not your natural form?"

Tarynn shook her head. "I'm a shapeshifter from Konisteri"

"I've heard of Konisteri but never met a Konisterian before."

"What's your race? I don't want to give you something that'll kill you, no matter what my half Varian friend says."

Kaelen glanced around furtively, then leaned closer and Tarynn did the same. "I was told this is a safe place so I can admit it to you, correct?"

Tarynn smiled. "Yes, you can."

"Argonian."

"Fascinating. To my knowledge, Earth has never hosted an Argonian. That makes a lot of sense now."

"Sense?"

"You're Scion."

"What?" Nalla's mouth opened with shock. The revelation having rendered her strangely speechless. "Holy fuck, Kaelen. I mean, I kind of suspected it but—" She lowered her voice and looked around to make sure no one could listen in. "Who all knows this?"

Kaelen scowled at the bartender then whispered back. "You do, now. The Tucks all know, as well as Einstein." Nalla frowned. "He admitted to knowing a little over a month ago. He recognized the house symbol on my ship suit, but I should have anticipated that someone of his intelligence would put it together. Leah thinks that Gabe suspects, but she insists he's loyal and wouldn't tell the CORP."

"She's right, but plenty of other people are looking for you." She reached out and squeezed Kaelen's arm. "Also, I don't care what any of them are saying on the news or what the CORP has declared. You're a hero in my book."

"Thank you." The sentiment touched Kaelen and she enjoyed knowing that at least some people appreciated her contributions.

"Okay, understanding that you're the person who carried a crashing plane on their back a few months ago, I'm going to make you a mixed drink with Guldronan Rum. You said sweet, right?" Kaelen and Nalla both nodded. Tarynn checked behind the bar. "Malibu Sunset. It's usually made with coconut rum, but I'll adjust it by using the alien liquor and cream of coconut. It also has pineapple and orange juices, grenadine, and maraschino cherry."

"Oh, yum!"

Tarynn pointed at Nalla. "Do not touch her drink and don't let anyone else touch it either. Guldronan rum is fatal to humans."

Nalla pouted and crossed her arms. "As you pointed out, I'm half Varian."

"And you'd be all the way dead."

"Fine," Nalla huffed. "Hands off my friend's drink."

When they got back to the table, everyone *ooh*'d at Kaelen's colorful cocktail, but Kaelen took Tarynn's words to heart. When Leah reached for it, Kaelen quickly pulled it away. "No one can touch my Malibu Sunset on the bartender's orders. It wouldn't be healthy and I like you all too much."

Gabe made a face. "Seriously? I've had some pretty strong alien alcohol. How bad could it be?"

Nalla systematically went around the table, starting with Leah and included herself in the pointing. "Dead, dead, dead, dead, dead, and dead." Then she pointed at Kaelen. "Pleasantly buzzed."

Gabe gave Kaelen a penetrating stare but sighed when Leah scowled at him. She shook her head and he let it go. "Fine. You know, we used to tell each other everything back when we were hacking and cracking together," he said.

Kaelen sensed the tension between them. Leah was kind, if firm. "At one time, we did. But things change, Gabe. You work for a government agency with some pretty stringent rules, and we're currently in a bar with a lot of ears, some more sensitive than others. I do trust you, but your boss is one of the most powerful aliens on the planet and the head of CORP-LA."

"You know he doesn't read minds casually."

"I know. But some of the secrets we keep are for your benefit as much as ours."

Nalla suddenly pounded the table twice, causing glasses to rattle. "I hate to break up," she waved her hands back and forth between Leah and Gabe, "whatever this is, but I'm going to because they called my name."

Distracted, Gabe protested. "Hey, why do you get to go first?"

Nalla rolled her eyes. "Because, genius, not only did I have to show Kaelen how to use the system, but there is no way in hell I was going to follow either one of you. I know how good you are, and I can make a bet about our newest squad member." She smirked. "By the way, the DJ is convinced Kaelen is The Bolt. It's pretty funny."

Maddy scowled. "What did you do, Nalla?"

Nalla pointed at herself and mouthed, "who, me?" while the rest of the table laughed. "I didn't do anything. But I have a feeling social media is going to blow up later."

Suddenly Maddy began laughing and pointed at Leah. "You've totally got the Alley Cat scowl perfect!" Leah frowned even more but took the time to raise a black glove covered middle finger.

Within minutes, Nalla was singing "Girls Just Wanna Have Fun." It was upbeat and Kaelen liked it. Leah, Einstein, and Gabe were discussing antiquated network operating systems. Not knowing anything about that particular Earth technology, Kaelen was content to sip her drink, feeling strangely loose.

"Hey, Kaelen. What song will you sing?" Tasha leaned closer, as did Maddy.

"It's not like Nalla's song. It's more, uh, emotional. I heard it playing through the walls right after I moved into your old apartment. It made me feel melancholy, but also, what's the slang? Seen. I believe that's the correct word."

"What's the song, darling?"

"It's what you call an oldie. Something called 'Superman.' Which makes sense given how many aliens and Chromodecs are here on Earth." Kaelen gulped a few more swallows of her drink as she watched Leah process her words. "Have you heard of it?"

The table had gone quiet and Gabe nodded. "Yeah, we all know it. It was pretty popular nearly forty years ago. It kind of became an anthem for aliens once they started landing on Earth" Then he made eye contact with Leah. Kaelen wasn't stupid, even though the drink was significantly slowing her higher functions. She assumed he'd gleaned information about her from the song and that their silent communication was an agreement of sorts. Kaelen hoped so because she didn't want to see Leah upset with any of the squad on her account.

Nalla finished her song and the crowd applauded, members of her own table clapping loudest. The DJ's voice cut through the cacophony. "Well done, Xena. Girls just wanna have fun, indeed! Next up, we've got the blue blaze herself. Give it up for The Bolt, everyone!"

Kaelen sucked down the rest of her drink, then sped out of the booth. Nalla seemed to think it was a good idea to give them a show, and since Szot's was a safe space, she did. Using her maximal speed, Kaelen blurred with motion and stood on the stage two seconds later. The crowd quieted a bit, with quite a few people whispering expletives. Kaelen didn't pay any attention to them. She only had eyes for the other end of the room where Leah sat watching her through that silly black cowl.

"*Psst*, Bolt." Kaelen looked at Sparrow. "The screen with the lyrics is here, it will highlight the words when it's time to sing."

"Okay, thanks." She didn't need the screen for the song, but it wouldn't hurt to be polite. Ten seconds later she began. Kaelen sang soulful words about hating to fly and searching for herself. Some didn't apply to her life at all, but others directly correlated to her unique situation, such as the home she'd never see. "I'm only a girl in a silly blue suit, sweeping up cavorite with an old worn broom…and it's not easy to be me."

Whistles and cheers began as the final notes faded out. Kaelen carefully placed the microphone back on the stand and gave a little bow of respect for their appreciation. Then she sped back across the bar to Leah. Her lips were open slightly and she had a look in her eyes that was intimate and familiar. Normally Kaelen wouldn't have dared to kiss Leah so wantonly in front of all her friends, but the strange Guldronan rum made her brave. She carefully cradled the rubbery clad cheeks between her palms and gave Leah a kiss that barely brushed their lips together. It was Leah who surged forward, taking the contact much deeper.

Kaelen reached up and caught a peanut aimed at her head by Maddy as she pulled away from Leah's lips, causing her personal Alley Cat to whimper.

"Hey, none of that tonight, Ra-Evon. Defile my sister in private please."

Rather than head for the lips that were calling to her, Kaelen picked up the glass for another sip and realized it was empty. She scowled at it, then looked around the table to find her friends watching with various expressions of amusement. "It's gone."

All of them nodded. Tasha giggled and leaned closer to Maddy. "She's kind of adorable like this."

"Uh huh, at least when she's not sucking face with my sibling right in front of me."

Leah reached over and took Kaelen's hand. "Come on, darling. Let's get another round for the table."

Kaelen grew excited. "More shots?"

Everyone at the table yelled back, "yes" except for Einstein. He merely nodded and said, "Indubitably."

They were behind a reptilian man with four arms, a Dlygyn if Kaelen remembered her Argonian species classes correctly. Once it was their turn, Tarynn looked back and forth between them. She gave Leah a sincere smile. "Congratulations, Alley Cat. I was glad to see you *walk* in."

"Thanks. We're here to order the next round." She rattled off everyone's drinks, including the oatmeal cookie shots. She aimed a thumb at Kaelen. "And another of the mixed drink you made for Kaelen. It's definitely done the trick."

Kaelen grinned, feeling more than a little loopy. She hadn't smiled so much in a long time. Maybe not ever. "It was delicious."

"Okay, but I'm only making you one more. Guldronan liquors are strong and you look like a lightweight."

Kaelen puffed out her chest and put her hands on her hips. "I'll have you know that I'm—"

A black glove covered her mouth. "She's appreciative that you're making her another drink. Thank you." Leah pulled her hand away then shook a finger at Kaelen. "Never argue with the bartender. Take this one a little slower, okay?"

Kaelen felt those little flutters in her belly at the way Leah was looking at her. She was beautiful, even if half her face was covered by that stupid hero mask. "Okay." Tarynn stifled a laugh as she poured the beers.

Everyone at the table cheered when they returned with the trays of drinks. Kaelen quickly unloaded the glasses then sped the trays back to the bar and returned in time to grab her shot and raise it with everyone else. Like before, they all took turns giving a toast before downing the sweet liquor. It had no effect but Kaelen loved the flavor. It was tasty but different from her rum drink.

"So, Tasha has some good news." Maddy looked to her right. "Tell 'em, babe."

Tasha beamed at her. "Yesterday, my partners and I officially closed on a location for our practice. As you all know, it's been a dream of mine for a lot of years to have my own practice where we can serve underprivileged and marginalized communities."

Her statement was a bit confusing to Kaelen. "What does this mean, that you'll no longer be a social worker?"

"It means that I'm actually a trained therapist and while I like being a social worker helping families, I'd rather get to the root of the problem as a therapist than constantly put on band aids. I've got a few other doctors that I graduated with, one of which had previously been working out of Los Angeles General Hospital, and we're all going into business together."

"Dude, that's awesome! Up here." Gabe held his hand up and Tasha slapped it.

Einstein raised his glass. "Here, here. Well done, Miss Smith."

"I knew you could do it, Tasha."

Tasha ducked her head and smiled, then leaned against Maddy's side. "Thanks, Leah."

Maddy smirked. "Basically, this means that while her hours will still be long, they will be a lot more regular."

"Does this mean you'll have more free days together?" Kaelen turned to Leah. "Perhaps now they'll have time for sex *and* family dinners."

Leah covered her mouth as she laughed and Maddy sighed. "Dammit, Kaelen." Then she paused, and nodded. "But yeah, probably." The rest of the table joined Leah's laughter.

They hung out at Szot's for hours, singing songs between late night appetizers and the occasional round of drinks. It was Einstein who wowed the entire bar with his proton pack when the costume contest began. The crowd panicked for a few seconds when he shot it at a wall but quickly calmed when everyone saw that the gadget didn't fire anything at all. He explained to the DJ who was hosting the contest that it was all harmless holographic light and sound creating a crackling plasma effect. Leah and Kaelen refused to enter the contest to avoid calling more attention to themselves.

Kaelen was glad to remove the restrictive Earth clothing when they returned to the penthouse after saying their good nights. They wore soft sleep shorts and shirts as Kaelen made good on her promise to give Leah a massage. Whatever effect the Guldronan rum had on her quickly wore off when she stopped drinking. Even so, she was gentle with her ministrations.

Leah's eyes were closed but Kaelen could tell she wasn't asleep even if Leah hadn't said anything to her.

"Did you have fun tonight, darling?"

Kaelen slowed her hands until she was gently caressing Leah's back. "I did. Szot's bar is an interesting meeting place. There is something for everyone to do there, and they have food." She gave a light poke to Leah's side, making her squirm for some reason. "Why didn't you tell me they had food when you invited me before? I may have attended your friend gatherings sooner."

Leah's laughter served as answer enough. "Don't ever change, my love."

Feeling playful, Kaelen leaned down to whisper in her ear. "No? You mean you don't want me to change what my hands are doing to say, this?" Her hands moved to decidedly less innocent massage regions and Leah gasped.

"I take it back. Change however you want."

Despite their inclination toward flirtatious exploration, it was obvious that Leah was exhausted. Kaelen assumed that Leah had over-exerted herself with all the walking she'd done. Rather than escalate their touching into sex, Kaelen deliberately moved from where she'd straddled Leah's back and lay on her side to face her. "You need sleep, *zhee*."

Leah pushed her bottom lip out into a pout. "I don't want to."

"I know, but tomorrow isn't a workday. We can do anything we want, yes?"

"Like what?"

Kaelen thought of all the wonderful activities they'd shared since officially declaring themselves in a courtship. "We could take a long bath, have breakfast on the balcony—"

"It's nearly November, Kaelen. Definitely too chilly for that. Even in Cali."

"Okay, we can go out for breakfast, or brunch. We could stay in and cuddle, or watch movies, or both."

Leah smirked. "You're getting closer."

"What am I missing—oh." A sudden, powerful wave of attraction invoked a full body shiver. Her voice was lower with arousal when she responded. "We can do that before breakfast—er, brunch, then maybe again later before cuddles?"

Leah pulled her into a tight hug. "You have the best ideas." Suddenly her lips parted with a massive yawn, and she gave Kaelen a sheepish look. "And you're annoyingly right in that I'm beyond tired. Thanks for being there tonight, for having my back and standing with me."

"You never have to thank me for that."

"I don't need to but I want to. I appreciate having you in my life, Kaelen. I never want you to forget that."

The emotional moment was interrupted by the vibration of Leah's cell on the nightstand. "Shit, I forgot I put it on vibrate earlier." Leah turned onto her back so she could reach the offending object. "Who would be texting me this late?" Leah looked down at her phone, then her mouth dropped open in shock right before she started laughing. "Oh my God!"

She turned the phone so Kaelen could see the message sent by Nalla, a single word, "Whoops!" and a link to a website. She looked at Leah. "What is that site?"

"It's a popular gossip site. They're pretty much speculating that Alley Cat and The Bolt are in a relationship because someone sent in a photo of us kissing."

Kaelen grew concerned. "Is that bad?"

"Darling, it's Halloween and neither of those heroes live in LA. Alley Cat is in Chicago and I've heard rumors that Bolt calls Detroit home." Leah put it on mute and placed the phone on the wireless charger. "I wouldn't worry about it. Only our friends knew our identities." She snorted. "I bet the real Alley Cat and Bolt are going to wonder who their imposters were at a random Los Angeles bar."

They looked at each other for a few seconds before bursting into laughter.

Leah shook her head. "Whoops, indeed. Way to go, Nalla."

Chapter Nineteen

Leah had Jenna block the first few hours every Monday morning so she could go through the weekly scans. They were mandatory for phase one nerve regeneration test subjects. She also had Jenna reserve the executive gym right after so the physical therapist could work with her in private.

Thirty minutes after her session, Leah was back in her office prepping for an eleven o'clock meeting. Her computer chimed with a new email, and she scowled then punched in the number for her CFO, leaving her on speakerphone.

"Hey, boss. How are you this fine Monday morning?"

"Cox, Ana? I thought I told you I never wanted to see his name cross my desk again after the last time he broke contract with us, then tried to undermine our bid with OAS."

Ana snorted over the line. "Yeah, well, much like a communicable disease, the symptoms of Jeffrey Cox disappear every so often then come back twice as bad as before. And we still got the bid."

"How do you know so much about communicable diseases?"

"My roommate in college."

Leah sighed and rubbed her forehead. "Anyway, what does he want now?"

"He wants the property at fifty west Pier Drive."

The address didn't sound familiar, but the ports of Los Angeles and Long Beach were massive. Genius though she was, Leah couldn't possibly keep track of all the Lockheed holdings around the world. "I give, what is it?"

"It's currently a shipping yard with warehouses and a large dock.

It's primarily used for large cargo shipping. And before you ask, I have no idea why Cox wants it, only that he was willing to pay a quarter over market value."

Leah considered the offer then remembered how much she hated Jeffrey Cox. "That man is a slimy weasel with no positive intentions whatsoever. Wasn't Cox Holdings the defendant in a recent lawsuit? I think lead from one of his factories had been leaching into the local ground water somewhere outside San Diego. I shudder to think of what he'd do with someplace a few miles from Long Beach. No deal."

Ana laughed. "I told him you'd say no, and he came back with one and a half. To be fair, I looked at the real estate estimate and L-I currently has no use for the property. It's been sitting empty since Ellie shut down the weapons manufacturing production in California. They used the warehouse and dock to ship overseas, and to other major cities up and down the west coast."

"Dammit Ana, you're not making this easy for me. How did it land on your desk anyway?"

"The offer was high enough that it kept getting kicked up the line for someone bigger to make the call."

"And I'm involved with this why?"

"Biggest decision maker on the list." Leah could picture Ana's smug look. She was infuriating sometimes, but also a great CFO and phenomenal friend.

"So, what's it going to be?"

Leah typed in a quick computer search to bring up the property on Google maps. She took careful note of the placement of the warehouse and length of the pier wall. "I have no idea what he would want with the place. It's not a pretty piece of property and he's been involved in more real estate deals lately than anything else."

"And?"

"I hate Jeffrey Cox more than I want to take his money. Tell him officially that we decline his offer. If he asks, say that Lockheed International has plans to develop the property as a testing point for green energy water vessels."

"Is any of that actually true?"

Leah smiled, unseen. "It can be. I didn't say how far into the future."

Laughter came over the speaker again. "Fair enough. Okay, I'll draft the official rejection letter and have it sent to his people."

"Thanks, Ana."

The power in the building flickered and died before either of them could hang up on their own. Leah wasn't worried because the building had backup power for essentials like the labs, security, and server rooms. The downside was that nothing else would operate, including lights and elevators. The building would be illuminated solely by emergency lighting and the natural lighting from outside. Leah was glad for the abundance of windows in her corner office.

She jumped in her seat when the door pushed open. Leah's first instinct was to reach into her desk for the Taser. One could never be too careful. She relaxed again when she heard Jenna's voice.

"Ms. Lockheed, I have Ron Canter on speakerphone." She held a cellphone in her hand.

Leah addressed her head of security. "Hi Ron. What's going on?"

"We have a hostile in the lobby. My team got everyone out with only minor injuries, but the Chromodec, or whatever she is, overloaded the primary energy grid for the building. I initiated lockdown for all the labs in case the woman gets through our main security doors. As for monitoring, security and emergency power are still active since they're not on a circuit accessible by the rest of the building."

"I gathered that when the power went out. How is she doing it?"

"Looks like lightning coming out of her hands. I've got security feeds still on her. Let me see if I can patch her through to your cell phone."

Leah moved her hoverchair back over to the desk so she could grab her own cell from the desk drawer. Thinking fast, she kept her back to Jenna and spoke quietly, knowing only one person would be able to hear her. "Darling, I'm perfectly fine and safe in my office. Please don't leave the lab, stay down there with Einstein until the CORP arrives." Certain that Kaelen would have heard her, and hoping she'd stay put, Leah moved back to Jenna's side and brought up the security app on her phone. Leah recognized the woman immediately. "Shit." She quickly closed out the video and called Gabe.

"Hey, LT, wassup?"

"Are you not on duty today?"

"Yeah, just came back from break, why—oh shit! Massive energy surge at—gotta call you back." She heard an alarm sound in the background as Gabe gave her a hasty, "We're on it, Leah," then hung up.

Jenna would never outwardly show anything but calm capability, but Leah had known and trusted the woman for a long time, and she could tell that her admin was rattled. "It's going to be fine. This is the same Chromodec that confronted my van the night I came back from Michigan." She brought up the app again so they could watch the feed. While the woman was doing a lot of damage in the giant three-story lobby at the front of the building, she hadn't destroyed the security cameras yet. They didn't have sound, but Leah could guess what she was saying.

Her office door opened again and Ana rushed in. "What's going on?"

Leah held up her phone so Ana could see the video. "Chromodec attack in the lobby."

"What does she want?"

"Apparently for me to pay for the sins of my family. Whatever that means."

Jenna frowned. "Do you think she's behind the attack in the parking garage?"

Leah shrugged. "Who knows. The police handled that one because he was human, but the man kept insisting that he forgot what happened and had no idea why he had a gun when Scion apprehended him. I got a tip that the CORP was going to investigate it as a potential mind control, but I don't think it's happened yet."

"This is most disconcerting, Ms. Lockheed. Who would want to hurt you?"

"It's Leah, and you know how it is. I still receive threats from the occasional crackpot."

Ana gave her a concerned look. "Sins of the past…and you say this is the same woman that attacked your van a few months ago after your trip with Kaelen?" Leah nodded. "The last event that caused controversy for the company was the mass shooting more than a decade ago. What was it, about a year before your parent's accident?"

Leah glanced back at her phone and sighed. "It wasn't an accident."

"What?"

"It's not something I wanted made public, but our car was attacked by a Chromodec. I requested the details be kept private because I didn't want to cause fear and panic. An entire subset of people shouldn't be judged by the actions of one."

Ana shook her head. "You're a better person than I am."

The video feed was replaced by Kaelen's face as her phone lit with an incoming call. "Ana, can you pull up the security app on your phone while I take this?" Ana nodded and Leah answered then moved her chair toward the balcony door for a little privacy. "Hello, darling."

"Leah! I can hear the attacker's heartbeat. It is the same woman from the street, the one that escaped your CORP."

"It's okay, love. I already know and the CORP should be here any minute now. We're all safe upstairs and security got everyone away who was downstairs."

"We have no power and large steel walls came down to seal the lab. Einstein says we can use a release to open the doors from the inside in case of emergency. But there are people stuck in the elevator and stairwell cameras are still active, and I—Einstein says I can't come up to you without risking my identity or the people in the elevator."

Leah said, "Sealing the labs is protocol in case of terrorist attack. And Kaelen, I told you that I'm safe. Please don't worry and do as Einstein says. If she escapes the lobby and heads my way, you'll be the first person I call. I won't think twice about the property damage. But for now, stay there and stay safe."

"Leah…"

"Please. Promise me."

A sigh whispered over the phone line. "I promise."

"Good, I'll let you know when I have an update."

Kaelen grumbled, "If only we'd completed the portal generator already, I could have handled that woman before she damaged the building."

Leah smiled. "My dad used to say that 'what ifs' are useless, that we should plan for the future rather than regret the past."

"He sounds like a wise man."

"Eh, he had his moments." Leah caught sight of Ana trying to get her attention. "Hey, Ana needs me for something. I'll call you back in a little while, okay?"

"Okay. You be safe, too."

"Always."

Ana called out, "Leah, you should see this. The CORP arrived and it looks like Jove himself is trying to apprehend the woman."

The three women crowded around Ana's cell phone. They watched as the head of the CORP turned to mist and disappeared, then a squad of CORP agents distracted the lightening wielding woman. She'd been smart enough to put her back to a wall. Unfortunately, that didn't protect her from someone who could form anywhere. Agent Garen Grath rematerialized to the space between her and the wall and tried to subdue the woman from behind.

The maneuver would have worked fine, but the second he touched her, the woman suddenly changed shape and two Joves stood facing one another. One swung and the other Jove blocked. They fought each other for a minute, then one of them ran toward the wall and turned to mist, disappearing from the camera's view. The remaining Garen held his fingertips up to his temples then pulled them away after a second and shook his head.

Ana gaped at her phone. "What the hell just happened?"

Leah pounded her palm with her fist. "That's it! This woman is a mimic. That's why she always displays different powers." She redialed Gabe's number and he answered after one ring.

"Dude, we're a bit busy at the moment. The woman just—"

"Escaped, I know. We saw it on the security feed. What I wanted to tell you is that she appears to be a mimic. You may want to look for any of those in the system. She wielded plasma a few months ago when she confronted my van and teleported away after touching Portis. Then she shows up today with lightening. As soon as she touched Garen, she picked up his shape shifting ability."

"Oh, shit! Space daddy is gonna be pissed." Gabe cursed. "Fine, I'll check the database and see what I can come up with. Mimic is not a common ability, for Chromodecs or aliens."

"Sounds good. And keep me posted, okay?"

"Leah," he whined. "That's not following proper channels and you know it.”

"Listen, this woman is targeting my company and me specifically. I think I have a right to know. And besides," she paused for dramatic effect. "I've seen your work and I can still hack circles around you."

"You'll get me fired someday."

Leah laughed. "No, I won't, the CORP likes the toys that Lockheed creates for them too much. But if it will make you feel better, I'll speak with Garen myself."

"Thanks, LT. Catch you later." Gabe hung up and Leah breathed a sigh of relief that she at least got him to agree to check the government's database for aliens or Chromodecs registered with that particular power signature.

Ana closed out the app on her phone. "So, what happens now?"

"I call Ron back and have him direct the facilities team to unseal the labs. After that they'll work on getting the power back. Jenna, please send a notice to LALT-all, that I want essential personnel only onsite for the rest of the week. Everyone else can work from home until next Monday. That should be enough time to have the lobby repaired and make sure our building-wide electrical failsafe worked to prevent damage anyplace else other than the front entrance."

"But productivity—"

"There is a reason everyone has laptops and VPN dongles, so we can work from home if necessary. It may be slower than normal but still feasible." She pointed at Ana but looked back and forth between her and Jenna.

"That includes the two of you."

"I'm not leaving you here—" Ana and Jenna both stopped speaking and looked at each other with eyes wide.

Leah shook her head and smiled. "You two are funny. And don't worry about me. I plan to make sure the right people are in place then go home myself. I can't do anymore here. I imagine that once everyone is evacuated, they'll shut off all but essential lab lines, backup systems, and the server farm until they verify circuits." She gave them both a wry smile. "It will be nice not hearing the desk phone ring."

Jenna huffed. "Like I'd ever let someone ring straight through without them being on your priority list."

Leah's cell rang and she answered the private number. "Hello?"

"Leah Lockheed-Tuck, I heard you have intel for the CORP. May I come up?"

Leah had spoken with Agent Garen Grath, Jove, numerous times. She wasn't worried about him discovering Kaelen's identity from a short meeting because she had no intention of letting him touch her. Not that he'd ever been less than professional in her presence. "The balcony doors would be easiest, but they're locked without power."

"I'll mist through the seal. See you in a few minutes."

Both Ana and Jenna looked perplexed, so Leah explained. "It was the head of the CORP. He'll be here soon, and I can share with him what I know of the attacker. You two pack your things and be ready to go as soon as lockdown has been cleared." Jenna nodded and left the office using her cell phone light to see in the darkened hallway beyond the doors.

"Leah," Ana's tone was indicative of how worried she was about Leah.

"I know, but it's going to be okay. They'll catch the woman eventually and until then, I've got a little ace up my sleeve."

"Are you talking about your hot alien girlfriend? She's a bit, eh, not particularly intimidating. Maybe have Hans expand your security team again."

Leah smirked. "Kaelen can be a handful when needed, but I'm not giving you any more details in the office."

Ana sighed. "Fine, but you owe me a girls' night soon."

"How about dinner this week?"

"Despite working from home, it'll be a hectic week for me. Who do you think is going to approve the contractor budget for the repairs and read through the onsite facilities team's findings for the full list of damage?"

"Make time. I'll handle facilities if you hire the contractors. Put money enough into it that we can get the repairs done asap. Boost security in the meantime."

After a few seconds, Ana nodded. "Fine. How about Thursday? I'll come to yours, you just invite your girlfriend over too so I can speak with her properly and not be drowned out by the Tuck sisters bickering over Monopoly."

Leah grinned. "I can swing that, and I'll let Kaelen know when I see her after Garen leaves."

"Speaking of." Ana pointed at the balcony where Jove stood in all his black-armored glory.

Unlike most other CORP agents, he didn't wear a black helmet. Leah assumed it hindered his various abilities. He shifted to that of his most common image, a dark-skinned human man known as Special Agent in Charge, Garen Grath. The person leading the LA Chromodec Office of Restraint and Protection.

"On that note, I'm going to go pack up my computer." Ana turned on her own cell phone light and walked out much the way Jenna had done minutes before.

Garen misted and his incorporeal form snaked around the door seal as Ana disappeared. "Miss Lockheed-Tuck."

They met in the middle of the open space of her office, and she held out her hand to shake once she saw he was wearing gloves. "How many times do I need to remind you that I don't stand on such formality. It's Leah."

He gave her a kind smile. She'd had enough contact with Garen to understand why Gabe called him space daddy. It was pretty funny but uniquely suited to the competent and protective man in front of her. "Leah then. Gabe says you have intel?"

"I'm sure you've already put it together, but you weren't there the night the woman came after my van." Leah went on to detail all her evidence while Garen listened with an inscrutable look upon his face.

"I did have an idea about mimic abilities but it's good to know she's not limited to either alien or Chromodec. It's also valuable knowledge that she copies both passive and active powers."

Leah considered his statement. "You mean because she used energy projection with the plasma and electricity but could also teleport and copy your shapeshifting ability?"

"Exactly. It's a small list of people who can do that. Gabe has already found three names, but they're all deceased so he's still looking. I'd like to speak with you about security though. We have direct evidence that this mimic attacked you before, or was going to attack you." Leah nodded. "I was also able to confirm that the man who shot at you in your parking garage, Derek Paules, was a victim of telepathic suggestion. Though I'm not sure if it wore off naturally after time elapse, or if the adrenaline of his ride courtesy of Scion was responsible."

"Say what you will about this Scion, but I'd be dead if she hadn't come rushing into the parking garage that day."

He narrowed his eyes and Leah was careful to keep her face neutral, a skill perfected after years of boardroom meetings full of people twice her age. Garen spoke again. "Either way, I was able to tap in and easily see the results of such tampering."

Concerned about the life of someone who was potentially innocent, Leah asked, "What will happen to him?"

"Oh, don't mistake his guilt. The man was actually a hired gun. While the weapon he used wasn't his, he has a rap sheet as long as my arm and he's wanted in three different states."

"I wasn't expecting that."

Garen smiled. "Neither were we." He cleared his throat. "Anyway, I'd like to put a team of agents on you until we catch this woman."

"I have my own security."

"They're not CORP."

"Exactly. And I'd like to keep it that way. No offense, Garen."

Garen crossed his muscled arms and frowned. "We're not going to steal any of Lockheed's secrets, Leah. I only want to make sure you're safe. You are a valuable member of the community and a precious resource for the CORP."

She scowled. "So, it's not about me, it's about what I can do for you."

He sighed and rubbed a hand down his face then back up through his short-cropped hair. "It's not like that and you know it."

"I know, Garen. But I have my own security which chafes already. I'm also confident in the CORP's response time should she come after me again. I'll be fine."

"We're fast, but you may need an immediate response that we can't accommodate. I wish you'd reconsider."

Leah looked up and tapped her lip. "Hmm, perhaps I should see if I can hire this Scion then. I mean, she blew in out of nowhere to catch a bullet. I bet she'd protect me again for enough money."

He shook his head. "You're being facetious."

"I'm actually being serious. She's fairly amazing from all I've seen on the news."

"She's a criminal."

Leah waved a hand in the air. "Yeah, yeah, and technically so are all the sanctioned heroes. Apparently, you either have to work for the CORP or be on the VIP list."

"You may have a point, but we're getting off topic."

Leah tilted her head and looked up at him. "Are we though? Because I'm serious about hiring someone like Scion as a protector, at least temporarily."

"Yes, well something tells me that Los Angeles's newest vigilante isn't moved by such things as money."

"You may be right. I mean, a person would have to be a certain level of self-sacrificing to risk the wrath of the CORP to save that plane." Leah suddenly remembered that there was a common element to Scion's rescue efforts, herself, but before she could panic her phone lit with an incoming call. She held it up. "Sorry, Garen, but it's my chief of building security with an update. I should take this." She answered, "Hey, Ron, give me a second, will you?" Then she hit mute and stared at Garen.

Garen looked as if he wanted to say more but nodded instead. "Of course. I'll let you get back to work. If you change your mind about those agents, give Gabe a call."

"I will, and thank you."

He gave her a little salute then walked over to the balcony doors and misted outside. Seconds later, he was flying away and Leah blew out a sigh of relief. After getting the update from Ron, she called Ellie and filled her in on the events of the previous few hours. Ellie was visiting a lab across the city so at least she hadn't been at risk.

The lights came on not long after Leah's last call. Ron told her they were bringing up the building power long enough to evacuate the labs and let people exit the elevators. Then they'd shut it down until electricians could come in and check all the lines. It would be a tedious process, but Leah was confident she had the right people managing things onsite.

"Leah!"

Leah crossed her arms and leveled a stern gaze at Kaelen. "How fast did you run up the stairs?"

Kaelen blurred across the room and pulled Leah into a hug. "Not as fast as that." Leah hugged her as tight as she was able then pulled back and raised an eyebrow causing Kaelen to expand her answer. "Einstein and I took the elevator to the first floor, then I came up the stairs. And it wasn't enough to make the security team suspicious."

She rubbed Kaelen's arm but didn't let her go. "I'm fine, darling. I promised you, didn't I?"

"You did, but this woman is powerful and unpredictable."

"That she is."

Kaelen stepped back again and paced in front of Leah's hoverchair. "I've been thinking about this while we were locked in the lab. She's not only found you late at night when few people knew of your itinerary or when we'd be back, but now she's attacked you here at the office."

As much as Leah didn't want to say anything, it was only fair to inform Kaelen of what Garen said. "Actually, she was most likely responsible for mentally controlling the man that shot at me in the parking garage too."

Kaelen stopped and faced Leah. "Did Jove tell you that?"

"Garen did, yes."

"You need more security."

Leah snorted. "He said that as well."

"Despite your CORP wanting to arrest me, they do seem to have a wise leader for this city. Will you increase your normal security team? I didn't see them the day of the parking garage attack. Do they stop their duty when you enter the building?"

And now they'd hit a topic she was afraid to admit to Kaelen. "Well…" She sighed.

"Your heart rate changed." Leah gave her a sharp look and Kaelen put her hands up. "I'm sorry, but I can't block it out. What aren't you telling me?"

"I told you that I initially cut back on my security when we first began spending time together."

"But you said you were increasing it again."

Leah nodded. "I increased security after both attacks, but I've limited them to outside surveillance only since we started dating."

"Vos, why would you do something so foolish?"

"Because I didn't want anyone to guess who you are. I was trying to protect your identity!"

Kaelen froze and stared at Leah with wide eyes. She dropped to her knees next to Leah's hoverchair and took Leah's hands gently between her own. "My identity isn't worth your life. What if she targets your home next? She has displayed an uncanny ability in finding you."

"Kaelen, even if I hadn't cut back on my personal security, it wouldn't do any good at my penthouse. The ones who are on duty have always stayed outside the main entrances to the building. If someone wanted to get to me, they could and that's a fact. Especially someone with powers."

Kaelen scowled. "I dislike your facts. You can't be unprotected. Please, I can't lose you like I've lost so many others."

Leah contemplated her options. She could enhance her own security by giving them more access, but they probably wouldn't do as good of a job as having a squad of CORP agents following her every move. Then again, they'd have to be even more careful that no one discovered Kaelen's powers if agents were always around. It was a conundrum.

She suddenly remembered her promise to Ana earlier. "Are you free to come over Thursday? Ana wants to have dinner and get to know my girlfriend better."

Kaelen accepted Leah's subject change and stood. "I'm always free, you know that."

"You were supposed to find a hobby for your off time."

"Yes, well, even hobbies couldn't fill all my time when I don't need as much sleep as a normal human. Besides, I enjoy staying late and doing good work. We're solving the problems of the world down in SPL. I'm happy to be a part of that."

"What about that show on Netflix you were watching?"

"I finished it. Besides, my couch isn't as comfortable as yours."

Leah smirked. "No?" Kaelen shook her head. "What is it about my couch that makes it so comfortable?"

"Well, your blankets are soft against my skin."

"Only the blankets?"

"Your cushions sink the perfect amount beneath my weight."

Leah rolled her eyes. "And?"

"And you're usually sitting with me on your couch. That's what makes it the best."

Delighted, Leah laughed outright. "You're ridiculous. You can come over whenever you want. I don't mind your company. Actually, I quite like having you around." Inspiration struck Leah like a bolt of lightning. "That's it!"

A familiar wrinkle appeared between Kaelen's pale blonde brows. "What?"

"Would you like to stay with me until Mimic has been apprehended?"

Kaelen was already nodding. "That's a brilliant idea. I would need to establish some boundaries if I'm going to be staying there as protection."

"What are you talking about?"

Kaelen continued with her rambling plans. "Yes, I need to be focused on protection duty whenever you are home. Which means staying in the guest room and refraining from any sexual activity for the interim so I can best guard your person—"

Leah placed her pointer finger over Kaelen's lips. "Executive decision, we are not avoiding sex until this woman is caught. I'm still making up for lost time and you're entirely too good at what you do for me to go without now. I have full confidence that you'll protect me with half an ear listening. It will have to do, love."

Kaelen's shoulders slumped as she breathed a sigh of relief. "Okay. I wasn't looking forward to that level of sacrifice while being around you all the time."

Leah gazed off in the distance, preoccupied by thoughts of her and Kaelen in her penthouse together every night. Kaelen must have mistaken her distraction for something else. "I'll protect you. I promise."

Leah laughed, "Who said I was worried? I'm simply trying to come up with places at home that we haven't had sex yet."

"That's something I'll gladly help you with later."

"Oh, I'm looking forward to it. Now, you should probably go back down to the lab and gather anything you'll need for the coming week while I finish packing my own things." Kaelen tilted her head. "I'm leaving shortly and you're coming with me."

"What about our projects?"

"Use the private lab at my place if you're working on something portable that you don't want to leave behind."

Kaelen followed Leah to her desk and watched from her space on the other side of it. "Why haven't you mentioned that you have a private lab in your penthouse?"

Leah grinned at her as she slid the laptop into its case. "Because it's not in my penthouse, it's the next floor down. And you haven't needed it yet." Leah waited for Kaelen to dispute her statement but she only nodded.

"Fair enough. I'll be back in a few minutes. I'm going to retrieve my own belongings from the lab."

Leah smiled at her as Kaelen left at a fast jog. Then Leah realized she'd agreed to her girlfriend moving in with her for the foreseeable future. "Fuck me."

Chapter Twenty

Kaelen watched Leah cook their dinner a half hour before Ana was supposed to arrive Thursday night. Because she was in the privacy of her own condo, Leah had forgone the hoverchair while working at the stove. She called over her shoulder, "Do you have those vegetables chopped for me?"

Startled, Kaelen returned her gaze to the round white vegetable. "Oh, sorry." She used her maximal speed to finish mincing the onion as Leah had demonstrated earlier. Then she moved on to the celery, carrots, and garlic. When she was finished, she carried the cutting board to Leah and observed as they were all carefully scooped into the large skillet. "What are you doing now?"

"I'm going to sweat these for a few minutes then add some broth and flour. I'll let it simmer for a little while before incorporating the rice and letting it cook."

The savory smell tantalized her. "Will there be enough for all three of us?" Kaelen didn't have to spell it out for Leah. Her main concern was whether there would be enough to satisfy her high calorie dietary need.

"Actually, can you bring me the container in my laptop case?"

Kaelen sped through the condo to Leah's office. She found the resealable container and returned to the kitchen, blowing a few pieces of mail from the counter, which she quickly picked up. She held the container out to Leah. "You may want to go normal speed while Ana is here. I'm aware that our friends know you're an alien, and a few probably suspect that you're Scion, but you should still be careful."

"Will you tell her about your recovery like you did with the group on Halloween?"

"Yes. I can't keep something like that from her, she's one of my best friends outside you and Maddy."

Kaelen smiled, loving how close the two sisters were. "If you trust her with your secret, then so can I. Besides, the entire squad already knows I'm an alien like Einstein and Nalla."

"Technically, Nalla was born on Earth."

"My point is that none of our friends have a problem with it." She held up her hand when Leah's mouth opened. "But if you're concerned, I won't come right out and admit it to anyone, and I'll watch my power usage while she is here."

Leah lowered the flame on the burner then approached Kaelen where she leaned against the counter. "Darling, you know that your powers don't bother me in the slightest. I only brought it up because I worry about you."

Kaelen looked down. Logically she knew it was necessary to be cautious, but now that she'd been using her powers a lot more, she felt stifled whenever she had to pretend that they didn't exist. "I know, and I love you for it."

"Well, you may love me a lot more for this. I know you struggle to eat enough food to satisfy your immense nutritional need. How you were surviving on CLIF bars alone for all those months is beyond me."

Kaelen frowned at the memory. "They were quite tasty, but I was hungry a lot and I cleaned out many grocery stores in the surrounding neighborhood."

"Knowing that you still struggle, and to save on your food budget, I had one of my labs work on this for you." Leah opened the container to reveal dense, brick-like bars inside, similar to the ones she'd been living on when she first arrived on Earth.

"What are those?"

"Super-compacted, high protein, nutritional bars for extreme caloric need."

Kaelen was skeptical. "How do they taste?"

"Eh," Leah looked down at the container and shook it a bit to rattle the bars inside. "Actually, nobody knows because they are so dense. Clearly the only people who can eat them are ones with incredible strength and digestive capabilities."

"So, only me then?"

Leah laughed. "Perhaps. Go ahead, try one. You're my lab rat for this. If it works out, I may ship some to the Millers. I can only imagine how much Michael will eat when he hits his teen years, especially since some of his powers have already kicked in."

"Given what I know of lab rats, I'm not sure that's an enviable title. Do you at least know the flavor?" Kaelen picked one up and Leah wasn't kidding when she said they were highly compacted. She gave it a sniff.

"Dr. Folkston said they went with chocolate to keep it simple."

Kaelen bit down on the bar and chewed it thoroughly. While the texture wasn't as preferable as something softer, her strength meant that it was easy enough to masticate. The flavor began quite subtly but by the second bite, it hit her in full and she grinned at Leah. "This is tasty. How many calories?"

"Three thousand."

She stopped chewing for a second and looked down at the bar in her hand. It was hard to believe that such a relatively small thing could hold so much. Kaelen had investigated alternatives online once she'd become more acclimated to the internet and its purchasing possibilities. The highest calorie bar she'd found was seven hundred. "This is amazing and it will help me immensely. How easy is it to produce, and when can you make more?"

Leah shrugged. "It wasn't that big of a deal. I knew we had a hydraulic press that had previously been used to compact fibrous material to test its potential for the construction industry in third world nations. I wondered if a few adjustments could be made to add the right ingredients for a nutritional bar for you and I was right. It's only a matter of mixing up a new batch whenever your bars run low." She laughed. "Dr. Folkston hasn't asked me what they're for yet, and I'm not sure what I'll tell him when he inevitably does."

"Tell him you're creating them for aliens with strong teeth and high energy needs." Kaelen finished her bar and dusted her hands. Then she moved closer and gave Leah a hug and a chocolatey kiss.

"You smell delicious. And that's actually a brilliant answer. Now, I need to finish the vegetables or dinner won't be ready on time."

Kaelen made a face. "Or you could skip the vegetables since they are an inferior food with low caloric value."

"Darling, not all of us have, well, alien metabolism. Regarding that, I have noticed I'm burning a lot more calories between walking around my apartment and the physical therapy. Though," Leah tapped her bottom lip and Kaelen recognized the twinkle in her eye, "it could have something to do with my ravenous girlfriend."

Kaelen grinned. "I have been known to amaze even Gabe on game nights with the amount of pizza I can eat."

"I'm not talking about food, love."

"Oh." Kaelen blinked at her, then Leah's meaning hit. "Oh!" Her grin grew as she moved even closer to Leah.

Leah put a hand against her chest. "Oh no you don't. We have company coming over and I need to finish dinner."

"Maybe Ana could visit tomorrow."

"She's already on her way."

Kaelen opened her mouth to say something but heard the telltale sound of the elevator rising. "She is literally nearly here. Do you want your chair?"

Leah sighed. "Fine." With a burst of speed, Kaelen fetched the hoverchair. Leah got herself situated in the seat seconds before the doors opened. Ana stepped out carrying her purse, another bag, and a bottle of wine.

"Sorry, I'm a little early but I brought dessert."

Kaelen looked from Ana back to Leah. "I changed my mind, she can stay."

Leah rolled her eyes. "I'm glad your sweet tooth is so accommodating with our friends."

Dinner was delicious, and surprisingly, Kaelen didn't mind the abundance of vegetables. It wasn't that she didn't care for that type of Earth food. It was exactly as she indicated to Leah. They didn't provide enough sustenance for her, so she didn't want to waste time eating them. Since food didn't seem to affect her health in a negative way, like it did for humans and a few other species, she was free to eat whatever she liked. A fact that annoyed Leah immensely.

The three women sat in Leah's living room after dinner and dessert were cleared away. They were enjoying the wine that Ana had brought with her. Ana was telling Kaelen a story of when she and Leah attended the Los Angeles campus of MIT together. "And so, every time someone called the administrative office, they got a recording of R2D2's scream."

Leah covered her eyes, laughing at the memory. "Oh God, I remember that! I actually hacked the system and had it run through a secondary programming loop as backup. It took a month for them to disable my security code."

Kaelen looked back and forth between them. "Who or what is R2D2?"

Ana opened her mouth to speak but nothing came out. Then she looked at Leah. "Are you telling me you two haven't watched any *Star Wars* movies?"

"Are you aware of how many films Earth has? We're slowly making our way through them. We started with musicals and Disney."

"Still…"

"Ana, I didn't even watch those movies until I was at MIT with you. Television wasn't exactly encouraged before I was taken in by the Tucks."

Ana's expression softened and she reached over to pat Leah's hand from where she sat on an adjacent chair. "Sorry, Leah. Little baby genius, I forgot. But that means you two need to watch them soon."

"Not all of them. You know I don't acknowledge the prequels."

"You're such a snob!"

Kaelen interrupted the verbal sparring. "Will I like the *Star Wars* movies?"

Leah tilted her head one way, then the other, considering the question. She leaned over and bumped her shoulder against Kaelen and gave her a smile. "I think you will—" Leah suddenly frowned. "On second thought, maybe not."

"What? You literally forced me to watch each one…numerous times!"

"Alderaan."

Ana gave Kaelen a strange look, one she couldn't identify. "Oh, shit. Sorry, Kaelen."

"I don't know why you're sorry or what this Alderaan is. It sounds like one of the liquors from Szot's bar."

Leah rested her hand on Kaelen's knee and hesitantly explained. "Um, one of the scenes shows the home planet of a main character purposefully blown up."

"Oh." The air left her lungs in a rush and the blackness of loss rose inside her. The sudden emotion took her by surprise. Kaelen looked down, clenching her fist.

Ana drained the last bit of wine from her glass, then held it up. "Either of you want some more?"

Kaelen understood that she was doing it to move them away from a suddenly heavy topic, and she was grateful. She took a deep breath and released it, letting go of regret, sadness, and heartbreak at the same time, then she looked at Leah. It was the perfect moment for Leah to shock Ana. Leah hummed quietly and made eye contact with Kaelen, who gave a little nod in return.

Leah casually said, "I've got it," then stood and plucked the empty wine glass from Ana's limp fingers.

"Holy fuck! You really did it, you secretive bitch." She got to her feet and followed Leah to the kitchen counter where they'd left the wine. Ana stared at her in disbelief while Leah uncorked a new bottle. She narrowed her eyes. "How long?"

Leah smirked. "A few weeks now. If you'd come out with us on Halloween instead of your hot date, you'd have known then."

"What?"

"You remember the headlines about Alley Cat and Bolt in a possible relationship the day after we all went out?"

Ana lifted a dark eyebrow in a look that was similar to one Leah had given Kaelen many times. "Yes? It was big news in all the gossip rags, especially since both heroes insisted that they weren't even in Los Angeles on Halloween."

Kaelen grinned. "I was The Bolt and Leah dressed as Alley Cat."

Ana gave her an inscrutable look. "There was video proof that the person dressed as Bolt had super speed. Can you explain that?"

"Uh—" Kaelen looked at Leah for an answer, or maybe permission. Leah nodded and Kaelen let out a sigh of relief. She wanted to tell Ana, but there was still a part of her that urged caution. "Well, you see, that's actually one of my powers so I was able to convince the DJ and it spiraled from there. I didn't encourage it though."

Leah nodded. "It's true. It was mostly Nalla's fault. She's the one that told people that Kaelen was the real Bolt and that she was off duty for the night to celebrate Halloween."

Ana laughed and shook her head. "Of course, she did." Then she froze and narrowed her eyes at Kaelen, looking first at Kaelen's short hair, then moving down to her toned arms and overall build. Her eyes widened and she whispered, "It's you."

"Me?" Kaelen pointed at her own chest.

"You're her, the woman that saved Leah and Ellie's plane, and Leah's life in the parking garage. You're Scion."

"Ana," Leah's tone was a warning. "You can't tell anyone."

She looked back and forth between Kaelen and Leah. "Who does know?"

"Me, Ellie, Maddy, and Tasha. Einstein guessed but insisted that he wouldn't say anything to anyone, even Nalla."

Kaelen shook her head. "Nalla knows too. The bartender at Szot's, Tarynn, she uh, outed me as Scion."

Ana held out her wine glass. "I think I need a refill for this discussion. You know the CORP is going to put it together eventually. I mean, I'm no genius but it doesn't take much to see the connection between two of the three Scion sightings."

Kaelen frowned. "You have a good point. Maybe I should go out and do more, what's the word, heroing? Heroics?"

Leah poured more wine for her and Ana before putting the bottle down and gripping Kaelen's forearm. "What you should do is lay low. We discussed this. You're technically a fugitive and while the CORP isn't looking too hard for you, all that will change if you start showing up more often."

"I may not have a choice if that Mimic woman keeps coming after you." Ana laughed and shook her head. Kaelen found it extremely odd. "What is so funny?"

Ana waved toward Leah. "I realize now why Leah was so unconcerned about that deranged Chromodec targeting her. She literally has a super-powered girlfriend with who knows how many abilities. I mean what," she looked at Kaelen and ticked items off on her fingers, "you're able to fly, are strong enough to lift freaking planes, you can catch bullets. Bullets, people!" She patted Leah's cheek. "I feel much better about your safety now."

Leah shifted a bit where she leaned against the kitchen counter. "That's actually the real reason Kaelen is here tonight. She's going to stay with me for a while until Mimic is caught."

"Excellent." Ana nodded at Kaelen. "I knew I liked you for more than your buff bod and ability to make Leah smile."

"I, uh, thank you?" Her words were confusing, but Kaelen smiled anyway as she watched Leah roll her eyes.

"Let's go back to the couch and I'll tell you all about my plans for announcing the nano serum treatment at CES."

Ana's face lit up with realization. "They're going to go bonkers. L-I's bottom line will hit the ceiling."

"That's exactly what I'm counting on." Leah gave Kaelen a conspiratorial wink. "After all, I've got to fund those green energy projects somehow."

Everything was quiet for the next few weeks. While there hadn't been any leads on Mimic's identity or location, at least she hadn't made another appearance. Leah told Kaelen that she was hosting a gathering she called Friendsgiving. It was comprised of the small Tuck family, as well as all their friends who had no place else to go for the holiday… which was all their friends. They'd also been invited back to Michigan to have dinner with the Millers the Saturday after. Leah arranged the flight and Kaelen looked forward to seeing Michael again.

Kaelen stared at the massive roasted animal that Leah stood over. She was using a brush to wipe liquid all over its skin. Basting it was called. "Does everyone celebrate this date with a large dead bird?"

Leah finished and placed the brush and bowl on the counter before sliding the roaster back into the oven and shutting the door. "Not everyone celebrates Thanksgiving at the end of November. For starters, this one is only observed in the US. Not only that, but there are many negative things associated with the holiday, mostly having to do with white settlers overtaking the native population in the Americas. None of us, the found family, actually celebrate the holiday itself. We made it into a time where friends can come together and share a meal, play some games, and eat pie."

The stove was filled with pots containing various types of food. Root vegetables, a shredded bread dish, and things Kaelen couldn't identify. She sniffed the air and closed her eyes. "It smells wonderful." Then Leah's last words hit her. "Wait, did you say pie?"

"Yes, darling. One of the main features of this holiday, besides the turkey, is an abundance of pie."

Kaelen moved closer and pulled Leah into an embrace. "Tell me more about this pie."

Laughter spilled from wine-stained lips. "You are ruled by your stomach."

"And my teeth, the sweet ones specifically."

"And your sweet tooth. Anyway, I've made blueberry and peach. Nalla and Einstein are bringing pumpkin pie and homemade macaroni and cheese. Let's see…Maddy and Tasha are making lasagna, garlic knots, and wild rice pilaf. Ellie made her famous chocolate pecan pie."

"Chocolate pecan pie? I've heard Maddy mention that before."

Leah smirked. "It's Maddy's favorite dessert."

"Better than my birthday cake?"

"Definitely. It's so good that Ellie bakes about half a dozen, to make sure there's enough for everyone to take some home. Though Maddy and I each get our own."

Kaelen hugged her. "That's because Ellie loves you both very much. What about Ana, Gabe, and Devon?"

Leah's eyebrows drew together. "I'm sure she loves them too."

"No, I meant what are they bringing?"

"Gabe said he's bringing homemade cranberry sauce and rolls. Devon wasn't sure yet, he didn't fly in from New York until this morning. And Ana is bringing plenty of wine."

Kaelen covered her eyes and laughed. "Oh no. I hope everyone is Ubering today."

"Taking an Uber, and they usually do. We'll either play games later or lower the big screen and watch a movie. It depends if the guys take over the game room to put on football."

"I've heard of football, and uh, the other football. Is it fun to watch?"

"It's lame, but I try to humor them."

"By lame, do you mean people are injured?"

Leah snickered. "Usually. It's a sport, one that is extremely physical and often televised. Boring if you ask me."

"I see."

Kaelen ate two of her special compressed chocolate bars before everyone showed up. She had no choice. The smell of all the cooking food made her nearly delirious with hunger but Leah wouldn't let her have any. Maddy, Tasha, and Devon were the first three to arrive, which proved to be a good thing since Devon brought a few appetizer trays as his contribution.

He shrugged as he unloaded the bags. "Sorry folks, but this was the best I could do. I'm still jetlagged and didn't trust myself to cook."

Leah walked around the corner smiling. "That's perfect, Dev. No one else thought to bring snacks."

"That's pretty lucky then. I've got—" He turned to look at her as he spoke, then did a double take. "Holy shit, you're walking!"

Leah looked at Maddy and Tasha. "You didn't tell him?"

Tasha shrugged. "We wanted it to be a surprise."

He moved closer and slowly circled Leah. "It worked." Then he paused and grinned. "You're shorter than I thought you'd be."

"What?" Everyone in the room nodded in agreement, including Kaelen. Leah looked around at them. "Why in the world would you think I'd be taller?"

"It's your—" Devon stopped speaking.

Kaelen had no problem giving her reason. "You exude a certain level of power and confidence that makes you larger within one's mind. People associate personality with physical size."

Devon pointed at Kaelen. "What she said." Then he looked back at Leah. "Hey, since I'm here early, can I put the game on?"

Leah rolled her eyes. "If you must. Though I have no idea why you like watching such a tedious and wasteful pastime. It's boring."

Maddy snickered. "Oh yes, not everything can be a thrill-a-minute chess match."

Leah flipped her the bird. "On that note, I'm going to make the whipped potatoes. Kaelen, darling, I could use your arm."

Kaelen wasn't sure what Leah would do with her arm. Before she could ask, Maddy made a motion with her hand, accompanied by an odd noise. "*Wapish!*"

"I don't know what that means."

"It means you're whipped like a herd beast, Ra-Evon!"

"But Leah has never—"

"Kaelen, are you coming? I want you to whip the potatoes for me."

Kaelen gave Maddy a smug look. "The potatoes are going to be whipped, not me. Now I know for certain that Leah is the smarter sister." She turned and walked around the large island and joined Leah at the far counter.

"Uh huh, keep telling yourself that." Maddy and Tasha laughed, then made their way down the hall toward the game room. It didn't have as large of a screen as the one that came down from the ceiling in the living room, but it was still nice.

Eventually the rest of the group arrived, including Ellie with her pies. She had so many that she'd called Maddy for volunteers to help carry them up to Leah's condo. The smell alone was enough to make Kaelen's stomach growl. They'd expanded the table and added chairs from a storage closet earlier in the day. Once the food was ready, everyone helped set it for dinner. Seeing the amount of food available, Kaelen had no doubt she'd walk away satisfied.

Leah and Ellie were on each end of the long table. Kaelen sat to Leah's right, while Maddy was on the opposite side of the table to Ellie's right. Maddy pointed at Kaelen from her seat. "I see that look on your face and no, you can't eat it all. The rest of us are expecting to take home leftovers, Kaelen."

She scoffed, "Even I have my limits. I wouldn't have eaten it all. Besides, there's pie!"

Maddy turned to Ellie. "One of those pies is for me, right, Mom?"

The eldest Tuck chuckled. "Yes, Maddy. Well, each household gets a pie, so you'll have to share with Tasha." Maddy frowned, but Ellie was adamant. "That means share, or you won't get your own next year."

"I'm excited to try it," Kaelen said. "I've had most of the others by now, except for Ellie's pie and the pumpkin. Are those seasonal?"

Nalla nodded. "Yup. Well, the pumpkin is. I don't know about chocolate pecan."

Leah asked Maddy to carve the turkey and once everyone had full plates of food, Leah raised her wine glass. "I'd like to propose a toast to celebrate my closest friends and family, having good people by my side who can make dreams come true, and finding love where I never expected."

Maddy raised her glass as well. "Mom's pie." The rest around the table followed suit, calling out things they were appreciative of.

"Making it back from New York in time for Friendsgiving."

"An abundance of leftovers so I don't have to cook the next few days."

"Nalla and the rest of my friends."

"My hot sparkle pants robeux—" Einstein made a little sound of protest. "Er, boyfriend…and Ana's case of wine." Nalla winked at her Anna while she said the last part.

Ellie raised her glass. "Having my daughters and all the people they love in one place."

"Nalla's humor, and my case of wine." Everyone laughed at Ana's comment.

Kaelen raised her glass. "I'm grateful for this group, for my new family and this planet. I—" She paused as a wave of emotion made her conscious of the strong grip she had on the fragile glass. "I didn't know that I could find so much happiness after suffering the loss of my people. But you're all here right in front of me, and my heart is incredibly full. I've found love and acceptance. Thank you."

"Aww!" Nalla jumped up and ran around the table so she could hug Kaelen.

Leah wiped a discrete tear while Maddy had the opposite reaction. "Well, it was a hell of a lot more sentimental than ours!" She asked, "Okay, who's left?" Einstein pointed at Tasha. "It is Miss Smith."

Tasha looked around the table, stopping on her older brother. He smiled and nodded, then she stood. Kaelen found the interaction curious.

Rather than lift a glass, Tasha put her hands in her pockets. Kaelen heard her heart race, and the stuttering breaths that indicated the woman was nervous, which was strange because she was usually the calm one.

Tasha took a deep breath then lifted her eyes to meet Maddy's curious gaze. "I, uh, well I wasn't certain I was going to do this today, but I thought it may be something we'd both want to share with our friends. I love you Maddy, and I love the life we've built together. After talking to my pushy brother," she glanced at Devon who chuckled. "He made me realize that if I love it, I should put a ring on it."

"Oh, my gawd, she just quoted the venerable Queen Bey!" Nalla practically vibrated in her seat, while Leah and Ellie covered their mouths with some unidentified emotion. Kaelen had no idea what was going on.

Tasha stepped away from the table, then pulled a ring from her pocket, and dropped down to one knee in front of Maddy. "Madison Tuck, would you do me the honor of becoming my wife?"

Maddy sat in shock for a few moments, then practically tackled Tasha after lunging from her seat. "Yes!"

Half the table stood from their chairs and moved to congratulate the couple. Kaelen looked at Einstein where he sat with a smile on his face. She asked, "Does this mean they are permanently partnered, uh, married?"

Einstein moved his gaze from the happy pile of people. "No, this was merely a formal way to ask someone for a permanent partnership. By exchanging jewelry and accepting Tasha's offer, it now means they are engaged. It is a state of relationship that leads to formal bonding, or partnership. The formal ceremony will come at a later date."

"And how do you know when you should offer permanent partnership with someone? We didn't have much control over this process on Argon. The match program decided who you would be joined with, though there was no definitive timeline for such things. Some pairings were announced soon after birth, others not until both individuals had joined guilds."

Einstein tilted his head. "Did you have an assigned mate?"

"No, even though I was gifted with my bonding torques after guild induction. Those and my holocube are the two mementoes that came with me from Argon. Well, those and the cloak given to me by my grandfather and grandmother."

"Interesting. As for your question, everyone's relationship moves at varying speeds. No couple is alike and as such, they will have different needs. Some couples never join formally. You simply do what is in your heart and hope that the person you wish to bond with feels the same way. Though from my experience, it rarely gets to the point of asking unless you already know the answer."

Kaelen nodded at his sage advice. "Thank you, Einstein. You've given me a lot of good information."

Their celebration continued into the evening. The ones that didn't want to watch football opted to play games at the large dinner table once it had been cleared off. Eventually, the abundance of food, family, friends, and fun left everyone content and sleepy, with the exception of Kaelen, and people began filing out with containers of leftovers. Once everyone was gone and the rest of the food put away for the night, Kaelen and Leah sat on the couch in front of the gas fireplace.

Leah held her hand and leaned her head against Kaelen's shoulder. "Did you have fun?"

Kaelen sighed and stared into the flickering flames. "Do you remember when we spoke of loss, and how to make it hurt less?"

"Yes." Leah tilted her head to look up at Kaelen.

She met Leah's gaze, admiring her pale blueish-green eyes. "You've filled my life. My friends, this found family, you… I've expanded so much since arriving on Earth that the pain is merely a discomfort in the background, barely noticeable unless I specifically probe it. Not only do I have you and my new friends, but we'll see young Michael and the Millers in a few days. I can't wait to visit Saturday and see how he is progressing with his Argonian studies."

"Kaelen,"

The rambling woman focused once again on Leah. "Yes?"

"Ovo te zhee."

Kaelen's heart raced and she smiled so wide it made her cheeks hurt. She pulled Leah into her arms. "That was perfect, barely an accent!" She leaned back slightly so she could thoroughly kiss her. "I love you, too."

When they pulled away for air, Leah was flushed. "I've been

practicing with that silly program. Your Wex is extremely judgmental when the pronunciation isn't quite right."

Kaelen giggled and squeezed her hands. "Yes, well, Wex is a dick."

"Kaelen Ra-Evon! Are those the same sweet lips that devoured Ellie's chocolate pecan pie earlier?"

"Yup. They're also the same lips that will devour you later." Leah lifted an eyebrow. "Uh, I learned that phrase from Nalla." Kaelen added, "Unless you're too tired from the day."

Leah squinted and got that familiar look in her eyes. "Why wait?" Leah stood from the couch and drew Kaelen up with her. She called out, "Fire off," then pulled Kaelen along as she walked backward toward the stairs.

Later while they lay in bed with sweat cooling on their bodies, Leah sighed contentedly within the circle of Kaelen's arms. "That was…I know I've mentioned how different sex is for me now since I've regained full function."

"You've said it is better now than before."

"Yes, but not how many would think. Believe it or not, it doesn't have as much to do with the sensation as people may assume. It's about not being afraid I'll lose control of basic bodily functions. Honestly, that was one of the worst parts of my paralysis. This has been such an amazing journey for me, learning all the things I like and dislike now that I have control over my body."

It was something Kaelen had never considered. She assumed that not having sensation and not being able to walk were important to Leah. She was open about the rest, though still somewhat private, and Kaelen knew she was a little embarrassed about her lack of control. She didn't realize until that moment exactly how much it bothered Leah. It made sense and she'd be hard-pressed to say different if it were her that were injured.

"I'm happy to make this journey of self-discovery with you. It's—" A heavy emotional pressure squeezed Kaelen's heart and her eyes filled with tears. "Your love fills my life in previously unimaginable ways."

"I adore you."

Kaelen kissed the crown of her head and looked down to see Leah staring at her in the dimmed light of the room. "You've also surpassed every romantic expectation I've ever had."

"Didn't you leave home at thirteen?"

"That doesn't mean I didn't think about what others had in their lives. I know my parents loved each other, but it was different. They were fairly accurate representatives of society, and they didn't possess the passion I see here on Earth. Outward expression of intense emotion wasn't normal or popular on Argon. But I witnessed a few passionate romances and secretly yearned for such, hoping the genetic program would match me to my preference."

Leah grew quiet for nearly a minute. When she spoke, her voice held hesitancy, sounding as though she were afraid of Kaelen's answer. "You don't bring it up much. Did you have a match that was lost on Argon?"

"Einstein asked me the same question earlier and the answer is no. I thought perhaps I'd receive my match name after my guild induction, but instead I was gifted my bonding torques from my parents." She turned so she could look into Leah's eyes. "I would have wished for a match exactly like you."

"Even though I'm not an Argonian, nor a member of any guild?"

Kaelen smiled. "Even though."

"I'm not going to lie; I've suffered a lot of heartache. Though I tried to temper my expectations after the injury, I also dreamed of finding love one day that would accept all of me."

The moment felt heavier than most of their conversations, and Kaelen turned on her side so she could give Leah her full attention. "I don't accept you, Leah Lockheed-Tuck." Leah sucked in a breath and Kaelen rushed forward. "I revel in your intelligence, humor, beauty, and compassion. Despite the high probability against the notion, I'd like to think that we met for a reason. You feel more important to me than a random connection. It's like—" Kaelen paused while she tried to explain her rationale.

"Quantum entanglement."

Kaelen translated Leah's words and smiled. "Yes! When two or more objects have to be described with reference to each other, even though the objects may be separated by a distance."

Leah reached up to brush a few whisps of hair from Kaelen's cheek. "Perhaps it was destiny and that's why you were never given a match."

She contemplated the notion before shrugging. "While improbable, the possibility isn't zero. I like the notion."

"That we could be entangled on a quantum level?"

"Yes, because it helps to explain the depth of my feelings for you." Leah nodded then her mouth opened wide with a yawn. Kaelen pulled the covers over Leah's shoulders and gave her a kiss on the forehead. "You should sleep. We can talk more tomorrow."

She got a squeeze for her words. "Night, love. You're the best part of this adventure I'm on." Leah fell asleep before Kaelen could respond to the heartfelt statement.

Chapter Twenty-one

Leah and Kaelen flew to Michigan on the hybrid Lockheed jet first thing Saturday morning so they'd have the entire afternoon with the Millers. She knew that Leah hated maintaining the ruse that she still needed the hoverchair, but it was necessary to preserve Leah's secret. That's not to say it wasn't useful at times. She'd come a long way in building up her lower body strength, but she still needed the occasional rest as the accelerated healing process took a lot of energy and she refused to slow down or sleep more.

Kaelen was nervous because they'd be meeting Paul and Shelly's eldest son, Tate. But it wasn't the same kind of worry she felt when they first met young Michael.

A familiar van was parked in front of the Gerald R. Ford main terminal building. The driver came around to open the large side door and Leah held out her hand to shake his. "Hey David, I'm glad you agreed to drive us again today. How's your mom and the rest of your family? You have a good Thanksgiving?"

He grinned at them as he pumped her hand up and down excitedly. "Good morning, Miss Lockheed-Tuck, Miss Ra-Evon. I was surprised to be personally requested but excited too because the holiday weekend bonus will sure be nice come Christmas time." He gestured toward the running vehicle. Kaelen entered first and lifted the arm rest for Leah. They didn't have any luggage because they planned to return late that evening.

Leah maneuvered her hoverchair so she could move to the seat. Kaelen laughed when Leah rolled her eyes and made a face. She whispered, "Soon." Six weeks and she'd be free for good.

Once the hoverchair was loaded and David in the driver's seat, he turned so he could see both women. "The family is doin' good. And I want to tell you again how much I appreciate what you've done for my mama. She zips all over in that daggum chair, chasing the kids everywhere and they love it. But those photography lessons you included got her smiling more than she has in the past year. I had no idea she could take such pretty pictures with a drone."

He looked away for a second and Kaelen listened to the truth of his words by his heartbeat. His eyes watered with emotion when he met their gaze again. "I don't know how I can ever thank you for what you've done. I know that people still grumble about the Lockheeds, but I gotta say you're an angel in my book."

"I…I'm not sure what to say except thank you. I want to do what's best for people. I know where I came from, but I also know where I want to go. I'm glad your mom is experiencing life again, and that your family is happy and safe."

Kaelen felt a wash of joy every time someone praised Leah for her good deeds. She also planned to dedicate the rest of her life helping Leah succeed with whatever she focused her mind on because her projects only ever led to amazing advancements. Kaelen smiled at David, mentally adding him to her list of people she felt protective over. The list was constantly growing. "Thank you, David. I know that means the world to Leah. And did you receive my message yesterday?"

"I did, Miss Ra-Evon. I'd be glad to join you all for another Thanksgiving meal. 'Specially if Shelly makes more of her apple pie."

Leah looked from David to Kaelen. "What message?"

Kaelen laughed. "After they discovered that David and Shelly were distant cousins on David's pappy's side?" She looked at him. "Is pappy right?"

"My grandpappy, yes. Uh, that's grandfather."

"Thank you, the slang is still a bit confusing. Anyway, Shelly and Paul told me to invite David for dinner, rather than make him sit out in the van for hours. Shelly's exact words were 'the more the merrier' when I asked."

"Aww, that was sweet of them." Leah glanced back at David. "I'll admit, I was a little concerned about you waiting for us for so long while we were inside eating a nice meal."

He shrugged, suddenly looking younger than his forty-two years. "It's no big deal, ma'am. Literally my job. And you don't have to worry about anything else." He touched the side of his nose. "Those papers you had me sign cover everything I see or hear within you, Miss Ra-Evon, or the Millers' presences. So, mum's the word."

"Thank you. And please call me Leah. As a warning, you may see even more strange stuff at the Millers, so don't be alarmed."

"Oh, I won't be bothered at all. In this crazy world, my motto has been to expect the unexpected. Why, just last week a giant oak tree grew right in the middle of the old River Town Crossings mall in Grand Rapids and it made the evenin' paper. Said some tree hugging Chromodec was trying to make a statement."

Kaelen perked up. "I'm a tree hugger."

He frowned. "I don't have any problem with folks who value the environment and all, but they did it in the middle, below the skylights where the kids' play area is located. A few kids and their parents got hurt. That's not okay."

"That's different. I don't condone that kind of behavior, or property damage. Hopefully they caught the person."

"Still looking, I'm afraid. They even called CORP agents in from the closest office in Detroit."

"I'm sure they'll find the Chromodec then. The CORP is very capable."

"Thanks Miss—er, Leah."

Kaelen wasn't so enamored with Earth's Chromodec Office of Restraint and Protection. "They still haven't caught Mimic."

Leah patted her hand. "She's a unique case, Kaelen. And they'll get her."

"Mimic?"

"A Chromodec or alien who wants to do Leah harm."

"She's probably a Chromodec," Leah added helpfully.

"This Mimic has attacked her a few different times."

His lips twisted with dismay. "Oh no, I hope they catch her. I'd hate to think of harm coming to either one of you in that big city of yours."

A knock on the window interrupted any further conversation. It was a police officer indicating they should move the van from the loading and unloading zone. David rolled down the window. "Shoot, sorry, officer. We're heading out now."

It was a little faster than before with roads clear of winter weather and construction. David mentioned the lack of snow was unusual for west Michigan in November. Kaelen took note that fields they passed on either side of the highway near their exit were plowed under. Leah worked on her laptop, catching up on some reports, while Kaelen continued the movie she'd begun watching on her tablet during the flight. Instead of typical headphones, she used her Argonian communicators as Wex's jump system could easily connect to the rudimentary device.

The movie was an epic superhero film that Gabe had recommended. It was entertaining, but her enjoyment was tempered because of Wex's constant commentary.

"Kaelen Ra-Evon, I analyzed the plot of what you are viewing and found it to be highly impractical. An object of that size moving within Earth's atmosphere would cause significant damage."

"It's a movie, Wex. It is not based on truth but rather fantasy."

Ten minutes later, another comment interrupted the sound of her movie. *"The level of lives lost as well as infrastructure damage would cripple a society for many decades. They would not be able to—"*

"Shut up, Wex. Please refrain from speaking for the rest of the movie, unless there is an urgent matter that needs to be addressed that does not relate to the movie."

Leah snickered next to her. "Is Wex being a dick again?"

Kaelen huffed. "Yes." Leah patted her knee and they continued with what they were doing.

Between the movie and Leah's work, the forty-five-minute drive passed by quickly. Kaelen could already see the changes Paul had made since their last visit; the influx of money having helped immensely. There was a brand-new mailbox on the post at the end of the driveway. The house itself had a fresh coat of paint, as did the garage and barn.

"Looks like Paul got himself a new roof. I remember him saying they had a few leaks when we were here last."

Kaelen found David's observation confusing. "People replace entire roofs here? Home ownership is complicated on Earth with all the upkeep that's required. We didn't use materials on Argon that were degradable or flammable in such a way. We had no leaks or fires."

Leah laughed quietly. "I know, darling, but Earth isn't there yet."

Despite all the changes, the old pickup truck still sat in the driveway. David parked the van a few yards away from it. Paul lay on his back beneath the vehicle with a box of tools nearby. "What is he doing?"

"Probably fixing it, though I don't know why he didn't use the money to buy a new one."

David shut off the engine and turned slightly in his seat. "He's proud, that's why. The people around these parts don't like to ask for help. My own grandpappy's family was especially stubborn."

Leah frowned. "What kind of truck is that?"

"Hmm, beneath the rust and dents I'd say it's an extended cab Ford Seeker. More than a decade old by the looks of it. It's a good small bed truck with decent passenger room, but not very practical if you have a big family."

Kaelen watched as Leah pulled out her cell phone and began texting her administrative assistant. Then she quickly averted her gaze out of respect for Leah's privacy. David got out of the van and made his way around to open the back doors and the side door. Leah was seated in the hoverchair and maneuvering back out of the van when David called out, "Hey, Paul. Whatcha working on?"

"Hit a rock on the way back from picking up Tate at the train station last weekend and took out my muffler. Had it hanging by some twine for the past couple months, I'm not surprised it went."

"Want any help?"

"Naw. I just need to put some elbow grease into this bolt so I can get the last bit of pipe off."

None of what he said made much sense to Kaelen. She'd never heard of elbow grease and was unsure why he'd use something as flimsy as twine to attach a vehicle part. What caught her attention was the way the truck rocked with his actions.

Something, the tiniest of sounds, made her look at where the lift mechanism sat. Time slowed as she saw it tip, indicating an imminent collapse that would surely injure Paul. She was out of the van in a blur of motion, catching and lifting the vehicle before it could crush him.

Everyone stopped and looked at her in shock. Rather than acknowledge what she'd done, she met Paul's wide eyes where he peered up at her. "Finish what you're doing. I won't let it fall." He nodded and slid back beneath the truck.

A few minutes later the bolt came free, and he shimmied out from under the truck holding the remaining section of the broken muffler. He tossed it into the cargo bed as Kaelen lowered the vehicle until the tires were once again on the ground. He took off the gloves he'd been wearing and held out his hand to Kaelen. "Thanks." He glanced toward the house. "And please don't tell Shelly what happened. She was already mad that I wanted to get this off today before y'all got here. I don't want her to worry."

Kaelen shook his hand. "I won't say anything and neither will they, though I'm surprised Michael or Tate didn't hear us pull in."

Paul grinned and waved them all toward the house. "Oh, Tate had his earbuds in talking to his newest love interest back in Chicago and Shelly has Michael listening to music with those noise cancelling earmuffs on so he'd stop pestering her to ask when you all were arriving. Clearly it worked."

"Clearly." Leah moved her chair closer to Kaelen and held out her hand. "Good to see you again, Paul."

He shook it. "Likewise. Shelly's got a nice spread for us. I helped some, as did Michael and Tate. Then she shooed us all out of the kitchen to get us out from underfoot and to keep us from snackin'."

Leah glanced up at Kaelen. "Oh, I know exactly how that feels."

Paul was shaking David's hand when Kaelen responded, "Hey! I'm not that bad."

The other three laughed as they made their way up to the house. Paul pushed through the front door first calling out, "Shelly, boys, guess who's here?"

Shelly came out of the kitchen wiping her hands on a kitchen towel. Her cheeks were red, probably from the heat, and she was wearing a red and white checkered apron. "Oh, you made it. How was the drive?" She gave Kaelen and Leah hugs, and squeezed David's arm. "Good to see you too, David. I made your favorite pie for after dinner. I remember you saying how much you liked it when you were here last time."

He ducked his head. "Thanks, Mrs. Miller."

She wagged a finger at him. "None of that, we're close to the same age." She glanced toward the stairwell. "I should go fetch Michael. He's going to be so excited. And you'll get to meet Tate."

Paul kissed her cheek. "I'll get him. I want to toss these coveralls in the laundry and wash up some. We'll meet you all in the kitchen."

They'd barely made it through the kitchen door when Michael rushed in and wrapped Kaelen in a hug from behind. "You made it!"

Rather than chastise him for running in the house, Shelly merely shook her head and put the tea kettle on. "What would y'all like to drink? I've got coffee, iced tea, water, and juice."

"I'll have coffee, please. It was early when we took off from LA." Leah said.

David nodded along. "I'll have the same."

Kaelen returned Michael's crushing hug, appreciating the fact that she wasn't going to hurt him with her strength. "I'll have water, thank you." She looked down at Michael when he pulled back. "How have your studies been?"

He made a face. "I told you last week on our video call."

"True, you did. However, you also said there was a big test coming up that you were worried about."

Shelly placed glasses of water on the table and said proudly, "He got ninety-eight percent on his advanced math exam."

Kaelen beamed at him. "Stellar!"

Michael said, "Mom, should I do it now?"

She winked. "Sure, why not?"

He stood with hands straight down to his sides, then bowed and gave her a formal Argonian sign of honor. *"Shruv i relarh krys: magzheb kvon."*

Kaelen grinned and gesture back. *"Ni relarh krys shlikeh."*

She clapped him on the shoulder and looked at the others. "He welcomed us to his house, and I told him we honor his house."

Leah smiled. "I actually got most of that. What a fascinating and complex language." She directed her next comment toward Shelly, David, and Paul, who had pushed into the kitchen as well. "Argonian is structured by verb, subject, object. We have a few Earth languages that operate the same way like Irish, Scottish Gaelic, Classical Hebrew, Māori, and Tagalog, for example."

"Well, I'll be darned, that's certainly interesting how a language from out beyond the stars could function a lot like one here on this planet." Paul turned to Michael. "Why don't you go get your brother so he can meet everyone before dinner."

Michael was gone in a flash, only to return a minute later with a tall, auburn-haired young man in tow. He had Paul's build but slimmer, and Shelly's smile and rosy cheeks. Shelly stepped forward. "Tate, these are the guests I was telling you about."

He grinned and held out his hand to Leah. "Mom, I know who Leah Lockheed-Tuck is. She's kinda famous, even in my art circle at school."

Leah snickered and Shelly sighed before continuing. "The other woman is Kaelen Ra-Evon. She's from the same planet as your brother. They both escaped just in time and came here."

He reached out to Shake Kaelen's hand as well. "Yeah, Mikey never shuts up about his Argonian kin."

Michael beamed. "Tate does art like I do math. He's amazingo!"

Kaelen looked at Leah to see if she knew the unfamiliar word and she merely shrugged so Kaelen said, "Uh, cool."

Tate ruffled his brother's hair and turned to their driver. "And you must be David. I'm glad you could all make it for dinner with us."

Kaelen lowered her voice and asked Leah, "I thought Nalla said youths were all rude and mannerless?"

The entire room heard the question and laughed, even Tate. "Well, Miss Ra-Evon, my mom raised me right."

Michael gave him a little shove before tattling. "Mom told us to be on our best behavior or we'd get no pie."

"Now *that* sounds more like the truth!" Leah shook her head at both boys.

"No, it really is cool to meet you three. I'm glad that Mikey has someone to help him with stuff." Tate glanced toward his mom and dad. "I knew he was struggling with his powers but he was afraid of telling the rents. So, this worked out, you know?"

Shelly broke the mood with a single hand clap. "Now that everyone's introduced, supper is about ready. You all can take a seat in the dining room while I finish whipping the potatoes. Tate will you grab drinks and Michael, you want to set the table?"

Both boys answered in unison, clearly a familiar response. "Sure, Mom."

Kaelen moved toward the counter where Shelly stood. "I can help with the potatoes. It's one of the jobs that Leah will let me do in the kitchen."

Shelly raised a salt and pepper eyebrow at her, and Kaelen demonstrated by moving her hand in fast circles. "Huh, that's certainly handy." She heard Leah laughing as she maneuvered her hoverchair through the pocket doors that Paul slid open.

It didn't take long to move all the food to the large table in the dining room. Shelly assured everyone that there was plenty to eat, even for Kaelen and Michael. Paul carved the turkey and Leah praised Shelly's gravy recipe. When it came time for dessert, Kaelen and Michael had a slice of all the pie flavors. Tate ate pieces of pumpkin and cherry, David stuck with his apple crumble, and Leah enjoyed a slice of pumpkin with Shelly's homemade whipped cream. Kaelen volunteered to help Tate and Michael clean up, then everyone moved to the living room where they could sit more comfortably.

Kaelen leaned down to whisper in Leah's ear. "Will you be okay here for a bit by yourself?"

"Of course, darling."

Kaelen gave her a kiss on the cheek and caught Shelly's knowing smile when she pulled away. She admitted, "Leah and I are in a courtship now. *Dolem*-Lockheed and *Dolem*-Ra are well-matched."

"That sure sounds like a complicated way to say you're dating."

Leah blushed and Shelly swatted Paul's arm. "Ignore him, not a romantic bone in his body. I'm sure happy for you both."

"Me too! You're dating the coolest scientist!" Tate snorted at his brother's enthusiasm.

Kaelen shot Michael a look. "Hey, I'm a scientist too."

He shrugged. "Well yeah, but she's Leah Lockheed-Tuck." He spoke as if that were all anyone needed to know to determine the coolness of a person. Leah snickered and Kaelen made a face.

"Well, I may not be as amazing as Leah, but would you like to take a walk with me?" She turned back to Paul and Shelly. "If that's okay with you. We won't be gone long."

Paul smiled. "It's fine. Michael, why don't you show her the duck pond out back?"

"Okay, Dad."

Five minutes later, the two of them stood near the large barn behind the house. Michael was explaining the purpose of each rusting tool along the edge of the one side as they walked around the structure. It wasn't long before the duo wandered down a track that led to a stand of trees. Michael turned to Kaelen when they were halfway to the woods. "What other powers will I have besides increased speed, hearing, and strength? You've mentioned more but haven't told me much about them. Tuk only gives details when I display something new."

"My guess is that you'll grow into many as you age. Some may be triggered by puberty, or length of time under the yellow sun. Others may be a combination of both. I also don't know what difference it will make that you didn't live as long on Argon, if that will make you more or less powerful than I am once you're full grown."

"Oh. I guess we'll find out, huh?"

She clasped his shoulder. "We will. I'll help you every step of the way, okay? Together we can find the answers to anything."

"Kymeth Sal ne Ra."

"Exactly that. My house was a proud one, but their status under the light of Vos was inarguable. Ra hosted the brightest thinkers in every generation, and you became part of that line with the passing of your house members before you."

"What do you mean?"

"You know how my grandfather was the head of the Thinker Guild when Argon exploded?" Michael nodded. "Well, your parents were also part of the Thinker Guild. As I'm now the head of our guild, and with the absence of your parents, you become a guild ward. That makes me your guardian. Of course, I'd be your guardian anyway since I'm the last guild inducted Argonian. The greater house always absorbs the lesser house, which means you would be part House of Xe and House of Ra."

"Oh." They walked along for a few more paces before Michael

asked, "Do you miss your mom and dad?"

Kaelen considered the question. While time in the ship was strange, enough of it had passed that the sharpest pain of grief had dulled within her heart. She'd come to the realization that most of her sadness was centered around the life that could have been. Kaelen had been truthful with Leah when she admitted that her life was filled with people and passion that she never had before, which tempered the loss.

"Kaelen?"

She sighed. "Sorry. I do miss my parents, friends, and all the people I worked with back on Argon. But it's different for me. Even though I was a working adult, I was still young and a social minor. I wasn't much older than you when I traveled for ten years to reach Earth. The combination of time and programming from Wex means that I never had to grieve."

"Maybe your loss of grief is the biggest one you have. Mom says that we should always get to say goodbye when we love something. That's what I got to do when we had to put Hank to sleep a few years ago. He was the best dog, but Dad said it was his time to go."

His words startled Kaelen and she could see the stirrings of a great Argonian mind in the making, despite living the past decade on Earth. "You're pretty smart, you know that? I think the loss of our world overshadowed the loss of my family, so I didn't feel justified to mourn a few over the many. I suppose it's just easier for me not to think about it most of the time."

"Yeah, I get it. But sometimes I still think about Hank and what a good boy he was. It makes me sad, but it also makes me feel good too. Does that make sense?"

His words hit a particularly poignant note with Kaelen, and she had to take a few deep breaths to regain control of her emotions. "It does." She shook off the melancholy mood Michael's unique insight draped upon her shoulders and pulled him to a stop. "Why don't we go through what I can do one by one. Please keep in mind that this is all I've discovered since landing and that I'm still learning too."

Kaelen suddenly rose into the air and hovered a few feet above the ground. "I can fly."

"It looks like you're floating."

"Sure, I can hover in place if I want, or I can travel at near the speed of light. At least that's the calculation by Wex. I can also go a long time without air, as well as survive on less oxygen. Both can happen when I fly high into the atmosphere." To display her flying speed, she pointed at a small building off in the distance. "I'll race you there, you on the ground and me in the air."

"Done!" Before she could say go, Michael took off in a spray of mud. She easily caught up and passed him before hovering above the tiny hut in such a way that it looked like she was sitting on it. His mouth dropped open. "That's so cool! What else?"

Kaelen pointed at a nearby puddle. "Sub-zero breath." Then she exhaled and the water froze solid. Without missing a beat, she hit the same puddle with twin laser beams from her eyes, causing it to melt and steam. "Laser vision." His mouth dropped open after the second demonstration. Kaelen floated to the ground and put an arm around Michael's thin shoulders. He would probably be a large man like his father from Michael's holocube, but until then he was still only a boy. "Wex and I have also documented telescopic and x-ray vision, maximal speed and hearing, enhanced reflexes, maximal strength, and invulnerability."

He was quiet for a minute before remarking, "That's a lot of power for someone to have."

She nodded solemnly as they began walking back toward the house. "It is. One of your American presidents once said, 'Great power involves great responsibility,' and he was right."

"That was Franklin D. Roosevelt. We learned about him in history class last year."

"And I learned it in my history lessons from Wex on the way to Earth. On Argon, we are all taught that our purpose in life is to contribute to society in a meaningful way. I don't know what that way means here on Earth, or whether or not it involves our minds or encompasses all the special gifts we have beneath the yellow sun. What I do know is that whatever way we contribute, we should leave the world better than we found it."

"But how? We go to church most Sundays and your powers make it sound like you're practically a god."

Kaelen stopped and gently turned Michael so he was facing her. "Because we hold such immense power on this planet, it's imperative that we understand that every action has consequences. Michael, under no circumstance is it our place to play gods to the people of Earth, even if our power deifies us."

His voice was a whisper. "I've gotten a lot stronger in the past year. Sometimes I worry that I'll accidentally hurt Mom or Dad. Tate told me to be extra careful anytime I touch someone else."

"That's good."

Michael glared at her. "You think hurting my parents is good?"

"No, I think that you worrying about it is good. If you're worrying, then you're taking care. That's an important step in learning how to control your powers. Tate was right."

"But how do I control it?"

They'd made it back to the barn and Kaelen looked around for something to demonstrate her idea to him. She picked up a fist-sized stone. Then she sped to a nearby oak tree, broke off one leaf, and sped back to stand in front of Michael. "Hold out your hands."

He obeyed and Kaelen placed one item in each hand.

"Can you feel the difference in weight?"

"Yeah."

"Good, now grip the stone in your hand and pinch the leave between your forefingers and thumb." Michael obeyed her request. "What if I wanted to hit the rock from your hand, how would you hold it?"

"I'd tightened my grip a little, like this."

Kaelen could see the skin tense and heard all the little muscle fibers tighten during the slight bit of pressure increase. "Good. Look at the leaf, let it settle back into the palm of your hand."

Michael opened his palm and the leaf lay flat once again, as perfect as when she'd picked it off the tree. "It's still a leaf."

She lifted the leaf from the palm of his hand and held it out to him. When he took it from her, she gave another instruction. "Now pinch the leaf as hard as possible between your fingers again." He did it and the leaf shredded from the pressure. "Squeeze the rock as hard as you can."

Michael gritted his teeth and Kaelen watched as the boy's knuckles turned white then the rock broke into a spray of pieces. He dropped them in shock.

"There. You see potential danger of your strength, but you also know that you can be gentle when you need to be. Unfortunately, unlike other kids your age, you'll always have to be careful to temper your strength and keep the rest of your powers hidden. Strong emotions will make this difficult, but I think you're fully capable of learning control. Trust yourself, Michael."

He gave her another hug before they walked up the steps of the porch. "Thanks, Kaelen. I'm glad I have you and Tuk to help me. Before you showed up, I felt lonely, like I was a freak or something with the powers I had. Tate helped but he doesn't really understand what it's like. But I don't feel so alone now."

She ruffled his hair as they pushed open the door into the house. "Neither do I, Michael. Neither do I."

In the living room, the other five were laughing at some story that David was telling about his mom and some interesting shots with her drone camera. Michael ran over to his mother and gave her a hug, despite not being gone for long. "Hey, Mom. Can I show Kaelen and Leah the project I built in my room?" His grin turned into a frown when he looked over at Leah's hoverchair. "Oh, shoot. Sorry, Miss Leah, but I don't think your chair will make the turn going downstairs to my room."

Leah met Kaelen's gaze and she lifted a shoulder.

Kaelen smiled and Leah blew out a breath. It was in that moment that Kaelen realized they'd reached a level of non-verbal communication that she'd previously envied in other couples.

"Actually, this is top secret, but you four are family and David has signed a non-disclosure agreement. I'm going to unveil the nerve regeneration nanobots and serum at the CES conference in Vegas in a little over a month. I suppose I can give you a preview of my success now." With those words, Leah abruptly stood from her chair.

"Oh, my Lord! You've gone and done it."

David shook his head and smiled at her. "Young Michael was right. You really are the coolest scientist."

"It was a team project and I'm happy with how things worked out." Leah turned to Michael who still stood with his mouth open. "Now, you wanted to show us your room?"

That snapped him out of his daze. "Oh yeah! Follow me." He ran down the stairs in his excitement, leaving them behind.

Paul chuckled. "First door on the left from the bottom of the stairs. The other door is basement storage and laundry."

Tate stood as well. "I think I'm going to my room too. It was nice meeting you both. And don't worry about your secrets, Kaelen. We already keep plenty for Michael. Not even Brandon knows about his powers."

Kaelen looked at Shelly. "That's your nephew that's in the CORP, right?"

"Yup. Good man, honest, and loyal as all get out. He sure grew up right but there are some things you keep close to your chest."

"Yeah, one of my good friends at school is an alien but they're not out. I'm the only one they've confided in and I'd never tell anyone who it is. It's safest that way."

"You're a wise soul, Tate, and it was good to meet you too. Looks like Michael has a pretty great older brother." The twenty-one-year-old's cheeks flushed even darker as he grinned and gave them both a wave goodbye.

Kaelen offered her arm and Leah took it gratefully. It was a lot of stairs to navigate when she spent most of her days still in the chair. "Thanks, love." She patted her arm as they made their way downstairs so they could humor Michael.

The happiness wasn't held by Michael alone. When Leah said that the Millers were family, it lit another spark within Kaelen's heart, and she knew that three more people were added to her list of those under the protection of *Dolem*-Ra. The Millers were her people. They were family.

Chapter Twenty-two

Lockheed scientists and engineers only had a few weeks after the Thanksgiving holiday to wrap up, or reach a safe stopping point for any ongoing projects due to a mandatory end-of-year shut down. A skeleton crew would check all experiments that needed close monitoring, as well as take care of any lab animals. Other than that, everyone was instructed to take the last ten days of the year off, not returning until January second. The small group that volunteered to work were trained on each lab's needs ahead of time and would receive two full weeks off later the next year.

The teams in SPL and Lab 12 would be gone even longer since they were attending CES after New Year's Day. That added even more to their to-do list in preparation for their absence.

Leah, Kaelen, Maddy, and Tasha had plans to take their holiday with Ellie at the house in Sello Bay. They'd invited the rest of their friends as well, but Devon had a gig in London for the week, Einstein and Nalla were spending their time off with Nalla's family in Portland, Gabe would be out of town on a CORP assignment, and Ana had tickets to see a few off-Broadway shows, one of which starred an old university friend.

In the meantime, Leah and Ana had a string of business lunches scheduled, starting with the chief geneticist at Organic Advancement Solutions, Dr. Stephanie Young. They were at a new fusion eatery that opened a few blocks from their corporate office. Stephanie had flown in from Chicago that morning and met them at the restaurant. She agreed to hear them out because OAS had technology that Lockheed was hoping to incorporate in a future project, and Leah promised to make it a profitable partnership if they signed on.

Leah thanked the server when her dish was placed in front of her, then focused on Stephanie. "How far have you gotten in your investigation of live cell genome editing to cure anomalies associated with cancer? I heard there were concerns with stability."

Stephanie leaned forward. She didn't look at all like the fifty-something years that Leah knew her to be. "There have been many questions speculated upon and investigated extensively. At OAS, we've—"

Leah's cell phone went off and she frowned when she saw the name of her security chief. "Apologies, Stephanie. But I need to take this." Leah backed her hoverchair away from the table and spun it so she was facing away from the other two women. "Hans, this better be important."

"I'm sorry, Miss Lockheed. But my team has spotted your stalker outside the restaurant that you're currently in. I'm sending two to intercept her before she can move any closer, and I've got two more coming in the back of the building to help you to safety."

"Fuck. Did you call the police?"

"And the CORP. Retreat to the back of the restaurant and await extraction."

The line went dead and Leah glanced around nervously. She spun the chair in place and spoke to Ana and Stephanie. "We have to go, now. All three of us."

"What's going on?"

"Mimic is outside the restaurant. My security team called to warn me. Hans sent in two guards through the back door to get me out while the rest confront her outside to keep her distracted."

"Mimic?" Stephanie's face was awash with confusion.

Leah shook her head. "Sorry. A rogue Chromodec or something that has a personal vendetta against me and my company, though I have no clue why."

Stephanie muttered, "It's always the rogues," and gave Leah a grim look.

Ana stood and dropped her napkin on the table. "Well, if Hans says we need to go, then let's get out of here." She looked around until she spotted the hallway leading to the back entrance. Stephanie stood with her.

Rather than follow suit, Leah moved her chair deeper into the restaurant. "Take Stephanie out of here. I can't leave everyone without a warning."

"Leah, we have to go." Ana grabbed at her arm and cast a worried glance toward the bank of windows on the street facing side. There was a woman outside that appeared to be in a standoff with men and women in black tactical gear.

"Please, Ana. Take Doctor Young toward the back hallway, I'll be there in a minute." After a few seconds hesitation, Ana nodded and made a beeline to their table. Leah flagged down the restaurant manager. "Excuse me!"

He strode over to her. "Is there something you need, Miss Lockheed?"

"Yes. The woman outside is extremely dangerous and is currently wanted by the CORP. You have to evacuate everyone out the back, or at the very least, have them move away from the windows."

"But everyone is still eating."

Leah glanced toward the windows in time to see a ball of flame heading toward her security team. The ones that weren't blown back off their feet, dove to the side to avoid serious injury. Mimic looked up and it felt as if she could see Leah where she sat twenty feet inside the windows. She whispered, "Too late." Then she snapped out of her fearful daze and yelled as loud as she could, "Everyone get down!"

Leah spun her hoverchair around in time to see Ana and Stephanie standing near their table. A massive explosion of glass and debris blew her chair toward the back of the restaurant. She could smell smoke and feel heat from nearby flames, then something hit her head and everything went dark.

Kaelen and Einstein were eating hotdogs near the food cart outside the building when she heard Leah's heart begin to race. "Leah."

He looked around in confusion. "Didn't you say Leah was at lunch with someone from OAS today?"

"No, she's in trouble."

Einstein's gaze narrowed. "What kind of trouble?"

Kaelen tried to focus, but she shook her head as she went too deep and Leah's heartbeat pounded in her ears. "I don't know, I only know she's scared." Before she could pinpoint Leah's location, they heard an explosion somewhere nearby.

"That was close." Einstein craned his head around. "Where do you think that—" Kaelen was gone before he could finish his sentence.

She'd already changed her suit and raced toward where she could hear cries of pain, flickering fire, and that familiar heartbeat. The scene when she arrived at the restaurant two blocks over was chaos. First thing she did was race inside and use her freeze breath to blow out the flames. Unfortunately, the explosion meant the ceiling above was unstable with many casualties on the ground. Kaelen grabbed a few support beams and used her laser vision to weld them in place to buy herself some time.

Once the restaurant wasn't in danger of imminent collapse, she scanned the room to find Leah. The hoverchair was on its side, and she lay unconscious next to it. Ana knelt on the ground near Leah's head, calling her name. "Come on, Leah, you need to wake up." Ana had a bleeding gash on her arm. Another woman with pale blonde hair near them was also unconscious and bled from a wound in her abdomen.

Kaelen sped to Leah's side, eyes glowing with anger and fear from deep within her hood. "What happened here, who did this?"

Ana looked up and gasped. "Ka—uh, Scion! It was Mimic."

If anything, the name of the rogue Chromodec only served to make her eyes glow brighter. Kaelen could feel the heat of them but her fire would not be tamed. Her voice came out as a low growl. "Where did she go?" Kaelen looked around, searching for the person who would dare to harm her *zhee*. Fury exploded within her and she struggled not to simply blast through the ceiling to hunt down Mimic once and for all. A moan caught her attention and she focused on Leah. Even under such dire circumstances, she was careful with her identity. "This woman needs help."

"She does, but they all need help." Ana gestured around the restaurant. "We were pretty far away from the windows, but the rest weren't so lucky. Leah will be okay. But many of these people need hospital care as soon as possible."

Ana spoke quietly but urgently. Cries broke through the cacophony of

Leah's heartbeat, and Kaelen realized she'd been ignoring the suffering all around her because she was so full of rage toward Leah's attacker.

Kaelen took in the scene inside the restaurant with wide eyes, fully seeing the destruction for the first time. "Holy Vos." She searched the room, looking for anything she could use as a transportation aid. Her eyes lit upon a giant slab of painted wood decor hanging on the wall. "I'll be right back."

She rushed to the hanging and pulled it down, then inspected it for sturdiness and size. Using her x-ray vision and super hearing, Kaelen determined the ones who were most in need of immediate medical care. None appeared to have neck or spinal injuries, so she carefully loaded all the ones in critical condition, including the woman near Ana and Leah, then flew them through the blown-out windows at the front of the restaurant. The nearest hospital happened to be LAGH. Kaelen was familiar with the location, so she took her collection of injured straight there.

She noticed a police officer coming out of the doors when she touched down next to the ambulance lane. "There was an attack downtown a few minutes ago. The restaurant contains more injured, but I determined these people were most in need. Please see that they receive immediate medical attention."

"You're Scion."

She nodded. "Will you help them?"

The man looked at the wooden platform full of injured people and launched into action. "Shit!" He called for help using the microphone hanging from his shoulder, then ran inside to fetch medical personnel.

Satisfied that they would get the care they needed, Kaelen flew back to the restaurant as fast as she dared. She arrived in time to see police cars and ambulances pull up, as well as the familiar black vehicles used by the CORP. Agents were already on the ground, speaking with men and women in black. Kaelen recognized one of them as a member of Leah's security team. She wanted more than anything to go to Leah, but she didn't dare. Leah's words of warning rang in her ears, so Kaelen pulled her hood up from where it had fallen back during her return flight. She remained floating a couple blocks away where she could still see into the building with her x-ray vision.

Leah's chair had been righted, and the woman herself sat slumped in the seat. Ana stood next to her and held a napkin to the gash on Leah's head. Police, firefighters, and paramedics rushed in and out of the building until all the diners and staff were safely removed. She kept watch as Leah and Ana were led to the back of an ambulance by a paramedic, where they were both checked over. The paramedic bandaged Ana's arm and told her she'd need stitches. The woman also wanted Leah to go in for testing because she was exhibiting signs of a concussion, but Leah refused. She insisted everyone else needed to be treated first.

Even from such a distance, Kaelen saw Leah shiver and wrap her arms around herself. She was about to go down there, despite the risk, when she saw a CORP agent point her way. "Quark." Kaelen shot straight up into the upper atmosphere and did a few circuits around the planet, coming in low over the water the same way she'd done before. She decided the only way she'd be able to reach Leah's side was to go as an employee of Lockheed International.

Kaelen landed in an alley near the restaurant and changed her suit to what she'd been wearing earlier with Einstein. Then she jogged the last few blocks to where she knew Leah waited.

Neither Leah nor Ana faced in Kaelen's direction when she got to the ambulance, but a police officer was. "Ma'am, you need to stay back. This is an active crime scene and they're still treating wounded."

"Kaelen!"

Ignoring the police officer, Kaelen rushed to Leah's side and gently cradled her hand. "I'm so glad you're okay. I…I don't know what I would have done if she'd critically injured you."

"We're both a bit banged up, but we'll be okay, darling. I'm more concerned about everyone else."

"Mimic?"

Ana shook her head. "She got away."

Leah frowned. "Hans found us inside and said that she bolted as soon as she blew the windows in with a massive fireball. Two of the team are also injured, sporting second and third-degree burns."

The paramedic frowned as she taped a gauze pad in place over the cut above Leah's brow. "It would have been a lot worse if it weren't for that new vigilante, Scion. She flew a ton of people laid out on a big wood board. I think she was heading for LAGH. I can only imagine how many trips it would have taken to get them all there otherwise."

"You saw Scion?"

Leah, Ana, and the paramedic all jumped when a woman spoke from nearby, but Kaelen heard her approach. The paramedic nodded. "Yeah. My partner was driving the bus and we'd just turned onto the block when I saw her lift a bunch of people and head toward the hospital. Got a call from another bus saying she'd dropped them off near the ambulance lane and left."

"Nothing else?" The paramedic shook her head. The CORP agent turned to Leah and Ana. "What about you, Miss Lockheed? This is the second time Scion has been spotted near an attack on your person."

Leah's lips quirked up on one side. "Well, in case you didn't notice, I'm not one of the folks she saved this time. Maybe she's got a beef with this Mimic character."

"Maybe. Either way, if you see her or know any information pertaining to the identity of Scion, be sure to call it in to the CORP. She's a wanted vigilante."

Kaelen wasn't a fan of the agent's attitude but apparently, neither was Ana, who scoffed. "I don't know if you noticed, but it wasn't the CORP who arrived moments after the explosion and saved our asses. You weren't here! I saw her put out the fires burning inside the restaurant, then weld support beams in place when the ceiling threatened to come down. Those people who were flown to the ER weren't the only ones she saved. How about you find the person that actually did this? From where I stand, as someone who's hurt, tired, scared, and done with today... Scion is a hero and the CORP can go to Hell!"

"Ana." Leah placed a hand on her friend's arm while Kaelen stared at Ana with wide eyes.

The woman scowled but didn't reply to Ana's rant. Instead, she turned and stalked off toward the CORP vehicles.

"That was stupid. Please don't antagonize the CORP. Lockheed International has a great working relationship with them. They're good at keeping this city safe, it's what they do."

"Yeah, well they're wrong this time." Ana was looking at Kaelen when she said it and Kaelen knew that she had Ana's full support. Ana sighed and rubbed her forehead, then winced and cradled her arm. "Damn. I need a drink and I should probably head to the hospital to check on Stephanie. Oh, and I need to call Doctor Turing at OAS and let her know their chief geneticist was in an accident while lunching with us."

Leah hung her head. "This is all my fault."

"No, it isn't. Why would you say that?"

Leah gestured to the chaos around them. "She's targeting me and doesn't seem to care if she puts others in danger if it furthers her agenda, or gets the vengeance she's seeking."

Kaelen rubbed her shoulder. "You can't control what other people do."

"I know I can't, but I can control how I react." Leah removed her cell phone from the pocket on the inside of her chair. She scrolled through her contacts until she found what she was looking for. Kaelen heard the other end pick up, then Leah began to speak. "Susan, this is Leah. Has the explosion at Saffronette's made the news yet? Okay, good. I need you to take down the following statement, then issue an immediate press release. Ready? Okay."

Leah took a deep breath and let it out before speaking. "I want to give my sincerest condolences to those injured in the attack on Saffronette's today. As one of the diners inside, I'd also like to express gratitude to both Scion and the emergency responders who were first on the scene to help those of us who were injured. To the woman responsible, the one referred to as Mimic, I beg you to stop your attacks within Los Angeles. Innocent people have been injured, buildings destroyed, and everyone is terrified. Please turn yourself in so that nobody else is hurt. You have all that?"

Leah waited and Kaelen could hear the woman on the other end of the line reading the statement back. "Perfect. Now, I want you to contact Davinia and tell her to arrange funds for the victims of today's attack, as well as for the businesses that were damaged. Call it a charitable donation, I don't care. Please take care of it before the end of the day." She waited another second then smiled. "I'm okay, just a little banged up. Ana is injured as well, though still fighting fit from what I just saw." Leah laughed. "Thanks, Susan. Talk to you later."

Ana shook her head. "You didn't have to do that."

"I know, but I wanted to."

Kaelen looked toward the black CORP vehicles and gritted her teeth. "Your CORP has been useless in finding Mimic. Why aren't they looking harder when she is such a danger to the people of this city?"

"Kaelen!" Kaelen tore her gaze from the agents standing near the entrance to the restaurant and looked down at Leah. "Douse the glow, darling. You'll give yourself away."

Kaelen immediately shut her eyes. "I'm sorry. Mimic makes me furious and sometimes it leaks out. I warned Michael on our recent visit that strong emotions affect our powers. I've been here more than a year and should have better control."

"Or—" Ana waited for Kaelen to look at her. "Give yourself a break because you've only been here a year. You're allowed to make mistakes, Kaelen."

Rather than let Ana's words pacify her guilt, Kaelen's mind flashed back to the day her planet exploded. Then her memory flew forward and she saw Leah's hoverchair laying on its side. She swallowed and tightened her fist. "Some mistakes have permanent consequences and should be avoided at all costs. People like me can't make mistakes, so I need to be stronger."

"Not on your own you don't." Kaelen looked at Leah, confused about how Leah could help when it came to controlling her powers. "With intellect, we overcome, darling. *Kymeth Sal ne Ra.* We'll figure it out together."

Kaelen took a deep breath and carefully let it out, much the way Leah had done earlier when speaking on the phone. "You're right. Thank you for reminding me."

"Anytime. Now, what do you say we go home?"

"I'd rather go for a drink."

"Not back to work?" Kaelen shot Leah and Ana a confused look.

Ana snorted. "Definitely not back to L-I. Is Maddy off today?"

"Pretty sure she is."

"Well, you either need to go to the hospital to be looked at, or your big sister should come over. And if Maddy is coming over, I'll let her give me stitches too."

Leah smirked. "Let her, huh?"

Ana muttered, "Shut up. I got over that ages ago."

Kaelen looked back and forth between them. "Got over what?

"Ana had a crush on Maddy for the longest time."

"Really, LT? You spilling all my secrets now?"

Kaelen shrugged. "Maddy is intelligent and a worthy mate, but unfortunately not available. If you were open to a variety of genders, Nalla says that Devon Smith is currently unpaired."

Leah laughed and pointed at Ana's face, then winced and rubbed the temple near her injury. "He is single but I'd say your attempt to matchmake with Dev has failed spectacularly based on the look she's giving you."

"Pity." Kaelen contemplated the dilemma. "I'm afraid your only hope would be if Maddy and Tasha practiced polyamory." Her comment made Leah giggle more.

"Or I could find my own dates, thank you very much." Ana rolled her eyes then changed the subject. "Now, moving off that topic, hopefully for good, where's your driver?"

"You're such a spoilsport. Kaelen, will you call Maddy while I call my driver?"

Kaelen nodded and pulled out her cell phone to make the call while Leah was busy with her own. It didn't take long for Leah's van to arrive, but they had to walk more than a block to meet it because the CORP had cordoned off the area of attack. Specialists would need to do a thorough check of the immediate infrastructure, verifying the safety of things like power, water, sewer, and gas lines. Suddenly Leah's chair stopped. "Fucking hell."

"What's wrong?"

"The explosion must have damaged one of the drive circuits. I've got hover capability but no motion."

Ana moved behind the hoverchair. "How about I push you then?" She gave an easy push then grunted. On her second try she leaned into it but the hoverchair didn't budge.

Leah sighed. "Great, looks like the emergency stabilizers have activated."

Kaelen looked from Leah to the hoverchair. "Stabilizers?"

"Yes, they kick in and act as a lock of sorts whenever it reads that I'm moving outside directed parameters. Clearly both the drive and stabilizers are damaged which means the chair isn't going anywhere until those are fixed." Leah pulled out her phone again. "I'll call for another hoverchair and request a hauler come and take this one back to the propulsion lab."

"Will it harm the chair if it's moved while the stabilizers are on?"

Leah shrugged. "Not more than what's already broken. It's just incredibly difficult, which is the point. Why?"

Kaelen stepped behind Leah and began pushing her toward the waiting van. She saw Leah's panicked look and smiled. "Relax. No one but the three of us knows that the chair is malfunctioning."

"I won't be able to raise and lower it into the van for me to slide onto the passenger seat."

"We can use the ramp to load it into the back. And with your permission, I can lift you into the seat. I know you hate that but it's the quickest way and takes no effort on my part."

Leah sighed but relented. "Fine. I know it can't be helped."

The lunch rush was over, so it didn't take long to navigate across the city to Leah's penthouse. Unfortunately, her lack of functioning hoverchair meant that Kaelen had to carry her into the building and in the elevator on her back, to maintain the appearance of Leah's condition and not give away Kaelen's alien strength in front of the security cameras. Leah called Ellie and updated her on the events at the restaurant and asked her to have another hoverchair sent to her penthouse.

Maddy arrived about fifteen minutes after they did. Kaelen heard the elevator coming up so was looking toward the doors when they opened. Neither Leah nor Ana noticed as they were in the middle of a full-blown argument.

"What's going on here?"

"Both wanted a drink but Ana told Leah she couldn't have any because she most likely has a concussion."

Maddy sighed and rubbed her forehead before striding across the room and pulling the wine bottle from Ana's hand.

"Hey! I'm not the one with a cracked skull."

"Both of you are injured and the last thing you need is alcohol in your system. How about you settle for some water and painkillers?"

Ana flipped her off and stalked over to one of the lounge chairs. She slumped into it and winced. "Fine. Fucking know-it-all doctors anyway."

"I'm pretty sure this know-it-all doctor is the one that's going to suture your arm here and save you a trip to one of the hospitals."

"Kaelen could probably sew me up. She'd only need to read about it online or something first."

"She probably could, but I'm the one with the doctor bag so zip it, Pérez." She looked around and addressed everyone. "It's probably good the three of you decided to come back here. One of my friends called and apparently, LAGH is a zoo with all the people from the attack. The next closest hospital had victims incoming from a multicar pileup on the I-5. Jonah said the injuries at Saffronette's would have been a lot more serious if not for that Scion chick." Maddy winked at Kaelen.

Part of her was stuck on Maddy's use of the word zoo to describe the hospital, and part of her was hyperaware of Leah. She was pale, sweating slightly, and squinting at the light coming in from the large, windowed wall. She gently clasped Leah's shoulder to get her attention. "You have a headache. You should let Maddy see to your injury then get some rest."

"No shit, Kaelen. Tell me something I fucking don't know!" No sooner were the words out of her mouth when Leah's eyes widened with dismay. "I'm sorry, I didn't mean to snap at you like that."

Kaelen swallowed and nodded. While the comment startled her, it wasn't unexpected. "I understand. Pain can make us react negatively, outside our normal state of mind. But please, sit down and let her take care of you."

"Your girlfriend is pretty smart…even if you aren't. Come on, Leah. Let's have a seat at the table where light is better, and I'll look at your head."

Leah made it obvious to all three of them how much pain she was in and allowed Kaelen to help her to a kitchen chair without further complaint. It didn't take long for Maddy to do a standard exam. Leah wasn't experiencing amnesia or disorientation, her pupils dilated evenly, and she wasn't having trouble with balance. But she did have a terrible headache, some nausea, and ringing in her ears.

"Definitely a mild concussion. It wouldn't hurt to have an MRI—" She held up a hand to forestall Leah's protest. "I already know what you're going to say. Maybe Mom can do a scan at Lockheed, but no working while you're there. I'll inject Lidocaine into your cut and suture it."

Ana had already moved into the dining area to sit next to Leah. Kaelen stood near her shoulder, shifting anxiously from foot to foot. She took care not to block Maddy's light. "What is the recovery for a concussion?" Maddy looked up at her and addressed them both. "The only thing she can do is rest and restrict things like physical activity, screen time, and a lot of socialization. I can write you a script for Ondansetron if your nausea gets too bad. Let me know, okay?"

"Thanks, Maddy." Leah frowned when she saw the needle headed for the skin above her eyebrow.

Kaelen moved closer and took her hand. *"Te hehd udolka ovo."*
"Ne ovo etsah."

Neither Maddy nor Ana acknowledged their quiet Argonian words. Instead, Maddy warned, "This is going to feel like little pinches. Try not to move." She made a series of six injections into the subcutaneous fat along the one inch cut while Leah squeezed Kaelen's hand. Maddy waited a few minutes before suturing the wound. When she was finished, she cut the thread and removed her gloves.

"You're not going to bandage it?" Ana was as fascinated with the process as Kaelen.

"Not for her. Face and scalp can generally be left open as long as they're kept clean. If the cut were smaller, I would have used Steri-Strips, but it was pretty deep and gaped open so better suited to stitches." She put on a new pair of gloves and moved to the seat next to Ana. "Okay, let's unwrap your arm and take a look. Did the paramedic say anything about deeper damage?"

Maddy helped Ana removed the gauze and bandage that covered the cut on her outer forearm. "She didn't think there was any other damage but said I should have it sutured to speed up healing time."

"Ouch, definitely right about stitches. Sorry, Ana, but this is going to take a lot more."

Kaelen looked away from Leah to see that Ana's injury was roughly four times longer than Leah's. "That looks like it could be painful."

Ana snorted. "No shit, Kaelen…the indestructible alien."

Kaelen held up her hands in defeat. "I'm sorry. I'm going to help Leah to her bedroom. Is there anything either of you need before I return?"

"Hey, Lee-lee, you want something for the pain or nausea?"

Leah shook her head and Kaelen didn't understand why she said no. It was apparent by the little stress lines between her eyebrows that she was in pain. "I'll be fine. I only want to close my eyes for a bit."

"Is she allowed to sleep with that rattled brainpan?"

Maddy chuckled at Ana. "She is, but we should keep an eye on her."

"Kaelen can listen for me, right?"

Kaelen was perplexed. "You'd allow that?"

Leah gave her hand a squeeze. "In this instance, yes. I only want to sleep."

Maddy stood and moved to Leah's side to give her a careful hug. Then she kissed her on the cheek. "I'm glad you're okay, sis. Get some rest."

"Thanks."

Leah and Kaelen started across the living room toward the stairs when Maddy called out, "Ra-Evon," she turned to look over her shoulder. "Make sure it's only rest she's getting."

Kaelen was offended at her insinuation. As an answer to Maddie's warning, she held up the middle finger on one hand while her other hand supported Leah as she made her way up the steps. Maddy and Ana's laughter followed the couple up the stairs.

Chapter Twenty-three

Kaelen confirmed Leah was sound asleep then made her way downstairs twenty minutes later. She'd heard Ellie arrive earlier and found the three women at the table. All the medical supplies were cleared away and Ana wore a new, clean bandage.

Ellie stood. "How is she?"

"She's tired and sore but otherwise fine. Thank you for bringing her other hoverchair. Do you know if Leah has the schematics for the upgraded one that she was using? I'll try to repair it when I return to work—"

Kaelen stopped speaking as Ellie wrapped her in a tight hug. "You don't have to fix anything. We have a special team that will repair the chair. It's the same lab that was responsible for many of the advancements in its current version. In the meantime, she can use the spare. It's not as fancy but it will do for a while." Ellie sat down and Kaelen joined them at the table.

"I'm going to grab a beer. Anyone else want something to drink?" Maddy stood and looked around the table.

"Wine?" Ana said hopefully.

"Not a chance. How about some water or juice?"

Ana huffed. "Fine. I'll have some water. We should probably order lunch because we didn't get to eat and I'm starving."

"I'm good, honey."

Kaelen's hot dogs were long forgotten in the aftermath of Mimic's attack. "I could use food as well. I'll order from Fleet Eats. Is there something I should avoid feeding Leah, or food that is beneficial to human brain healing?"

The beer cap popped off with a *psshht* sound, and Maddy walked over to sit down again. "Not so much avoiding foods, I recommend certain things for brain injury recovery. Let's see…" She handed the glass of water to Ana and placed her own beer bottle on the table in front of her. Maddy ticked off items on her fingers. "Food that's heavy on antioxidants like dark chocolate and blueberries. Fatty fish, dark leafy greens, walnuts, pumpkin seeds, eggs, avocado, and meat. Basically, she needs those antioxidants, Omega-3s, and protein."

Kaelen looked toward the kitchen, scanning the pantry with her x-ray vision. "She has dark chocolate and walnuts in the pantry." She swung her sightline to the oversize refrigerator. "Blueberries, eggs, kale," Kaelen shuddered at the bitter leafy vegetable. "There's some sort of meat but I can't tell what it is without looking." When she switched her sight back to normal, she saw them staring at her with their mouths open. "What?"

Maddy shook herself first. "It's freaky how you're able to do that."

"But so handy, especially if you're looking for your keys."

"Why don't I make something for everyone instead of ordering food?"

Maddy raised a dark eyebrow and Kaelen found it reminiscent of Leah. "What are you thinking, Mom?"

Ellie tapped her top lip, then smiled. "How about blueberry walnut pancakes with a side of eggs."

Kaelen smiled. "You can cook all that?"

Maddy snorted. "Not everyone survives on takeout and protein bars, Kaelen. Mom makes the best pancakes. Though I'm not sure if she wants to make enough to fill your bottomless pit."

It was a fair assessment of Kaelen's appetite and she frowned. "You have a point. Make pancakes for everyone else and I'll order food from Fleet Eats."

Ellie stood and walked around the table to squeeze Kaelen's shoulder. "Nonsense. I'll make you a large stack…if you come help me. Tell me what put that wrinkle between your brows while you're at it."

Kaelen rubbed between her brows feeling the telltale wrinkled skin that always gave away her thoughts. "But I can't cook."

"I know for a fact you help Leah in the kitchen. That's all you have to do. Measure and stir and I'll do the actual cooking."

Kaelen wasn't about to turn down Ellie's pancakes, not if they were as good as Maddy stated. She hadn't been wrong about Ellie's pecan pie. "Okay."

As promised, Ellie put Kaelen to work measuring ingredients into a comically large bowl. Leah ordered it online as a joke but had used it a few times when making dinner for both of them. Kaelen suddenly remembered what she wanted to ask Ana when she came downstairs after making sure Leah was sleeping soundly. "Ana, were you able to learn the status of your friend? The one I took to LAGH?"

"They couldn't give me any details about her because I'm not family. However, I received a call from Stephanie's wife." She turned to look at Ellie. "Did you know that Doctor Young happens to be married to the long-running director of the CORP?"

"Rocket?"

"Yup, the very same."

Kaelen looked back and forth between the two women. "What or who is a rocket?"

"Agent Romy Danes is the famous director of the Chromodec Office of Restraint and Protection. She's one of the leaders that stopped Marek Meza during the Chromodec uprising nearly two decades ago." Ellie shook her head and frowned. "I remember when Congress grilled that woman about the identity of the two civilians who helped save the country. Then Nova and T'ala showed up—"

Maddy laughed. "We watched footage of the hearing in school and those suited gasbags about shit themselves when they flew down from the gallery."

Super intellect or no, not much of what they were saying made sense to Kaelen. She'd had Earth history during her voyage, but it gave a vaguer overview of major events without going into some of the details that the other women in the room were familiar with. "You mentioned them at a game night once. They are in the state of Washington, yes?"

"Yup. Came to Earth as babies. Seems weird to be born as someone's soul mate."

Ana nodded. "Weird but kind of romantic, I suppose."

"Were they already in the CORP when they helped quell the uprising?" Kaelen was genuinely curious how people joined the government agency, not that she was likely to ever do something like that.

"I think they were recruited after. Right, Mom?" Ellie nodded. "Who can say how it all went down though behind the scenes? Leah and I were just kids when it happened. Anyway, both women are geniuses like another alien I know."

The timing seemed odd as most people aged out of action focused careers, like the previous LA SAIC that Gabe mentioned, Lingua. "You said nearly two decades ago?" Ana nodded. "How is it this T'ala is still working as an agent?"

Ana shrugged at the same time Maddy muttered, "Aliens."

"Anyway, back to the phone call. Agent Danes reassured me that Dr. Young was doing fine. Romy said that Stephanie took a piece of shrapnel and had some internal bleeding, but thanks to her quick arrival at the hospital, they were able to stabilize her. She's also got a concussion and broken ribs, but overall, it could have been a lot worse."

"Okay." Kaelen felt guilty that she wasn't faster to help. Perhaps if she hadn't let rage consume her, she may have taken note of the casualties sooner.

"Hey," she looked up when Ana spoke. "Thank you. Your quick actions inside that restaurant prevented a lot of bad stuff from happening. You saved her and the rest of us, and I want you to know how much I appreciate that."

"What did you do in the restaurant, Kaelen?" Ellie asked.

Ana answered before Kaelen could. Instead, Ellie pointed to a few more ingredients while Ana told the short tale. "I'm not sure how she did it, but Kaelen put out the fire that had started inside. As for Mimic, I don't know what power she stole, but if I had to make a guess, I'd say it was pyrokinetic. It happened so fast… the entire front of the restaurant blew in." She shivered. "Anyway, Kaelen put out the fires then did something to shore up the collapsing ceiling."

Ellie had a large electric griddle heated on the counter as Kaelen shoved the giant bowl of mixed batter closer to her. It turned blueish purple once the blueberries were added. Ellie used a ladle to make a series of four-inch circles in two rows on the griddle. Afterward, she placed the ladle back in the bowl and turned to lean against the counter.

"Now, tell me what was on your mind when you came downstairs."

The most recent attack on Leah as well as the damage done to her chair put the initial concept in Kaelen's head. "Leah's safety. Her guards, the CORP, none of them are enough while Mimic is still loose and terrorizing Los Angeles. I can't hunt for Mimic properly because of the CORP, and I can't be with Leah all the time."

"You have an idea." Ellie stated it as a fact, displaying insight on Kaelen's thought process and logic.

Kaelen nodded. "I have an idea for something that can help but would need the time and resources to work on it. As the Lab Director at Lockheed International, I'd like to ask you for approval."

"What are you thinking?" Ellie glanced at the pan and held up a finger. "Hold on a second." She grabbed a spatula and flipped all the pancakes, then turned to resume the conversation. "Okay, what have you got for me?"

"I believe the closest Earth comparison is called a shockwave attenuation system. It uses an energy shield to protect objects from explosion shockwaves and shrapnel."

Ellie lifted her pale eyebrow, highlighting the fine wrinkles around her eyes and across her forehead. "I've heard about that. I think Boeing created the original system decades ago. It supposedly generates a plasma shield using lasers, electricity, and microwaves. But as far as I know, that is a complicated and large system and so far, only the military has made use of it."

"Holy shit, are you talking about a forcefield?"

"Maddy, language!" Ellie began scooping cooked pancakes onto a large tray while she asked, "How would it work to protect Leah?"

Kaelen took the tray that was handed to her and sped it over to the oven to keep warm, then returned to answer Ellie's question. "Einstein is putting together a super high-efficiency battery. It will be able to hold a larger, longer-lasting charge, while a fraction of the size. However, I'm confident that Lockheed's existing battery technology would be sufficient to power a scaled-down version of this system."

Ana asked, "How can you build something that another company created? I highly doubt they've released specs or schematics for such a thing. And what about copyrights?"

Ellie finished ladling on the next batch of pancakes. "Copyrights and patents wouldn't matter because this would be a one-time, not for profit, build, right Kaelen?" She nodded. "One way is to reverse engineer an existing system. But that won't work in this case for two reasons, we don't have any samples, nor would it be possible to adapt in its current large-scale format."

"I read a few articles about it not long after I landed on Earth. I also read a lot of science articles during the Lockheed International holiday shutdown last year. We had a similar system on Argon that we used in our small, personal ships, the same kind I traveled here in. I think I can replicate the field in a size that will fit in her hoverchair."

Maddy drained the rest of her beer as Kaelen retrieved the tray of pancakes from the oven, sans mitts, when Ellie was ready to remove another griddle full. "That's all well and good, but how does it actually work?"

"A small area is ionized, making the temperature, density—"

Maddy waved her hand in the air. "Never mind, forget I asked. This is my day off and I've already gone over my quota of thinking."

Ana turned to her. "I'm surprised they didn't call you in after the explosion."

"I'm not on call, and seniority has its perks."

"Kaelen," she turned to look at Ellie. "Do it. I want my daughter protected." Kaelen nodded and recognized the look in Ellie's eyes as the same one her own mother had when she sent that ship out into the unknown. Clovi Ze-Est had loved her, but her mother's lies still cost Kaelen her world. It was hard to reconcile.

"As long as Leah is well enough on her own, I'll start first thing tomorrow."

"If she's not, email me a list of what you need, and I'll have it sent here. Use the lab downstairs to work on it."

"Thank you."

Eventually the pancakes were finished and Maddy volunteered to cook scrambled eggs and the ham steaks she found in the fridge. Kaelen was setting the table when she heard Leah's heart rate change.

"She's waking up."

Ellie frowned. "She hasn't been sleeping that long."

"She—I think it's a bad dream." Kaelen sped up the stairs and to Leah's room in time to see her thrash for a few seconds, then bolt upright as she woke abruptly.

Leah groaned and grabbed her head and lay back down. "Ugh, it feels like someone is hammering my head from the inside.

"I'm sorry. If you're feeling up for it, you should try to eat some food."

Leah made a face. "I'm still a little nauseous." She sniffed the air. "What did you order?"

"I didn't order anything." Kaelen grinned. "Maddy mentioned a list of foods that could help you recover, and Ellie offered to make blueberry walnut pancakes. We have that, scrambled eggs, avocado, and ham steaks."

"Wow, that's a lot—oh, I forgot." She smiled at Kaelen. "Okay, I suppose I can eat something. I feel better after my little nap. Did Ana get an update on Stephanie?"

Kaelen held out her hand. "I'll tell you on the way downstairs."

Leah didn't go to work for the next few days, per her sister's orders. She also wasn't happy to sit home with nothing to do but rest. As promised, Ellie sent over all the items requested by Kaelen, which she then had to explain to Leah. Rather than shut down the idea, Leah spent her time resting in the lab where Kaelen worked so she could watch the process. She asked a lot of questions, offered some input, and simply enjoyed the spectacle that was Kaelen's genius.

Maddy assured Leah that eighty percent of people with mild concussions fully recover within the first fourteen days. While Leah didn't tell anyone, even Kaelen, she already had plans to go back to the office early. The persistent headaches were the only thing bothering her after the first week.

Leah went back to work the following Wednesday, despite protests from Kaelen, Ellie, and Ana. Kaelen frowned and went downstairs to the

SPL when she realized Leah wasn't going to go home. That left Ellie and Ana. When Ellie called Maddy, hoping she would convince Leah to be reasonable, she simply responded, "I already knew Leah would go back early. If the headaches persist, take acetaminophen. You should probably follow up with your normal doctor for an MRI scan. Though Mom could do it onsite there."

"Thanks, Maddy." Leah disconnected the call. "Satisfied?"

"I will be after you've come downstairs for that scan."

Seeing no quarter given by her mom or best friend, Leah sighed. "Fine. May as well get it over with now." She pressed the intercom button. "Jenna, when is my first meeting? I've nothing on my calendar."

"Friday, Miss Lockheed."

"It's Leah, and today is Wednesday."

"I'm well aware, *Leah*, but that's the first day you have any meetings scheduled."

Leah scowled. "Thank you, Jenna." She glanced around to see Ana smirking from her seat on the couch.

"I smell a rat."

"I have no idea what you're talking about."

Ellie chuckled quietly. "Don't be angry because we care about you, honey. Let's go downstairs and get your test out of the way, then you can come back up here and push around some papers if it makes you happy."

"I should have you both fired," Leah grumbled.

Ana stood from the couch and burst into laughter. "Don't threaten me with a good time. Anyway, I have to go. Unlike a certain CEO, I have a full day of meetings."

Leah refrained from flipping her off while under the watchful eyes of Ellie. Instead, she made a shooing motion with her fingers. "I'm ready. Do we need to call ahead to the lab?"

"We've got an hour before the biomed team comes in, so plenty of time to fit you in." Ellie brought up the hoverchair forcefield on the way downstairs. "Was Kaelen able to finish the shockwave attenuation system?"

Leah nodded. "She installed it early this morning before I even got up. We haven't tested it yet, and, for obvious reasons, I don't want to."

"Without testing, how confident is she that it will work?"

"Kaelen told me that she was certain of the design. Mostly because the materials and technology were at or near-Earth level. It was only the configuration of components and settings that our planet had never seen. It helps that she also had Wex bring up the schematics for her ship's attenuation system to use as a comparison."

Forty-five minutes later, after Leah's MRI, they entered the SPL. Ellie picked up the conversation where they'd left off on their way downstairs. "Will you run a test on the new system, to confirm that the forcefield works?"

Kaelen entered the main lab from the hallway leading to the secondary labs. "Please bear in mind that this is not a true forcefield like you see in Earth movies. I keep hearing people say the word, but this isn't that kind of technology. The system wasn't designed to prevent direct impact from shells or shrapnel. Rather, it protects the target from the shockwaves of a nearby impact. Once the shockwave is detected, it sends a signal to an arc generator, which in turn ionizes a small region between the shockwave origination point and the hoverchair. It can deflect some debris, but not all." She shrugged. "It was the best I could do under the circumstances."

"It's certainly better than having some vengeful Chromodec blasting me from my chair with a firebomb."

"We can test the system now if you like. Take your chair into the impact chamber and leave it at one end."

Leah raised a single dark brow at her. "And how will you create the shockwave?"

"You'll see." Kaelen turned to Einstein. "Do we have a bin of scrap metal I can use as simulated shrapnel?"

He nodded. "I'll retrieve it and meet you at the end of the hall."

Once the lab cameras were off and everything was in place, Ellie, Leah, and Einstein stood outside the chamber, watching Kaelen through ten-inch-thick reinforced plexiglass. Kaelen held the bin of scrap metal in both hands and suddenly tossed it a foot into the air ahead of her. Then she clapped her hands together with such force, the watchers felt the vibration of it on the other side of the shielded wall. The metal pieces exploded outward toward the hoverchair, only for most to be stopped, deflected, or destroyed by the plasma field. As soon as the shockwave dissipated, the plasma field disappeared.

Leah looked to her left where Ellie and Einstein stood. "I'd say that was a success."

Kaelen picked up the chair and brought it out of the room with her. She set it down next to Leah, who grimaced with distaste before settling into the seat once again. "Did you doubt my design would function as promised?"

"Darling, you didn't give me a one hundred percent certainty so there was a chance of failure." She shrugged.

"True."

Leah's cell phone rang and she answered it after verifying the caller. "Hello, Garen. You know I prefer for you to go through my administrative assistant for all calls. My private number is for emergencies."

"Apologies, Miss Lockheed—"

"Leah."

A sigh echoed over the phone. "Apologies, Leah. We still haven't been able to trace Mimic's whereabouts, and I was hoping to convince you to accept CORP protection after her latest attack."

"The same CORP who has failed to stop or find this menace despite her numerous attempts to murder me? Forgive me if I don't have a lot of confidence in your people."

"If you would only reconsider—"

"While I appreciate the offer, the answer is still no. If it makes you feel better, one of my best engineers made a downsized version of a shockwave attenuation system and installed it on my chair. It should go a long way toward protecting me. If you want to serve my safety and that of Los Angeles's citizens, you'll find wherever Mimic is hiding and bring her in. Surely you must have some clue as to her identity or hidey-hole."

"I don't think—"

"If you can't help, perhaps the director of the CORP can. After all, we were meeting with her wife when the restaurant exploded." The other end of the line went quiet, and Leah suspected she struck a nerve.

Garen's voice was a deep rumble over the phone. "I spoke with the director before they returned to Chicago. Rocket is concerned about Mimic *and* our new vigilante."

Leah scoffed. "While I was unconscious for most of it, I heard that Scion saved Doctor Young. Perhaps Agent Danes should be more appreciative."

She had to admire Garen's composure. "We've got some leads, with one person gone undercover in C-town in hopes of coming up with a name. I promise to keep you posted."

"Thank you." Once the call disconnected, she looked up to see three concerned faces. "Don't give me that look. I have a valid reason for not wanting the CORP as my immediate security."

Kaelen frowned. "I've told you before that my identity isn't worth your life."

"Please respect my decisions about personal safety. I think I have a right to choose how I move forward under the given threat, don't you?" Leah looked at Ellie and Einstein to let them know she included them in her statement as well. She could tell Ellie especially wanted to argue. "You know me, I would never take foolish risks. If I thought that the CORP could do a significantly better job than my own team, protective measures, and Kaelen, I'd find a way to make it work. But they've been one step behind this entire time."

Ellie gave her arm a squeeze. "You make excellent points. I'm worried about you, but I'm glad to know that you've considered all the options here. I trust your word, Leah. I always have."

"I know, and I appreciate it. Now, I believe we have a meeting with finance in," Leah looked at her watch and frowned, "a little over fifteen minutes. That gives me enough time to pee and grab a coffee."

"You mean I have a meeting. You've got nothing until Friday, remember?"

"I promise I'll only tag along. I won't even bring my laptop, okay?"

Ellie gave an uncharacteristic groan. "Fine. I'll be happy for your company. I'm not a fan of end of calendar year finance meetings, but they're infinitely better than end of fiscal year finance meetings. You may as well come with me as long as you lay off the screen time. I need to stop in my office for my laptop."

Leah snickered. "You act like I'm ten and grounded." She looked at Kaelen. "What will you be working on?"

Einstein answered for both of them. "I didn't have a chance to tell her yet, but I'm finished with the battery prototype and ready to install it into the case for the portal generator."

Leah was torn. "How long?"

Einstein steepled his fingers while he wore a look of thought. "I'd estimate another thirty to thirty-five minutes before we have something we can test."

Ellie frowned. "Well shoot. We'll be right in the middle of the meeting, with two more back-to-back after that." She looked at Leah. "You could always stay here instead."

"No." Leah sighed. "There was actually a budget item I wanted to address. Besides, if I'm here I'll be tempted to help."

Kaelen appeared concerned. "Would you like us to wait to test the prototype portal generator?"

"No. The faster you test it, the faster you can work out any bugs."

"Bugs? There will be no bugs! We are twelfth caliber—"

"I'm well aware of how intelligent you both are, Mister Trog. Let's call it fine-tuning, if the other word offends you so."

He stared at her for a few seconds then nodded. "I suppose that is an acceptable bit of foresight. Untested technology can be problematic. Something my race knows well."

Kaelen smiled at Einstein and clapped him on the shoulder, using a little more force than intended. He stumbled a bit as she told Leah, "We'll keep you updated on our progress." Then to Einstein, "Come along, Clevna. Today we're going to make our own escape route from the bowels of this building."

Kaelen and Einstein worked for the next half hour on the portal generator. She helped him layer the battery then assemble it into the case. It was delicate work, nearly too much for two people to do. But both had steady hands and precise spatial sense. Thirty-three minutes after Leah and Ellie left for their meeting, Einstein placed the watch band on the work bench and stepped back.

"Should we test it?"

The controls were fairly simple. It was the tiny microprocessor and motherboard inside that made it more complex than nearly anything else on the planet. While the face displayed the time, much like any other smart watch, with a swift twist of the case ring, a display popped up. It was there a person could enter latitude, longitude, and altitude.

"This could be dangerous, at least for whomever tests the device. I think it was a good addition to put in the location slide."

The location slide was something that shifted the portal to the side in the event solid matter was detected in the same location as the destination point. "If this works, I have an idea to program satellite connection so we can have real-time scanning of the destination to verify location ahead of time."

Einstein pursed his lips. "That would certainly be beneficial. We could also expand the programming so it doesn't move the end point from the destination. Instead, a warning would pop up with an alternate location suggestion that the user can select if no safe, nearby shift is possible, given environmental factors at the time."

Kaelen nodded. "Excellent thought. In the meantime, we should only select destination points that meet the following criteria," she ticked off items on her fingers, "away from witnesses, empty—with no chance of someone or something in its place, and not visible by any recording equipment. But for now, perhaps we can set it to open in the impact lab."

"I would say that makes the most logical sense." Einstein opened a drawer at his personal workstation and pulled out a satellite phone, then indicated that Kaelen should pick up the watch. "I'll go to the lab and record the coordinates. I'd previously calculated SPL's distance below sea level for another project." He told Kaelen the altitude and she entered it into the interface. Einstein was only gone a minute before he returned and read off the latitude and longitude. "That will put the destination point right in the middle of the lab."

"Okay. Should we throw something through as a preliminary test? We can turn on the camera in here, and in the impact lab to record the simultaneous matter transfer."

With a few keystrokes on his laptop, Einstein brought up the camera feeds for each room and switched them to record. Then he handed Kaelen the stress ball sitting next to his monitor. "Try this first. Once I verify it has gone through with no defects, perhaps we can try the test with organic matter."

Kaelen and Einstein looked around the lab and their gaze fell on a plant beneath a grow light. They said, "No," at the same time.

Einstein frowned. "Leah would be extremely displeased if something were to happen to her special plant."

"True. Let's do the inorganic test and decide after."

Three minutes later, Einstein gave her the okay to activate the portal. He spoke normally, aware that she'd be able to hear from an entirely different section of the lab. Kaelen had already put in the coordinates so all that was left was for her to hit the activation button. A second later, a swirling vortex opened in front of her. It was about seven feet in diameter, plenty large enough for someone to step through. She could see the impact lab on the other side, so she tossed the ball then shut the portal to preserve power.

Einstein called out, "I've got it and I don't see any damage or deformation. Should I come back now, or have you found something else to test?"

Kaelen reactivated the portal and stepped through before she could overthink it. She shut it off and turned around to see Einstein smiling from the other side of the room. She grinned back at him. "It worked."

"It did. We should narrow down coordinates for a safe location that will take us out of the lab."

"What do you think of the roof? What are the odds that someone will be up there at any given time?"

Einstein's look turned grim. "Not zero. There is also the real possibility that any location you choose on the roof could be seen by passing planes, helicopters, surrounding buildings, and especially the CORP. I would say it is too risky."

Kaelen considered the problem. "If it is me going through the portal, does it have to be where anyone could see? For instance, I could set the altitude to 60,000 feet and come down from there."

"We'd have to compensate for the difference in rotational spin of the Earth between that height and our sublevel, but I think it could be achieved."

"Do we though? It's not like it matters where it opens at that altitude because I can fly. My speed is such that any drift resulting from rotational speed differentiation would be negligible."

"True. Unfortunately, we'll have to find a way to compensate for the rotational spatial shift for you to come back to the lab the same way."

Both stood in silence for a moment before Einstein held up a finger. "You have super speed. I think it is within the realm of possibility that if you speed to an alley, you could make use of the portal without anyone seeing, so no adjustment would need to be made. However, the CORP is good at picking up energy surges throughout the city, so we should endeavor to both make a dedicated space for you to return within the SPL, and to shield it properly so the portal's energy signature isn't picked up by their equipment."

"I think we could make some additions to the impact lab that would help shield any surges from detection no matter what kind of equipment the CORP is using. Though why they'd track anything here within Lockheed property baffles me. I think our distance below ground will help with the shielding efforts."

"The impact lab is a good choice in case of energy malfunctions that need to be contained. And while anomalous energy signatures would not normally be questioned by law enforcement within the labs here at Lockheed, it is another matter if they are actively tracking someone that they consider a vigilante. We cannot be too careful with your safety or the company's reputation."

Chapter Twenty-four

A few hours later, Leah returned to the SPL to see their progress. Einstein and Kaelen were successful in shielding the impact lab and explained the reasons for it. They even demonstrated by having Kaelen go through, exactly as she'd done before during the initial testing with Einstein. Leah was congratulating them when Kaelen heard something strange and tilted her head to look up and outward.

"What is it?"

"An explosion, alarms, and sirens. Many of them. It is…" She extended her hearing more, trying to decipher details of radio chatter, voices, and comments. Kaelen heard a police officer and screams. She turned wide eyes back to Leah and Einstein. "Guardian Technologies is on fire. Emergency personnel on the scene report that the building is leaning. I need to go!"

"Nalla!" Einstein appeared panicked. "The Guardian building is right next to Meta News Network."

Kaelen quickly set the watch for her current latitude and longitude, but with an altitude far above what anyone in the city would detect. She looked at Leah before stepping through. "I'll be back as soon as possible."

There was fear in Leah's eyes but she nodded anyway. They'd discussed Kaelen's need to help many times over the past few months, but this would be the first real test that didn't involve a threat to Leah. "Be safe." Her quiet words chased Kaelen through the swirling blue portal.

Kaelen exited high in the atmosphere near the Armstrong line.

Atmospheric pressure is so low at 63,000 feet that water boils at the normal temperature of the human body. Exposure to pressure below this limit for humans meant a rapid loss of consciousness and eventual death. Luckily for Kaelen, her Argonian biology kept her safe. She quickly rocketed her way back to Earth toward Los Angeles and the skyscraper that was spewing flames and black smoke.

There were no CORP agents or other emergency personnel on the scene, but Kaelen could see flashing lights approaching from a few blocks away. She assessed the most dangerous threat first and flew down to put out the fire.

It burned hot, more so than she'd ever felt before, and it smelled strongly of chemicals. Her suit burned away in spots and reformed nearly as fast thanks to the nano-infused fibers. Without knowing the cause of the original fire or explosion, she was hesitant to blow it out with her ice breath. Then Kaelen calculated if she moved fast enough, she could use cyclonic air currents to draw the oxygen out of the floor she was on.

Kaelen listened intently for any signs of life and grimaced when she found none. Plan in place, she sped to one of the blown-out windows and began circling her arms rapidly until she'd created a funnel of smoke and flame, drawing all the air out the window. After a few minutes, the majority of the blaze died down from the lack of oxygen, but a lot of damage had been done. She used her ice breath on the rest.

The skyscraper shuddered beneath her feet, and she peered down through every floor, taking special note of the supporting girders that had been damaged in the blast. The building shuddered again and suddenly shifted. She sped out the window to see it tilting farther than what any skyscraper was designed for, even in earthquake prone locations such as LA. Thinking fast, Kaelen flew to the side tilting toward the MNN tower and found the most stable place to apply pressure. The façade crumbled beneath her hands, leaving behind a bare steel girder. She slowly straightened the building but couldn't let go.

"Scion! You are under arrest. Please stay where you are and prepare for detainment."

Kaelen looked to her left to see two CORP agents floating next to her. She used her x-ray vision to identify the bone structures of Sinter and

Gauss beneath the helmets and suits. Not that it was necessary because she recognized their voices and heartbeats. "As much as I appreciate your dedication to duty and law, do you think you could help me save the people inside this building first?"

The dark helmets swung to face each other, then they looked back at her. As one they raised their hands, and she felt a slight reduction of pressure. The woman spoke first. "We've got agents in the building trying to evacuate the workers."

"That's all well and good, but we still have the building itself to contend with."

Gauss swore and Sinter said, "It's too heavy, even for us. We'll have to call in Jove."

Kaelen heard their intercoms and knew that the SAIC would arrive soon. She had a plan but needed someone of appropriate strength to hold her place while she went inside.

A large muscled form wearing the familiar black armored suit flew in from the same direction that the other CORP agents had come from. "Do we have a plan yet?

"No, sir. Agents are inside evacuating the people. We found Scion out here, uh, holding up Guardian Technologies."

"They may not have a plan, but I do. Unfortunately, it won't work unless you're strong enough to take my place."

"So, you can do what, escape?"

Kaelen felt another odd vibration through her hands. "The building isn't stable and if I wanted to escape, I would have done so already. Better yet, I wouldn't have shown up to help. Please, we need to prevent more loss of life and property damage. The angle of the building will cause it to impact Meta News Network and possibly create a chain reaction with the other nearby skyscrapers."

Agent Garen Grath, the infamous Jove, nodded. He flew down and added his considerable strength to Kaelen's. "My plan is to go inside the building and repair the damaged girders that are failing."

"They'd have to be welded in place—"

She slowly released the building, confident in the agent's strength. "I can do it. Please?"

"Fine. You get this one free pass, but I don't trust you in this city.

You need to promise me that you'll leave Los Angeles, or stop using your powers."

Kaelen hesitated for a moment then shook her head and sped inside. She found her way to the section where the girders had been melted and damaged in the explosion. She looked around for metal she could use and found it in the steel frames of heavy work benches. Using a combination of her strength, laser vision, and ice breath, Kaelen was able to stabilize the building. It would have to do until it could be brought down safely.

She flew back outside and hovered twenty yards from the agents. "It's done. The repair should hold until construction crews can begin demolition."

Garen lowered his hands and approached her slowly. "You didn't answer my question."

"Because I don't have an answer. I can't promise not to help people or use my powers any more than you can. Your laws may be practical, to an extent, but they're also callous."

"That's answer enough. Go!"

Kaelen suddenly found herself held by some external force and surrounded by flying agents. Three were the original ones she'd come into contact with, Gauss, Sinter, and Afterburn, the guy with a jetpack. A few more surrounded her that she'd not seen before. Some appeared to have mechanical means of flight, others were either Chromodecs or aliens. "I'm afraid I won't allow your people to detain me, Jove."

One of the new black-clad figures spoke. "You're not an agent so I don't think you get much say in it."

"You're right. I'm not one of you and that's exactly why you can't detain me." Then with a casual amount of effort, she flew straight up in the air. She didn't realize until too late that one of the agents had grabbed onto her leg at the last second. The heartbeat thundering through the woman's veins let Kaelen know that it was Sinter.

"Let go, I'm flying too high for humans."

"No! I have a…job…to d-do."

Duty or no, the woman couldn't function with barely any oxygen at such a high altitude. Her grip slackened and released entirely, then she fell away back toward Earth. "Vos!" Kaelen flew after her, catching the woman in her arms so she could carry her back to safety. Rather than take her to where all the agents were waiting, Kaelen flew Sinter directly to the CORP headquarters. A quick scan with her x-ray vision showed thick walls capable of extreme defensibility. She couldn't chance leaving her by the front door. Instead, Kaelen gently placed the woman on the roof as she was starting to wake.

"Wha—what happened?"

Kaelen floated above her, listening intently for the return of the other CORP agents. "You flew too high in the atmosphere and suffered from brain oxygen deprivation. You fell unconscious and began to drop, so I caught you and flew you here. Are you well?" Kaelen could hear panicked calls over Sinter's com channel and knew they'd find her soon. She assumed the agents would have some sort of tracking capability in their suits or helmets.

"I'm fine." The helmeted head turned left then right. "Looks like I'm back at the CORP facility." Sinter reached up to push something beneath the edge of her helmet as she pulled herself up to stand. Then she raised the shielded faceplate and held out her hand. "Thank you. You saved my life."

Kaelen took in the high cheekbones and medium brown skin; details she couldn't see with her x-ray vision. She clasped Sinter's hand. "I would never have let you die, though you were brave in what you tried to do."

Sinter put her hand down again and made a face. "More like foolish." She shook her head and met Kaelen's gaze. "We're not the enemy here."

That earned Sinter a smile. Kaelen picked up the sounds of approaching CORP agents. "Funny you should say that, because, neither am I." Kaelen flew up into the air and looked back at the woman. Then with a nod, she blurred down to street level and into an alley that was out of sight. Once she was certain there was no one following or tracking her, Kaelen activated the portal watch and stepped into the lab she'd left not long before.

Leah rushed to embrace her. "Kaelen! Are you okay? The news showed you working with CORP agents, then you disappeared straight up with one of the agents." Einstein was there along with Ellie, whom they must have called after Kaelen went through the portal.

"Once I had enough people to prevent the structure from toppling,

I went inside and reinforced the damaged girders. They'll still have to demolish the building, but it should hold well enough to keep the surrounding blocks safe from unplanned collapse."

"Kaelen Ra-Evon, your actions show much honor. Nalla called me right after you left and said that the Guardian Technologies building began to tilt toward MNN before they even realized they'd need to evacuate. Apparently, they had cameras on you as soon as you arrived."

Ellie also pulled Kaelen into a hug. "You were a hero out there. They've been replaying the scene of you flying up to the side of the skyscraper and pushing until it was vertical, speculating about your strength and identity."

"I'm glad I manipulated the suit hood into a cowl for this particular duty. Even with the hood, I would have been close enough during the daytime for the agents to see my face."

"Fuck." Everyone looked at Leah who'd paled with Kaelen's words. "Agent Garen Grath is telepathic."

Kaelen shook her head. "He wore gloves and I was fully covered by my suit. No skin contact was made between us. The positive from this situation is that we know the watch works. It could stand to use a few improvements as Einstein and I discussed before the trial. But overall, it serves its purpose. I wonder if we can locate Mimic without garnering the attention of the CORP."

"Or," Leah looped her arm through Kaelen's. "We can take a deep breath and start planning for the holidays. The end of year shut down is a week away. You, me, Ellie, Maddy, and Tasha will be in Sello Bay for a week. We'll have a few days before heading to Vegas. I thought we could celebrate the new year there since CES begins on Tuesday, January third."

Ellie rubbed her forehead. "What is it about this time of year? The weeks always get away from me. I still have too many things to do at the house to have you all over."

Leah grinned at her. "You literally say that every year."

The next day, the front page of the Los Angeles Tribune featured a picture of Kaelen holding up Guardian Technologies. "Hero or Vigilante: The Scion of Los Angeles," filled the rest of the page and continued inside. It was also on the main page of their website. Reader opinions seemed split on whether they were for or against Kaelen's heroic alter ego. The photo was probably taken via drone because the CORP had kept news helicopters away from the building.

Conversely, Meta News Network, the very building Kaelen saved from destruction, published their own article praising Scion. It featured eyewitness accounts and described her heroic activities since first appearing. Another article speculated about her identity and race. The second write-up posed questions, such as was she a Chromodec or an alien, and how many powers did Scion possess?

Not only was MNN's newspaper cover photo larger and in high definition, but it was also taken from a bird's eye view from their balcony on the side facing Guardian Technologies. They even had video looping on their website showing Scion's actions in preventing the skyscraper from coming down and taking out other buildings along the way. The CCTV footage of the explosion, along with the abrupt tilt toward Meta News Network was frightening to watch.

Perhaps as a final middle finger to the Tribune's mediocre support of Los Angeles's newest hero/vigilante, Meta News Network had an entire page inside the paper and on the website, that listed every life Kaelen had saved since making her first appearance. The list included the passengers and crew from Flight 327, Leah Lockheed, Dr. Stephanie Young and the mention that she was the current CORP director's wife, the people trapped inside the restaurant, and everyone still inside Meta News Network and Guardian Technologies before Kaelen caught the skyscraper and prevented its collapse.

The evening before Kaelen and Leah were scheduled to travel to Sello Bay on holiday, they sat snuggled together on Leah's couch with the fireplace burning. Kaelen discovered Taylor Swift, a fifty-year-old music artist, weeks before and was halfway through listening to all the songs in her discography. Leah had never been exposed to the artist so gamely

 The Last Scion of Ra

listened along. Unfortunately, Kaelen couldn't seem to relax.

"Darling, what's wrong?"

Kaelen was reclined into the corner of the L-shaped couch and Leah reclined against her, wrapped securely within her lover's arms. Understanding that Leah could feel the tension behind her, Kaelen consciously relaxed her muscles. "I'm sorry. It's nothing important."

Leah turned so she could see Kaelen over her shoulder. "It's important if it affects you. Are you worried about our Sello Bay trip next week?"

"No—yes. I mean, I'm worried about many things. Mimic has shown an uncanny ability in finding you wherever you go. Sello Bay won't have resources like law enforcement or the CORP nearby to draw on for your protection."

"I'll have my security team, and Sello Bay does have a police department, even if it's on the small side. Most importantly, I'll have you."

Kaelen froze as Leah's words prompted another line of thought. "Is Sello Bay far from Los Angeles? Where does your security team stay when you visit?"

Leah laughed. "Sello Bay is a few hours north of LA. It's far enough away to be a long and tedious drive, but it won't kill an entire day on the road. The team stays in the same hotel as me when I travel to another city. But when I go home, I always stay with Ellie at the house."

"Is that safe?"

"Sello Bay is a bit different because Ellie's house is in a secluded location about ten miles from town. That means Hans and his people will follow behind us in two large motorhomes that were customized for my security team. Their duties are to watch the perimeter, and Hans will assign guards to follow me whether I go into Sello Bay proper, or simply take the hoverchair out to the beach."

"Beach. I've never actually been to a beach since coming here."

"To Los Angeles?"

"No, to Earth."

Leah twisted a little farther and raised her arm so she could slide her hand around to the back of Kaelen's head. She pulled Kaelen close and kissed her. "It's not exactly beach season, but I promise we'll come back next summer. We can swim in the ocean together, and it can be a first for both of us."

Kaelen smiled down at her. "I'd like that."

"As for worrying about Mimic, I had Jenna put out a press release stating that I'd be going to Europe for the holiday. Hopefully that will throw her off the trail so we can relax, and I can prepare for the CES presentation on the opening day of the conference."

"And you think it will work?"

"I don't think that it won't work. All I can do is hope."

Leah turned back around to stare into the fire and Kaelen contemplated her words. "What is there to do in Sello Bay? Are there many restaurants, or shows like this Las Vegas we are visiting to celebrate the new year?"

Laughter shook Leah, carrying through to Kaelen's chest where they were pressed together. "Sello Bay is a small town. There are a few typical eateries, half a dozen chain restaurants, fast-food places on the outskirts of town, and an old-fashioned diner. It's not exactly a hub for culinary delight, nor for entertainment. However, one thing I love about Sello Bay is the Winter Festival that takes place every year near Christmas. It doesn't celebrate any one religion or holiday, just winter and the end of the year in general."

"I've never been to a festival. What's it like?"

Leah paused. "Well…it's like a carnival, or a fair."

"I've never been to those events either."

"It's easier to show you than explain. I think you'll like it and I'll be honored to introduce you to my hometown with the Tucks."

Her phrasing was curious and Kaelen considered the notion of multiple families. "You mentioned once that you lived in New York before. Did you like one place or the other better?"

Leah grew silent for a minute. "I loved both places differently. Obviously, New York reminded me of my parents and brother. We saw plays, musicals, and operas in the city. There was fine dining, art, culture…everything that wasn't in Sello Bay. But things were different living in the manor there. I had less freedom of body and mind with my birth parents. There was a lot of emphasis put on us to look and act the part of a Lockheed. I know Mother and Father loved us, but it wasn't shown the same way that Ellie and Charlie displayed it."

"How do you mean? The hugging thing?"

Leah shrugged within Kaelen's embrace. "In part. The Tucks were certainly more physically affectionate. But they were a lot more open with praise and encouraged me and Maddy to problem solve and think for ourselves. They weren't worried about appearances because they didn't have the legacy that came with the Lockheed name. Instead, they wanted us to be happy."

"What does that mean when it comes to a preference over one city or another?"

"It's strange to admit, but I think I've been happier with the Tucks than I ever would have been with my own parents and brother…but that happiness is offset by the loss I felt for my family and the sadness that followed. I think your wisdom on the topic of loss was accurate in that I grew with my adoptive family and eventually the hole of loss became small compared to all I gained. While I have fond memories of New York, the city, and Lockheed manor outside the city, there is something truly comforting about coming home to Sello Bay."

Kaelen gave her a little squeeze. "I can't wait to experience that with you."

Leah turned her head and beamed back at her. "Me too."

Worried about Leah's safety where Mimic was concerned, Kaelen asked if they could do the new nanobot injection before leaving work for the holiday. The procedure was painless because they were introduced the vaccine way, in the large muscle mass of Leah's upper arm. The new nanobots would alter the previous set's programming to aid in overall health and healing, well beyond the spinal specific injury. Kaelen took the liberty to add a few new objectives since her second set was more advanced and could handle multiple job routines.

Per Hans's request, Leah sent one of her vans to the airport with a decoy member of her security team dressed to look like her in one of her spare hoverchairs. They were hoping the decoy would help sell the idea that Leah was leaving the country for the holiday. They actually scoped out a rendezvous point ahead of time and used the portal watch to leave

Leah's condo undetected and meet up with another transport van a few miles outside the city. It seemed to work well because neither Hans's team, nor Kaelen could detect anyone following them.

Ellie met them at the door with hugs and cheek kisses for Leah and Kaelen. Once Leah was inside in her hoverchair, Kaelen went out to fetch their bags while the security team set up their fancy motor homes around the back of the house by the barn.

"I put you both in the den since there is a foldout bed in there and a pocket door that closes for privacy. Maddy and Tasha can have the upstairs room when they arrive." She led the way through the house to show Kaelen where to put the suitcases. The curtains were open because it was a bright and sunny, mid-winter day.

Leah scowled.

Kaelen saw the look. "What is it?"

"While I love having the curtains open this time of year because the sun is so scarce, I was hoping to ditch the chair while inside the house. I know I'm fairly safe and out of the way here, but my security team doesn't know about my recovery as I'm still trying to keep it as secret as possible."

"Hmm…" Ellie looked at the large bay window that faced the front of the house. "If only I had some reflective film on hand. If I'd thought of this sooner, I could have installed it before you arrived."

"Are you referring to the material being stored in the optics lab? Einstein and I were up there a few weeks ago and I remember him pointing out the rolls to me."

Ellie nodded. "Unfortunately, you're already here. I suppose I can call and see if Maddy could swing by and pick it up before they drive up in a few days. It's too bad they both have to work until the twenty-third. I suppose not everyone gets nearly two weeks off like Lockheed employees."

"It would take no time at all for me to retrieve a roll. Then I'll install the film when I return." Kaelen grinned at them both. "It's one of the benefits of enhanced speed, it cuts easy work down to nothing."

Ellie planted her hands on her hips. "Kaelen, no. It's too much of a risk for you to fly there while the CORP is still looking for you. I saw the news before I left. You've made Agent Garen Grath fairly unhappy. The

CORP put out a tip line asking for any information as to your identity or whereabouts."

Kaelen held up her left wrist and slid the sleeve back so Ellie could see the sleek watch. "That's why I'd use this. I can teleport right into the back room of the SPL, retrieve the material from upstairs, then teleport back here with no one the wiser."

"Darling, security cameras will pick you up."

"No, this could work." Ellie looked at her own watch. "Holiday staff is still on site. I'll call and have one roll transferred down to SPL immediately. I can log in remotely and shut off the cameras within the lab, and Kaelen can use the watch to retrieve the roll. Excellent idea."

"Ellie—"

"Honey, I want you to be as comfortable as possible while you're here. This plan has no risk. Let Kaelen get the film and we can be free for the rest of our time in this house, okay?"

Kaelen watched the struggle on Leah's face before she gave a nod. She knew that Leah was extremely independent and had a hard time accepting help. Not only that, but Leah hated having others do a lot of work to suit her comfort.

"Okay, fine. And thank you. The reflective film wouldn't have crossed my mind."

Ellie turned to head back toward the kitchen that Kaelen had spied when they first entered the house. "I'm going to make the phone call. We'll shut off the cameras remotely once we know the film has been delivered. I'd prefer not to have irregular staff unmonitored in that lab."

Leah called after her, "That line of thinking is exactly why you're the VP of operations and lab director."

Kaelen moved her gaze from Ellie's retreating back to Leah. "What do we do now?"

"Now we eat cookies. Can't you smell them?"

"I can but I didn't want to assume. I remember Maddy mentioning once that Ellie always made cookies to celebrate her homecoming. Won't she be mad if we eat them all before her and Tasha arrive on Wednesday?"

Leah laughed, a light, joyous sound that never failed to lift Kaelen's spirits. "Ellie will probably be baking every day during the holiday break. She'll bring some to the holiday festival, she'll send some back with both me and Maddy, and she'll probably mail some out, and freeze some. We won't lack for cookies, pies, and other sweets, I promise."

Kaelen was skeptical. While she was a superpowered alien, and despite the fact that Maddy swore an oath to protect and heal, Leah's sister was overprotective and sometimes scary. She didn't want to be responsible for the elder Tuck sibling not getting her promised cookies. "If you're sure…"

"Smell the air and tell me what you notice."

They'd played the game before, testing Kaelen's senses. She sniffed the air. "Spices, overall sweetness, and something—a sweet nutty smell. It reminds me of the tiny glasses of alcohol Nalla bought the first time I went to the bar with everyone."

Leah grinned at her then maneuvered her chair through the large pocket doors, following the same path that Ellie had taken minutes before. "That's right. What you're smelling isn't Maddy's favorite chocolate chip cookies. Today's cookie is my favorite, oatmeal raisin."

Kaelen sped after her, not wanting to be left behind with such amazing smells permeating the house. "Will I like oatmeal raisin? Is it similar to the shot?"

Leah smiled at her when Kaelen caught up. "I guess there is only one way to know. Pour us some milk and take a seat at the counter. I bet Ellie already has a plate made for us."

Ellie answered, "I bet she does, too." She addressed Kaelen while retrieving milk from the fridge and three glasses from the cupboard. "The lab technician said they were scheduled to water Leah's plants in the SPL shortly, and they'd take the reflective film down at that time. About twenty minutes."

Kaelen licked her lips when she saw the large plate mounded high with fresh cookies. "That is good news. I'll go when we're finished here. After all—" she looked from Leah to Ellie and grinned "—it's important to have sustenance for such an important mission."

Leah laughed and selected a large one from the top. "Ooh, they're still warm." She held it up in the air. Kaelen copied her motion, unsure why Leah didn't immediately eat it. Ellie picked up her own cookie and they moved them together so they could touch, much like the toast that

Kaelen witnessed many times during game nights and at Szot's bar. She moved her cookie to touch theirs as Leah said, "To family, and all our sweet traditions."

Kaelen nodded and took her first bite, moaning at the explosion of flavor. She chewed and swallowed while Leah and Ellie looked on.

"Well, do you like it?"

"Significantly better than the alcohol with the same name. I've added 'plates of Ellie's oatmeal raisin cookies' to my list of favorite things. Does that answer your question?"

Leah giggled and said to Ellie, "Looks like you have a new fan."

"Nonsense, Kaelen isn't a fan, she's family." She smiled as Kaelen shoved another cookie into her mouth. "We'll have to learn what your favorite is so I can make you a special batch too."

Cheeks bulging with cookie, Kaelen rushed to Ellie's side and gave her a safe, tight hug. Initiating such contact communicated the level of Kaelen's comfort and appreciation far more than words ever could.

Chapter Twenty-five

Kaelen opened the door wide enough for Leah's hoverchair to glide through, causing the bell hanging above it to ring sharply. The D-Street Diner hadn't changed much over the years. Leah smiled as she took in the teal booths along the front wall, the jukebox, and pie case with its rotating selection of sweets conveniently placed next to the register. Leah watched Kaelen look around at the décor on the walls. It was a mixture of 1950's era collectibles and pastel paints. "What do you think?"

"It's quite colorful. What kind of food do they have here?"

Leah pointed above the main counter where there was a food list written in chalk. "The menu is up there, or they have printed ones on the tables. Why don't we sit down and decide what we want to eat."

Leah led her to a table that was out of the way from most of the foot traffic. Kaelen moved one of the chairs out and over to the wall next to the jukebox. She paused to stare at the beautiful machine that was comprised of rounded chrome edges and neon lights. "What is it?"

"It's a jukebox, a record player."

Kaelen gave her a curious look. "Records, as in recorded data?"

"Um, no. An old format for musical recordings."

"Oh! How does it work?"

Leah realized that she didn't have any change on her for the jukebox. "I'm not sure I have—"

"Why if it isn't Little Leah! I haven't seen you in a few years. What brings you back to Sello Bay, my dear? Still running the show over in LA?"

Leah smiled at the older woman with curly black hair and quickly raised her hoverchair to accept a hug. "Hi, Monae. I'm glad to see you today. It's definitely been a while for us, even though I stop in at D-Street this time every year. Usually it's with Maddy."

"Yeah, I wasn't here last year. Had myself a bad cold all through Christmas. And the year before I had to go out east to help my daughter with her newborn. I've sure missed seeing you and Maddy's smiling faces. Most people move away and never come back but not you two. Ellie is one lucky mama."

"Ooh, I didn't know Carmen had kids. Congrats to her then. Maddy and her fiancé will be up in a few days. Until then, I'm showing my own girlfriend around."

Kaelen held out her hand. "Hi, I'm Kaelen. It is my pleasure to meet you."

Monae took the offered hand. "Aren't you the cutest thing, and so polite!" She winked at Leah. "Don't let Miss Kaelen get away now. I'm guessing if you're bringing her here to Sello Bay, things are pretty serious."

Kaelen nodded as Leah said, "Definitely serious. She's my one."

Monae tucked a notebook into the front pocket of her apron with one hand and wagged the pen at Leah with the other. "Well then you better listen to Queen B with this young lady."

At Kaelen's confused look, Leah explained. "She's talking about the old Beyoncé song, 'Single Ladies.'"

Her eyes widened. "Oh, the one Nalla mentioned when Tasha proposed formal marriage with Maddy. It's a strangely popular song given the fact that it was released thirty years ago."

Leah shrugged. "What can I say, she was one of those formative artists."

Kaelen smiled up at Monae. "I have no plans of escape because Leah and I are courting. She is my match by a probability of at least ninety-nine-point-four percent."

"Oh my, another sweet face with a big brain is more than a match for Miss Dimples here."

"Wait, when did you—how did you calculate that?"

Kaelen shrugged. "I had Wex run the predictive algorithms a few weeks ago with the DNA match program found in its database." She paused and appeared worried. "I'm sorry I didn't tell you when it completed. I wasn't sure if you put a lot of emphasis on such things the way my pe—uh," she glanced at Monae, then back to Leah. "Family used to."

"Are you kidding? Kaelen, it's amazing!"

"You two are funny. Since this is Kaelen's first visit to D-Street, would you like some time to look over the menu or do you know what you want?"

Leah grabbed two of the menus that were in the holder next to the wall. "Give us a few minutes, okay? I'll start with some coffee and orange juice. What about you, Kaelen?"

"Water and iced milk, please."

Monae raised a dark eyebrow at the strange drink request but shrugged. "I'll be back in a few minutes." She pointed her pen at Leah. "And be sure to save room for dessert with whatever you order."

"I will."

Monae left to check another table while Kaelen and Leah looked at the menu. "Since you are so familiar with this restaurant, what is your favorite thing to eat?"

"At Christmas time? I literally order the same breakfast every year, cranberry walnut pancakes with a side of bacon."

Kaelen looked at the menu, her eyes scanning up and down each page as she turned. A few seconds later she closed it and placed it on the table. "Okay, I'm ready. Do I need to temper my appetite here or can I order what I want?"

Leah winked at her. "Eat what you want, Kaelen. I'll enjoy watching Monae's face as she's forced to write it all down."

"Okay."

"You two girls ready? Let me guess, Leah will have her usual, the cranberry walnut pancakes and a side of bacon. Right?" She winked at Kaelen. "That girl's been ordering the same thing for years."

Leah laughed and put her menu back in the holder. "It's not my fault your recipe can't be beat or replicated." She shook her finger at the older woman. "Someday…"

"Yeah, yeah." Monae turned to Kaelen. "And for you, dear?"

"Hey Monae, you may want to take out your order pad for Kaelen.

She has quite the appetite."

Monae looked from Leah to Kaelen. "Nonsense, lay it on me, Miss Kaelen."

Kaelen took a deep breath and began, "Reuben omelet with sides of bacon, hash browns, and rye toast. The waffles with bananas foster and whipped cream. The cranberry walnut pancakes, because Leah wouldn't lie about something that was good enough to eat every time that she comes in."

"Is that all?"

Kaelen shook her head. "I'd also like the biscuits and gravy, a piece of chocolate mousse pie, and the peanut butter bliss." She put her menu in the holder with Leah's.

"Uh—" Monae's mouth opened then shut. She looked at Leah. "Is she for real?"

"I warned you."

With a shrug, Kaelen explained, "Leah says I have sweet teeth."

"It's a sweet tooth, darling." Leah knew Monae would be okay with the order. She was a smart woman and Kaelen wasn't the first alien to come through Sello Bay. When Leah first moved there after the death of her family, Monae had Trigeri twins working for her in the kitchen and had proven to be quite open over the years.

Monae tutted, "Sweet teeth she says. Fine, I'll put your orders in."

Kaelen lifted her eyebrows. "You remembered all that without writing it down?"

"Miss Kaelen, I've been doing this a long time and have an impeccable memory. I'm good at watching the world around me and remembering every detail." She tapped her temple then rattled off Kaelen's entire order. "We'll have that up right quick. At least it's not too busy." Then she turned on her heel and walked toward the swinging door and into the kitchen.

"I forgot to ask because everything got busy the last few days, did you mail your packages before we left the city?"

Kaelen had been looking around the diner, appearing puzzled. Leah assumed that some of Earth's historical junk may be a bit too primitive for her advanced mind to understand. Kaelen brought her gaze back to the other side of the table to answer Leah's question. "Yes. I sent them with the fastest delivery option so they'd arrive in time. And you're sure that the Millers are Christians who celebrate this holiday? I don't recall ever asking when we were there."

Leah snorted. "Pretty sure."

"How do you know?"

"For one, they are white, middle-American, and living in the Midwest."

A wrinkle appeared between Kaelen's eyebrows as she said, "They live in Zeeland in a state on the northern border of this country."

Leah shook her head. "The Midwest is a region that encompasses the northern middle of America. Anyway, that particular region skews toward conservative Christianity."

"I see. But they didn't act particularly conservative. Not like what I've seen on the news. And Tate said he was pansexual on our last trip."

"You're right in that they don't seem socially conservative based on our visits. After all, they're raising an alien boy and have another queer son in art school. However, they do have a cross hanging on the wall in the living room and mentioned they regularly attend church. So, there is your proof of religious affiliation."

"Oh yes, Michael told me about that. Proof is good. No matter where they live, I was assured of a speedy delivery so Michael will receive his fancy telescope that you recommended I buy, as well as the leather-bound journal set. I hope it is okay, but I put your name on the gifts with mine. After all, most were your idea since I wasn't sure what was appropriate."

"Kaelen, you didn't have to do that."

"I know, but I'd like to think that we both wanted to gift him the items, so I addressed them as such. I also picked out gifts I thought Paul, Shelly, and Tate would like and labeled them the same."

Leah reached across the table and clasped Kaelen's hand to give it a squeeze. "Thank you."

"You're welcome. Michael was a little disappointed that I couldn't come visit this month, but he understood given how busy work has been with us getting ready for the trade show. I did tell him that I'd be there in February." Kaelen looked thoughtful. "I don't understand why your February is so dramatic and odd."

"What?"

"Your calendar and leap events are strange. Argon was advanced enough to have a time keeping system that split days into precise increments, thus not needing such adjustments. After all, a second was an artificial construct and nothing but what a society says it is."

Leah snickered. "Darling, Earth's time increments were created long before humans knew much of anything about space, planets, or even science."

Kaelen frowned and only hummed at the new knowledge. "It still could have been adjusted, as you'd need to do every centum millennium anyway, once you reach that far into your recorded existence on this planet."

"Perhaps you should send an email to NIST with your thoughts on the subject when we finish with the conference." Kaelen nodded as if it were a serious suggestion, and Leah hid a smile behind her coffee mug.

After breakfast, Leah took Kaelen to a park in the middle of town where the Winter Festival was set up. There was a selection of tents full of everything from hot chocolate vendors to folks selling arts and crafts. Leah explained that the festival ran for fifteen days, starting the week before Christmas and running until the week after. She said it was a lot busier on the weekends, with games, pony rides, music, and more.

She mentioned that besides the interactive stuff that was sponsored by local businesses, the other side of the park was a wonderland of colorful lights. They could see strands spiraled high up trees. Others were twisted along wire frames to form animals and famous structures.

"Why aren't the lights on?"

"Because it's daytime and they won't be as visible, so there's no point in wasting power. I promise that the entire family will come back to see them when Maddy and Tasha arrive." She squeezed Kaelen's hand. "It's a Tuck tradition to go to dinner then walk through the park with hot chocolates."

"Dinner, chocolate, and colorful lights?" Leah nodded. "I don't know if I've mentioned it to you, but I find Earth holiday traditions endlessly fascinating. I've read about many religions, past and present." She paused. "Why do they call unpracticed religions mythology?"

Leah laughed quietly. "Funny you should ask because that's

a question I've wanted to know the answer to for a long time." She shrugged and Kaelen continued.

"Despite not believing in the same thing as humans, I love the idea of togetherness that many religions celebrate at the coldest, darkest end of the year."

"It's only cold and dark in the northern hemisphere, darling."

Kaelen shrugged. "Even still, all the gatherings of friends, food, gifts, and decorations of lights are enchanting, more so than anything else I've discovered on Earth." She sighed and looked back at the wonderland path as they exited the park toward the van. "I can't wait for Maddy and Tasha to arrive so we can experience even more."

On the night of Christmas Eve, they sat around the living room of the Tuck house. Over the past week, Leah and Kaelen had seen everything in Sello Bay they wanted to see. They'd gone to the beach and watched the ocean at moonrise and sunset. Kaelen was enamored with the great watery expanse, not having anything like it on Argon. The entire family had gone to dinner earlier to give Ellie a break, since they knew she preferred to do most of the cooking on Christmas day. After dinner, they all went to see the Sello Bay Winter Festival of Lights. Hot chocolates in hand and laughter in the air, Kaelen had never felt so included or full.

It was close to nine o'clock and all the lights were off except for the tree, a few LED candles in the windows, and the television. As Leah already explained, it was time for the annual, non-traditional, Christmas Eve movie viewing.

"Is this a good movie?"

Maddy waggled her hand back and forth in answer to Kaelen's question. "Eh…"

Kaelen glanced left where Leah was snuggled next to her on the couch. "Will I like it?"

"Probably. Just remember that it's a comedy and not a serious sci-fi flick."

"Okay." Kaelen directed her gaze over to Tasha. "And you've seen this movie before, last Christmas?"

Tasha snorted. "Unfortunately. Last year was actually my first year seeing it. The movie is ridiculous, but fairly entertaining."

"You can say it, dear. It's just plain stupid but it grows on you. Of course, after a decade I would hope so for my sanity."

A beeping microwave interrupted the conversation, and Kaelen stood since it was her popcorn they'd been waiting on. "Be right back." As promised, she returned seconds later with a steaming bag in hand and resumed her seat. "If the movie is so bad, or questionably bad, why do you watch it every year?"

"Tradition." The word was spoken by Maddy and Leah at the same time.

Ellie held up the remote. "Ready?" When everyone gave their okay, she pushed the play button and the title for *Mars Attacks* displayed on the screen.

Kaelen laughed when the movie was over. Everyone stared at her until she got her humor under control. Leah placed a hand on Kaelen's thigh, concern written all over her face. "Are you okay, darling?"

Kaelen grinned. "I was picturing Nalla and Einstein as the news person and the scientist." That comment sparked laughter from everyone else.

Maddy shook her head. "I would pay money to see his reaction."

Kaelen took care of the popcorn trash, and Ellie turned off the television and put on Christmas music. Then the entire group was allowed to select one gift each from beneath the tree. It was yet another Tuck tradition. Tasha gave Maddy a brewery passport for the many craft breweries scattered throughout Los Angeles and the surrounding region. Maddy gave Tasha a delicate, gold necklace.

Kaelen was shocked by the gift and asked Maddy, "I thought you were already engaged to join houses. Why would you choose to bond without a ceremony or your friends around?"

Maddy's eyes grew wide. "What?"

"The torque—" Kaelen pointed at the gift clasped around Tasha's neck. "On Argon torques are exchanged at the time a couple permanently bonds, or marriage as you call it." Rather than clear up confusion, Kaelen watched as Maddy grew noticeably pale. "Did I say something wrong?"

Tasha was smiling, as was Ellie, but Leah laughed. "Oh my God,

Maddy! Look at your face."

"Talk about skipping a few steps!"

Leah turned to Kaelen. "You're freaking her out. Unlike Argon, the Earth marriage ceremony only involves rings. It's traditional for the person asking to give a ring when a couple is engaged. Then they exchange different rings at the time of the actual marriage ceremony. Necklaces, or torques in this case, are just a nice gift to show you care about someone."

Kaelen thought about her own bonding torques in the *palda* at her apartment. She wondered if she'd ever be able to give them to someone here when Earth customs were so different. "Oh."

Apparently recovered from her scare, Maddy sat back on the couch. "I guess I never considered how different your people's customs were compared to ours. You say you've got permanent bonding, but how does it work? Do you give the torque as an engagement gift, or what?"

"When Argonians bond it's a joining of houses. Our tradition is to have a match assigned to you by the DNA match program. Match assignment usually occurred after the age of induction, though families had been known to run the test when children were younger so they could best prepare for the merging of the houses. Some Argonian houses, especially higher ones like *Dolem*-Ra, would gift guildmembers with their bonding torques right after induction."

Tasha's eyes widened with alarm and Maddy blurted out, "Wait, you had arranged marriages?"

"Does that mean you have bonding torques, or were they lost with your planet?"

Leah answered for her. "Their marriages weren't like what you're thinking. Argonians had an advanced computer program that analyzed genetics, intellect, personality, and physical potential, as well as compatibility between two houses."

"Kaelen, you mentioned that you were inducted before you left Argon. Did you have a match?"

Tasha was one of the most astute and emotionally mature people Kaelen had ever met. She shook her head. "They were going to run the analysis later in the year as I'd only inducted not long before I was sent away. I—" Kaelen sighed because the memories were still difficult.

Leah rubbed her thigh. "You don't have to talk about it. I know this is hard still. We'll understand."

And Kaelen knew they would. If any group of people, any family could, it was the four others in the room with her who'd all lived with their own losses. "It's okay, I don't mind sharing with you. I was only thirteen when I was inducted and had barely begun work and research full time since I'd completed all Argonian education available. My *vrenesh*—family—thought it would be good to wait until I was older before requesting a match. Now I'm happy they did."

"Why?"

Kaelen considered Maddy's question. "Argonians bond for life. The bond wasn't always for sexual purposes as most were," she glanced at Ellie, understanding that Earthlings were hung up on topics of sexuality, "ace or asexual. They were a bond of friendship, love of one sort or another, and house strength. And while you could request a new match, the program provided the best one first, so it wasn't considered sound. Most didn't unless there was an unforeseen accident and one of the matches died."

"What do you mean by love of one sort or another?"

"On Argon we have many types of love. *Shofl* is non-romantic or familial, but rather for inanimate objects or pets. *Zhee* is romantic love, or lust. And *kinec* is familial love."

Tasha nodded. "We have the same notions with different words. Philial is non-romantic between friends or family members. Eros is romantic love. We actually have many different words for all the various states. Ludus is playful, mania is obsessive, agape is selfless love, uh, and more. You can google types of love and find all the forms. Believe it or not, love is a common topic that comes up in therapy."

Ellie spoke up, "Kaelen, you mentioned that this computer sets matches for your people, but what was the bonding ceremony like? How will that work for you and young Michael now without your match program?"

Kaelen glanced at Leah and found an intense look on her beloved's face. "Technically, I brought the program with me in my ship. Wex is fully capable and has already run a match analysis. As I said, Argonians bond for life. Our society has no, uh, divorce like Earth."

"Holy shit."

"Maddy, language."

Tasha held up a hand. "Wait, you said Wex has already run match analysis for you?" Kaelen nodded.

"And it found someone here on Earth?" "Yes."

Maddy narrowed her eyes. "Who?"

Kaelen glanced at Leah again and grew warm at the smile directed at her. "I was matched at ninety-nine point-four percent with Leah Lockheed-Tuck."

Ellie's eyebrows lifted. "Is there something you girls need to tell me?"

Leah's cheeks turned pink. "Not yet."

"Isn't it a given though with your matching thingy?" Maddy waved her hand vaguely back and forth toward where Kaelen and Leah sat on the love seat.

"No." Kaelen felt Leah tense next to her and rushed to explain. "I'm not on Argon and would never assume that Leah would comply with Argonian customs. While I am certain of our courtship, I will always respect her wishes concerning the length and future of our relationship."

Maddy raised her hand. "Wait, you never answered the question about your own bonding torques. Did you receive them after induction?"

"Of course. I keep my torques in a secure place."

"You still have them?" Leah looked at Kaelen in surprise. They'd discussed her torques previously, but never that she still had them in her possession.

"Yes. They're in my apartment, along with my holocube. But I would never expect you to follow my traditions, should we reach the point where you want to progress to a more permanent bonding." Kaelen didn't mention to Leah or the rest that within her heart, she knew there would be no one else for her but Leah. But after many lunches with Nalla Bel, she'd come to understand that humans were much slower to bond and move forward in the progression of love. She had time and would have patience with her chosen.

Leah lifted Kaelen's hand and kissed the back tenderly. "I want you to know right here and now that I'm open to other cultures and traditions. Perhaps we can discuss the differences later?"

The rest of the room faded away. "I'd like that."

"Get a room!" Kaelen felt the air change and caught the pillow that Maddy threw at them. With a casual flick of her wrist, she sent it back with impeccable accuracy. "*Oof*! Leah," Maddy whined, "you need to find yourself a clumsier, less perfect, girlfriend."

Everyone laughed and the evening progressed from where it left off before the strange, culturally-heavy, discussion began. Since eyes were on Kaelen and Leah, they retrieved one of their gifts for each other from beneath the tree.

Kaelen had trouble coming up with gift ideas for Leah, until she remembered that family was one of the most important things to her. With Wex's help, Kaelen made a holocube, similar to what she'd traveled from Argon with, and filled it with images of both Leah's families, the Lockheeds and the Tucks. Leah got Kaelen a soft knit beanie with matching scarf and mittens. Even though Kaelen couldn't feel the discomfort of cold weather the way a human could, she appreciated the gift because Leah said she looked adorable.

The last gifts to be opened before everyone went to bed were for Ellie. Leah bought Ellie the Alaskan cruise she'd been wanting to go on for ages, and Maddy bought her a new digital camera with a zoom lens.

Later, when everyone had retired for the night, Kaelen and Leah lay curled up together on the sofa bed in the den. "Darling," Leah said.

Kaelen opened her eyes to see Leah watching her in the low light. "Yes?"

"I meant what I said about your culture. I want to share your customs in regards to relationships and bonding, whenever you're ready to take the next step."

Kaelen blinked. "Your wording…it sounds like you're implying that we're at different emotional levels." She took a breath and let it out, contemplating how much to admit. She was afraid of pushing Leah or putting an unfair amount of expectation on her shoulders where their relationship was concerned. "I want you to know that I'm already where I need to be. I simply await your word and permission to move forward."

"Permission?"

"Leah, the match program predicted our success. But more than that, my heart feels you inside where no computer program can touch.

You're my person, whether you believe in bonding houses or not. I'll wait as long as I need for you. Forever if necessary."

"Oh."

"And I know that we are very different people, disparate races. So, I understand that as a human, things take much longer to develop emotionally for you, if they develop at all. I want to give you all the time you need— " The desperate press of soft lips against her own cut off Kaelen's remaining speech. The kiss lasted so long that eventually Leah had to stop to breathe. Kaelen found herself breathless as well, for completely different reasons.

Leah smiled at her in the near-darkness. "In case that didn't answer your declaration, I'll tell you now that my love for you is immeasurable. I would be honored to wear the symbol of your house, should we mutually decide to make our relationship permanent."

"Is that something you wish for? A permanent romance with someone?"

"More than anything."

Kaelen was silent, understanding exactly what Leah meant. It wasn't a future promise, but rather a statement of now. She moved away from Leah on the bed before leaving it entirely. Kaelen turned on the light in the den, and Leah quickly got out of the bed, looking concerned.

They stood in silence, separated by nearly two feet.

"Darling, what's wrong?"

"Nothing is wrong. Please be patient. I've only seen this performed once." Leah nodded and Kaelen brought her palms together in front of her face, pointed up the way some Earthlings pray. She slowly lowered her hands until they rested at the base of her breastbone, then rotated her wrists to point the tips of her fingers toward Leah. Without breaking eye contact, Kaelen opened her hands to show her palms and recited the ages-old Argonian bonding request.

"Leah Lockheed-Tuck, *vrenesh i cluhz ut zhetinao ne ra pret ne Dolemn*-Lockheed."

"Kaelen…" Her name was a whisper from Leah's lips and Kaelen waited, understanding that it would take her love a minute to translate and respond.

Leah took a deep breath and sent a beauteous smile her way. "I, uh…

as house… *Dolemn*-Lockheed, I accept a bond of heart and intellect with *Dolem*-Ra." Seemingly unsure what to do after that, Leah placed her hands atop Kaelen's so they pressed palm to palm.

Kaelen pulled her into a hug. Tears fell and she didn't care because she'd never felt more loved or accepted in her entire life. "Thank you, *zhee*. I promise to cherish you as long as I live."

When they pulled apart, Leah wiped the tears from Kaelen's face. "Does this mean we're engaged?"

"I, uh—" Kaelen rubbed the back of her neck. "Yes. We are now matched and committed to bond. Ellie and Maddy won't be angry with me, will they? Was I supposed to ask them?"

Leah laughed quietly. "No, Kaelen. I don't need anyone's permission to dedicate myself to someone. You are exactly who I want to spend my life with. We can discuss possible ceremonies at a later date but rest assured, this is what I want."

"Okay. Thank you for the gift of your heart. There is no greater treasure in life than love."

"Is that an Argonian saying?"

Kaelen shook her head and leaned forward to give Leah another kiss. When they pulled back again, she said softly, "It's mine."

Chapter Twenty-six

Ellie, Maddy, and Tasha were overjoyed to learn of Leah and Kaelen's strange engagement. Kaelen mentioned her fear that Maddy would caution Leah against an official pairing because she was so overprotective and their courtship had been rather short by human standards. Instead, she clapped Kaelen on the shoulder and said she trusted her sister's judgment. After celebrating the holiday with Leah's family for a few days, the entourage found themselves on the move again.

Leah, Kaelen, and Leah's security team flew into the Las Vegas McCarran International Airport on Tuesday, three days after Christmas. Ellie, Einstein, and the rest of the scientists, sales, and setup crews would follow after the first of the year.

To best mask Leah's itinerary, the team switched vehicles outside Los Angeles and arranged to have the motorhomes driven to their normal storage location. They went from that point straight to the airport to avoid leaking any news of Leah's presence to Mimic. They couldn't do anything about Leah's highly publicized presentation scheduled for the first day of the CES, but at least her travel there would be relatively safe.

It was late when they approached McCarran, and Kaelen watched out the window toward the famous Las Vegas strip with something akin to awe. She glanced at Leah, looking conflicted.

"What is it, darling?"

"You know how much I hate waste, and I suspect diverting this much energy and water to a large desert city is excessive, even by Earth standards." Leah nodded. "Despite that, I can find something beautiful about all the lights below. You mentioned we would be partaking of the local entertainment, but I had no idea the main street was going to be a visual wonder."

"It's true that Las Vegas is known by many nicknames, including the City of Excess, and Sin City. But you're right in that it's become a playground for entertainment of all kinds. Gambling, music, stage shows, oddities, and everything in between."

Kaelen frowned. "Should we be enjoying this?" She waved her hand toward the lights below as the plane began its descent.

Leah squeezed her fingers. She'd been afraid to fly after the disaster of Flight 327. But the person who had saved her then was in the next seat, so it helped immensely. "You know I hate waste as well. That's why I chose our activities carefully to mitigate our carbon footprint. What you probably don't know is that Las Vegas is one of the testing grounds for our most recent solar grid. On top of that, another company has built an express underground transportation solution to help eliminate some of the cars and congestion in the city."

Leah scowled. "While the visionary responsible for The Boring Company is full of narcissism and ego, he has had, and implemented, some great ideas. The Loop was created so people can move around in automated electric vehicles in a more efficient manner. The tunnels require less cooling, maintenance, and energy than the streets above."

Kaelen lifted her eyebrows at Leah's description. "Impressive. Will we be able to see this loop?"

"It's actually referred to as the Las Vegas Convention Center Loop, so yes. CES is so large that it's hosted at a dozen different venues, grouped into three geographical areas. Tech East, Tech West, and Tech South."

"It sounds as though you've attended often."

Leah smiled at her as the plane gave a bump when it touched down. "Tech is big business and if I want my company to stay on top, I have to know what and who I'm up against. I go every year." She glanced out the window before training her eyes back on Kaelen. "The Loop will take you from one end of the convention to the other if you need. There are also shuttles, taxies, and a monorail."

Twenty minutes later, Kaelen stood to disembark, head tilted at an odd angle beneath the overhead compartment. Kaelen always seemed to be aware of the space around her. Perhaps she'd learned such awareness when also learning about her yellow sun gifts. Leah imagined that someone of such immense power and invulnerability had the potential to accidentally do a lot of damage if they weren't careful. It was one of the many questions she had yet to ask.

"Where are we staying?"

"Jenna booked the Grand Lakeview suite at the Bellagio. Ellie will stay with us when she arrives. Jenna also booked a block of rooms for the security squad that came with us. Hans has another team he hires whenever we're here, but they won't need rooms onsite. It's a standing job with a reputable Las Vegas firm."

Kaelen frowned. "I'm not going to let anything happen to you."

"I know that and truthfully, I'm not worried. We've kept my itinerary secret and Jenna says nothing was leaked to the Los Angeles press about me coming back into town before flying here. I think we've given Mimic the slip for the time being. Hans's main concern will be the actual conference where I'm slated to present."

Leah observed Kaelen intently watching around them as they disembarked. The wrinkle meant she was worried and probably listening with her enhanced hearing as well. Even so, Leah was startled when Kaelen pulled out her phone and spoke quietly into it.

"Wex, continuously scan local channels for any mentions of a rogue Chromodec while we're here."

"Yes, Kaelen Ra-Evon. I've also taken the liberty to access a geosynchronous satellite to monitor the region for strange anomalies and energy signatures. I am ignoring any readings from the secure government training complex located northwest of Las Vegas."

Leah found Wex's words curious. They stepped aside to wait for Hans and his team to join them and asked, "Secure government training complex? Wait, is Wex referring to Area 51?"

"Yes, Leah Lockheed-Tuck. That is the place I am referring to."

Leah frowned at the phone in Kaelen's hand and Kaelen snickered at her. "Apparently it is. What is significant about that place?"

Hans and his team joined them for the walk to baggage claim and Leah explained. "It started as a secret government research base hidden in the middle of the desert. It's actually the place where Chromodecs were first created—er, discovered? The details on that government debacle are still redacted despite the fact that it happened nearly ninety years ago."

"It's no longer used for research?"

Leah shook her head. "The CORP took it over as their main training center after the Chromodec Uprising. It's far enough out of the way so people with power aren't a threat to anyone nearby. Before that, their training and detention centers were located down at Guantanamo Bay."

"Yes, I remember you telling me about it, and I read about the event on the internet. Why was it moved to Nevada? The information I searched didn't mention the reason."

Leah shrugged. "It's pretty common knowledge now, I guess. The region around Guantanamo Bay was rendered a heap of slag after Nova took out Colonel Marek Meza by turning a missile he launched back onto him."

"Oh, that incident."

"Yes, well, no one knew she was an alien at the time and there was a lot of fear and anxiety about Chromodecs because of the Uprising. The CORP launched a campaign of rebuilding and rebranding, which has gone a long way toward mitigating the negative image that came with such a terrible tragedy."

"I can see how humans would fear such an event and the people who perpetrated it. The powerless often fear those with power."

"It's true. I think that's why transparency was a key objective with the CORP agencies located in each city. Protecting the citizens and places of Earth is also a top priority for the government, and that's probably why they allow for the sanctioned heroes. While their identities are unknown, they've proven many times that they'll follow the CORP code."

"Which is?"

"Peace, prosperity, and protection."

"Interesting."

Once they were outside the airport, they found two electric transport vans waiting for them, courtesy of Jenna. Both had a cargo area large enough to accommodate Leah's hoverchair, like the one hired in Michigan. A third of the security team rode with them, while the rest took the other van. Leah shivered a bit in the chilly air and zipped up her jacket. She watched as Kaelen looked around, taking in others doing the same, and copied their motion. Her alien biology forced her to keenly observe her surroundings to best fit in with the humans.

It didn't take long for the group to arrive at the hotel and check in. It was early evening. They had spent an entire day traveling between the drive from Sello Bay and the flight to Vegas.

Leah wasn't tired and knew that Kaelen wouldn't be either. However, she didn't want to tax her team more than necessary. Hans would need some time to put his security detail in place. She'd given him the itinerary for what she planned to do before CES, as well as what the schedule was once the conference started.

"Hans, it's been a long day and it's probably best if Kaelen and I take dinner in our suite tonight. We'll head out tomorrow to see the local sights. I trust that Jenna already sent you the itinerary?"

"Yes, Miss Leah."

"Excellent. We'll have breakfast in the room as well. After that, the vans are scheduled to pick us up and drop us off at the Grand Canyon tour company."

He nodded. "I'll have the team ready. Four from the local crew will stay outside the suite, but the rest will come with us. The Vegas team will also help cover off shifts and late evenings."

"That sounds good. Once everything is set, I don't see why you all can't enjoy your evening on the strip. Here," Leah reached into the case that was attached to her chair and pulled out a wallet. From it she withdrew a handful of large bills. She counted out one for each member of the security team that came with them from Los Angeles. Leah held out the stack of cash to Hans and he took it with a serious expression, the same he always wore. "Tell them that money won is twice as sweet as money earned."

Her words garnered a smile. "That was a great movie and I will." Then he nodded to them both. "Good evening, Miss Leah, Miss Kaelen."

Kaelen gave a little wave. "Bye, Hans." Then she turned to Leah. "I read about the Grand Canyon. How will we tour that with you in your hoverchair?"

"I certainly don't plan on hiking! I found a specialty tour company that uses brand new Sikorsky Dragonfly electric helicopters. They are larger and faster than the original firefly and can take a few passengers. The company promises only renewable energy sources by utilizing solar charging for their battery packs. After the Grand Canyon tour, we'll take a much shorter one to visit the Hoover Dam."

"I'm excited to see such wonderous features on Earth's landscape. Perhaps someday I'll travel the planet to see more." Kaelen paused before continuing. "That is…if it's something you'd like to do. I don't think travel is as enjoyable when doing it alone."

"I'll admit that I've been solely focused on running my company from a relatively young age. Not to mention all the difficulties involved with traveling while disabled and limited to a chair. What I'm trying to say is that while I've gone around the planet for business many times, I've never really traveled for pleasure. I'd love to see the world with you."

"That makes me happy."

Kaelen was far from stupid and not nearly as naïve as when she first began working at Lockheed. There was something special about seeing her face as she experienced each new and wonderful thing. Ellie's homemade cookies, random puppies in the park, the beauty of a sunset that apparently looks remarkably similar to the rose light found on Argon. Leah wanted a million more moments with her like those. She tilted her head when she noticed Kaelen's attention wander. "What is it?"

Kaelen beamed. "The door is locked and no one's around. The suite doesn't contain cameras or other sub or supersonic listening devices. That means—" she held out her hands to Leah, who immediately raised her own arms to interlock their fingers together. Kaelen pulled her up from the chair. "You can walk around as free as you like."

"Thank you." Leah used the moment to embrace Kaelen and burrow her nose against the soft skin of her neck. She loved the smell of her and decided months before that it must have something to do with Kaelen's own unique biology.

Kaelen returned the embrace. Her voice was quiet in Leah's ear. "I know how much you want to stop using the chair now that your injury is fully healed. How have you felt since the last injection?"

Leah considered the question. "I feel better than I've ever felt in my life. It's pretty exhilarating, actually."

"It's only a few more days, then we'll unveil our project and revolutionize the world. I can't wait to help all the people who want to recover from paralysis."

Leah pulled back and met those heartbreaking blue eyes. "You know what I can't wait for?"

"What?"

"I can't wait to walk by your side for the rest of my life."

Kaelen pulled her close again and they reveled in each other's touch. The mood was abruptly shifted when Kaelen's stomach gave a loud growl.

Leah smirked as she stepped back. "Dinner?"

"Yes, please. I ate one of my special bars on the plane, but I'd enjoy real food now."

"I'm sure we can make that happen in a place this expensive. Let's go find a room service menu."

The next day they saw the most famous landscape from the air. Leah had been there before, but she was excited to watch Kaelen witness the world wonder. Her face glowed with joy and it made Leah's heart happy to share it with someone she loved.

At one point, Kaelen turned to Leah within the fairly quiet helicopter. "There was nothing like this on Argon. We had some rivers and local flora and fauna, but much had died along with the planet. A lot of our geology was crystalline in form and didn't erode like Earth rock."

"Fascinating." The more Leah learned of the alien planet, the more she longed to explore beyond the boundaries of Earth. Perhaps someday they'd be able to fly to the stars together.

It was going on five p.m. by the time they arrived back at the hotel. They had dinner reservations for seven, which gave them about an hour and a half to get ready for a night out before they had to leave. Once again, Leah lamented the fact that she was still stuck in her hoverchair. Then she immediately thought of all the less fortunate people who had no special nanobot therapy or serum and would continue to be plagued by various injuries and difficulties. Leah Lockheed was well aware that she was in a place of privilege. She sighed.

"What's wrong?"

"Nothing. I'm reminding myself of all the things I have, rather than act like a spoiled child because I can't have something exactly when I want it. Did you get a chance to program a new dress outfit for our dinner tonight?"

Kaelen gave her a smile that was strangely reminiscent of her sister when Maddy was keeping a secret. "I did."

"Did you peruse some of the design links I sent?"

"No. I asked Maddy for ideas while we were still at Ellie's."

"When was this?"

"When you rode with Ellie into town the day before we left. I asked Maddy for advice and she brought up a few pictures of things she thought you'd like."

"Oh really? And will you show me before we head out to dinner?"

Kaelen shook her head, still wearing that mischievous smile.

"Whyever not?"

"She also told me that it would be better received if it were a surprise, and that I should listen to your heartbeat when you saw me."

Leah crossed her arms and grumped. "Maddy and I need to have a discussion about coaching a person's significant other into keeping secrets."

Kaelen caressed the side of her neck, following her fingers with feather light kisses until her lips were next to Leah's ear. "Trust me."

Leah shivered and sucked in a breath. "I do."

"Good. Now, you mentioned that you wanted to bathe and change." Kaelen brought out her cell phone to look at the time. "Based on how long it usually takes you to get ready for an upper echelon event, you should probably begin soon."

Leah shook her finger in the face of the woman who knew too much for her own good, and Kaelen playfully caught it gently between her teeth. "You shouldn't test my resolve, or you'll find us dining in for a second night in a row."

Kaelen cocked her head, then returned her gaze to Leah. "Is it still considered eating in if we're eating out? That's the correct phrase, right?"

That comment brought Leah to a full stop. "Oh my God! Who are you and what have you done with my awkward alien fiancé?"

Kaelen shrugged. "Nalla told me that it was okay to be playful in both speech and deed. I learned the phrase from her and thought you may enjoy flirtatious banter, but I can stop if you like—"

Leah cut off her rambling with a passionate kiss. When they pulled apart again, Leah was panting and Kaelen appeared slightly dazed. "Don't stop. I think it's a wonderful thing. Now, I'm off to get ready since apparently my readiness needs are predictable."

Leah returned to the main suite a little over an hour later. She looked around but didn't see Kaelen anywhere. "Darling?"

The faintest of wind gusts blew against Leah's face as Kaelen suddenly appeared in front of her, mouth hanging open as she stared at Leah's lavender jumpsuit with the plunging neckline. The color complimented her complexion and dark hair. "You look amazing!"

Leah looked Kaelen up and down and shook her head. "So says the goddess made flesh in front of me." The sides of Kaelen's short blonde hair were smoothed back, and the top had a slight amount of lift to it. She wore a simple black suit with a crisp white dress shirt beneath the jacket. The necktie was also black and skinny, left slightly loose. Leah used it to pull Kaelen closer, licking her lips.

"Are you sure this looks good? Your increased respiration and dilated pupils indicate heightened attraction, but I'm concerned that it will not fit the aesthetic of the—rfmrf." Leah made sure Kaelen couldn't finish her statement.

As the kiss ended, Leah released her gentle grip on the tie and they pulled away from each other. "Darling, you look positively sinful, perfect for an evening in Vegas. But you have to tell me where Maddy came up with this idea."

"She mentioned that when you were younger, you had a crush on an actress by the name of Kate Winslet, even though most of her movies were made decades previous. You apparently watched all her movies and had pictures of her and someone named Robert Pattinson hanging on your side of the room." Leah felt her face heat as Kaelen continued. "Then Maddy showed me photos from a magazine where the woman was wearing a suit…this suit, so I scanned the image into my nano program to add to the design files."

Leah laughed. "Unbelievable."

"I'm not lying—" Leah's finger pressed against Kaelen's lips.

"*Shh*, it's only a saying. Now, we better head to dinner before I decide to cancel the reservation and have you instead!"

Kaelen flushed. The pink washing across her cheekbones only added to the allure. Leah winked as she reapplied her lipstick and settled into her hoverchair.

Many hours later, back in their suite for the night, Leah panted on the bed with her arm thrown over her eyes. The suit didn't stay on long when they returned, but then neither did Leah's outfit. The day had been full of fun and new experiences and Leah smiled to think of all the adventures they'd share together in the years to come.

Leah paced around the suite while Ellie and Kaelen looked on. In less than two hours, she would introduce their revolutionary new treatment to the world.

"Honey, try to relax. Everything is going to be fine." Ellie said. She'd warned Kaelen earlier that Leah would stress all the way until she gave her presentation. Only then would she settle into the role of a charismatic and informative speaker.

"I know, I know! But I need to bleed off some of this manic energy." Leah stopped abruptly. "This is the first time I've been able to physically work it off before a conference. I didn't know I was someone who paced!"

Ellie gave her a hug. "I think you've got a lot of learning to do in regards to habits and hobbies now that you're no longer limited to the hoverchair." She pulled back and held Leah by the shoulders. "This medical advancement is going to help so many people."

"It really is. And we owe most of that discovery to Einstein and Kaelen. Speaking of, where is Einstein?"

"He said he wanted to leave early to make sure the presentation was set up exactly to your preference." Leah made to speak and Kaelen held up her hand. "He also said that he knows you pay your people well to do the things you ask them to do, but he would feel better to double check the details himself."

Leah smiled and breathed a sigh of relief. "And you two don't mind that I'm the one presenting this to the world? After all, it was mostly your collaborative discovery."

"*Zhee*," Ellie had stepped away and Kaelen moved to fill the space right in front of Leah. "You are Lockheed International and the best way to show the world what we've achieved. I'm honored to have you present our project. Now, we should leave soon. Even with the speed and efficiency of our security team, I've seen enough of the convention crowd milling around Las Vegas to know that it is sure to be busy on the first day."

"Good point." Leah looked around the room. "Are we ready then?"

"When you are, dear." Ellie slung her purse across her chest.

Kaelen knew that everything they needed was already at the venue. She herself only wore her ship suit, programmed to something Leah referred to as business casual, and her communicators. She figured it was the easiest way to stay in touch with Wex while it monitored Las Vegas.

Leah settled into the hoverchair and took a deep breath. "Let's do this."

The security team dropped off Leah, Ellie, and Kaelen where Leah was scheduled to present. They would be at the venue for the entire day so wouldn't need transportation again until later. Leah and Ellie wanted to check on Lockheed's booth after the presentation, but everyone anticipated an influx of interview requests once the big announcement was made.

Kaelen and Ellie each gave Leah a kiss and hug before she made her way backstage with her security personnel. Hans had two men at every entrance to the auditorium, as well as guards backstage with Leah. Kaelen was thankful that she'd be surrounded by her team.

Wex hadn't reported any anomalies, but Kaelen kept her senses heightened as a precaution. She was seated next to Ellie in a section reserved for them in the front row. Einstein sat on the other side of Ellie, while the scientists from Lab 12 were in the next row back.

When it was time for Leah to speak, the murmuring of the crowd fell to a hush as she made her way centerstage in her hoverchair. She was wearing a wireless headset so she could move around as she presented.

She gazed out into the crowd, seeming to look for something before spotting Kaelen. Leah smiled and Kaelen nodded back, mouthing, "*zhee*," to reassure her.

With that, Leah squared her shoulders and began to speak as a video played in the background on a large screen. She had a controller in her hand that she could pause or interact with the presentation as needed. "Many of you already know who I am. After all, why else would you be here?" The crowd chuckled around them. "For those of you that don't, my name is Leah Lockheed-Tuck and I'm the CEO of Lockheed International."

Leah moved around the stage as she spoke. She made eye contact to connect with the crowd while explaining the different points of their discovery. Leah spoke on how the project was split between multiple labs working on two different cure vectors. She discussed the breakthroughs made by Lab 12, calling out each member of their team by name.

"The genetic modification and expansion of regulatory T-cells broke boundaries we only dreamed possible. But it wasn't until we combined the serum with the medical nanobots created primarily by Clevna Trog and Kaelen Ra-Evon, that we saw the breakthrough we'd been searching for."

Murmuring rose from the crowd as people speculated on the nature of the breakthrough, then Leah began speaking again.

"I'm here to officially announce that my company has found a way to repair spinal cord injury."

The noise around them grew and Kaelen heard more than one person talking about proof. Ellie leaned over and whispered, "This is where she grabs them. I cannot wait to see how they react." She chuckled and Kaelen joined her, knowing the humans around them were sure to be "blown away" according to Maddy.

Leah smiled and looked around the massive room. "I know you have doubts. Any logical person would. What if I told you we've been running trials for months and I have a dozen individuals who have achieved partial mobility? That those same people are only halfway through the treatments?" Leah paused for effect, and Kaelen watched her take a deep breath, perhaps to ready herself for what was to come.

"What if I told you that Lockheed International had one trial candidate who started earlier and already had one hundred percent mobility, with full recovery from an L2 spinal cord injury and subsequent paraplegia?" Murmuring got louder and Leah raised her voice to be heard clearly. "The spinal cord was severely compromised and the injury itself more than a decade old, which compounded the complications involved with full recovery."

Leah looked around one last time, then while keeping her gaze fixed on Kaelen, pushed a button on the hoverchair and lowered it all the way to the ground. She figuratively brought the audience to their knees when, as if it were no big deal, she neatly hopped out of the chair and stood before the crowd. "I was patient zero, but I'm certainly not going to be the last. Not only will I ensure this treatment is available to the entire world, but Lockheed International intends to make it affordable."

Leah pushed a button on her watch to send the chair away while the crowd devolved into astonished chaos. Leah laughed and motioned for quiet. People began taking their seats again as she moved the presentation to the last question and answer screen. "Now, what would you like to know? I've got about twenty minutes left with you so make them count."

Kaelen turned to tell Ellie that she thought Leah was enjoying everyone's amazement, but before she could speak, Wex's computerized voice filled her ear.

"Kaelen Ra-Evon, I am detecting a magnetic anomaly in the region directly over your location. The last satellite scan indicated an abnormal field of magnetism approaching Las Vegas from the southwest."

"Magnetic anomaly?"

"What was that, honey?"

Kaelen turned to Ellie. "Wex said it registered a magnetic anomaly over our location." Kaelen listened but couldn't hear anything out of place. Unfortunately, the conference boasted thousands of attendees and it would be nearly impossible to detect one unfamiliar heartbeat amongst the masses.

"Do you think it's Mimic?"

"I'm not sure. I've met two with powers of magnetism who are CORP agents, but I don't know how Mimic would have gotten their power unless—"

The ceiling above the stage suddenly exploded inward, raining debris everywhere. People screamed and threw themselves to the ground between the seats. It happened so fast and with so little warning that Kaelen only had time to protect Ellie, Einstein, and the people right behind them from flying metallic shrapnel. She changed her suit configuration and was about to ask if they were okay when the inconceivable happened.

Thump-thump. Thump…thump. Thump—

Leah's previously steady and strong heartbeat slowed, then stopped.

She turned her head toward the stage and screamed, "No!"

"Honey, what's wrong? Can you see Leah, is she okay?"

Kaelen shook her head. "Her heart, it's stopped— she's gone!" Kaelen sped onto the stage and found Leah's body pinned beneath one of the fallen girders. She was bleeding from numerous cuts and her neck was twisted at an odd angle. Kaelen lovingly cleared the largest debris from around her and straightened Leah's body. Kaelen's x-ray vision showed a severe skull fracture at the back of Leah's head, probably from the same impact that broke her neck. Her love's heart remained silent and Kaelen grieved.

The death of her family was nothing. The loss of her planet and people couldn't compare to the woman lying still beneath her hands. Tears fell and Kaelen clenched her fists.

Hearing another loud heartbeat nearby, Kaelen looked up and spied a familiar face floating above the opening in the roof, one she recognized from Lockheed's security footage. Mimic smiled down at the destruction below and Kaelen's eyes glowed nearly blue with rage. "You!" Kaelen Ra-Evon began to rise from the stage and the expression on Mimic's face changed to one of fear.

Despite Kaelen's abundance of love and affable personality, she was a woman who had lost too many people in her relatively young life, and now Mimic had cost her one more. The most significant one. Anger was familiar to Kaelen, but the rage was something new and poisonous. It was destructive and incredibly difficult to control when suffering the agony of infinite loss. In an instant, Kaelen disappeared under an avalanche of painful emotion and Scion lifted to the surface.

She had no time for the CORP or their precious laws. Mimic would face justice for her ruinous actions.

Chapter Twenty-seven

As soon as Kaelen cleared the hole in the collapsed roof of the convention center, she found herself battered by steel beams leftover from the destruction. She quickly collected each one before they could do more damage and put them safely on the ground, then raced after Mimic. Even filled with rage, she was aware of the people around her and didn't want anyone else to be hurt in the chaos.

Mimic chose to flee after seeing Scion shrug off the beams as if they were nothing. It was the Chromodec's first mistake. Kaelen caught her easily over the desert north of Las Vegas. The region was uninhabited and she felt it safe enough to confront Leah's killer without a lot of collateral damage.

Kaelen grabbed Mimic by one leg midair and threw her toward the desert below. She was surprised to find the woman unscathed as she crawled out of the crater created by her impact.

Mimic smirked. "Thanks for letting me borrow your power, bitch."

"Who are you?"

"I'm the one who finished what I started, avenging the death of my family."

The image of Leah, broken and bleeding below the collapsed roof flickered through Kaelen's mind and she saw red yet again. Her laser vision flared, shooting a beam straight into Mimic's chest. The blast sent the woman tumbling backward, her motion ripping a rent in the desert landscape. She cried out but pulled herself up once she came to a stop. Mimic's shirt was burned away but she wore strange alien armor beneath that protected her.

"You have that power too? Ooh, I can't wait to taste them all." Mimic's eyes glowed and a beam shot toward Kaelen. She dodged the well-telegraphed attack.

Kaelen scowled as she realized that the brief contact she had with Mimic when she threw the woman was enough for Mimic to copy her Argonian powers. Her mind raced, attempting to discern whether the Chromodec would have the same strength as she did, or if Mimic would be slightly weaker, much the way a clone or copy of an image was less than the original.

The ground cracked beneath Kaelen's feet as she took off toward Mimic. Her speed and acceleration were so great she broke the sound barrier seconds later. Kaelen was ready for Mimic to dodge her fists but she didn't need to worry. Mimic wasn't practiced enough in her new powers to react the same way as someone who had been using them for over a year. Kaelen plowed into Mimic and sent her into a low range of hills. The ground shuddered and dust filled the air. She pummeled her for a few seconds before Mimic was able to strike out with a fist and drive Kaelen back.

Mimic flew up into the air and hovered while Kaelen pulled herself off the ground. "Why the fuck are you so concerned with the Lockheed's anyway? They're nothing but murderers, the whole family. Putting guns into people's hands. The company road was paved in blood, which eventually killed my parents. My older brother sought revenge and nearly succeeded if he hadn't died the night their car went off the road. I was too young at the time to help."

Calculations, trajectories of attack, and the mystery of what Mimic revealed to her filled Kaelen's head. She wanted her own revenge but something was telling her to listen, to understand. "A family is not one unit, but a collection of individuals. Leah Lockheed-Tuck has done nothing but help society since the day she took over her company. No, before she took over. You were too young to do harm at the time and so was Leah!"

"Yeah, what's your point? She comes from bad blood and it's only a matter of time that the Lockheed greed has her going the same direction as the rest." Suddenly, Mimic copied Kaelen's move from minutes before and took off straight toward her. Kaelen left her position as well and they collided midair over the low mountain range. The sound was heard for miles away.

Unfortunately, with both of them having the same strength and invulnerability, they were too well-matched for a decisive victory. In frustration, Kaelen's anger grew. She blasted Mimic again with her laser vision, but the woman got an arm up in time to block the beam from hitting her face. She yelled in pain and Kaelen hit her again. Mimic tumbled away until she struck the ground. She rose slowly, cradling her arm to her side.

Kaelen had never been in a position where logic and rage warred inside her for control. "You've killed innocent people today, injured and endangered the lives of many more. You need to be stopped."

"And how will you stop me?"

"I'll do whatever it takes," Kaelen growled.

Mimic cocked her head and floated off the ground again, perhaps ready to flee. "I see. So, not only do you defend murderers, but you have no problem becoming one as well. Kill the ones that kill, is that it?" She paused, then added with another smirk. "No matter what you do, the bitch will still be dead." Then without warning, Mimic spun and rocketed away as fast as possible, heading northwest.

Kaelen grew furious and went after her. So focused in her rage, she never heard that precious heartbeat stutter and start again.

The convention center was in chaos. Emergency personnel swarmed the hall looking for wounded and trying to verify that the rest of the auditorium was structurally sound. Rather than flee from the room like everyone else, Ellie and Einstein ran to the stage where they could see Leah's body lying uncovered from when Kaelen had dug her out of the debris.

Ellie checked Leah's pulse and stifled a sob. "Her heart's stopped. Help me do CPR." She cleared more space on the stage so they could work but Einstein put a hand on her arm.

"I'm sorry, Doctor Tuck, but I saw one section of the roof strike Leah on the head before she went down. I suspect the blow broke her neck and killed her instantly." He gestured toward the stage where the blood was pooled around Leah's head. "Notice there—"

"I refuse to believe that!" Ellie dropped to her knees and began doing chest compressions. "We didn't heal Leah with all this technology only to lose her now."

Einstein didn't argue. He knelt on the stage to help her, despite all medical signs that the effort was futile. He gave the appropriate breaths when indicated and in-between, he tried to ascertain the full extent of Leah's injuries. He gave another two breaths, then carefully felt behind the head to inspect the wound.

"Quark!"

Ellie glanced up at him. "What is it?" She was tiring but refused to stop.

Einstein immediately grabbed her shoulders to prevent further compressions.

"What are you doing?"

"Stop. Her heart is beating."

"What?"

Leah's chest suddenly arched from the floor, and she sucked in a dramatic breath before exhaling and lying flat again. She didn't wake, but Einstein could see she was breathing on her own. Einstein carefully turned Leah onto her side and showed Ellie the back of her head. He moved the blood-soaked hair so she could see the unmarked skin of Leah's scalp.

"I…I don't understand."

Einstein was in awe. He never imagined that the replicated nanobots in Leah's body had reached a point where they could respond so fast. This was world changing science. "It's the nanobots. It must be. The serum was good, but Kaelen said they were going to inject the nanobots she personally programmed before leaving for the winter break."

Ellie's mouth dropped open as she looked at Einstein in shock. "What did Kaelen do?"

"Truthfully, I have no idea. She was responsible for that portion of the project. Once the preliminary trials started on the other test subjects, I switched my focus to the micro battery, per Leah's instruction."

"We need to tell Kaelen she's okay."

Einstein thought about the look on Kaelen's face when she realized that Leah was dead. He'd never seen anyone so full of heartbreak and rage, and he feared what Kaelen would do. "She's gone after Mimic."

A phone rang from the edge of the stage and Einstein retrieved it from Leah's hoverchair that was knocked on its side, despite the built-in stabilizers and forcefield. He recognized the name and used Leah's fingerprint to unlock and answer the call, putting it on speakerphone so both of them could hear.

"Miss Lockheed, the CORP fears your life is in great danger. Mimic was able to copy the powers of a CORP agent, one of our mag twins."

Ellie spoke up from where she knelt on the stage holding her daughter's hand. "I'm afraid you're too late, Agent Grath. Mimic already attacked the convention while Leah was speaking."

"Is Leah all right?"

Ellie swallowed thickly. "She—she actually died for a few minutes but she's recovering already."

"How?"

Einstein answered him when Ellie froze as she looked down at her unconscious daughter. "Jove, this is Clevna Trog. I'm one of the scientists working on an experimental nanobot and serum treatment that Leah was unveiling at CES. She was the first recipient and we believe that not only has the treatment fully restored all spinal function, but the nanobots themselves are continuing to work on her body, thus saving her life. She is healing at an unprecedented pace."

"Amazing. And where is Mimic now?"

He was unsure how to answer without giving away Kaelen's identity. He looked at Ellie but she only shrugged back at him. "Scion showed up right after the attack and went after Mimic."

Jove was silent on the other end of the line for a few moments and Einstein heard him sigh. "Scion's abilities are like nothing I've ever seen. She's incredibly powerful and if Mimic copies them, I'm afraid for all the citizens of Las Vegas."

"Actually, Director, I heard two sonic booms so I'm certain they have already left the city. But in all honesty, I too fear the outcome of such a super battle. I've never seen Scion react in anger in all the news coverage nor from eyewitness accounts. But she appeared to be in a rage when she saw that Mimic had killed someone. I hate to think of what could happen to a person under such circumstances who, to date, has done only good."

"I'll keep that in mind, Mister Trog. I'm scrambling agents to teleport to the CORP training facility now. We'll get our two rogues under control. I'd appreciate it if you could update me on Miss Lockheed's condition when you're able."

Einstein knew the rules when it came to divulging medical knowledge. "That will be up to Leah, when she wakes. But I'll pass along your request at that time."

Jove hung up and Einstein set Leah's phone on the ground next to her side. He observed her strong breaths as well as the returning color to her cheeks. "She looks much better." When Ellie didn't answer, he met her intense gaze. "Did I do something wrong?"

"Kaelen is Leah's fiancé and you've sent the CORP after her."

"I'm sorry. I took the logical route. It is better that the CORP stop her from doing something she'll never return from than to let her take out unnecessary vengeance on Mimic. Kaelen is my friend, and I wouldn't act in any manner that sees her take harm, unless she loses control. The person I saw hovering over the stage wasn't Kaelen. It was Scion and she was not in her right mind. I don't believe my friend and fellow scientist would ever kill someone…but when her eyes glowed blue as Scion, I have no calculation that could predict what actions she'd take."

Ellie let out a long breath and gazed back down at Leah. "Perhaps you're right."

In the desert, not far from the CORP training facility at Area 51, three highly decorated CORP agents stood in conference.

"Sir, it's your call on what we should do here. Scion has eluded us to date, but I'll admit that she's never harmed anyone or created unnecessary property damage with her actions. She's prevented both during her sightings."

A woman with a whiteish blonde mohawk stood at Garen's left with her arms crossed. "She is an alien of untold power who by eyewitness reports is acting unpredictably. I say we take her out and ask questions later."

It may have appeared strange to some for the tall, well-built alien agents to defer to the small middle-aged woman, but Rocket was infamous for her leadership skills and composure under stressful conditions. She made to run a hand through her hair and cursed when she hit the top of her helmet. A few years had gone by since she'd last been in the field. Truthfully, she wouldn't have suited up this time if not for her wife's pleading on behalf of Scion.

"I think it's important to separate them and talk Scion down. Perhaps if we can let her know that Miss Lockheed-Tuck is alive it will help." She turned to T'ala. "You are our ace in the hole. From all reports of her power, all she can do is juice you up. I want you to hold her if nothing else works."

Jove cleared his throat. "The only problem with that plan will be if she flies into the upper atmosphere, as she's done many times. We can't track her there, and she can go higher than any human or Chromodec can survive with no ill effects from oxygen deprivation. That's not even mentioning her speed."

T'ala frowned. "Fuck."

Rocket waved it off. "We'll deal with that if it becomes an issue. For now, let's move out before they wreck all the natural beauty here." She looked around and scoffed. Director Romy Danes was well known for her hatred of the desert.

A few miles away, Kaelen was locked in battle with Mimic. They both bled from numerous cuts and burnt exposed skin. Though to be fair, Kaelen had hardly any exposed skin with the way the nanotech suit covered most of her body. One simultaneous blow sent them tumbling through the air away from each other, floating in place, panting, and staring at one another.

Mimic broke the silence. "You don't seem to get it. We're too well-matched and I can tell that I've been fighting a lot longer than you have. You may as well give up and let me go."

Kaelen drew in a ragged breath to answer. "I will never let you go. You killed the most important person in my life and yours is now forfeit!"

Mimic laughed and waved a hand toward Kaelen. "Look at you, exhausted."

"Kaelen Ra-Evon, your opponent is correct. You've depleted much of the stored energy within your cells and you have no practical fighting experience. Perhaps it is unwise to continue the battle in such a manner."

"Wex," Mimic tilted her head curiously when Kaelen spoke, clearly not understanding who or what she was talking to.

"Yes, Kaelen Ra-Evon?"

She screamed, "Shut the fuck up!" Then Kaelen rocketed straight up in the air, all the way to the edge of her atmospheric limit and caressed inside the suit to retract it into two bracers on each forearm. The rest of her was left completely nude. Radiation from the yellow sun flooded her system, providing a much-needed recharge. Then she engaged the full suit again and dove toward Earth, heading for the heartbeat of Leah's killer.

Her impact with Mimic far below looked like a bomb going off. When the dust cleared, Kaelen stood in the center of a massive crater, lifting Mimic from the ground by her throat. The woman was bleeding, and her eyes were glazed with disorientation and injury. "Now you'll pay for your crimes." Kaelen's eyes began to glow with intense, blue light.

"Scion! Stand down! That is an order!"

Kaelen recognized the voice though wasn't sure how the man had come so far in such a short amount of time. She didn't think Jove possessed that kind of flight speed. "You don't understand. Mimic has killed and injured countless people. She must pay."

"She will be held accountable for her crimes, but first you need to release her and let us handle it legally."

Kaelen shuddered with emotion. "She—she killed Leah... Lockheed."

"You're wrong. Miss Lockheed is alive."

She turned to glare at the man, eyes burning with fury. "You lie! Leah was dead. Mimic killed her when the roof caved in."

Jove was accompanied by two other agents, one with a helmet and one without. When they rose into the air, the woman with long, spikey hair down the middle of her head changed her visage and became a negative image of herself with glowing black hair and eyes. Neither of the newcomers had heartbeats she recognized. The rest of the agents stayed far back. The smallest agent of the trio opened her helmet.

"You don't know me, but I'm Romy Danes, or Rocket. I've been the Director of the CORP for nearly two decades."

"You won't change my mind. Your CORP is why Mimic was free to hurt so many people. The same CORP that hunted me for doing what was right!"

The woman shook her head. "I'm not disagreeing with you. You may not realize that you saved my wife a few months ago when she met with Miss Lockheed-Tuck."

Kaelen faltered. "I—I wanted to help, to save people."

"And you have. Now it's time to let us handle Mimic, to put her away where she can't hurt anyone else. You've proven to be a person of honor many times, and I'd hate to think you'd tarnish that honor by seeking needless revenge."

Her voice broke. "But she's dead! Mimic killed someone and I don't know how to reconcile that with all my other losses. I don't know how to move forward."

Jove held out a hand. "I swear to you on everything that I stand for that I tell the truth. I spoke with one of her scientists, Clevna Trog, as well as Ellie Tuck. Leah was alive more than fifteen minutes ago."

His words gave Kaelen pause and she loosened her grip enough for Mimic to suck in a desperate breath. She couldn't tell if he was lying by heartbeat alone because he was an alien and didn't have the same responses as a human. She looked at Rocket.

"He's not lying. Doctor Lockheed-Tuck is alive, and Mimic's attack caused no other casualties, only injuries and damage to the auditorium."

Kaelen gasped and began to hope.

"Now, you've done your job by preventing more harm and getting Mimic away from civilians. It's time to let us do ours." Jove signaled to the rest of the agents, and they moved to surround the crater.

The action filled Kaelen with doubt. "How can I believe you when lies are nothing more than a crushing weight I've had to bear my entire life?" The blue radiation leaking from her eyes intensified.

The strange glowing woman spoke. "Scion, I don't know who you are or where you come from, but I too know loss. You don't have to let it define you. Trust me when I say that anger is a path that leads to self-destruction."

"T'ala is right. You've been nothing but honorable in all your deeds and actions so far. You've saved many lives, including the life of a CORP agent who was trying to arrest you." Jove enunciated clearly, "You are not a killer. Stand down."

Kaelen froze and extended her hearing. She ignored the heartbeats all around her, the sounds of the desert and overhead planes. She stretched her senses even farther to the ringing bells and sounds of the Las Vegas casinos. Then she heard familiar voices, and one all-important heartbeat. "Leah," whispered between her lips into the wind. Her laser vision winked out and multiple sighs of relief hit her ears.

Kaelen released Mimic, who fell to the ground with a curse. She'd clearly recovered while Kaelen wavered between rage and indecision. Kaelen moved away from her before she could be tempted to cause more harm.

Rocket, Jove, and T'ala touched down not far in front of Kaelen and she grew fearful. They were powerful and could take her away from Leah, but she wasn't going to run anymore. Kaelen had crossed a line and she knew it. It was time to face her own justice.

Garen moved to apprehend Mimic as she pulled herself upright. Unfortunately, he wasn't fast enough and she screamed, "Fuck the CORP!" as she unleashed twin laser beams toward Rocket. Kaelen sped in front of her, but T'ala was fast. The energy struck her right in the chest, and she sucked in a breath. It didn't injure her in the slightest. Instead, Kaelen was amazed to see the blackness grow brighter somehow.

"That's what you've been throwing around? Woof!" She raised a fist and shot a beam of white right back at Mimic, knocking her unconscious. Jove merely shook his head then waved the other agents in.

Kaelen looked around then stepped back abruptly when she realized how close she was to Rocket. "Sorry. I was afraid she'd hurt you."

Rocket shook her head and clapped Kaelen on the shoulder. "You've got good instincts, kid. Have you thought about becoming a CORP agent?"

"Oh no, I'm much too intelligent for that."

T'ala snorted and Rocket pointed at her. "I wouldn't laugh because you know it's within the realm of possibility that she is."

"Sure, she is." T'ala began laughing and Kaelen didn't understand what was so funny.

"I'm a twelfth caliber intellect."

The laughing agent fell into silence. "Oh, shit."

That only made the others laugh and Rocket crowed, "I told you so." Then she turned back to Kaelen and observed her for a few seconds. "Thank you."

Kaelen shook her head, ruefully. "No, thank you. What I've done today…I'm sorry. It wasn't normal behavior for me, and I accept your judgement. I only wanted to help people."

Rocket smiled kindly. "I've been doing this job a long time and one thing I've learned is that some people don't want your help. Mimic was one of them. She was so blinded by her anger at one family that she refused to see the truth."

"Truth?"

"That vengeance doesn't end pain, it continues it."

Kaelen swallowed the lump in her throat. "Are you going to arrest me now?"

"No. I've spoken with the powers that be and the CORP is going to put out an official press release thanking the new hero, Scion, for her help in apprehending an extremely dangerous, rogue Chromodec."

Kaelen cocked her head. "I don't understand."

"I hold a lot of power as the head of the Chromodec Office of Restraint and Protection, but even I have to answer to the people above me. I'd previously consulted with the president on this matter, and I've updated him again before coming out here. He was well aware of the situation and approved my suggestion."

"Suggestion?"

Rocket held out a hand. "Welcome to the sanctioned list, kid. Keep doing what you can to uphold the CORP motto of peace, prosperity, and protection, and I'll look forward to working with you in the future."

"Oh."

Rocket nodded and Jove stepped forward to shake her hand as well. When T'ala moved closer, she did something to make the black glow disappear. "Perhaps someday we can discuss where we come from. My *Q'sirrahna* and I arrived on Earth as babies, lost to our home planets years ago. We've been trying to find updates on whether or not they survived the civil war that plagued our people."

"Unlike you and your soul mate—"

"You know my language?"

Kaelen nodded, recognizing the word from many interplanetary languages she'd studied when she was a child. She switched back to English. "Yes, though it wasn't common. As I was saying, my world was lost to me. I was sent away right before my planet exploded."

T'ala paused for a moment to take in the new information. "Well, the offer still stands. As I said, I'm familiar with loss and if you ever want to talk, I'm a good listener."

"Thank you."

With that, Rocket and T'ala flew toward the rest of the agents in black. Jove reached into a pouch on his thigh and retrieved a collar, which he secured around Mimic's neck. She suspected it was a power inhibitor. Then he lifted the unconscious woman and slung her over one shoulder to follow the rest. A portal opened about twenty feet from Kaelen's location and all the agents went through it. Kaelen looked down at her watch and back to the empty space where the large glowing opening had been moments before. The sheer size of it made her jealous.

She realized it probably wasn't mechanical when she remembered that the CORP had a few teleporters on staff. That certainly would have been handy rather than inventing portal tech small enough to fit into a watch. Before her brain could go off on another tangent, Kaelen heard her name whispered on the wind by the person she remained attuned to.

"Kaelen, come back."

Like a bullet firing from the barrel of a gun, Kaelen took off in a black and silver blur, toward Las Vegas and her heart.

Kaelen noted all the destruction, including at least one fire. As much as she wanted to be by Leah's side, that familiar heartbeat was strong in her ears, so Kaelen took a few minutes to put out the fire and help clean up some of the mess that was impeding the first responders. There was less damage than she'd initially assumed. It was mostly confined to the immediate location of the stage in the room where Leah had spoken in front of the large crowd.

Kaelen eventually floated down through the hole in the roof but stopped when she saw paramedics kneeling next to Leah on the stage. Ellie and Einstein stood nearby wearing relieved smiles when they spotted her.

One paramedic noticed Kaelen hovering overhead and grew pale. "Scion!"

Understanding that she still had a role to play, Kaelen responded appropriately. "Fear not. The vigilante known as Mimic has been turned over to the Chromodec Office of Restraint and Protection. If you'll excuse me, I'm going to clean up some of the debris for emergency personnel while you tend to Miss Lockheed-Tuck."

The other paramedic stepped to the side seconds later, and Kaelen caught her first glimpse of Leah since hearing her heart stop. Leah looked tired. She smiled when she saw Kaelen and whispered, "*zhee.*" Of course, Kaelen was the only one who could hear it.

That single word gave Kaelen more energy than a hundred yellow suns, and she swiftly moved around the stage, gathering fallen metal sheeting, wires, beams, and other materials. Minutes later, the stage was clear of debris. She took it all outside to a nearby construction dumpster and when that ran out of room, she made a pile in an empty lot. In an effort to save the convention center energy from the lost climate-controlled air in the desert, Kaelen meticulously bent and welded the roof back into place with the scraps she found.

Unfortunately, she welded herself out and had to go back in via the entrance that the small group of Lockheed employees had taken hours before. It was probably for the best because she came in dressed as her civilian identity, Kaelen Ra-Evon. Police and firefighters tried to stop her from entering the damaged room, but she was too fast for them. Instead, she bolted straight for the stage and yelled, "Leah!"

Despite the protestations of the two paramedics flanking her, Leah pulled herself upright and took a step toward the stairs leading down from the stage. Kaelen wrapped her in a strong embrace and trembled with emotion. She whispered into Leah's ear, "I thought I'd lost you."

When they pulled apart, Leah lifted her hand to caress Kaelen's cheek. "On the contrary, darling, you're the one who saved me." She glanced toward the medical personnel who continued to mill about. "I'm afraid we've baffled the paramedics, and they're requesting that I let them take me to the hospital for an examination. Apparently, I lost a lot of blood on the stage, but they can't find any wounds on me."

Tears pooled in Kaelen's eyes. "I—you were dead and I lost myself. Leah," she looked away and swallowed, "I almost did something horrible."

"But you didn't."

"It was a close thing. If Jove and Director Romy Danes hadn't told me that you were alive…I don't know what I would have done."

Leah squeezed her even tighter. "I have faith in you, love. I know in my heart you'd choose good over evil even when things look darkest. You carry a spark of hope inside you."

Kaelen didn't answer because she knew the shameful truth. She was ready to end Mimic's life, ready to impart her own pain on the person responsible for it. Even now, Kaelen wasn't certain if she would have stopped without outside interference. She'd been blinded by grief and rage. Rather than respond to Leah's statement, she asked, "What do you want to do?"

The triumphant look on Leah's face seemed out of place after such a harrowing ordeal. "I'm going to return to the hotel for a shower and change of clothing, then I'll come back to the conference and deal with the press."

"Honey, maybe you should let them check you out to be safe. You may be healed now but the fact remains that you lost a lot of blood."

"Ellie, I'm fine. And I refuse to back down from this. Mimic has been taken care of," she glanced at Kaelen, who nodded. "So, we can continue as planned. It's not the first time an attack or other damage has occurred during CES. Thankfully, the homicidal Chromodec left the rest of the place unscathed. They'll adjust by moving around some of the speaking engagements that were previously scheduled in this room."

Ellie glanced around and whispered, "Why are you so adamant about this? You died, Leah!"

Leah left Kaelen's side to pull Ellie into a hug. "I understand your fear and I'd feel the same way if I were in your shoes. But this is our moment. Don't you understand what this means?"

"Means?"

"Ah!" Everyone looked at Einstein as he held up a finger. "The cure she unveiled today. If having Leah walk across the stage wasn't proof enough, then the live feed of her presentation from all the cameras that were left running puts our company on the highest level in regards to medical advancement. Not only did Leah appear critically injured, audio, and Ellie's actions on the stage will show that she was indeed dead for a few minutes before we performed CPR. Then we have the paramedics who come in and express disbelieve that Leah has no injuries. This is all irrefutable proof that we've accomplished something amazing, and Leah wants to capitalize on that as much as possible."

Ellie's lips pressed into a thin line. "It's grim and callous and a bit dark even for you." She sighed and her shoulders drooped as she gave in to Leah's wishes. "I'll admit that you're both right. Fine, let's gather your security team and head back to the hotel. But as your doctor," Leah snorted. "I want you to have some juice and crackers to help replenish your body after the blood loss."

Kaelen looked around. "Where is Hans and his crew?"

"The debris had blocked them backstage. It wasn't until you cleared the large beams that they were able to come out here and check on me. The police made them leave the room once they were free, so Hans said they were going to regroup outside the hall doors."

The paramedics packed up their gear and stood awkwardly off to the side. One tried yet again to persuade Leah. "Miss Lockheed-Tuck, are you sure you don't want to take a ride with us to Mountain View? Given the nature of your incident, you should have tests run to check for internal bleeding."

Leah laughed and shook her head. "Internal bleeding is the first thing my medical nanobots would have repaired. Trust me when I say that there is nothing wrong with me that a hot shower won't cure. Thank you both for your attention and care, but I'm sure other people out there need you more."

"If you say so." The woman nodded, then she and her counterpart made their way off the damaged stage and through the doors that were guarded by the police.

One officer called out as they left, "Miss Lockheed-Tuck, and the rest of you, we'd like to get a statement before you leave." He looked at Kaelen with irritation, clearly still angry that she'd gotten by him. "Starting with you. Where were you during the incident?"

"I had to pee. I already knew what the unveiling was about since Clevna Trog and I were the two scientists who worked on the project with Miss Lockheed-Tuck."

Leah rolled her eyes, playing along. "You pick the worst times to go to the bathroom."

Einstein chimed in, "Or the best. At least she wasn't here during the attack."

The officer continued. "We heard reports from others that ran out that Scion showed up and chased Mimic away. Is that true?"

"I certainly can't tell you because I was busy being, well…nearly dead." She shrugged at the nonplussed look on the police officer's face.

Ellie spoke up. "Yes, Scion showed up after Mimic attacked through the roof. And she did chase the Chromodec away. We have no way of knowing what happened after that. Einstein pointed out that he heard two sonic booms, so we assumed they flew away from the city with great speed."

"Scion said that Mimic had been apprehended and turned over to the CORP when she came back to clean up the auditorium."

Ellie smiled at Einstein. "I forgot about that."

The officer nodded and recorded Einstein's statement in his notes. He asked a few more questions before letting them go. After all, it wasn't as if they were responsible for what happened at the convention center. They were victims like everyone else, perhaps more so. Three hours later, the entire team was fed, clean, and ready to take on the world.

When Leah walked into the area where her company had their massive display, she was mobbed by the Lockheed International staff on site. Each one had heard of the momentous unveiling, then of the attack after. They had all seen the video. The Lockheed employees cared for their CEO and Kaelen knew it warmed Leah's heart. Leah Lockheed-Tuck only wanted to do good in the world, and to do right by her people.

Kaelen decided in that moment that she would endeavor to follow more of those same principles. She liked the CORP motto and knew that she could abide by their creed with a clear conscience as well. Peace, prosperity, and protection. They were good words to live by.

Chapter Twenty-eight

"Lockheed International is a trailblazing force of innovation. We are leading medicine and technology into the future, one cure at a time. And that is why I'm proud to break ground on our new biomedical lab, here in Lennox." With those words, Leah planted her shoe on the step of the shovel blade and dug into the dirt below. Ellie stood a little to her left while Kaelen and Einstein were farther off to her right side. As the highest-ranking scientists in the trial, they had the honor of being present for the groundbreaking event and press conference after.

Applause and a multitude of clicking shutters drowned out any other words. The tumultuous events at CES, as well as Leah's revelation to the world about Lockheed's advancement, sent a shockwave through the scientific community. The company's stock increased significantly, and investors lined up in droves to get in on the new technology. As a result, it only took six months to fund and staff a manufacturing site dedicated to nanotechnology and the serum needed to reverse the effects of spinal injury on the human body. Leah had plans to investigate cancer treatment possibilities, but she wanted to get the Nerenase production up and running first.

What they didn't tell the world was how badly Leah had been injured at the convention, especially not the fact that her treatment essentially brought her back from the dead. Panic and tragedy alter people's perceptions, so everyone assumed Ellie had overreacted on the stage the day of the attack. No one believed that the genius CEO of Lockheed International had actually died.

It was something that Leah thought about a lot. None of the other test subjects showed the same type of cellular healing as Leah, and she suspected it had to do with that last nanobot and queen injection, the one that Kaelen programmed herself. After discussing the issue with Kaelen and Ellie, they decided that the world wasn't ready for that kind of science. Human mortality tempered many of their rash actions and overreach.

Once the applause slowed, Leah moved to the assembled stage for the actual press conference. "Now that the dirty work is finished, literally, I'm ready and willing to answer your questions relating to the Nerenase project." The crowd chuckled at the pun as hands went up. Leah saw one familiar smile and pointed toward the woman. "Yes, Meta News Network?"

"Miss Lockheed, is it true that rather than sell to medical facilities or state corporations and charge insurance companies exorbitant fees for Nerenase treatment, Lockheed International medical centers around the world will handle both the sales and administration of it?"

"Yes, that is true. There were many reasons behind the decision, but a major one is because the formula and technologies are proprietary, with multiple copyrights filed on behalf of Lockheed International." Leah raised her hand to call on someone else, but Nalla was tenacious.

"Sorry, to finish that question, is it also true that the cost of the treatment will be income based for the afflicted person?"

Leah smiled and met Nalla's gaze. "Yes. It's yet another reason for our facilities to administer the treatment. As someone who once experienced a spinal cord injury, I know firsthand the impact paralysis has on all parts of your life. But unlike most other people, I was also born into privilege and never had to worry about the significant cost of treatment, therapy, mobility, and assistive devices. Not everyone is so lucky, and I don't believe they should be penalized for their wealth or lack thereof."

Leah answered another twenty minutes worth of questions about the project before someone moved the press conference in a slightly different direction. "Miss Lockheed, Joe Minot from the Scientific American. Now that Lockheed International has achieved something never thought possible, what's next? Will the company focus on producing and refining Nerenase, or is there another big project in the works?"

"I'm happy you asked, Joe. As everyone knows, we always have a lot of innovations in the pipeline of discovery, even some that are built upon the platform of Nerenase. However, I've tasked the Special Projects Lab team to work on a cost effective, solar-powered desalinization system." She waved toward Kaelen and Einstein. "Mister Trog and Miss Ra-Evon have made significant advancements in compact battery technology and are currently working to improve the efficiency of Lockheed's proprietary photovoltaic cells."

Ellie glanced at her watch and cleared her throat to signal Leah that she should bring the press conference to an end.

Leah smiled and moved her gaze around the crowd. "Okay, it looks like my time here is nearly finished. I can take one last question." Hands waved in the air, and she picked an unfamiliar person near the back. "You there, go ahead."

"Miss Lockheed, David Bennett of the New York Post. What exactly is your relationship with Scion? There have been rumors that the two of you are involved given the number of times she has saved you, up to and including the attack in Las Vegas."

Leah sucked in a breath at the question, not expecting it in the middle of her groundbreaking revelations about their new cure. She wasn't prepared for anything along those lines, but she thought it would be a good time to make another announcement. "I consider Scion a friend." She laughed. "As you pointed out, she's saved me too many times to be an enemy."

The reporter pressed, "And you assert that there is no romance between the two of you?"

Leah was careful to answer without actually lying. She smiled widely at the man. "I'm afraid my heart is quite taken." She gestured for Kaelen to move to her side. "I'd like to introduce my fiancé, and one of the brilliant scientists behind the nanobot side of the Nerenase project. Kaelen Ra-Evon." Then she reached out to clasp Kaelen's hand and mouthed, "I love you," to her before meeting the gaze of the reporter. "Brains and beauty, why would I look anywhere else?"

He sputtered, "But Scion is literally a hero!"

"Scion may have saved me, Mr. Bennett, but Kaelen is my real hero." Laughter and more than a few "aww's" went through the crowd.

"I'm afraid that's all the time I have today, but I want to thank you for coming. And please, stay and enjoy the refreshments. I've been told by a good friend that reporting is hungry work." More chuckles followed her remark as the crowd began to disperse.

Kaelen hugged her. "You were amazing and brilliant."

"She's right, honey, you handled everything, including the question at the end, with style and grace."

Hans gestured to Leah, and she recognized his request to exit the stage. Just because Mimic was locked away didn't mean others with an axe to grind weren't out there. It was better to be safe than sorry. "My security team is getting antsy. What do you say we all crash Lotus Garden for an early dinner?"

"That sounds great."

Leah looked up when she heard the familiar voice. "Maddy! I thought you and Tasha had to work today?"

Maddy shrugged. "I called in a favor and switched shifts with Patel, and Tasha didn't have any appointments this afternoon, so she blocked her schedule." She held her hands out to the side. "And here we are."

Leah pulled them both into a group hug. "You two are the best. Thanks, sis."

"Yes, we are." Maddy paused when Leah pulled away. "I know I've told you this before…but I really thought you'd be taller."

"You've only got two inches on me."

"That's a lot."

Leah sighed. "No, it isn't."

"I'm literally looking down at you, it's plenty."

Suddenly Kaelen stepped closer and brushed against Maddy's shoulder and looked down at her. "Yes, two inches is a good height difference, isn't it? I'd estimate it to be the thickness of a cinnamon roll. You remember that one breakfast at The Bean Bag, right, Maddy?" She shook her head and said, "Their butter knives are so flimsy."

Maddy swallowed. "Yup." Then she turned to Leah and gave her a pained smile. "I'll stop. You can call off your girlfriend now."

Leah laughed and wrapped her arm around Kaelen's waist. "Please, she wouldn't hurt a fly." She looked up at Kaelen in time to see her frown, before her features smoothed into a pleasant smile.

Nalla joined the group then, interrupting whatever else Leah was going to say. "I'm pretty sure you broke every news outlet with that last declaration about Kaelen."

"You can't be serious. We literally created a treatment to repair spinal cord injury and you think the press is going to focus on the fact that I'm engaged?"

"Oh, for sure. The world has known about Nerenase for months, since CES. But this…this is big news. I'll bet you fifty dollars that your engagement garners more front-page headlines tomorrow than Lockheed's new miracle cure."

Leah held out her hand. "Make it one hundred dollars and you're on."

Einstein spoke up. "I'd have to agree with Leah, Nerenase is a major scientific breakthrough. There is no way it will be less important than what amounts to relationship gossip about the company CEO."

Ellie, Maddy, and Tasha all spoke at once, taking sides in the argument. As they quieted down, Leah turned to Kaelen. "What about you? Do you have an opinion about the headlines tomorrow?"

Kaelen shook her head and smiled. "I'm not making a determination, but I have kept track of all the bets." She tapped her temple.

Maddy snorted. "Of course, she did. Come on people, my stomach isn't going to feed itself, and I'm pretty sure my sister promised to buy everyone an early dinner."

"That's not at all what I—fine. You call ahead though to make sure they've got seats available."

Ellie startled everyone with her laughter as they walked away from the stage. "Honey, I'm the oldest one here and even I don't eat this early. Maddy should still call ahead but I think we'll be fine because it will take at least forty minutes to make our way to Xiuying's restaurant in Koreatown."

Leah met Hans's gaze where he stood close to the group. He nodded and pressed a finger to his ear so he could communicate the plans with the rest of her security team. She trusted Kaelen, but if they wanted to keep up appearances, she couldn't go around without security every time she was with her fiancé. That would be too obvious.

Once they'd announced Leah's recovery to the world, she wasted no time donating her electric vans to a service that helped people with disabilities. The vans could be converted for use with a standard driver's seat, or left as is. She replaced it with an electric SUV and spent many hours over the past few months re-learning to drive using foot pedals in conjunction with the steering wheel, instead of only hand controls.

Ellie rode with Maddy and Tasha, leaving Leah alone with Kaelen during the drive to the restaurant. Kaelen was unusually silent. "Are you okay?"

"Why wouldn't I be? Everyone I love is healthy and happy, plus I'm here with you."

Leah maneuvered onto the highway, sparing a glance for Kaelen. "You seem quieter than normal, like you're lost in thought."

"I—" Kaelen sighed, an unusual sound from her. "I have been thinking about something you said to Maddy earlier."

"Something I said?"

"You told Maddy that I would never hurt a fly but you were wrong. I have hurt someone. I would have killed her if I hadn't heard your heartbeat. Wishing death upon another is a moral failing in Argonian society. I have failed a test of citizenship with my actions."

"Oh—" Leah made a quick decision to exit the highway so they could talk someplace more secure, sensing that Kaelen's guilt was weighing heavily on her.

"Leah, where are you going? We told everyone we'd meet them at the restaurant."

"This is more important. You're more important." She pulled into a parking lot not far from the off-ramp and brought the vehicle to a stop. Leah saw her security team pull into the lot after them. She turned in her seat so she could face Kaelen, noting the white knuckles where Kaelen gripped her own hands. "You are one of the most noble and honorable people I've ever met. Why would you think you're a failure?"

"I researched Argonian law."

"Darling," Kaelen met Leah's intense gaze. "You're not on Argon."

"Yes, but—" Leah covered her soft lips to stifle the words.

"Tell me, would you expect a human on Argon to only abide by their home planet's laws unconditionally?"

"No."

Leah pressed on. "And if a visitor to Argon acted in a way that were noble, true, and worthy of the highest house, would you call them a failure if they didn't meet their own planet's moral and intellectual standards?"

Kaelen shook her head.

"Planets and their people are all distinct. Earth has a mix of humans, aliens, and Chromodecs. Much like science involves a mix of different materials with their unique properties. Some elements are volatile and require different procedures, fail-safes, and levels of interaction, while others are harmless and inert. You won't always be able to act and react like an Argonian when dealing with more volatile races."

"But I would have killed her." Kaelen pounded her fist against her own thigh. "I held her life in my hands and wished for nothing more than to snuff it out!"

"You didn't kill her though."

"What's the difference either way between intent and action? The dark thoughts were poison in my heart."

Leah gave Kaelen a tender smile. "The difference is choice. You chose to spare a life that day."

Kaelen looked fearful, tears shimmering in her eyes. "What happens next time, or the time after? How can I be sure I'll always make the right choice?"

"You can't. Darling, we all have lines that we'd cross when pushed to our limit. If you think I wouldn't feel the same way if something were to happen to you, Maddy, or Ellie, you're sadly mistaken. I don't believe it makes me a monster. On the contrary, it makes me human."

"But I'm not human, Leah. With my power, I can't afford to be."

Leah covered Kaelen's hands with her own. "I can't tell you what to do or how to act. But I believe in you, Kaelen. Follow your heart and stop trying to live up to a people who did nothing but let you down."

Kaelen was silent for a minute before drawing in a slow breath and releasing it. "You're right. I've said this before but it clearly encompasses so much more of my life than I originally anticipated." She looked at Leah. "I need to forge my own path here on Earth. Yes, I am *the* Ra. I'm the last of my house and people. But as the last, how much does my birthright mean here? I'm doing good work, I've received my match, and I have friends and found family I never expected to experience again after the loss of my planet."

"Perhaps…" Leah trailed off, unsure how to make her suggestion.

"What is it?"

"Maybe Tasha can recommend someone for you to speak with about your losses and experiences. I think you could benefit from actual therapy and not the Wex kind. Grief is an odd emotion and can affect our thoughts and actions in strange and unexpected ways."

Kaelen frowned at the suggestion but nodded. "I'll ask Tasha later after dinner. Thank you."

"You never have to thank me for caring about you, for loving you and wishing you all the happiness in the world. That is what best friends and true partners strive for. I consider you both."

Kaelen smiled. "You match what's in my head perfectly." Suddenly her stomach gave a loud growl and she clutched at it. "Perhaps we should head to dinner now."

"Are you okay?"

"Yes, much better."

Leah put the vehicle in drive and made her way out of the lot and onto the highway. Hans and his team followed behind them. "Good, because I hate to think that you'll be too upset during dinner to enjoy dessert after."

"Dessert? Is there a new offering at Lotus Garden? I didn't know they had a dessert selection."

"I'm talking about later, once we're home alone."

Kaelen's head tilted when Leah looked her way. "I don't understand."

"Darling, dessert is a euphemism."

"Oh." Leah glanced at Kaelen and smirked at her wide eyes. "Oh! Yes, dessert sounds like a great idea. Uh, then maybe we can have real, non-euphemism dessert too?"

Leah laughed, delighted that she knew her love so well. "Of course. I'm sure I can find something to satisfy your sweet tooth."

"I'm nervous." Kaelen's jiggling leg stilled at the touch of Leah's hand.

"Darling, don't be nervous. Michael is going to be beyond happy."

With no hoverchair to worry about, they'd actually rented an SUV at the airport to drive themselves from Grand Rapids to Zeeland. Leah wanted electric but there wasn't one available so they had to settle for a hybrid. Unlike their earlier trips to see Paul, Shelly, Michael, and occasionally Tate when he was home from university, Leah had the bare minimum of two security guards with her. They'd visited often enough by that point that there was still a risk someone would guess her destination and cause trouble.

Kaelen was the one who suggested they tell Hans about her powers and secret identity to save the man from heartburn every time Leah dismissed her team. He understood her reasoning better but still insisted she have at least two with her when traveling out of the city. Hans handpicked Ron Patchett, or "Patch," and Jules Yang. Both were skilled, dedicated, friendly, and would never disclose Kaelen's alternate identity.

Leah glanced down at the navigation screen, then returned her gaze to the dusty road ahead of them. "You've got about fifteen minutes to tell me why you're so worried."

Kaelen turned slightly to look at the guards in the back seat. Patch and Jules studiously looked away, pretending to be part of the vehicle decor. Even so, she lowered her voice slightly. "He's been studying Argonian culture for a year now. What if he doesn't approve of our match? What if he thinks—"

Leah's laughter brought her spiraling words to a halt. "Sweetheart," Kaelen smiled when Leah used Ellie's familiar term of endearment. "For one, I know it bothers you, but Michael will always be more human than Argonian. He's too…too, Midwestern. Trust me when I say he won't hold, what to him is an alien culture, higher than the one he was raised with."

Her words made sense and Kaelen frowned. She didn't like that Michael wouldn't understand what it meant to be Argonian the way she did. But she also knew that it meant his life would be a lot easier. He'd never have to walk with a foot in each world, trying his hardest to do right by both. Perhaps that was where some of her fear stemmed from. Kaelen paused as the rest of Leah's statement caught up with her thoughts. "You said for one, what is the other reason?"

Leah turned her head so Kaelen could receive the full power of what

Nalla called Leah's *look*. The combination of head tilt, lip curl, dimple, eyebrow lift, flirtatious smile, and what Nalla said is "killer eye contact," had Kaelen sucking in a breath. "Michael adores me. I may not wear a cape, but he's told me often enough how I'm his hero."

"You think so?"

"Trust me, darling. Michael will be over the moon that he can say he's related to me in some way. Shelly already admitted that he tells everyone at school we're friends and that I've visited multiple times. It's pretty cute, actually."

Kaelen sighed, feeling significantly calmer. Then she turned to Leah with a bright smile. "You're pretty cute, and smart too. He couldn't have a better role model to look up to." Leah's cheeks pinked and Kaelen was satisfied that she'd said the right thing.

They turned up the driveway not long after that, and Leah parked between Paul's new pickup truck and Shelly's car. A blur raced from the house to their SUV as soon as they rolled to a stop. Whatever dust was kicked up by their arrival was blown away by one excited boy. Michael hopped impatiently from foot to foot while he waited for everyone to exit the vehicle, then he threw himself at Kaelen and gave her a hug not many others on Earth could replicate.

When he pulled away, she ruffled his dark hair and grinned down at him. "You're getting stronger, *bhejek*. And taller."

He beamed back at her. "I am! I even helped Dad when he changed the tires on the old truck last month, before he gave it to Tate."

Kaelen looked around and didn't see the old vehicle or hear Tate's heartbeat so assumed he was still in Chicago. "You're doing the exercises like I showed you? Control is important, both emotional and physical because one affects the other."

"Yup. Tuk says I'm doing well in my studies too."

"I would expect nothing less from such a bright young man."

At the sound of Leah's voice, Michael's eyes lit up and he rushed to her side. "Leah!"

"Careful, son." Paul and Shelly had come outside, albeit at a much slower pace than Michael.

"I'm always careful, Mom. But this is Leah and I haven't seen her in ages!"

"They were here a month and a half ago."

Leah laughed and hugged him. "It's fine, Shelly. I can't help it that I'm his favorite scientist."

He pulled away and looked from Leah to his parents. "I want to be like Leah when I grow up."

Paul laughed. "Weren't you saying the other day that you wanted to be a famous writer, changing lives with every word?"

Michael blushed and rubbed the back of his neck. "Geez, can't a person do both?"

All the adults laughed and Leah patted his shoulder. "If anyone can do it, I bet it's you."

"Come along everyone, I've got fresh pies made." Shelly looked beyond Kaelen and Leah toward Leah's bodyguards. "Hi Jules. It's good to have you and Patch back. I even remembered your favorite tea and soda, and ordered some special for when you visit."

Jules was the more serious of the two and simply smiled and gave a quick nod. "You didn't have to do that, Mrs. Miller." Kaelen could tell by the tone of her voice and elevated heart rate that Jules was secretly pleased.

Patch was a lot less restrained. "That's pretty sweet of you, Mrs. Miller. Thanks a lot."

"Nonsense! Call me Shelly and it wasn't nothin' big. I know you all have an important job and you've been here enough times that you're practically family."

Michael chimed in, "Like found family?"

Kaelen laughed. "Very close to it. What do you say we go have some pie?" She looked around at the group and rubbed her stomach. "I don't know about you all, but I'm starving."

Leah answered her at the same time she winked at Shelly. "Aren't you always?"

A few minutes later they'd claimed seats around the table in the Millers' dining room. Leah helped Shelly serve up slices of pie while Paul made sure everyone had drinks.

"Tate's not home for the summer?"

Shelly winked at Leah. "Tate and his *imzadi*, Sam, were here for a bit. But they were heading back early so they could spend time with Sam's aunts."

"*Imzadi*?"

Michael grinned at Kaelen. "That's what you call your datemate when they're gender neutral."

"Oh, like boyfriend, girlfriend, and *imzadi*?" Michael nodded. "I don't recognize the word."

"Darling, it's from a television show, *Star Trek*. It means beloved." Kaelen nodded, though she was unfamiliar with the show referenced.

Paul grunted. "I like that Sam. They've got a good head on their shoulders."

Michael had already moved on from the discussion about his brother and was focused on his dessert. He scooped up a large bite of blackberry filling but paused when the fork was nearly to his mouth. He looked back and forth between his two visitors. "Kaelen said you had something important to tell us. Is it bad news?"

Kaelen was caught with a full mouth of pie, her cheeks bulging comically like a chipmunk. Everyone looked at her and Patch hid a chuckle behind his hand. Not wanting to worry her young cousin, Kaelen swallowed the large bite with some effort and took a drink of her iced milk to wash it down. "Actually," she reached toward Leah's hand and was comforted by her soft skin as their fingers intertwined, "Leah and I wanted to tell you that we got engaged during the holiday break."

A look of hurt washed across Michael's face. "But— but that was last year, months and months ago! Were you afraid to tell me?"

Leah answered him. "Not at all, my darling boy. We've been keeping it secret from a lot of people because neither one of us wanted to face the scrutiny involved with what could be viewed as a fast engagement for such a high-profile relationship as ours."

Paul's deep voice questioned, "What changed?"

"Well, I had a press conference the day before yesterday where I was forced to announce my relationship with Kaelen, as well as our engagement."

"Forced?"

Leah blushed and Kaelen laughed. "Someone from the press questioned what her relationship with Scion was, speculating that they were involved romantically because of how many times Scion has saved her. So, she told them that her heart was already taken by me and that we were engaged."

"Hmm, good call."

Kaelen gave Leah's hand a light squeeze before picking up her fork again. "Now that we're official, we've decided to set a date for our wedding. It's going to be something small, very intimate, with no press allowed."

Michael's mouth dropped open. "Wow. Will you need a best man? Do you have rings and stuff? Uh, will you get married or whatever like people on Argon?"

Shelly chuckled. "Michael, slow down and let them answer."

Leah smiled. "It's fine." She glanced at Kaelen, who had another mouthful of food, and explained what details they had. "The place will be kind of remote, but we're working on a way for Kaelen to transport everyone there at once, undetected."

Paul paused his fork halfway to his mouth and his eyebrow lifted. "How remote?"

"Antarctica."

"What?" The word was loud in the kitchen because multiple people yelled it at once.

Kaelen paused while demolishing her first large slice of pie but Leah explained. "As Lockheed International moves farther into green energy technology, and researches ways to combat global warming, we thought it would be prudent to have a place specifically geared to study bell weather effects. Kaelen suggested a remote arctic location for a research station."

"When did you start it?"

"Right after the first of the year."

"Oh, my lord." Shelly took a sip of her cooling coffee.

Paul gaped at her in surprise. "I've seen a lot of construction in my day. How on Earth did you get it built so fast in such a harsh location?"

Leah laughed. "It helps to have a lot of ready money for materials and an extremely capable, fully-powered Argonian available. Kaelen has been invaluable."

Kaelen shrugged. "What she's not saying is that I've consulted with Einstein and Wex and they agreed it would be beneficial to incorporate a lot of Argonian technology into the facility, provided access was very limited."

Michael looked at her in awe. "Wow. Who is going to be allowed in?"

"For starters, only those with access to the SPL. Well, and those we invite to the wedding. Eventually, more scientists will be trained, given security clearance, and rotate to the station."

Shelly shook her head. "I didn't even know such a thing was possible. I guess I never thought about how other research stations ended up down there."

Leah answered like it was no big deal but Kaelen knew how much work it took to get the correct approvals for such an endeavor. "I did need to get special permission from the British government first, then from my own government. Then I had to give a detailed plan for the place, and a list of materials used in the facility's construction."

Paul's mouth dropped open. "How in the world did all that come about?"

Kaelen grinned. "Director Danes of the CORP called in a favor to help us out. Leah let me name it Adyta because it reminds me of the Thinker school in Kypl City on Argon."

"Golly! And we get to go there?"

"Yes. We altered a company shuttle so it can be carried at extreme speed."

Shelly put a hand over her stomach. "What kind of speed?"

Kaelen translated the speed into miles per hour even though they'd done all the calculations in meters per second to come up with an appropriate acceleration G-force that was safe for humans. "Roughly nine thousand miles per hour. We will arrive at the Adyta Research Center in a little over two hours once I take into consideration the deceleration speed."

"Jeez, that's a lot." Michael looked at his parents with a furrowed brow. "Is it safe for everyone? We studied G-Force in science class, and they said that too fast acceleration could make someone real sick, even die."

"Don't worry, Michael. Kaelen and I went over all the calculations thoroughly. Ten G can cause unconsciousness and death. As long as

Kaelen takes ten minutes to accelerate to cruising speed, the most we'll hit is slightly more than a commercial jetliner at point five three G."

Shelly let out a sigh of relief and Paul nodded. He took a sip of his coffee and asked, "So when is the big day? You need us to wear anything fancy?"

Kaelen smiled. "Wear whatever you're comfortable in as long as it's warm."

"How cold is Adyta?"

Leah shrugged. "Chilly, more like a cave right now. The last reading Wex took said the ambient air temperature inside was roughly fifty-five degrees but Kaelen is still bringing environmental systems online."

"Have you seen it?"

"Blueprints and pictures only, I'm afraid." She pointed a thumb at Kaelen. "This one wants to surprise me with it."

Once Paul and Shelly's questions ran out, Michael continued with his own. "When is the ceremony and will you pick us up or will we have to fly out to Los Angeles first? Is Tate invited?"

"We'll pick you up at noon on the twenty-second of September and have you back the same night. Is that okay?" Kaelen paused, unsure. "I know that it's a lot to ask but at least it's a Saturday. I don't even know if Tate would want to attend, but we chose that date specifically because we celebrate it as my Re-birthday."

"Re-birthday?"

She smiled at Shelly. "It's the day I landed on Earth. We celebrate it like an ordinary birthday."

Paul and Shelly shared one of their looks, then moved their gaze to Michael. "That's actually what we did for Michael too. He was born into our lives so we decided that would be as good a day as any to celebrate."

"Cool! That means I'm just like you." He beamed at Kaelen and her heart squeezed with affection. He was such a happy and outgoing boy. She could never thank the Millers enough for what they did for her people, for her.

Shelly reached over to affectionately run her fingers through Michael's hair. "Michael has his Argonian lessons every Saturday but missing one day is fine, especially for something as important as a wedding. And we'll have to check with Tate about his schedule."

Michael threw himself sideways to hug her. "Thanks, Mom. I promise I'll ask Tuk ahead of time so I don't get behind on any assignments."

Patch muttered from his end of the table. "I wish I'd been so studious in school."

Jules laughed quietly. "Same. There is a reason that important CEOs and scientists exist in the world yet we are the ones protecting them."

Leah looked up from her plate at their words. "Never sell yourselves short. You two are good at what you do and every one of us here appreciates your work and dedication."

Patch grinned and Jules gave her a solemn nod. "We know, truly. And speaking for both of us, you're probably our favorite assignment to date. You understand how to be safe in a public setting, not to mention you're literally engaged to Sc—uh, a super special woman who knows how to take care of business."

Kaelen looked back and forth between Leah and Jules. She whispered to Leah, "Is that a euphemism?"

Leah snickered. "Yes, but not the way you're thinking."

"Erm…" Kaelen blushed and shoved a forkful from her third piece of pie into her mouth. All the adults laughed but Michael blithely carried on eating as fast as Kaelen. Not much came between a hungry Argonian and homemade pie.

Epilogue

"Are we there yet?"

"Mikey, give it a rest." Tate had been watching a movie on his tablet but pulled one earbud out to reprimand his brother.

"Fine."

Five minutes later the boy asked, "How much longer?"

"Michael, weren't you listening when Leah said we were traveling more than fourteen thousand miles away from Michigan?"

He huffed. "Yeah, Mom. But riding inside when I could be outside flying like Kaelen is boring."

"Son," Michael looked up at Paul. "You can't even fly yet. Maybe someday you'll be able to go flying with Kaelen where it's safe, but until then we should let her handle our travel plans."

Michael slouched in the shuttle seat. "Okay, Dad."

Gabe grinned at the boy. "He's a real pistol, isn't he? I can totally see Kaelen's enthusiasm." He'd been fully let in on the secret but admitted he'd guessed it after Kaelen saved Leah in Vegas. Not only that, but he told the group of Lockheed friends that he suspected his boss knew as well.

Michael wasn't offended at what the strange man said. Instead, he gave Gabe a curious look. "What do you do? I know Kaelen said that Leah's sister is a doctor," he pointed at Maddy. "And her fiancé Tasha was a, uh, psychotherapist?" Tasha nodded. Michael continued around the shuttle. "Um, Miss Ellie is Miss Leah's Mom and another scientist and helps run Lockheed International, and Einstein works with Kaelen. But I don't know you four." He gestured toward Gabe, Devon, Nalla, and Ana.

Nalla wasted no time introducing herself. "You don't want to know anything about Gabe, he's boring. I'm a reporter and I work at Meta News Network in Los Angeles. Einstein is my boyfriend."

Michael's mouth dropped open. "Wow, really? I want to be a famous writer. That's kinda similar!"

"Hey, I thought you wanted to be a scientist like me?"

Shelly started laughing. "Oh, lately he's been going on and on about how he wants to be a superhero, like Scion, T'ala, or Bolt. But he wants to be a writer too. I suspect it will keep changing monthly until he's old enough to officially decide."

"Mom." Michael whined.

Tate laughed at him and gave the boy a light chuck to the shoulder. "She's totally right, Mikey. Remember when you wanted to be a trashman because they drove the coolest truck?"

Nalla winked at Michael. "I wanted to be a parking ticket officer when I was your age because they drove little cars around my hometown. But Kaelen tells us all how smart you are so I bet you can do whatever you set your mind to. A famous playwright, Edward Bulwer-Lytton, once said the pen is mightier than the sword. No matter how cool a superhero is, a well written paragraph is sometimes further reaching and more influential."

He grinned at her. "Saving the world one word at a time."

"Hey, that's pretty clever." She turned to Einstein, "I like this kid."

Devon used the lull in conversation to stand from his seat and shake Michael's hand. "My name is Devon Smith and I'm actually Tasha's brother. I'm a professional photographer who travels around the world."

"Gosh, you're taller than Tate. Do you think I'll be as tall as you someday?"

"Keep eating your vegetables and I don't see why not." Devon winked at Shelly as he sat down.

Paul scratched at his temple, obviously trying to puzzle something out. Leah tilted her head. "What is it?"

"Devon Smith, I know that name. You're the one that took the famous photo in downtown Chicago years ago. The one with Nova and T'ala absorbing the power of that human bomb guy."

He shrugged. "Yeah, that's me. I was only sixteen at the time. Me and my sister were at the Taste of Chicago with our mom." He glanced at Tasha. "Our dad died a few months before that, and she gave me his old camera." He chuckled. "I took it everywhere with me. Little did I know that one picture would start me on a path that has brought me so much joy and taken me around the world."

"Dad would have been proud, Dev."

Gabe interrupted the heavy moment. "Don't worry little man, I'm actually the coolest one of the group. I'm Gabriel Murphy and I'm a CORP agent, specializing in the tech side."

"The CORP, really?" Gabe grinned and nodded. "That is cool! My cousin Brandon is an agent in Chicago called Pulse. Do you have a codename and are you a Chromodec with powers too?"

"No."

"An alien with powers?"

"N—no?"

"Oh, you go into the field and stop bad guys like Brandon?"

"Uh, not usually—"

"Do you invent cool weapons and other stuff to stop bad guys?"

"I mean, sometimes."

Michael appeared vaguely disappointed. "Oh. Well, what do you usually do as a CORP agent?"

Suddenly, Gabe looked less sure of himself. "I use computers a lot. I coordinate field agent response and hack—er, I mean I investigate other people via the internet and help find folks who are missing."

"Hmm. That's fun, I guess. It's nice to meet you Mr. Murphy."

Ana chimed in after everyone's laughter died down. "I'm Ana Pérez and I work with Leah. I'm only here for the wine."

"Ana!"

Michael looked from Ana to Gabe and back again. "Are you with Mister Murphy then? He kinda wines a lot."

"Michael!" Shelly tried to be stern, but the twitch of her lips indicated she was on the verge of laughing with everyone else.

"What, Mom?"

"Nalla was right, this kid is great."

Leah snickered from her seat near the front, and everyone else soon followed.

Before they knew it, the shuttle began to slow. The hull didn't have windows because Leah didn't want to take any chances that Earth materials would fail when faced with such high speeds. As it was, they had to coat the outside in something that would reduce friction so they wouldn't burn up in the upper atmosphere.

Leah pushed a button on the console. "Darling, are we nearly there?"

Kaelen's voice came across the cabin speaker. "Wex says our time of arrival is imminent. I'm bringing the shuttle down now. I'll let you know when I have you inside and it's safe to depressurize."

"Okay."

Leah felt the shuttle shift as Kaelen set it down. Maddy used the opportunity to unclasp her harness and move toward the front where Leah was seated. "Are you nervous?"

"Yes and no. I think I'm more excited than anything."

Maddy rubbed Leah's back. "You said you haven't seen this place yet?"

"Not in person, and that's what's exciting. Maddy, this is the first step into Earth's future. She's put so much of her people's technology, it's probably the closest I'll come to seeing an alien world. It fills my heart to see Kaelen so committed to a company I've dedicated my life to."

Maddy chuckled. "I mean, she is marrying you, or whatever it's called on her planet. That's about as committed as you can get."

"True."

The shuttle gave a lurch and Maddy grabbed the back of one of the seats to maintain her balance. "She must be bringing us inside the shuttle bay."

Leah felt a bump as the small craft was settled on the ground once again. A few seconds later, Kaelen's voice returned. "The outer doors are closed. You can depressurize." Leah hit the switches as everyone donned the jackets they'd stowed beneath their seats. Environmental systems were fully functional but it was safety procedure for their guests to keep winter gear on them at all times.

Rather than file off the shuttle with everyone else, Ellie joined Leah near the front. "Is there anything I can do, honey?"

"No, Kaelen has already taken care of most of the preparation. The facility isn't stocked for occupancy yet so she brought refreshments down early this morning."

"What will you wear?"

Leah shrugged. "I have no clue. Kaelen said she was working on something for me. I trust her."

Nothing could prepare Leah for the sight that assailed her when she pushed through the doors into the vestibule of the Adyta Research Center. The ceiling was taller than expected with clean lines and recessed lighting that gave everything a white-blue glow. The length of the walls to her left and right featured unique friezes. One was of the Los Angeles skyline, and the other was unfamiliar and full of strange and fantastical buildings and spires. She knew then that Kaelen had brought both her worlds into one place. The rest of the group milled around in the same state of amazement.

Leah covered her mouth with her hand as Kaelen sped to her side. "What do you think? I used my laser vision to carve them."

"Kaelen, this is beautiful! You've described your planet and architecture many times, but words could truly never do it justice. I'm so happy you've found a piece of your home here."

"Leah," Kaelen reached out and took her hand. "My piece of home is you."

Kaelen showed the group to a large, high-ceiling room. There was a shimmering, eight-sided platform near the front that Kaelen had built herself. It was the closest she could get to replicating the Argonian crystal bonding spire, without having any of the native materials of her planet. "Please, everyone, sit and relax and we'll return shortly." As she led Leah away, she called out, "Wex play a mix of Earth and Argonian music in the interim, please."

Wex's voice came through the speakers all around the room. *"As you wish, Kaelen Ra-Evon."*

Off in another empty room, Leah asked, "You promised you'd have something for me to wear?"

"I did. I've been working on creating fabric that replicates the ship suit given to me by my parents. I also programmed traditional Argonian wedding attire into both. Are you sure you're okay with this ceremony, rather than one that is more closely aligned with a traditional Earth wedding? It's not too late to change."

Leah grabbed both Kaelen's hands. "Darling, Argon gave you to me. The least I can do is give you a little of Argon in return. I love your traditions and look forward to joining with you in front of our friends and family."

The joy in Kaelen's heart with her words nearly eclipsed the radiant light of Vos. Once she synched Leah mentally with the nanotechnology in the new suit, all it required was a bit of physical interaction to activate the change. Kaelen took a little time to show Leah how to alter the material.

Minutes later, Leah stood in a sleek, form-fitting white suit with a high collar. A regal matching cape flowed over her shoulders and down her back to the floor. The corners where the cape met with the front of each shoulder featured an obsidian black, stylized L, with both the horizontal and vertical lines doubled on the letter. Tilted one way, it looked like an LI, tilted another, it could be taken for LL.

"What—"

"I hope you don't mind, but I took the liberty of making that your house symbol. It was easier to have something to record in Wex's Argonian database." Kaelen caressed her own suit and it changed to nearly the exact replica, except Kaelen's outfit was deep black and her House of Ra symbols were gleaming white. She'd also trimmed her hair again so it was short in the back and sides, and hung down much longer in front.

"I haven't had a chance to tell you how much I like your new cut." Leah reached up to straighten a few strands. Her own hair was pulled into a French braid and twisted around in back, leaving her neck bare.

Kaelen wasted no time placing a kiss on the exposed skin. "I like everything about you." She held out her arm. "Are you ready to pledge your house to mine?"

"Darling, there is nothing I'd like more."

They re-entered the main gallery and the music quieted on Kaelen's command. Everyone who had traveled halfway around the world to witness their union stood from their seats. Someone gasped as they walked between the rows of seats toward the front, and Kaelen thought it may have been Ellie. Once they made it to the front of the room, Kaelen and Leah turned to face the gathered group of friends and family and bowed, then turned in the opposite direction to the little robot floating directly ahead.

"Greetings Kaelen Ra-Evon and Leah Lockheed-Tuck. Welcome to Adyta Research Center."

Leah exclaimed delightedly, "You gave Wex a body!"

"I did." Kaelen instructed, "Wex, we're ready to begin."

"As you wish, Kaelen Ra-Evon. Please step upon the spire and be still while it rises."

Kaelen and Leah held hands as they walked up the three steps to the platform. It rose into the air six feet once they were in place. Despite the height, they were easily another six feet from the tall ceiling. The platform itself glowed red, brightening at regular intervals. Kaelen saw Leah look down and whispered, "I built it to pulse with the light of Vos to symbolize the sacred heart of our people."

"It's beautiful."

"Thank you."

The ceremony was short, something that both Kaelen and Leah thought the rest of the crowd would appreciate. A beam of red light suddenly shone down from the ceiling to highlight the entire spire they stood upon, bathing both of them in the rose light of Kaelen's lost planet.

"Dolem-Ra is a powerful example of wisdom, intelligence, history, and innovation. Kaelen Ra-Evon was deemed the best of Ra at the time of Argon's destruction. Despite traveling light years away, across numerous galaxies, the last scion of Ra has found a suitable match within the House of Lockheed."

Kaelen hadn't programmed Wex to say the words but she knew what they were going to be ahead of time and approved.

"When two houses come together, they are not halved in blood, but rather immeasurably expanded because of Dolem-Ra's unique standing within Argonian society. Kymeth sal ne ra translated to Earth English means: with intellect we overcome. Despite the destruction of her planet, Kaelen Ra-Evon exemplifies the creed of her house. With her joining to

Leah Lockheed-Tuck, they become a whole greater than the parts."

Someone in their group of friends and family sniffled and Wex continued. *"Dolem-Ra and Dolem-Lockheed will be stronger together from this day forth. Kaelen Ra-Evon, you stated that you wish to say individual pledges at this point in the ceremony?"*

"Yes, Wex."

Wex removed two gleaming torques with colors woven around their surface. Emerald, sapphire, and silver swirled in a dancing pattern. Kaelen grasped one and Leah the other. Rather than back away again, another compartment opened farther down on Wex's torso, and the AI removed two more objects.

"Kaelen Ra-Evon, in deference to the merging cultures of Earth and Argon, I created two smaller bands for your fingers. That is the way of Dolem-Lockheed's people."

"Oh!" Leah's mouth dropped open in shock. "You didn't tell Wex to do that?"

"No."

"You may now recite your vows. Once you've placed the bonding torques on each other, I will give you the bands."

Quiet Argonian music played as Kaelen spoke. "Leah Lockheed-Tuck, I once told you that immense loss left a hole in our hearts that was impossible to fill. It has taken me two Earth years to learn that sometimes the hole can be filled." Kaelen met Leah's shining gaze and smiled. "When I look at you, I don't see the loss of my planet, my family, or my culture. I see nothing but love and a future full of stars. I lost one world to find you and I would sacrifice more to keep you. You hold my heart." With those words, Kaelen gently clasped the indestructible torque around Leah's neck.

Leah sniffled and wiped the tears from her eyes. Kaelen noticed more than a few people in the crowd doing the same. Leah gave a self-conscious laugh. "How am I supposed to follow that?"

"Zhee, don't follow. Lead and I will be by your side."

Leah drew in a deep breath and responded, "I've known many things in my life. Love, loss, family, brilliance, friendship, and pain. One thing I've never known is someone like you. Kaelen Ra-Evon, you've challenged me and helped me to become a better person. Not by what you've done for me, but rather, your faith in me. Your nobility, your intelligence, and your insatiable curiosity for the world around you—they're all qualities that convince me that our match is true whether we are here or anyplace else in the galaxy. I would follow you to the end of the universe and back, because you hold my heart, too."

Leah copied Kaelen's motions and clasped the torque around her neck. The weight of commitment and honor felt heavy and she cherished it. Wex moved closer and extended robotic limbs so they could each grab one of the bands.

"The bands are made from terzenite and struck to match your Argonian bonding torques. May your joining be as long-lasting and twice as strong." Leah and Kaelen took turns placing the rings upon the third finger of each other's left hand. Then they turned to face their friends as the red light changed frequency and they were bathed in yellow sunlight to indicate the changing culture. Kaelen lifted her hand to wave at their found family, but Leah pulled it back down again.

"Darling, you're forgetting the best part."

Kaelen was confused until she suddenly remembered the ending of many Earth wedding traditions. Wex prompted from its position behind them. *"Kaelen Ra-Evon and Leah Lockheed-Tuck, you may kiss your match."*

"You told Wex to say that, didn't you?"

Leah stepped close and giggled, though she kept her voice as quiet as Kaelen's. "I didn't actually but I'm starting to think Wex isn't as bad as I've always assumed."

Kaelen rolled her eyes, a terrible habit she had picked up from Leah. "No, Wex is still a dick."

"Come here, Darling. You owe me something." Leah pulled her close. As they kissed, Kaelen felt stronger than ever before. It could have been from the presence of their friends and family, or from the tide of emotion she felt while holding Leah within her arms. Either way, Kaelen made a mental promise that she was never going to let Leah go.

Maddy yelled from somewhere below, "Kaelen, if you don't come down soon, I'm going to eat all the cake!"

The spire suddenly lowered and the newly married couple settled back onto the steel portion of the platform with twin ringing sounds as the soles of their boots hit the surface.

The promise to hold Leah forever could start after dessert.

Acknowledgments

Scion was an accident. I set out to finish a different book during NaNoWriMo and accidentally conceived of, and churned out, a 150k word fanfic. I knew right away the story was so different from the source material that it would fold nicely into my superhero world, and that's exactly what I plotted from the beginning.

There are some people that deserve the moon on this one. My amazing beta reader, Anne Pace, is excellent at fixing my English, grammar, and sentence structure, despite having French as her first language. She's taught me a lot. Another person that was instrumental in getting this work off the ground was my sensitivity reader, Anne Hart. I learned so much about the disabled community and sensitivity writing and I know I'll carry the mindset forward to future novels and stories. Two others that deserve praise and thanks for slogging through my chaotic stories and poor grasp of the English language are my editors, Patty, and Micheala.

The Annes, Patty, and Micheala…you four are the true heroes and I'm honored to have worked with you. My other acknowledgements are to May Dawney for creating another gorgeous cover, and Flashpoint for continuing to put their faith in me and my stories.

Books by K. Aten

The Fletcher

Kyri is a fletcher, following in the footsteps of her father, and his father before him. However, fate is a fickle mistress, and six years after the death of her mother, she's faced with the fact that her father is dying as well. Forced to leave her sheltered little homestead in the woods, Kyri discovers that there is more to life than just hunting and making master quality arrows. During her journey to find a new home and happiness, she struggles with the path that seems to take her away from the quiet life of a fletcher. She learns that sometimes the hardest part of growing up is reconciling who we were, with who we will become.

The Archer

Kyri was raised a fletcher but after finding a new home and family with the Telequire Amazons, she discovers a desire to take on more responsibility within the tribe. She has skills they desperately need and she is called to action to protect those around her. But Kyri's path is ever-changing even as she finds herself altered by love, loyalty, and grief. Far away from home, the new Amazon is forced to decide what to sacrifice and who to become in order to get back to all that she has left behind. And she wonders what is worse, losing everyone she's ever loved or having those people lose her?

The Sagittarius

Kyri has known her share of loss in the two decades that she has been alive. She never expected to find herself a slave in Roman lands, nor did she think she had the heart to become a gladiatrix. But with her soul shattered she must fight to see her way back home again. Will she win her freedom and return to all that she has known, or will she become another kind of slave to the killer that has taken over her mind? The only thing that is certain through it all is her love and devotion to Queen Orianna.

Rules of the Road

Jamie is an engineer who keeps humor close to her heart and people at arm's length. Kelsey is a dental assistant who deals with everything from the hilarious to the disgusting on a daily basis. What happens when a driving app brings them together as friends? The nerd car and the rainbow car both know a thing or two about hazard avoidance. When a flat tire brings them together in person, Jamie immediately realizes that Kelsey isn't just another woman on her radar. Both of them have struggled to break free from stereotypes while they navigate the road of life. As their friendship deepens they realize that sometimes you have to break the rules to get where you need to go.

Waking the Dreamer

By the end of the 21st century, the world had become a harsh place. After decades of natural and man-made catastrophes, nations fell, populations shifted, and seventy percent of the continents became uninhabitable without protective suits.

Technological advancement strode forward faster than ever and it was the only thing that kept human society steady through it all. No one could have predicted the discovery of the Dream Walkers. They were people born with the ability to leave their bodies at will, unseen by the waking world. Having the potential to become ultimate spies meant the remaining government regimes wanted to study and control them. The North American government, under the leadership of General Rennet, demanded that all Dream Walkers join the military program. For any that refused to comply, they were hunted down and either brainwashed or killed.

The very first Dream Walker discovered was a five year old girl named Julia. And when the soldiers came for her at the age of twenty, she was already hidden away. A decade later found Julia living a new life under the government's radar. As a secure tech courier in the capital city of Chicago, she does her job and the rest of her time avoids other people as much as she is able. The moment she agrees to help another fugitive Walker is when everything changes. Now the government wants them both and they'll stop at nothing to get what they want.

Running From Forever

Sarah Colby has always run from commitment. But after more than a year on the road following her musical dreams, even she yearns for a little stability. Her sister Annie is only too happy to welcome her back home. When she meets Annie's boss, Nobel Keller, she's immediately drawn to the woman's youthful good looks and dangerous charisma. The first night together leaves Sarah aching for more, but the second shows her the true price of passion.

Embracing Forever

Sarah Colby is a musician, teacher, lover, sister, and so much more. In the past year, she learned that sometimes life takes you places you never even knew existed. For Sarah and her sister Annie, they found out that not only were the monsters real but sometimes you loved them. Now the Colby sisters and their friends are being targeted by someone with a grudge. They must discover who is attacking the people of Columbus or risk losing all that they hold dear. Nobel Keller is with them every step of the way but will she bring salvation or merely the end of their lives in Columbus?

Burn It Down

Ash Hayes was failed by the system at the tender age of sixteen and suffered an addiction. As a result she lives her life weighed down by the guilt of her past. To atone for childhood misdeeds, Ash trained as a paramedic after high school and eventually became a firefighter with the Detroit fire department, along with her childhood best friend Derek. Friend, confidant, brother, he has been her light in an otherwise dark life. When tragedy strikes on the job, injury and forced leave from the department are the least of her concerns. Suffering from even more guilt and depression after the loss of her two closest friends Ash is set adrift in a sea of pain.

When Mia Thomas buys the house next door, Ash finds friendship in the most unlikely of places. It's Mia's nature to help and to heal. Many would say she has a knack for finding the broken ones and leading them into the light. But Ash's secret still lives deep inside her. Before the firefighter can even think of a future, she has to amend her past. Like the phoenix of legend, Ash has to burn her fears to the ground before she can be reborn.

Children of the Stars

The world was forever changed when a government genetic experiment created the Chromodecs from a dead alien in 1952. Decades later, when it became apparent that society needed a way to deal with a hybrid humans with unheard of powers, the CORP was created. The Chromodec Office of Restraint and Protection was a special government police agency formed to keep track of the Chromodecs.

This particular tale involves two refugees, young babies who were sent down to Earth to escape being used as pawns in an interplanetary war, despite the fact that Earth itself wasn't so safe. Destined to be Q'sirrahna, or soul mates as the humans called it, Amari Losira Del Rey and Zendara Inyri Baen-Tor would grow to be more powerful than any other beings on the planet, if they could find each other first.

After being forced to hide from the CORP when it's realized their powers could level entire cities, Amari and Zen will have to answer one question. Who will save the world when it all falls apart?

Remember Me, Synthetica

What happens when a woman loses her memory but gains a conscience?

Dr. Alexandra Turing is a roboticist whose intellect is unrivaled in the field of artificial intelligence. While science has always come easy, Alexandra struggles to understand emotional cues and responses. Driven by the legacy of her late great-uncle, she dedicates her life to the Synthetica project at her father's company, Organic Advancement Solutions (OAS).

Her life is rebooted when she wakes from a coma, six months after being struck by a car. Traumatic brain injury altered Alex's senses, her memory, and her personality. Despite the changes, she feels reborn as she navigates her way back into her old life. Part of her new journey includes dating the alluring Doctor of Veterinary Medicine, Emily St. John.

Emily is enamored with the hyper-intelligent scientist, but there are things about Alex and OAS that don't add up. With Emily's prompting, Alex undergoes testing that leaves her with more questions than answers. What she discovers changes more than her life, it will change the world around her.

The Lost Temple of Psiere

As the heir to the throne, Royal Connate Olivienne Dracore cannot escape having a Shield team protecting her wherever she goes. But with the addition of Shield Commander Castellan Tosh, she has a team that doesn't just guard her person but also aids in her job as a historical adventurist. She knows without a doubt that together they can unravel the Divine Mystery of who the Makers were and why they created the great temples.

With the conclusion of their last mission, Olivienne acquired the map needed to find the mysterious third great temple of Psiere. And there is no one better to accompany than her beloved Cmdr. Tosh. But before they can leave to brave the dangers of the unknown, first they must brave their own oathing ceremony. They will need each other for the coming mission because as with all things related to the Makers, mystery often begets mystery and danger is always just a wrong step away. Especially when the prize is something that could change Psiere forever.

Elemental Attraction

Two people find themselves in a quandary. Aderri—a powerful dragon shifter with some light defensive magic and Ellys—a half-elven swordswoman for hire, one of the best across the six nations.

When Aderri gets news that she must come home for the naming ceremony of a new hatchling, she's forced to hire Ellys and her telepathic steed, Roccotári, to see her safely there. Of course, things are never simple as they seem. Not only do they have to traverse the land between two kingdoms on the brink of war, but Aderri's Clan expects her to return with a romantic interest. So, for the added promise of triple Ellys's normal fee, the half-elf agrees to pretend to be Aderri's suitor.

Ellys and Aderri have to convince a Clan full of magical mixed-shifters for a week that creatures of differing elements can burn with the flames of love, without actually lying. A situation made even more difficult by a matchmaking mare, steamy baths, and an innkeeper with mischief on the mind. Caught between the weight of the past and expectations of the future, they must find their true destiny within the heat of fire.